Then i

Floating and riding the drift of the breeze.

Stopped in her tracks, Memphis listened intently. This was not her imagination or a trick of the wind. A woman hummed a tune that sounded like a hymn. But sound carried in freakish ways in the mountains. In fact, the brief breeze that had brought the haunting sound had disappeared, and the night was still. From behind the house came an odd illumination. The lights again, she thought. A chill ran down her spine, as if someone had traced an ice cube straight down her back. She shivered and huddled closer into her jacket.

Don't look at the light. Move, Memphis. Get into the house.

Praise for Linda Anderson's first novel, *Over the Moon*

The
SECRETS
of SADIE
MAYNARD

LINDA
ANDERSON

POCKET STAR BOOKS
New York   London   Toronto   Sydney   Tokyo   Singapore

This book is a work of fiction. Names, characters, places and
incidents are products of the author's imagination or are used
fictitiously. Any resemblance to actual events or locales or
persons, living or dead, is entirely coincidental.

An *Original* Publication of POCKET BOOKS

A Pocket Star Book published by
POCKET BOOKS, a division of Simon & Schuster Inc.
1230 Avenue of the Americas, New York, NY 10020

Copyright © 1999 by Linda Kirchman Anderson

ISBN: 0-671-02768-9

First Pocket Books printing May 1999

10 9 8 7 6 5 4 3 2 1

POCKET STAR BOOKS and colophon are registered
trademarks of Simon & Schuster Inc.

Front cover photo of woman's face courtesy of Tony Stone
Images

Printed in the U.S.A.

For Hugh,
who helps me live my dream

Acknowledgments

Many thanks and love to my sister, Dr. Joan Mitchell, Jeanmarie Grimsley, and Linda Parr, for invaluable suggestions in the early stages of *Sadie*. Thank you to Debbie St. Amand, Marilyn Jordan, Marcia King-Gamble, Margaret Fraser, Sandy Madden, and Diane Miller for their knowledgeable criticism and emotional support. This book could not have survived without them.

A big hug of appreciation from me to all members of the Southeastern Writers Association, especially Becky Weyrich, Nelle McFather, Pat Laye, Cappy Hall-Reardon, and Margaret Pennycook for hours of talk about the agonies and pleasures of writing, and to my buddy, Harry Rubin, who makes me laugh.

My deep gratefulness goes to Buddy and Jean Ferrell for their graciousness on my book-signing visits to West Virginia. Sadie's story is loosely based on a true murder mystery that occurred many years ago. I thank Delores Stephens for reminding me of that mystery. Thank you to my West Virginia cousins for their warm hospitality and continued support.

It goes without saying that all of my children, Karin, Lani, Melissa, Alec, and Duffy get special thank-you's for putting up with my deadline nerves, and for their belief in me, but a special thank-you goes to my oldest daughter, photojournalist Kris Anderson-Barrett, who helped me with the camera scenes. Any mistakes are mine not hers.

Sincere appreciation to Meryl Sawyer, whose friendship and enthusiasm helped make *Sadie* a reality.

Deep gratitude and thanks to my talented editor, Caroline Tolley, and her belief in this book, and to my brilliant agent, Karen Solem, both of whom I thank God for every day.

The

SECRETS
of SADIE
MAYNARD

❧ Prologue ❧

May 1936

"Ain't nobody never gonna find her here."

"Nope." The older man's shovel cut sharp and deep through the soft spring earth, damp from the gentle rain. A feeble rainbow arched briefly over the ridge of the West Virginia mountain then disappeared. The sun could not penetrate this gray morning's murky fog.

"They say she's hauntin' places."

"Ain't even got her buried yet. How kin she be a ghost?"

"Dewey Puckett swears he picked up a hitchhiker who climbed in the backseat of his car, but who warn't thar when he turned to talk to her, and Granny Tucker says she runs alongside the road near Twenty-Two Mine where they found her body."

The old man's expression of disgust turned to one of belief. Granny Tucker saw spirits for true.

"Maybe so."

Though perspiring from exertion, the old man hunched his jacket around his neck to ward off the damp, unseasonable chill. The younger man, shivering with cold and apprehension, dropped his shovel to rub his hands together for warmth.

"Don't it seem cold for this time of year?" he asked the old man.

"Yep."

They dug faster, eager to be done with the gruesome task.

"I never dug a grave," said the younger man. "You?"

"Yep. You'll dig aplenty iffen you live long enough."

"They ever ask you to do anything like this afore?"

"None of your business." The older man cast the younger a worried look. "He's payin' us real good 'cause he knows we'll keep our mouths shut. You want to keep makin' money, you remember that."

"Sure, sure."

"Iffen you don't, I might be hyar diggin' a grave for you next year."

"I'll keep my mouth shut. I 'preciate the work a whole lot. I really do. My babies is hungry."

"That's why I picked you to help 'cause I knowed you was closemouthed, and 'cause I knowed your wife and babies is sickly. He thinks I'm doin' this by myself, but I'm gettin' too old to do some of their dirty work."

"Why they want to hide her grave?"

"Don't know, and you don't want to know either."

"They stick together, that bunch, don't they?"

"Yep."

"Are all town people like that?"

"Nope."

"Just them that's got secrets, huh?"

The old man straightened and wiped his wet brow with the back of his forearm. He kicked a big rock down the mountain and was silent as he watched it tumble down the steep slope, spitting up clods of earth as it disappeared from view. Then he turned to stare at the other man.

"Everybody got secrets, son. Town people, mountain people, everybody. God knows some secrets, the devil knows others. But I'll tell you somethin', these hills knows them all, and these hills holds secrets 'cause they respect them." His stare hardened. "Ye'd do well to remember that, elsin' you might lose your tongue, or your wife might lose a father to her children."

"Yes, sir. Yes, sir." The young man's voice trembled. Eager to hide his fear, and anxious to look away from the intensity of the old man's eyes, he bent to his task again.

Behind them, where the rainbow had been, a gold luster rose around the ridge. The gold shimmered for a moment, then wavered, then grew stronger as a pale-blue light outlined the nebulous form. The blue and gold merged and became an incandescent glow of pearly white floating eerily in the gray drizzle.

The young man scratched the back of his neck.

"You hear someone singin'?"

"Nope."

"Coulda swore I heard someone hummin' 'What a Friend We Have in Jesus.'"

"It's the early morning breeze comin' through the pines. Pay a mind to what you're doin', boy. Ain't nobody here but us," said the old man. But the hair rose on the back of his neck and he sneaked a look into the woods beyond the clearing. He resumed digging with a troubled frown on his face.

The incandescent form floated down the hill toward them, flared brightly and hovered for a moment about fifteen feet from their bent backs, then faded away.

The old man straightened, rubbed his ear as if to clear it and shuddered. He looked around again but saw nothing.

Hurriedly, they reached for the fresh-sawed wooden casket and pushed it without ceremony into the shallow hole in the earth. It landed with a thud and lay in its resting place at an awkward angle.

§1§

October 1996

Silence spread through the Yancey County Country Club crowd like spilled whiskey on a hostess's best satin tablecloth. All heads turned toward the tall, rugged man entering the room.

Most men would have checked to see if their tie was in place, or run a swift hand along their jaw to see if they'd shaved close enough, but this man wore no tie, and he'd long since given up worrying about the five o'clock shadow on his square jaw.

Pared lean and hard, his shoulders rectangular rather than rounded, his frame seemed more for the backwoods than this privileged gathering. But the cut of the expensive navy blue sport coat he wore over faded jeans and immaculate white shirt indicated an accustomed ease in such surroundings. One dark, craggy eyebrow rose derisively then settled back in place.

Mack "Cutter" Tate, focus of the scrutiny, seethed inwardly but managed a genial smile. After all, he wasn't angry at the people who stared at him, just at the reason for their stares. He knew their rabid curiosity about his reaction to the latest newspaper headline was to be expected. But that didn't mean he had to like it. Nearly every person partying at this annual Indian summer celebration had a hand in his growing up.

Through the years, one or another had nurtured him, fed him, cursed him, even hidden him.

The small combo, back from its break, blasted out a fifties version of "Stagger Lee," the lights dimmed, and the disco ball on the ceiling whirled red and green strobes around the large room. People began to dance again, and others were content to munch on their barbecued ribs and fried chicken. The spell was broken.

Cutter smiled down at the woman on his arm. Her pretty face showed confusion and embarrassment, although he also sensed a certain pride at the effect of their appearance.

"Don't worry, Alison. They won't bite."

"Are you sure?" she asked with a small laugh.

"Positive."

"Your lips are smiling, but those sexy gray eyes are grim," she teased.

"Having your life put on display by God and *People* magazine isn't the most pleasant of experiences."

"Jake Bishop isn't God, Cutter."

"No, God has his own agenda, which I have stopped trying to figure out," he said with a shade of bitterness. "But if Jake Bishop weren't a well-known reporter, and a master at revving up publicity, this whole thing would have been ignored. Only the *Yancey Record* would have run the story and that's bad enough. I'm just a poor, humble mining engineer, Alison."

She laughed. "A mining engineer you are. Poor and humble you are not."

He grinned hugely and tugged her into the dancing crowd.

"Hey, boy, how ya doin'?" A sweating, beer-toting fat man stopped his rock-and-roll gyrations to slap him on the back.

"Great, Billy, just great," shouted Cutter above the music as he quickly danced Alison past the fat man and his wife. He knew Billy Gus and Elva wanted to talk, find out how Cutter was handling the renewed interest in the old scandal, but he wasn't in the mood tonight.

"Don't let 'em get you down, big guy," shouted another man.

"Don't intend to, Bud."

The raucous music stopped and the band began to play a wobbly version of "Feelings." Cutter drew Alison close to him, but a young woman grabbed his arm.

"Cutter, I have to talk to you."

"Sure, Birdy, but later. Alison, this is Birdy Harless, a neighbor and old friend. Birdy, this is my date, Alison Gardner. Alison lives in Charleston. You have kin in Charleston, don't you, Birdy?"

Birdy nodded her head and flicked a quick smile at Alison.

"Yes, you know I do, but Alison and I can gab later. You don't mind if I borrow him for a minute, do you?" she asked Alison. Her grasp on his arm tightened, and she pulled at him.

Cutter firmly, but gently, pried her fingers loose from his arm. "Come over for coffee in the morning. We'll talk then."

"But, Cutter, there's something you should know tonight."

"It'll wait, Birdy." He ignored her look of annoyance, waved good-bye to her, and guiding Alison by the elbow, headed toward the doors and out to the terrace.

A raspy crickets' choir greeted them. Cutter placed his arms on the stone wall, and leaned into the night, gazing out at the manicured greens and the mountains etched in the distance. Alison knew him well enough to leave him to his thoughts for a while, and he appreciated that.

This was the widest expanse of acreage in the narrow-cut mining valley. The mountains held close and fast to the bottom land in Yancey County, but the hills here around the golf course, unlike the rest of the deep, claustrophobic valley, were spaced so the sky was spread wide and viewable. He was glad of that tonight for he could see the stars painted bright, close and almost touchable. The North Star hung low over the trees.

It was a warm night, sweet with summer's finale, but a skipping breeze held the cool promise of fall. A waiting night, a night marking time, he thought, and shivered. Marking time for what, he wondered? More heartache?

He hated the emotions Jake Bishop's latest television spots had stirred within him. He dreaded the resurrection of old feelings and fears he'd thought long resolved and buried. Memories of his childhood, the grandfather who loved him, the father who hated him, and the law man who delighted in torturing him flashed before him like silent-movie stills. Low in his gut, a deepseated pain he'd walled up and sealed away had already begun to gnaw its way to the surface. He hunched his shoulders forward, as if to relieve them of the tension gathering around him, and then stood straight, remembering the woman who waited patiently by his side.

"Sorry, Alison. I hope all this hullabaloo hasn't ruined your weekend. We should have left Yancey, maybe gone to Bermuda, or Vegas, or . . . hell, I don't know, anywhere but here."

"You love it here, and besides, you can't escape your past, Cutter, no matter where you go."

"You're right. But, I'd learned to live with it, had even managed to feel it was a minor part of me, hardly thought of it anymore until this damned Jake Bishop showed up. The thing that mystifies me is why and how a former prominent war correspondent, turned rotten author, would latch onto a stale mystery hidden in the mountains of West Virginia."

"I don't know, darling, except that Bishop is having huge success with his book series about unsolved murders. Obviously, he's found that revealing old scandals is more profitable than reporting wars."

"His weekly appearances on *American Notebook* promoting the book are getting more sensational. The town is beginning to grumble about the unfair exposure it's getting, and I feel like they're blaming me."

"It's true mountain people don't like any invasion of their privacy, but I'm sure they're not blaming you. Let's forget about it for now. The evening is too lovely to waste."

"Ever the wise Alison."

She pulled her lacey wrap close around her shoulders. He realized the breeze had quickened while he'd ignored her and she was getting cold.

He pulled her to him, enjoying the soft pressure of her breasts against his chest. For a moment he wondered if his grandfather, in the midst of his own travails and in love with a woman he couldn't have, had taken refuge in another woman just for the joy of reveling in her fragrances, her sounds, the feel of her and nothing else. Just the feel of a woman and the comfort she could so warmly give.

One thing he knew for sure. He was experiencing only a portion of the powerful emotions his grandfather must have felt when the whole town suspected him of murder. Fighting the fog of suspicion was like finding your way out of a smoky room. Smothering and almost impossible.

Memphis sat straight up, drenched in cold sweat.

The haunting cry that had awakened her still rang in her ears. As her eyes adjusted to the darkness, the shapes taking form in the room around her were familiar, and yet not. *Where am I?* The last time she'd felt this bone-wrenching fear was in the hospital in

Bosnia. But she wasn't in Bosnia. Not in her Manhattan apartment either.

She fought the cold panic that curled through her like drifts of dry ice.

The old pain in her knee shot upward and lodged in her hip, reminding her that she'd done too much driving today.

Her elbow met the corner of a bedside table, and she groped for a lamp, flashlight, anything. Nothing but a glass of water, which she almost tipped over during her fumbling.

From an open window, a waft of cool, clean, pine-scented air dried some of the perspiration on her chest and forehead, and she suddenly remembered where she slept: the antiquated Victorian house where her mother, Faith, had grown up, and where Memphis and her sister Margo had spent several childhood summers.

Had she dreamed the eerie scream, or had it been her own cry? Had Katie cried out in her sleep? Heart pounding, Memphis reached to caress the soft, warm form of her eighteen-month-old daughter, who slept beside her. Katie's small back rose up and down in relaxed slumber. Memphis resisted the urge to pick her up and hold her close for comfort.

Had the ominous scream come from the woods behind the house? Ordinarily not easily spooked, her reaction to the unsettling sound bothered her. It was as if something unimaginable was out there, something she couldn't rationalize away.

She tried to summon up the Memphis of old, the Memphis who took any dare, who traipsed all over the world unafraid, and sometimes alone. Alone until she'd met Jake.

"Good old 'Jake the Snake.' The last person I need to think of right now," she said to herself in the stillness. "Wouldn't he get a big laugh? Me, all shaky."

Accustomed to the twinkling, festive lights of Manhattan, and sounds of traffic on the streets below, she felt the blackness of the mountain night outside the window close around her, pressing into the bedroom, enlarging her feeling of aloneness. Often she'd been alone on battlefields, the only woman among whizzing bullets and cursing men, and had never felt as vulnerable as she did now.

Loneliness was something she learned to live with, something she'd accepted as part of her, something she expected she would always have, but she'd never felt fear or vulnerability until Katie came into her life.

The miracle of her daughter had brought monumental love. A feeling of fierce kindredship for the small bundle of dependent energy, and a corresponding sense of responsibility and maternal protection had created the care with which she now tread. She had learned to take better care of herself, to be more judicious in her actions and her work.

Yet here she was in West Virginia, with Katie along, determined to right an age-old wrong. There had been a time in her life when this trip would have been a kick, a challenge. Her mission here would have been just another fast chapter in the adventures of Memphis Maynard, *daring* photojournalist. No more. She had Katie to think about now.

The decision to leave Manhattan and come to Yancey had been hasty, but imperative as far as she was concerned. Her editor had berated her, telling her he'd given her time off to enjoy Katie, not to burn herself out on some wild-goose chase to West Virginia.

Her sister, Margo, had said, "Oh, God, Mem, leave the whole mess alone. It's best forgotten." Then she'd flung her hands dramatically in the air and whooped with laughter. "Besides, I can't imagine you and Katie alone in that horror of a house. It's probably got cobwebs on the ceiling and mice in the corners. God, remember how we used to scare each other, jumping out of hidden stairwells, and telling preposterous ghost stories? But we had fun, didn't we?"

A whippoorwill caroled in the woods behind the house, its repeated, rolling trill sounding forsaken in the absolute stillness of the night. The high, lonesome whistle of a freight train sounded in the distance.

Memphis shivered, then tucked a blanket over Katie, who had kicked off her covers. She massaged her knee as the physical therapists had taught her, assuaging the pain until it was a dull ache, then lay back down, pulling the sheet up close to her chin.

"This is ridiculous, Memphis Maynard," she whispered. "Get a grip. Everything seems spooky because we arrived so late."

Somewhere in the house a telephone rang. She shot straight up again, finally located the lamp on the bedside table, and turned it on. The big face of the round tin windup clock showed midnight. Good Lord, who would be calling at this time of night, and where in God's name was the telephone? As she drew on her robe, she searched her mind, frantically trying to remember whether she'd seen a phone in any of the rooms.

The insistent ringing came from downstairs. Yes. These old houses usually had a dim cubbyhole between the dining room and the kitchen that held a small desk with a telephone. She remembered the light switch at the top of the stairs, hit it, and raced down the steps, robe flapping behind her.

Bingo! There it was, exactly where she'd imagined it. She snatched up the receiver.

"Hello?"

"Hi, Mem."

"Good God, Margo, don't you know what time it is? It may be nine o'clock in Seattle, but it's midnight here."

"Oops, sorry, Mem. Tonight's Monday, our dark night, and I knew I wouldn't have a chance to call tomorrow. I can never get used to these time changes when we're touring in the West."

"How's the show going?"

"Great. *Phantom* is hard work, but a fun show to do. Your big sister got rave reviews. But, I called to see how *you* were, if you arrived safely and all that stuff."

"Sure, why wouldn't we?"

"Well, I know you're a tough cookie, or want everyone to think you are, but sometimes your sense of adventure combined with your generosity gets you in trouble."

"Oh, come now, Margo Maynard, who's usually rescuing whom in this sister act?"

"I will admit you've gotten me out of some scrapes, but I worry more about you now that you have Katie along."

"Katie's fine. We got in late, so instead of putting her into a strange bed in a strange house in the middle of the night, I put her in bed with me."

"Why did you get in so late?"

"I had car trouble and got delayed in Charleston for repairs, and then . . ."

She stopped short. It was just the sort of thing Margo was always telling her not to do. But what was life all about, if one didn't go the extra mile, if one didn't take a step into the unknown once in a while?

"What else? You didn't pick up any hitchhikers or anything like that, did you?"

"Well, I . . ." Damn, she knows me too well, Memphis thought.

"Memmy?"

"Well, yes I did. She was all by herself on this deserted road near one of the coal mines, and it was late. I felt sorry for her."

"Oh, God, Memphis. You're too trusting."

"Me, trusting? Not after what happened with Jake. Unfortunately, he trampled all over my 'trusting' nature, as you call it."

Silence hung for a moment as Margo realized she'd opened a sore subject. "Sorry, Mem."

"That's okay. Anyway, old habits die hard and I'm glad I picked her up, poor thing. I didn't notice until she climbed in the car that she was barefoot and had scratches all over her, like she'd been running through the woods or something."

Interested now, Margo asked, "Did she explain what she was doing on a deserted road late at night, or how she got there?"

"Didn't say one thing. Not even hello, good-bye, or thank you. She only stayed with me for about a mile. When she wanted out, she touched my arm, pointed, and smiled. I asked her if she was sure, because there was nothing around but the entrance to an old mine shaft off in the distance."

"And vat deed she say then, my pretty one?" asked Margo in her old storytelling wavery witch voice from childhood.

"She just nodded a yes, so I stopped and let her out. When I drove off and looked back in the rearview mirror, she'd already disappeared into the woods."

"Sounds weird to me."

"It was, kind of. But everything seems a little weird here. Probably because of those ghastly scary tricks we used to play on each other in this house."

"You've always felt some odd link to Sadie, but it must have intensified. I know you're royally pissed at Jake for writing the book you want to write, or you would never have taken Katie down there to stay in that dreadful house. God, it was bad when we were little. How is the wretched old thing?"

"Seems fine. Paint's peeling off the ceiling and wallpaper is hanging in shreds here and there, but the bedrooms are clean and there's food in the refrigerator, just as Nelsey Kinzer promised. Someone placed arrangements of wildflowers around, too. Probably Nelsey Kinzer."

"Who's Nelsey Kinzer?"

"Nearest neighbor, and unofficial caretaker of our modest estate. Grandpa's trustees at the bank pay her a small sum to come in and clean once a month."

"How long since we've been there?"

"Twenty-three years, I think, the summer Alma died. Mom had the big row with Grandpa and never brought us back."

"We had some good times there, too, Mem. I remember picnics near a cabin, and someone telling ghost stories and old mountain tales."

"Yeah, I don't remember what she looks like, but I think Nelsey may have been the storyteller. Grandpa never let us mix much with anyone so we didn't get to know many people, but we did go swimming in a lake, and we went to revival meetings where everyone sang gospel songs loud and lively like they believed every word they sang."

"I think they did."

"That would be nice to think, wouldn't it?" Memphis yawned. "Gotta go, Margo. It's been a long day."

"Okay. Love you. Don't let those mountain folk be mean to you, and Mem, if you don't get the whole story straightened out, remember that it's not the end of the world."

"I know. I love you. Bye."

With Margo's words echoing in her ear, Memphis decided to think only of the good times here, not the bad. Her jaw tightened with determination.

Her whole life had been shaped by a search for adventure, a seeking of knowledge and better under-

standing of human nature. Photography had fulfilled
much of her quest. It had led her to strange lands with
beautiful scenery, and war-torn countries with sad
stories. Here in her own country she'd retraced the
lives of depression families chronicled originally by
Margaret Bourke-White in the 1930s. The questions
and answers she found in the eyes of others in their
moments of despair or triumph had shaken her deeply.
The seconds she'd pinned in time, held forever in the
lens of her camera, exposed the commonality of everyone—their joy or pain, their courage, their bewilderment about this thing called life. For Memphis herself,
those photos held resolve and hope.

Underneath the determination to finally clear up the
questions surrounding her grandmother's murder,
Memphis realized that even here in Yancey her hope
for answers for herself burned strong as ever. They had
to do with a "coming home," for finding parts of herself
that struggled to come forth, but never quite surfaced.
They had to do with heart secrets, and soul secrets that
she'd captured in the faces of others, in the stance of
their bodies, or the plea of their hands, but had never
identified in herself. And for some unfathomable reason, she'd always thought that Grandmother Sadie's
story might hold answers for her.

Jake Bishop tilted his chair back, balancing on the rear
legs, his feet latched around the desk legs in front of
him. He pushed the warped green plastic eyeshade up
on his head, making his blond hair stand on end. His
old pals at the Associated Press ragged him about his
eyeshade affectation, which aped the style of veteran
reporters in the forties and fifties. Jake didn't care. The
eyeshade was his good luck charm. He even wore it on
the TV spots he did for *American Notebook,* and women
seemed to adore it.

A pencil clenched between his teeth, he watched the

printer spit out his work for tonight. When it was finished, he let the chair settle to the floor, grabbed the stack of papers, and read them.

Pleased with the results, he clicked off the computer and got up to pour himself a cup of coffee. His fourth that night.

"This should bring her running," he muttered to himself, as he reviewed his copy again.

He paced the small, nondescript hotel room, finally stopping to snap up the paper shade and look out the window at the town of Yancey. The hour was late. Only two cars traveled on the one-way street that circled the courthouse and the square.

"Kids cruising. Who else would be awake and moving in this hick burg except a teenager with some life in him?"

Popcorn spewed from the machine in the yellow-lit window of Murphy's Five & Ten on the corner. Someone had forgotten to turn off the automatic popper for the night.

Jake whistled between his teeth and smiled. "Gonna be a helluva lot of stale popcorn to eat tomorrow. Maybe they'll run a special on it."

He'd become accustomed to talking to himself. He hadn't made many friends in Yancey. In fact, he'd made a few enemies, but it didn't bother him. He was having the time of his life. Teasing and titillating the citizens of Yancey County and southern West Virginia had become a source of amusement.

What had started as a lark, a small project to fill time until another big story like Bosnia came along, had become the focal point in his life. It was no longer a lark. His book series about unsolved murders of the last one hundred years had become a huge success. He intended on playing this particular tale to its fullest, yanking the string until he loosened the knot at the end. His intense curiosity had been piqued, but the

chance that Memphis might show motivated him even
more than curiosity.

The possibility that the story might bring Memphis
back to him hadn't entered his mind until he realized
she couldn't avoid knowing about the success of his
books. His television appearances on *American Notebook* reporting this third and newest subject, the murder of Sadie Maynard, would almost insure that
Memphis would know about his forthcoming book. He
knew her well enough to know it would anger her.
Maybe enough to bring her to Yancey.

He hadn't finished the book, and he'd structured the
1936 murder as an ongoing five-minute spot on each
week's show. It required that he spend more time in
this backwater, dead-end place than he wanted to, but
he was almost certain she would show sooner or later.
Sooner, he hoped. He wanted her back in his life.

Across the street the blue and orange neon lights of
the Rainbow Diner flashed on and off, then on and off
again. Dewey Puckett, owner of the diner, was signaling Shine McCoy it was time to go home.

Jake watched as Shine picked himself up off the
loafer's bench, brushed the coal dust off the seat of his
baggy pants, and shuffled up the street. Other regulars
on the bench had long since gone home to bed, either
sobered-up enough to know it was past bedtime, or
been discovered by a family member who had come
and led them home by the ear. Shine drank until he
passed out, then seemed surprised when he woke up
around midnight to find himself alone. He lived by
himself and had no family to care about him, so Dewey
Puckett always let Shine know when it was time to go
home.

"If I'd spent my life here, I'd drink myself into
oblivion too, Shine old boy," muttered Jake.

Yancey was a rough, hardscrabble place, an abrasive
remnant of its early coal-mining days. But beneath the

gritty exterior of the citizens, there existed a genuine caring for one another. Even Jake, who had been given the cold shoulder, had witnessed the warmth of the community when they thought he wasn't watching. He wasn't fool enough to think they were going to open their hearts to him, but he knew the people in this town were fiercely protective of their own, no matter how ill or evil the person or deed.

Which brought to mind Yancey's own Huck Finn, Cutter Tate, bad boy turned grown-up successful businessman. Tate had killed a man and so had his grandfather, and both had gotten away with it. Trying to get information from the locals, though, was like pulling teeth with eyebrow tweezers.

Jake smiled. He hadn't needed them. He'd dug up everything essential through newspaper files, old deeds and records, eavesdropping, and by listening carefully to what people weren't saying, or by what they avoided saying when he interviewed them. There weren't many still living who could give him firsthand accounts of what happened all those years ago, but he'd found enough. Enough anyway to whet the appetite of his viewers. Jake Bishop had every middle-class housewife in America wondering who really murdered Sadie Maynard sixty years ago.

Cutter Tate had refused to talk to him. *Well, Mr. High and Mighty Tate, you may not want to talk to me, but I've finished your grandfather's story and now maybe I can scare up the dirt on you.* Cutter Tate was going to make great copy. He knew Tate had led an odd life here as a child and teenager. Though son and grandson of one of Yancey's wealthiest families, Tate had lived a hand-to-mouth existence, often fed by neighbors, or chased by irate homeowners.

Jake had disliked him on sight. He knew the dislike was irrational, but it was instinctive and he hadn't figured out why. Perhaps it was the man's big Scotch-

Irish good looks. Typical of many of the descendants of the region's original settlers, Tate had a healthy complexion and a shock of unruly dark-brown hair. If he didn't like you, and he didn't like Jake, his mercury eyes cut through you like laser beams. Standing tall next to the Welsh descendants, who were stocky, dark, and built well for work in the coal mines, Cutter Tate looked like he could be king of the mountain.

Just the thought of the arrogant bastard made Jake crave a cigarette. He dug into his shirt pocket, and remembered too late that he'd quit three months ago. Jerking the window shade down again, he soothed the immediate nicotine urge by downing the rest of his cold coffee. Smoking irritated Memphis. He'd quit when he realized there might be a chance to get her back.

For a moment he took the luxury of remembering her slim body in his arms, her very satisfying supple satin breasts in his fondling hands. He closed his eyes and heard the small moan she gave when she was ready to climax. A tightness gathered in his loins. He groaned with frustration. Opening his eyes, he wished again that Memphis was here. They'd had some great times together in the Gulf War, in Bosnia, all over the world. He wondered where she was this moment, and willed her close to him.

He didn't have to wonder where Cutter Tate was on this autumn night. At the "club," of course, the Yancey County Country Club. Yancey was a tacky, blue-collar town, but it had its share of aristocracy and privileged citizens. It always had, and they stuck together like flies and flypaper.

That's how they had gotten away with murder sixty years ago.

§2§

Nelsey Kinzer wiped her hands on her calico apron and looked around the Maynard kitchen. The faded speckled-yellow linoleum was cracked and buckling but sparkling clean. The old-fashioned lime-colored gas stove was forty years old but it worked. *Well, Lord, the place looks good enough. Smells good enough, too. You'd think they'd be up by now. The sun's shinin', for heaven's sakes. Don't care how late they got to bed, don't know how a person can sleep after the sun's up.*

She popped her biscuits into the oven and let the door slam shut with a bang. She poured hot coffee into a carafe on the table, then smacked the empty battered tin pot on the old stove with a clang. *That oughta do it,* she thought, and with a small smile of satisfaction heard a baby whimper from an upstairs bedroom.

A flurry of activity erupted over her head, and soon hurried footsteps came down the back stairs. A slim woman holding a toddler in her arms appeared in the doorway, an alarmed look in her river green eyes. Sun-streaked bronze hair floated about her face and shoulders in a wavy cloud. Slender bare feet, toenails painted flaming red, showed beneath her white terry cloth robe. The baby rubbed its eyes with a curled-up fist and stared at Nelsey.

"Who are you?" the woman asked, bewildered. "What are you doing in my kitchen?"

"I'm Nelsey Kinzer." *Who'd she think I was, Hillary Clinton?* "Thought you might like some breakfast. Have a seat."

"Look here, I . . . well, sure. I didn't expect . . ."

Didn't expect some hillbilly woman to be neighborly, did you?

"Don't know what you expected, but I expect that baby of yours is hungry. Do ya mind introducin' us?"

"This is Katie." She smiled. She lost her look of alarm and her whole face lit up as she kissed the child on its flushed cheek.

"Set Katie in the high chair there. I'll watch her while you brush your teeth, or whatever it is you need to do when you get up in the morning."

The woman needed nothing. Memphis Maynard was the prettiest woman Nelsey had ever seen. As far as Nelsey was concerned, Memphis Maynard could march right outside in her cloth robe and bare feet and into the town of Yancey as she was. *Wait'll those horny old lechers in town get a gander at this. She sure don't look like those pictures in* Life *magazine. Combat helmet she wore in those pictures hid all that springy hair. With the black sunglasses, the mud on her face, and the pack on her back, she'd looked more like a man.*

Nelsey watched Memphis struggle with the decision of whether or not to leave the baby alone with her. Acting unconcerned, Nelsey turned and poured pancake batter onto the hot iron griddle.

"Okay, sounds like a good idea," she finally said. "Thank you. I would like to wash my face and brush my teeth. I, ah, didn't know we'd be getting up so early." Nelsey heard her settle Katie into the high chair. "Katie loves pancakes, and I see you've made bacon. She likes bacon, too. Katie, you be a good girl. Mom will be right back."

She left the kitchen, then hurried back in. "Just cut

up Katie's pancake, and break the bacon into small pieces, and . . ."

"Needn't worry. I know about babies," Nelsey interrupted dryly. "Raised four of my own."

She left again and the baby began to fuss.

Nelsey placed bacon bits on her tray and a soothing hand on her head. "Don't be a worryin' child. Your mama will be right back."

"Mama," said Katie.

Katie grabbed the biggest piece of bacon and smiled at Nelsey, flashing two top and four bottom white teeth. Nelsey smiled back. "That's right. We're going to be friends, aren't we?"

By the time Memphis returned, Katie had eaten all of her pancake and bacon. Her face and pajamas were a mess of maple syrup and bacon crumbs.

"Look, Mrs. Kinzer, it was kind of you to come over this morning, but I really didn't expect to hire anyone right away, except to baby-sit Katie sometimes. I'll be interviewing people."

"I didn't expect to get paid when I come over here this morning, Miz Maynard. I just come to welcome you. Sit and have some breakfast. How do you like your coffee, black or white?"

"Black, please."

Out of the corner of her eye, Nelsey watched as Memphis busied herself cleaning up the mess Katie had made. She had changed into a pale-blue chambray shirt that she'd tucked into formfitting faded jeans, and tied a navy blue sweater around her shoulders. A straw summer belt circled her waist, and she wore red moccasins on her feet. She'd piled all that wavy hair on top of her head and secured it into a ponytail with a red bandanna. Feathery strands had already escaped. They bounced airily around her face and the back of her neck.

With quick energy she wiped the tray, washed the baby's face, and kissed her cheek.

"Your food's gettin' cold," said Nelsey.

"Right. I'm sorry. Thank you, Mrs. Kinzer. This breakfast is wonderful, delicious." Nelsey noticed she attacked the food with the same intensity she'd employed to clean up the baby's mess. Seemed like she kinda burned with energy. "We were tired when we got in last night, but I noticed how clean everything was. I do expect to pay you for opening the house and everything."

"Suit yourself. Call me Nelsey. Don't know who people are talkin' to when they say Miz Kinzer."

"Okay, Nelsey. I'll be looking for a baby-sitter. If you know anyone you can recommend, I'd appreciate it. Until I find someone who satisfies me, I'll be taking Katie with me everywhere I go."

"Don't think you'll be wantin' to take Katie with you to some of the places you'll be going."

"How do you know where I'm going?"

"Don't, exactly. But it don't take much to figure you're in Yancey County to look for your grandmother's grave because of that book Mr. Bishop is writing. Although I don't know why he thinks findin' her grave is going to change anything. Anyway, that'll mean going into rough country."

She gave Nelsey a hard look. "I don't think the grave will be that difficult to find. Jake Bishop just didn't look in the right places. Besides, my primary purpose for being here is not to search for her grave, but to find out who really murdered her. I'm sure that will only entail interviewing people in town."

"We already know who murdered Sadie Maynard."

"If you're talking about Amos Washington, that poor black handyman they railroaded to jail, I don't believe a word of it. I've read the transcripts of the trial, and I stopped by the state penitentiary on my way here. I went through every microfile they had on Amos, his conversations, behavior, and illnesses while he was in prison. There's no way that old man killed my grandmother."

"Suit yourself." Nelsey shrugged and got up to clear the table.

"And this nonsense about her ghost has got to stop."

Nelsey sighed. "You're not goin' to change mountain ways, Miz Maynard. For sixty years, Sadie Maynard's ghost has been seen up yonder on Twenty-Two Mountain, usually alongside the road wanting a ride to God knows where."

Nelsey saw the woman's face pale and wondered why.

She continued. "And some people say they even seen her around this house and back in the woods where Amos first hit her over the head." With a noisy splash Nelsey dropped the plates into the filled dishpan in the sink, then turned around to face Memphis Maynard. "If you think you're going to convince people otherwise then you got another think comin'."

"You don't like me much, do you?"

"Don't know you. Haven't made up my mind. But I do think your comin' here was foolish. Some things is best forgotten. Why don't you let your grandmother rest in peace?"

She watched Memphis's hazel eyes turn deep green with purpose. *This lady is not going to back down easy.*

"Because I don't think she's resting in peace, and if there *is* a ghost, that's the reason why. Her reputation has been grossly maligned. I didn't mind it so much when the story was a local folktale and was confined to this area, but now Jake has seen to it that millions of people know about the so-called Mysterious Case of Sadie Maynard."

"The case was solved. The only mystery is findin' her grave. People here haven't paid Jake Bishop no mind.

Only a few people in town who it'd make a difference to anyway, and they seem to be handlin' it okay."

"Well, I'm not handling it okay. Jake Bishop and I do agree on two things, though. Not only has Amos Washington been impugned, but somebody got away with murder. This town has been hiding a secret for sixty years, and I intend to uncover it."

"Jake Bishop has only implied things. He hasn't proved anything different than they did sixty years ago. What makes you think you can?"

"Jake is not the most subtle person in the world, and he wouldn't understand the people here. At least I have family ties here, a personal stake in the story, and a vague knowledge of the area."

"That'll buy you a cuppa coffee and a day-old doughnut at Leroy's."

Memphis ignored Nelsey's sarcasm. "I'm also more determined than Jake. He gives up easily."

Nelsey noticed a touch of bravado in her voice and wondered if Memphis was as tough as she pretended to be. She poured them both another cup of coffee and sat down across from her. "Sounds like you know this Jake Bishop."

Memphis hesitated for a moment, then looked Nelsey straight in the eye. "I know Jake Bishop very well. We haven't seen each other in over two years, but he's Katie's father."

"I see," said Nelsey. Startled, but struggling not to show it, she sipped her coffee. *Sure was more goin' on in Bosnia than a war.* "Well, he's not very popular around here."

"That's understandable. Jake's going to look for the dirty part of any story, and he doesn't care how he digs it up." She rushed on, as if she didn't want any further discussion of Jake Bishop. "Nelsey, I know you're not thrilled about my being here, or maybe just the *reason* for my being here, but you've been good enough to give us a lovely welcome this morning and, I wonder . . . well, if you could just kind of help me get started."

She smiled, and Nelsey could see how Memphis could charm a story out of someone. The smile lit up her face like her eyes lit up when she looked at Katie.

"How would that be?" Nelsey asked.

"Well, just information about some of the principal families involved. Aside from Amos Washington, Macauley Tate was the principal suspect. I understand he has a grandson living here."

"Yep. Cutter Tate lives here with his father, Bill Tate."

"Umm, so Macauley Tate's son is still living. I'm surprised Jake didn't mention him in the series. I'll put him at the top of my list to interview."

"Won't do you no good. Bill had a stroke years ago. Paralyzed. Sits in a wheelchair and can't speak. Has a male nurse, Victor, takin' care of him."

"I see. What about the grandson? I know he's a mining engineer, but he's also considered a wealthy man. How can that be? Mining engineers don't make much money unless they own mines of some kind, and there's no money in coal mines anymore. And now that I think of it, though he was older than I was, I vaguely remember Cutter Tate as some sort of juvenile delinquent." Nelsey watched as she puckered her forehead in concentration. "Seems as if my grandfather mentioned him as a troublemaker."

Nelsey decided it was best to ignore the remark about Cutter and Sheriff Maynard.

"Nothing suspicious about Cutter's money. He's just good at buying up real estate and mineral rights. Owns lots of property around here, some of it inherited from his grandfather. He's a lawyer, but don't practice except in the wintertime." Nelsey heard the note of pride in her voice and reminded herself that pride was a sin. "Mostly he uses his other degree. Cutter went to school to learn how to reclaim land stripped by the mines."

Nelsey stopped, telling herself that sometimes she talked too much.

"What do you mean, reclaim the land?"

"Senator Elizabeth Brady got a bunch of laws passed about restoring land. Now the mine owner is required to replace and replant any land ruined by mining operations. That's what Cutter does. He travels all over, designing landscapes, planting trees, stuff like that."

When he isn't fightin' to get back what's rightly his. Nelsey clamped her mouth shut.

Katie had been banging her tray with a spoon. Now she wailed impatiently. Memphis stood and lifted her swiftly out of the high chair. Katie's wail turned to laughter as Memphis swooped her through the air like a bird. The sight of the two of them warmed Nelsey's heart. Can't help but like them, she thought grudgingly.

"Don't remember me, do you?" asked Nelsey.

"I'm sorry, should I? Our grandfather never let us associate with many people around here."

"I know, but your step-grandma Alma used to bring you to visit with me when I still lived on the mountain."

"You're the storyteller! I told Margo that's who you might be. We sat around a bonfire and roasted marshmallows while you told stories."

"Yep."

"It's been a pleasant memory."

"I'm glad. You were sure a talker then. Always had a lot of questions about your real grandmother. Wanted to know what Sadie was like, and did I ever know her."

"Did you know Sadie?"

Lord, help me to tighten my tongue.

"Kind of. I was a child when she was alive," she said shortly and turned to find a towel to dry the dishes.

"Katie needs changing and cleaning up," said Memphis. "Thank you, Nelsey. Just leave the dishes. I'll clean up when I get back. By the way, where is your house?"

Nelsey pointed out the kitchen window. "Just got a new roof. You can see it over there, that red patch showing through the big oak tree down the hill. Five-minute walk. You have my number if you need me."

"Thank you again." She hefted Katie on her hip and walked to the door. "Oh, by the way, where would I find Cutter Tate this morning?"

"You'd have to call his office, but Cutter's not much of a talker even if you can find him."

"I called his office before I left New York. They said they couldn't give me his schedule."

Nelsey hesitated. She knew where Cutter would be this morning, and she also knew Memphis Maynard would drag that baby all over the county until she found him. Would be better on the baby if Nelsey at least pointed Memphis in the right direction.

"Cutter can't help you, but if you're set on seein' him I expect he'll be at the latest site, top of Cat Teeth."

"Cat Teeth?"

"Cat Teeth Mountain. It's up Route Sixteen." She'd tell her where, but she wouldn't draw her a map. "Get a map of the county roads at the chamber of commerce in the courthouse."

"Thank you. I will." She left, running up the stairs with that baby like she was superwoman or something.

Nelsey reached for the black rotary-dial telephone that sat on a scratched-up pine desk. Cutter's line was busy. She'd try him again later.

The early morning sky was a clear blue; the air, cool and crisp. Cutter watched a pair of cardinals flash red and ginger through the air and settle in the fading gold of the maple tree next to his rear terrace. The birds were a reassuring sight. Cardinals mated for life. To Cutter that was intriguing.

Alison had just driven off, back to Charleston, and he missed her. She was good company. He looked at his watch and sighed. He liked to be up on the mountain early, but when Birdy phoned he'd promised he'd wait until she got here. Somewhere along the way, Birdy Harless had appointed herself his guardian, probably in high school. She was a best friend, but sometimes she could be a real pain in the ass.

He could hear her coming through the house now. Clippety clip, clippety clip, moving quickly in those eternal high heels of hers.

"Hi, Jackson," he heard her greet their houseman, whom she'd known since childhood. "Would you be a sweetie and tell Lulu I'd love a corn muffin? Mornin', Mr. Tate. Mornin', Victor. How ya doin' this mornin'?"

Cutter imagined her throwing her airy kisses to his father and his male nurse.

She fluttered through the open French doors, her gardenia-scented perfume preceding her, pecked Cutter on the cheek, and perched on the white, wrought-iron chair opposite him at the table. With a tiny frame, a small beak of a nose, and a whistling little voice, Beatrice Harless came by her childhood nickname honestly.

"Well, heavens to Betsy, Cutter, I know it's past time for you to be gettin' married, but I surely don't think Alison Morgan is the woman for you."

"Birdy, I don't recall asking for your sterling opinion. For Christ's sake, is that what you wanted to talk to me about?"

"No, and don't be so grouchy."

Amused, he held his tongue while he watched her pour a cup of coffee, her thin lips primly set.

"Birdy, darlin', speak or forever hold your peace."

"Sadie's ghost has been seen again."

"What's so unusual about that? People have been seeing her for years."

"It usually means something bad is going to happen, Cutter. You know that."

Sadie's appearances did seem to coincide with unfortunate circumstances. Once a tornado tore through the county an hour after Sadie had been sighted. Another time a baby drowned at the lake.

"That's a bunch of baloney, Birdy, and you know it. You're an educated woman. Use the brains God gave you."

"Remember the time she appeared the morning of your birthday? Nelsey had your party at Chief Logan Park. It stormed and Jimmy Mac got hit by lightning. He's been a soft-brained do-do ever since. Counts his toes and picks boogers out of his nose all day long."

"Well, his nitwit of a mother hid him under a tree, for Christ's sake. He's lucky to be alive, poor guy. Get serious, Birdy. Lightning strikes now and again."

"Okay, so you don't take any of it seriously, but I'm not finished. Wait till you hear this." She blew on her coffee and arched her blond eyebrows.

"What is it, Birdy?" he asked, trying to be patient. Birdy meant well.

"Guess who just arrived in town?"

"Who?" His patience was wearing thin.

"Memphis Maynard. Sadie's granddaughter."

Alarm crowded his impatience, but he took in a breath and let it out slowly.

"I do believe the Maynard sisters still own the old Maynard place," he said sarcastically. "I don't see anything unusual about one of them visiting. Nelsey says the place has been neglected and needs attention. No one's lived there since old Sheriff Maynard died ten years ago."

"Really, Cutter. Now who's being a dunce? If you can't see that it's no coincidence, her arriving here right after the publicity about Jake Bishop's book, then you're a bigger fool than I thought."

"So, she's a nostalgic person, or a genealogy buff, or she's come back to sell the house or something." But his curiosity got the better of him. "Which sister is it? The actress or the photojournalist?"

"Ah-ha! So you do know who they are?"

"Of course I do. I read the newspapers, Birdy. They're both beautiful women."

"Well, it's the photographer. They say she's going to write a book about the whole sordid thing, too."

Dammit. He wished they would all go away and leave him alone. The story was ancient history, but it seemed to have a life of its own. Just when he thought everyone had forgotten about his grandfather and Sadie Maynard, up it would pop again. He supposed it wouldn't bother most people, and though he hadn't even been born at the time, for Cutter the 1930s scandal held deep personal pain. He would do anything to defend his beloved grandfather's fragile reputation.

He knew the whole town had always felt that it was probably Macauley Tate who had killed Sadie Maynard and then let a black man go to jail for him. But because of their respect and affection for the mine owner, and because of the prejudices against black people at the time, they'd held their tongues.

So the whole town, and he supposed its descendants, hid a kind of collective guilt. He knew his grandfather had *not* killed the woman, either accidentally or on purpose. He also suspected that Memphis Maynard had put herself in harm's way in coming to Yancey.

He heard Birdy rattling on about something, a baby, Nelsey, Jake Bishop. She'd read in *People* magazine that the baby was Jake Bishop's but they'd never been married. He let her rattle. None of it registered. His mind was filled with the loving face of his grandfather. Cutter's life had changed drastically after the death of the only person who had truly loved him.

". . . I mean, really . . . Sally Junior is supposed to be practically engaged to H. A. the third. Well, finally I told Sally Junior she was an utter idiot if she dated that Bishop man. I mean, he is kind of cute and all, or maybe sexy is the word, with all that long blond hair and that Jaguar he drives, but I told her he just wanted to date her so he could get information out of her. Poor child's never had a lick of sense, but then her mother never did either, God rest her alcoholic soul."

"Birdy, darlin', the last thing I want to talk about this morning is Sally Hutton and Jake Bishop." He stood up. "I have to go."

"But I haven't had my corn muffin yet."

"Then go into the kitchen and tell Lulu what you want. You know, Birdy, you're the one who should be getting married. You're thirty-eight years old. If you had a family of your own, you wouldn't be worrying so much about me and my affairs."

Birdy stood up quickly, flushing bright crimson and sloshing coffee out of her mug onto the stone terrace.

"Why Cutter Tate, that was mean. I've lo—" She stopped, blushing even brighter, her eyes watering. She continued with difficulty, tripping over her words. "I've . . . I've known you since we were five years old. Of course I, uh, care about what happens to you, but you don't need to tease me about it."

With dawning embarrassment and concern, Cutter realized that Birdy was telling the truth. All these years Birdy had been there for him, and he'd always taken her for granted.

He gathered her to him and gave her an affectionate hug, ruffling her short curly blond hair.

"I'm sorry, darlin'. I know you care, and I care about you. But sometimes you get too nosey."

She snuggled into him with a big sigh. "I know, Cutter, don't worry about it. No problem."

He gave her a light kiss on the forehead and set her away from him. "Now, I have to go to work. Come over for dinner tomorrow night."

"Maybe. Cutter," she called after him as he walked away, "I don't think Sadie's sighting and Memphis Maynard's arrival are a coincidence. Please be careful."

Memphis loved driving when she wasn't in a hurry. Never knowing what to expect around the next bend gave her an unending sense of expectation and freedom, and Katie loved riding in the car. Memphis rarely used her Jeep in Manhattan, so this was a real treat for both of them.

The trip up Cat Teeth's winding road had been a gift assortment of surprises: a dipping, breathtaking view, a darting deer, a glimpse of a tiny community of white houses tucked away in a deep valley, a spreading sugar maple tinting gold with autumn. Unable to resist, she'd stopped several times to take pictures. She was beginning to feel better about being in Yancey.

"Look Katie, I think we're almost there."

Katie's garbled reply sounded like "most there." Just beginning to put two and three words together, she repeated everything Memphis said now.

The mountain peaks drew her eye skyward as they neared the top. The tall trees, feathery pines, and dense foliage along the sides of the road thinned, and the view spread out before her. Mountain peaks and saddlebacks shone dark-green, purple, and red against the sapphire sky. Her destination was a flattop section that looked as if it had been sheared off with a sharp knife. Residents in the mining camp at the foot of the mountain had told her that's where she would find Cutter Tate.

Expecting the ugly, bare devastation of a deserted strip-mining area, Memphis was surprised at the healthy, nurtured appearance of the landscaped site.

She followed attractive blue-and-white signs directing her to the Cat Teeth Mining Operations office and parked in front of a large square cinder block building. She unfastened Katie from her car seat, and carrying her on her hip, went inside.

Two men in gray utility jumpsuits worked at drafting tables. Wall-sized chalkboards behind them displayed handwritten charts, and figures flashed across green-screened computers. Willie Nelson's "Uncloudy Day" came from speakers in the ceiling. They looked at her in surprise, then both of them jumped to their feet. She wondered which one was Cutter Tate.

"Excuse me, I'm sorry to interrupt your work, but I'm looking for Mr. Tate."

"Uh, yes ma'am. Sorry we're so slow on the uptake. You startled us. We don't get many visitors up here. Cutter's at the mine."

"I thought this mountain was all mined out."

"Almost. We're cleaning out the last of the coal and then we replant."

"I see." She smiled sweetly, but couldn't resist a jab. "That's why they call it 'strip'-mining, I guess, because you strip everything you see."

"It's not called 'strip'-mining anymore, miss, it's called 'surface'-mining."

"How do I find Mr. Tate?"

They glanced at one another. "Well, I suppose one of us could show you the way, but I don't think the boss is expecting anyone. . . . And, eh, well, you sure you want to take the baby? It's kind of a rough road, and there's a lot of big heavy machinery at the site. . . . It's real noisy."

"Wait a minute, Bob, I don't think Big Molly is running today."

"You're right." He looked at his watch. "Cutter usually takes a break around this time in the morning. I suppose it would be okay. Come on, miss. You can follow my truck."

"I'm sure I can find the way if you'll just point me in the right direction."

"Well, it's against the rules for anyone to be wandering around up here. You can get lost easy."

"I don't wander, gentlemen, and I don't get lost. I've hiked and driven an army jeep over more rough terrain than you can imagine. I can take care of myself and Katie." She knew she sounded like some tough broad, but she'd learned the hard way that in this business you had to be.

"I'm sure you can, miss. Nevertheless, I'm showing you the way. Them's Cutter's rules, and that's the way it is."

Memphis gave up. Their surprise at her visit had turned to wariness, and now was not the time to anger anyone. She flashed her best smile.

"Okay."

The man put on a hard hat and walked out the door. Memphis followed him, fuming. She hated depending on anyone else for anything, even directions. If they knew how many battle-scarred fields and woods she'd maneuvered through, and how many bullets and bombs she'd dodged in the last ten years, they wouldn't be so bossy about their rules.

Fifteen minutes later, they arrived at a site more like what she'd expected in the first place. Huge earth-moving machinery sat in a whitish gray boulder-pocked shallow crater the size of a football field. It looked as if God, in a fitful fury, had squeezed the top of the mountain in his fist until everything had pulverized into chalky dust.

The engineer driving the pickup truck in front of her blew his horn, pointed a finger toward an enormous piece of machinery, then circled off and left her alone. A dust cloud mushroomed when his truck scratched off. Fine grit blew in puffs, entered the open Jeep windows, and settled on her and Katie. They coughed, and Katie started crying. Memphis closed the windows and turned on the air conditioning. She reached in the backseat to wipe Katie's face and give her a drink of water. Maybe bringing Katie hadn't been such a great idea.

"Don't cry, honey-babe. He was a rude man, wasn't he? As soon as the dust settles, I'll have you out of this car in no time flat."

But Katie's wail increased in volume. "Katie, quiet, honey. I promise we won't be here long."

She had to find a good baby-sitter soon. She fished in the canvas bag of baby supplies, found Opal Marie, Katie's favorite rag doll, and gave it to her. Katie poked her finger in Opal Marie's soft tummy, then hugged the doll, and quieted until her sobs became small hiccups.

The dust settled, and Memphis gingerly maneuvered the Jeep across the moonlike crater. The man she'd spotted stood next to an enormous yellow grader the size of a two-story building. She put the car in park, cut the motor, and considered the situation. Katie walked well enough, but the surface was rough. She'd have to carry her.

As she walked toward the man, Katie on her hip, an acute sense of déjà vu filled her, so strong that it almost stopped her in her tracks.

He stood with his foot on the scraper of the grader, studying a clipboard in his hand. Impervious to her approach, he made a notation and flipped a page. Of course, that's why she felt she'd been here before. With his hard hat, khakis, and heavy boots, and his blue shirtsleeves rolled beyond his tanned biceps, the man looked like a Clark Gable or Jeff Chandler character in one of those 1950s Texas oil-gusher movies.

He continued studying the clipboard, obviously ignoring her.

"Hi," she called as she drew closer. "Are you Cutter Tate?"

He didn't change expression or move a muscle. His eyes on his work, he asked in a gruff voice, "Where's your hard hat?"

"I beg your pardon?"

"Anybody with sense knows you don't come into an area like this without protection. Bob should have given you a hat. Bringing the baby wasn't a bright idea either."

Memphis knew he was right, but she quivered with indignation.

"Sorry. If I ever come again I'll be sure and follow the rules. In the meantime, are you Cutter Tate?"

"That who you're looking for?"

"Yes."

"Then I guess you've found him," he said, still not looking at her. He flipped another page over the clipboard and made a notation.

Talk about rudeness.

"I'm Memphis Maynard."

"I know."

He stuck the yellow pencil between his ear and the hard hat, and finally looked at her. His eyes dusted over her casually. She sucked in air, hard, trying to breathe normally as the alarming feeling of déjà vu hit her once again.

His eyes were an arresting silver gray, the color of early morning mist. The mahogany, hard-angled planes of his face documented his outdoor work. From the faint white lines slanting upwards alongside his eyes and firm mouth, she could tell there were times when Cutter Tate laughed a lot, but he wasn't smiling now.

"It wasn't hard to figure, Miss Maynard," he continued. "Yancey is a small town. I heard about your arrival. I don't get female visitors up here often, unless it's a state inspector. Are you an inspector, Miss Maynard?"

"You know I'm not, and you must know why I'm here then."

"I can guess. Is that your child?"

"This is my daughter, Katie."

"Do you always take her with you when you're talking to a man about murder and disgrace?"

His attitude was infuriating.

"No, I don't. I'm interviewing nannies this afternoon. Until I'm sure I've found someone appropriate, Katie comes with me."

"We don't have 'nannies' in Yancey, Miss Maynard. We have baby-sitters. You won't find anyone better than Nelsey, by the way. She's helped raise most of the babies in town."

Katie whimpered, "Mama."

"We'll be just a moment, Katie, then we'll go for another car ride. Mama wants to ask the man some questions."

"I'll save you some time." The misty gray eyes grew hard and cold, like polished moonstones. He removed his foot from the scraper and stood straight, towering above her. "I have nothing to say to you—no new answers to old questions, no startling revelations about my grandfather or your grandmother. So, please, leave me alone. I'm sorry you made the trip here for nothing."

Katie was crying now and heavy on her hip.

"After I went to the trouble to drive up here, you at least owe me the courtesy of a brief conversation, Mr. Tate. I will get to the bottom of this story, no matter what, with or without your cooperation, so you might as well talk to me."

His heavy eyebrows drawn together in one severe line, his lips hard against his teeth, he said, "I owe you nothing. I didn't invite you here, Miss Maynard, and I don't mean to be discourteous, but I repeat . . . we . . . have . . . nothing . . . to talk about. Period. Your child needs your attention."

Accustomed to having the last word in any interview, Memphis's fury mounted but Katie's wails grew louder and louder.

"I'll contact you at a later time, perhaps tomorrow at your home."

She hated being pushy. Jake had often said she wasn't pushy enough, so she'd had to develop an aggressiveness that wasn't natural to her, and she would use every skill she possessed to get to the bottom of this mess.

She spun on her heel and marched in double time to the car, as fast as she could with Katie bumping on her hip.

He called after her. "Don't bother, Miss Maynard. I won't be home."

In the Jeep she located a cookie for Katie, wiped her wet face with a Kleenex, held her close in her arms, and soothed her. "Shh, shhh, Katie, babe. Everything's okay. We're going home now."

Katie clung close to her, her fat little arms hugging her neck, her wet cheeks tucked safe into the fold of Memphis's neck. "I love you, Katie. Love you."

"Luv you, Mama," mumbled Katie sleepily into her neck.

She turned and saw that Cutter Tate had summarily dismissed her. He was walking away and was already near the center of the crater, heading toward a crew of men who stood on the far side. He had the walk of a big man, with narrow hips and long legs swinging forward slow and easy—an unstudied, but arrogant, sensual stride.

"Well, Mr. Arrogant Tate. I'm not dismissed easily. One way or another, you *will* talk to me."

§3§

Cutter shoved the book on Rolls-Royce engines back onto the library shelf. It didn't contain the information he needed, but he was lucky to have found anything at all on the subject in the Yancey County Library.

A project of the Yancey Women's Club, the library was housed in a gracious old home left to the organization by a deceased member. It sat on the banks of the Tow River among lovely oaks and sycamores, a quiet, peaceful place to while away idle hours. The women were well-meaning and earnest about their library, but even with the financial support of the town and county, their resources were limited.

He would have to drive to Charleston to do the research on the "Merlin" engine of his ML-407 Spitfire. Only two of the twin-seater fighters remained from World War II, and he was the proud owner of one of them. He'd paid too much for it, but owning the dainty but feisty plane had long been a dream of his. Everyone thought he was nuts, especially the previous owner: a Brit who had predicted he'd have trouble finding anyone to work on the engine in the United States.

"And where," the man had then asked condescendingly, "in West Virginia do you find a flat parcel of ground to wing off from, my friend?"

Little did the snob know that several of the mountaintop areas Cutter had reclaimed were perfect for taking off and landing the plane. The Spitfire needed scant room for takeoff and performed better on grass than on asphalt.

So far he'd been lucky. He and a mechanic in Charleston with good hands and a good brain had handled minor repairs and tune-ups. But he'd heard an odd rattle in the fifty-five-year-old engine this morning and had cut short his weekly Saturday morning pleasure flight.

As he reached for a book titled *The History of Engines*, he heard the bell on the beveled-glass door tinkle as someone entered.

"Good morning, ma'am. My name is Memphis Maynard, and I'm hoping you can help me."

"Why, I hope I can help you, too," said Carolyn Cabe in her shaky ancient-librarian voice. Carolyn had been in charge of the library when he was a child. Cutter couldn't see the two women, but he could imagine Carolyn's toothy, yellow smile. "You wouldn't be the lady war correspondent, would you? Why, of course you are. I remember pictures of you, and I think I remember someone saying you were in Yancey for some reason or another. Gracious! We're honored to have you in the library. We have some of your articles on Bosnia over there in the magazine section. Is that why you came?"

"No, ma'am, but thank you, I'm looking for . . ."

Though the politest and kindest of ladies, Carolyn was hard of hearing and sometimes talked right through someone else's words.

"The high school children use those articles a lot for current-event papers." Carolyn's chair scraped the floor as she got up. "We also have that wonderful series you did when you followed up Depression families. Here. You come with me. I'll find them for you."

"No, no, please keep your seat." Memphis spoke

louder. "Please sit down and finish your tea. I came for another reason. If you'll point me in the right direction, I'm sure I can find the information I need."

Cutter smiled. The sight of fragile, bowed Carolyn Cabe tottering among the dusty shelves must have alarmed the pushy Maynard woman. Well, at least she had some consideration for the elderly, he thought. They were on the other side of his aisle now. He could see the pink sleeve of Carolyn Cabe's dress through the books. He probably should reveal himself, but Carolyn knew where he was—or had she forgotten he was in here?

Admit it, Tate. The sound of Memphis Maynard's voice captivated him, and he wanted to listen a while longer. There was none of the New York clipped hardness, which surprised him. He supposed she'd acquired the lilting confident tone during her world travels.

"I'm looking for microfilm on copies of newspapers sixty years old," said Memphis to Carolyn.

"Oh, my gracious, child. We don't have such things in this library."

"But the clerks over at the newspaper office said you would have what I needed."

"Oh, no, child. You must be mistaken. They have microfilm there of newspapers back to 1925. I have nothing here except some old newspapers that were of special interest. What topic are you interested in?"

"The murder of Sadie Maynard."

There was a long silence. Cutter held his breath.

"I see," said Carolyn Cabe, her warm tone changing to chill aloofness. He could almost imagine her thought processes. "Are you kin to the Maynards?"

"Yes, ma'am. Sheriff and Sadie Maynard were my grandparents."

"I should have known, should have made the connection. In fact, I do believe I remember your step-grandmother, Alma, bringing you in here when you were a child."

"Yes, ma'am. She did."

"Well, I'm sorry, Miss Maynard. I have nothing that would help you. You've made a trip for nothing. Now if you will excuse me, I have work to do."

Cutter had already walked to the end of the aisle. He stepped around to intercept Carolyn before she could reach her desk.

"It's okay, Miss Cabe. Show her what you have."

Distress in her watery blue eyes, Carolyn Cabe said, "But I really don't have much, Cutter."

What the hell, he had nothing to hide. Besides, Memphis would find nothing that Jake Bishop hadn't already found. "I know, but give her what you have, and call the *Yancey Record* and tell Ed I'm sending Miss Maynard back over there. Tell him I said to let her look at all the microfilm she wants."

Carolyn tottered toward her desk while Memphis faced him.

"So, Cutter Tate loiters behind library shelves listening to private conversations, and the local newspaper lies about microfilm. What a nice town Yancey is," said Memphis. Her eyes blazed with indignation. "No wonder my mother left years ago."

"I wasn't loitering, and you were conversing in a public place. I apologize for the *Yancey Record*. We're not trying to hide anything here, Miss Maynard. There's nothing to hide. We're all just kind of private. If you'd ever lived in a small town, you'd understand how we take care of one another."

"Seems like a bit more than that. They're all pretty eager to protect you, Mr. Tate, which leads me to believe there *is* something to hide."

She wore a vivid green crewneck sweater over tan shorts, and ankle-high hiking boots with bulky white socks folded over the top. Except for a nasty white scar that bisected one knee, her legs were still tan from summer. The sweater made her eyes all the greener, the dark smoky jade of river water. Summer eyes, he thought, summer rivers reflecting leafy branches and crystal skies.

Though he stood six feet from her he saw the intensity of her anger, and he couldn't blame her. For the moment the anger didn't disturb him, for he was caught in a wondering time warp. He'd seen pictures of Sadie Maynard. Faded, colorless, grainy gray images. Did Memphis look like her grandmother? Yes, there was a resemblance. Had Sadie's summer-river eyes also heated to a hot emerald when she was angry?

"No one is hiding anything. They're just being protective."

"Of you."

"Yes, of me." He didn't mention there might be a few others who were being protected, too.

She placed a fist on her hip and leaned against the bookshelf.

"Why do they love *you* so much, Mr. Tate?"

"They don't. It's just habit. They've taken care of me since I was ten years old."

She nipped at her bottom lip, then let it go.

Cutter knew instinctively that she was fighting her curiosity, that she was dying to ask why the town of Yancey showed a proprietary interest in Cutter Tate, grandson of a suspected murderer. But she also knew the answer had little to do with her investigation, and if it did she would find out elsewhere. Somewhere along the way, Faith Maynard had made sure her daughters were brought up correctly. Good breeding dictated that unnecessary, nosey questions were not polite, even from the toughest of reporters.

"Going hiking?" he asked, changing the subject and looking pointedly at her boots.

"Yes."

"You'll wish you'd worn slacks or jeans. It's getting colder, and the higher parts of our mountains are rough terrain."

"I'll keep that in mind," she said, but he knew from her stubborn tone that she wouldn't.

"Where's the baby?"

"I took your advice and hired Nelsey Kinzer."

"Good. You won't regret it." He had no compunctions about being nosey. She came here to delve into his private life, so he had a right. "Looking for Sadie's burial site, I suppose?"

"Yes. That's one of the reasons I'm here, remember?"

"And the other reason?"

He watched as, unconsciously, she braced her shoulders, took a deep breath, stood straight and proud, then spoke out.

"I intend to prove that your grandfather killed my grandmother, and the whole town helped him cover it up."

He'd egged her on, knowing what she was going to say, so why was he suddenly so furious with her? He'd wanted to provoke her. It was as if he knew her eyes would glisten with anger again, and that her full bottom lip would quiver a bit, and that her forehead would crease and then smooth back to its former fairness.

Cutter felt the same inexplicable impulse he'd experienced when he first met her at the mine yesterday. He wanted to kiss her, hard and long. He wanted to sweep Memphis Maynard into his arms, hold her tight against him and explore her taut slimness, discover the secret places that ignited all that burning energy. He wanted to take her right there on the waxed library floor between Ibsen and Hemingway.

He shook his head to clear it, and a chuckle began to well within him at the consequences of what he'd just imagined. Carolyn Cabe would never be the same again, and the ladies of the Yancey County Library Board would have something to talk about for years to come. But the way Memphis Maynard affected him wasn't a laughing matter, and his humor left him quickly.

Instead, he shifted slightly to his right and barred her forward motion, for she'd started to walk away toward Carolyn Cabe's desk.

"It's quite obvious that you and Jake Bishop are working together on this." He heard the animosity in his voice and did nothing to hide it. "In fact, you probably sent him here. How else would he have known about a murder that occurred in 1936 in an obscure little town in West Virginia? Jake Bishop is the type of man who is motivated only by money, fame, or a beautiful woman. *You* fit the bill." His voice grew harder. "I'll tell you what I told him. My grandfather was a brief suspect in the case, as were others in the town. He had nothing to do with Sadie's death. Believe it. Go back to New York."

"Evidence shows otherwise, Mr. Tate. I'll stay until I prove it. Now get out of my way."

She placed a hand on his arm to move him aside, but snatched it back as if she'd been burned and looked at him strangely. He understood her consternation. He was sure she'd felt the same warm tingle that he had.

The tension that had grown between them stretched until it strummed and vibrated like a tautly tuned guitar string. Cutter knew he would never forget the smell of musty old books and the monotone ticking of the library clock as they stared at one another in the silence, stunned. Her touch had ignited an excitement and warmth he hadn't felt in years. It flickered and grew and rolled like a fireball burning a path between them.

She spoke first. "I . . . I'm sorry. I shouldn't have pushed you. I, uh, it was rude. I'm so sorry." She hung her head for a second and looked at her feet in confusion and embarrassment, emotions he thought were probably uncharacteristic of her.

"That's okay. I shouldn't have blocked your way. I'm sorry, too. We're acting like children."

Cutter held his hand out to her. He couldn't resist. He wanted to feel her hand in his. Would she take it?

Memphis hesitated, staring at his hand as if it were a hot coal in the fire that flickered and danced about them.

"I'm not offering my hand in friendship," he said, "because, under the circumstances, I doubt if we could ever be friends. But since you insist on staying in Yancey and pursuing this course of action, I'd like to think we could at least be polite to one another."

"Yes, you're right."

She placed her hand in his and gave it a brief, firm squeeze. He held the slim softness seconds longer than necessary and found the swift-beating artery in the tender vulnerability of her wrist. Instantly, his heart shifted to keep rhythm with hers, as if it had been waiting to rediscover this particular pattern of thrum and drum.

Behind them, he heard Carolyn Cabe approaching. Reluctantly, he released Memphis's hand.

"I called Ed Roberts, editor of the *Record*," Carolyn said coolly to Memphis. "He said come over and he'll let you search the microfilm."

Cutter watched relief spread over Memphis's face.

"Good luck," he said. "You won't find anything your friend Bishop hasn't already found, but good hunting. And good hiking."

She nodded, thanked both of them, and left quickly.

For Cutter, the library became a dull and empty place, devoid of light and warmth. He knew something momentous had just occurred, but he wasn't sure if he liked it or not.

"Everything all right, son?" asked Carolyn.

He realized then that he'd groaned. "Oh, sure, Carolyn. I'm just fine." But he knew that he wasn't.

"Carolyn, where are the books with Memphis Maynard's photos? I'd like to see them."

The trip to the cemetery, which was tucked back in a nook of hill and valley, had been fruitless. Unkempt and uncared for, the old place was tall with weeds, and leaning gravestones angled drunkenly into the earth. Memphis had searched diligently for a hidden sign—a half-buried marker, or a barren stone or plot—but found nothing.

Nelsey had asked her this morning why finding the grave was so important to her. Memphis had told her that it was Jake Bishop's discovery that no one could find the grave that had intrigued her. Why should it be so hard to find? It must hold a secret, or some clue as to the mystery of Sadie, or it would be more visible.

She hadn't mentioned the horrid, screaming argument she and Margo had overheard between their mother and grandfather the last summer they'd spent here. Crouched in a dark upstairs closet, ears covered, they'd cowered away from the angry, frightening words. Memphis remembered that Faith had returned from a visit to a cemetery that she'd assumed held her mother's grave site, but hadn't been able to find a commemorative marker. Grandfather Maynard had said someone must have moved it without his permission.

The argument had escalated from there. Faith had dispatched her daughters upstairs. As they ran, Memphis's heart had knocked so madly that she thought it would jump out of her throat and beat her racing feet to the top of the stairs.

"What have you done with her? Where is her grave? Everytime I come, you promise we'll go to it, and then you make up excuses. I want to know now." Faith had stomped her foot.

The sound of a slap had reached them, and a wounded cry from Faith. Memphis had jumped to open the closet door, wanting to go to her mother's rescue, but Margo had held her back.

"Don't you yell at me, girl," her grandfather had said. "You leave well enough alone. I know where she is on the mountain, and I visit the place by myself. She belongs to me, and you don't need to be lookin' for her last restin' place. Alma raised you, and you need to be thinkin' of *her* as your mother."

"I'm grateful to Alma, but I remember that my real mother loved me dearly, as I love my daughters."

"Them two need a hand taken to them. They're beautiful, but wild, jest like your mother was."

Faith's voice had lowered then, but the young girls had heard the bitter, fearful tones of their mother and grandfather, and a snatch of words now and then.

"You'll never touch them. . . ."

"If you know what's good for you . . ."

"There's more than you're telling me. . . ."

". . . never be safe around here."

Sobs and cries followed.

Faith had slept with them that night, holding them tight in her arms. In the morning they had departed and never returned. Memphis would never forget her mother's pinched white face as they drove through the mountains to their home in Tennessee.

She sighed and shoved the depressing scene away from her as she always did.

Parched, dusty, and itching with what she feared were chiggers, Memphis drove the Jeep over the bridge that crossed the broad, rushing creek at the bottom of the hill to her grandparents' house. The wooden planks vibrated and grumbled at the passage of her tires and the weight of the Jeep. Despite her weariness, she smiled at the creaky groans of the old bridge. It smelled of sun-baked tar, and she remembered the hot, sticky, splintery feel of the planked wood beneath her bare feet as she'd crossed it many times when she was a child.

At the end of the bridge was Leroy's, where she and Margo used to buy Popsicles and fresh lush juicy peaches on long stifling summer days.

She'd been dying for a cold drink since she'd left the cemetery. She'd stop at Leroy's before she traveled on up to the house.

The squeaking screen door into Leroy's Place closed behind Memphis with a whack. She remembered now that it always had, and she saw quickly that nothing else had changed much either.

The not-so-quick grocery store, a mile down the hill from the house, was one of the last of a dying breed. Leroy still sold pig's feet in stone jugs, and purple pickled eggs in gallon jars, bread, milk, brown eggs, and Coca-Cola of course, in small green glass bottles, and Royal Crown Cola, or RC as it was called. At the four-stool counter sat an aged, shoulder-bowed Leroy, a cigarette burning close to nicotine-stained fingers. With him sat two retired coal miners, their pale, seamed faces evidence of years below the earth's surface.

Their conversation stopped when Memphis entered. They watched in curious, although not unkind, silence as she walked across the canted floorboards to the squat red-metal drink box, which sat near the center of the store. The box had a silver lip of a bottle opener, and a scripted Coca-Cola logo was scrawled across the front. Memphis wondered if the Coca-Cola people in Atlanta knew they had an antique sitting in the mountains of West Virginia.

"Howdy," said Leroy. "What kin I do for you, miss?"

"I just need some milk, and a few Cokes," she answered.

"Hep yourself," he said, and the three went back to their gossiping.

She lifted the heavy lid of the drink box and searched around beneath the icy watery slush. Her fingers had just identified the crimped top of a Coke when a familiar voice came from the dim recesses of the store.

"We've been all over the world together, Memphis. Who'da thunk we'd meet up again at Leroy's?"

The bottle dropped from her fingers back into the icy water.

"Jake?"

He stepped into view, cocked a hip, and slouched lazily against the red-metal box to stare at her. "Hello, beautiful."

With careful deliberation, she stilled her fast-beating heart.

"What are you doing here?"

He took a swig from the Orange Crush bottle he held and said, "Don't tell me you didn't know I was in Yancey."

"I knew you were in Yancey, but how did you know I'd be at Leroy's?"

"Among other research I've done here, Memphis, I obviously took time to find your grandmother's old home and deduced that was where you'd be staying. I figured sooner or later you'd be stopping here, so I've kept an eye on the place. Leroy and I have become old friends."

"You could have just knocked on the front door, or used the telephone."

"Didn't know what kind of reception I'd get. This way, you had to talk to me, couldn't run away."

"I've never run away from anything, Jake. You, on the other hand, seem to have no problem escaping unwanted situations." She remembered the quick flick of fear in his eyes when she'd told him about her pregnancy, then the lightning retrieval of his composure.

The sun-bleached whitish blond hair, swept back in a ponytail and tied with a piece of rawhide, and the riveting sea blue eyes were captivating as always, but she found to her vast relief they hadn't the power over her that they once had. With studied nonchalance, she reached back into the icebox, retrieved the Coke, and opened it on the silver-lipped opener.

The last she'd seen of Jake Bishop was his retreating back as she lay on a cot in a field hospital in Bosnia.

Never would she forget the sight of his shoulders moving jauntily, his khaki shirt dark with sweat and dirt, his long blond hair swinging across his back as the distance between them lengthened, the yawing, twisting pain of desertion by the man she'd loved and trusted for four years growing with each step he took.

She'd heard her weak voice call out, "Jake," expecting him to turn around with the familiar teasing grin on his face, but he hadn't. The sounds of misery coming from the injured men on surrounding cots had faded as her ears filled with a high tinny sound. The sickeningly sweet antiseptic smells of carbolic acid and mercuric chloride had turned her stomach, but she'd swallowed her vomit. She'd watched in agonized disbelief as Jake Bishop walked out of the med tent and disappeared from her life.

She'd vowed then and there never to call out in weakness again.

"Go away, Jake. Leave us alone."

"Can't do that, honey-child. You and Katie are my family."

"When did you decide that, Jake? No, let me answer. You decided that when you got tired of the latest bimbo under your tutelage, the last sweet young thing who hung on your every word and wanted to learn everything the famous Jake Bishop had to teach her about journalism or photography."

"Not true, my love."

"Go away, Jake. Got bored, didn't you, when there were no more wars to chase? You sold out for the big bucks. Go away. You've got your story."

"The story isn't finished, the book isn't finished. If you hate me so much, why did you come here, Memphis? That strange fascination with your grandmother flare up, or maybe you couldn't resist renewing the old vibrations between the two of us?"

Her temper flared.

"I came here because you betrayed me, Jake." The three men at the counter were watching them now. She lowered her voice and hissed between her teeth. "I told you my grandmother's story one night after we'd made love, never imagining that you'd make it grist for national consumption. It was a personal story, Jake, a family mystery."

"Like I said, honey, we're family."

"Katie doesn't even know you. Wouldn't recognize you if you walked in and announced you're her daddy."

"I tried to find you in New York, but your family and friends protect you like a steel chastity belt fastened around a princess. Your editor and your sister are particularly sensitive. Brrr! I'm sorry that you feel I stole your story, Mem. I really am."

The note of sincerity in his voice almost got her, but then she remembered he had a doctorate in charm. She gripped the icy Coke bottle tighter, realizing that Katie's blue eyes looked at her from Jake's face.

"My first book was such a hit that I knew I'd stumbled on a bonanza," he continued. "I remembered your mountain tale of murder and mayhem, so traveled here to nose around a bit. Got intrigued, and well, that's how the whole thing got started."

"I see," she said with heavy sarcasm. "And it never occurred to you that you were violating a personal confidence and that it would hurt me terribly to think you cared so little for secrets told between lovers. Oh, and of course, you didn't remember that I said someday, when the time was right, I wanted to clear up the questions surrounding my grandmother's death and was considering writing a book that would solve everything?"

"Well, the time is now. I'm here and you're here and we always were good together." He smiled, and added, "In more ways than one."

"I wouldn't work with you again for love or money, Jake Bishop. I want to tell Sadie's story in a loving way, not as lurid gossip. Besides, why do you think a book about my grandmother will be such a bestseller?"

"Three reasons. People are always interested in how insensitive and noncaring previous generations have been to black people. It gives them a chance to feel noble. They'll eat up the story of poor Amos sent to jail in place of a rich white man. And it happened in the arrogant South, which the rest of the country considers backwards, ignorant, and insensitive, anyway. Northerners and Midwesterners will love finding fault with and pointing their fingers at the South again. For shame."

"That's hideous, Jake. The South isn't really like that, and you know it."

He ignored her, intent on the case for his book. "Secondly, there were rumors at the time of some unusual sexual high jinks going on amongst the powers-that-be here, and they might have had something to do with the murder. People love reading about secret sex stuff."

She'd expected most of what he said, but this was a shock. "Wait a minute, wait a minute. I never had any information like that."

"I found one mention of it in an early account of the trial."

"It certainly wasn't in anything I read today," Memphis said heatedly.

"Well, I expect old man Root had it removed after he found out I'd been digging through the files."

"I don't believe you."

He hiked his shoulders, and smiled. "Believe what you want."

"And what's the third reason this dirty book will sell so well, Jake?"

"You, Memphis. A beautiful, well-known photojournalist with a juicy scandal in her past concerning her just-as-beautiful grandmother."

"Only because you've built it all up so, Jake. Intimated much more than there really is. Which reminds me, aren't you concerned that these titillating spots you're doing on *American Notebook* will hurt sales of your book?"

"Nope." A cocky grin lit his face. "They're designed to tease, but not tell all. My publishers have agreed to rush the book into production. Each chapter is turned in, edited, and set in type, and the book will bust into the bookstores as a true-crime exposé one month after the final chapter is turned in."

She hated to ask, was afraid to ask, but she had to. "And when will that be?"

"First of March. Was it Shakespeare who said the winds of March blow ill? Fitting, don't you think?" he asked with the same cocky grin.

Furious now, Memphis didn't care if the men at the counter heard her.

She lashed out.

"No, I don't think any of this is funny, Jake. Not only have you ruined any sense of homecoming I might have had, you've antagonized everyone in this town. I went to the newspaper office this morning. They wouldn't let me see the microfilm on Amos Washington's trial until Cutter Tate intervened."

Jake came out of his slouch in a hurry. "So, you made friends with Tate. I should have known."

She glanced at Leroy and his friends, saw their vast interest in the conversation, and made an effort to lower her voice. "We're not friends. He dislikes me as much as he dislikes you. Nobody in Yancey likes us very much, Jake, not even those who remember me as a child, but I'm going to see the end of this, and I'm going to do it without you."

"So be it, beautiful." He swallowed the last of his Orange Crush and placed the empty bottle in a slotted wooden box on the floor. "But I would like to get to know Katie."

"No."

"She's my daughter, Memphis."

"You know why, Jake."

"I made a mistake. I want to make up for it." Memphis saw the determined look in his eyes. Jake usually got what he wanted. He was Katie's father. Was she right in denying him access to Katie?

"I'll think about it."

"Good. We'll be crossing paths, and I'm looking forward to that."

He took three steps toward her, and she thought he was going to give her arm a pat and walk on by, but he grabbed her shoulders and kissed her. His tongue slipped with practiced ease into her once eager mouth, and for a moment, shocked, she almost relaxed into his body. Swiftly, though, the hurtful memories reasserted themselves and she shook herself free.

Gasping, and so angry she couldn't speak, she swiped at her mouth with the back of her hand as he sauntered on by. The screen door slammed behind him.

The wet Coke bottle slipped out of her hand and bounced around, amber liquid spewing over the rough pine floor.

"You okay, missy?" asked an intrigued Leroy.

Embarrassed and angry, Memphis shook her head. "I'm fine, Leroy," she said softly. "He's just an old friend. I'm sorry about this mess on the floor. Please, give me something and I'll clean it up."

"Never you mind. I'll clean it up. You go on home now. Nelsey and that baby are probably waitin' fer ya."

So, Leroy had known who she was all along. That shouldn't surprise her. Everyone in this town knew everything about everybody.

Driving up the hill to the house, she scrubbed at her mouth again, trying to erase the memory of Jake's kiss. Even more disturbing were his words echoing in her ears. She had *not* come to Yancey because she wanted a reunion with him. He was fooling himself if he hoped for a renewal of their tumultuous relationship.

She maneuvered the last, narrow loop to the house too fast, and all of her enlarged microfilm newspaper copies slipped from the passenger seat and onto the floor. Damn! She pulled into the gravel driveway close to the house and parked the Jeep. A faded news photo of her grandmother Sadie stared up at her from the floor. She bent to retrieve the papers, and all thoughts of Jake left her as she became intrigued with her grandmother's face and the old scandal.

Flipping quickly through the papers, she stopped at a front-page story.

Across the top of the page were four photos: one of Sadie, one of Macauley Tate, one of Harvey Root, and one of Amos Washington, the hired handyman of both Macauley Tate and Harvey Root. The victim and three suspects.

She read the first paragraphs out loud.

"The trial of Amos Washington for the murder of Sadie Maynard, wife of Sheriff James Maynard, continued to be the sensation of the community and the state yesterday. Mrs. Maynard, found on Twenty-Two Mountain by a coal miner on his way to work at four o'clock on the morning of May eighteenth, died from a gunshot wound to the head. Her throat had been slashed and her face brutally mutilated.

"An estimated six hundred people crammed themselves into the courtroom to hear the testimony of Macauley Tate, CEO of Tate Mining. Tate, at one time a prime suspect although not indicted, admitted that the pistol used in the crime, and the knife, were his, but he had left them months before the crime in the converted limousine that was used for hunting trips. Many prominent men in town made use of the old car and Washington as their driver. Tate insisted that he didn't think his handyman, Washington, was capable of such a heinous deed. Pale, and visibly shaken, Tate was excused from the stand."

The article hinted that Macauley Tate and Harvey Root, who was chairman of the county commission and president of Yancey National Bank, were members of a secret organization of some sort that played prominently in the night of Sadie's murder. Oddly, Memphis hadn't found any mention of the clandestine group in later articles. The article further noted that the sordid story might not have taken on such sensational hues had prominent men not been involved, and had Sadie not been the wife of Sheriff James Maynard.

Late afternoon sunshine shone through the open car window and onto the photocopies. Oblivious to the sunshine and the chill October air, Memphis stared at the pictures, wondering what had really happened that May night in 1936. Where did each of these people fit into the story? She'd read a lot about Macauley Tate and Amos Washington, but Harvey Root was still an unknown to her. She had an appointment to interview eighty-year-old H. A. Root, Jr., son of Harvey Root, tomorrow. H. A. would have been twenty years old in 1936 and certainly would remember something of the scandal and his father's role in it.

H. A. Root, Jr. had followed in his father's footsteps and taken over the presidency of the bank when his father retired. Eighty years old, he himself had just retired, and was one of the few people still living who might be able to shed some light on the murder. Mr. Root's daughter had turned down Memphis's request to interview him until Nelsey intervened. Thank God for Nelsey.

Amos Washington's photo showed a diminutive man with a large head. He wore a big-billed cap that rested on protruding ears. He had a small, tentative smile on his friendly, dark face, and trusting eyes. As far as she knew, H. A. Root, Jr. was the only living person who'd known Amos Washington or his family, if Amos ever had any family.

Macauley Tate, with his 1930s slicked-back haircut seemed a dignified man—nice-looking, kind eyes, a cleft chin like his grandson. Meant nothing. Ted Bundy had been handsome with kind eyes, too.

Her thoughts slipped unwillingly back to her encounter with Cutter Tate in the library. Her first reaction had been one of total fascination with the way his bigness filled the aisle where they stood, the way he unconsciously dominated the whole large book-filled room. His dark, unruly hair, covered with a hard hat on their first meeting, was a surprise to her, and she'd had a ridiculous urge to reach up and smooth it into some sort of order.

In the crazy, shaken moment when she had touched him, she'd felt a fierce craving to know if the rest of his body was as tan, lean, and hard as the arms she could see and the hand she felt. Embarrassed now at the intensity of her longing, she blushed hot, then shivered. The animal attraction she'd experienced toward him was undeniable.

She shrugged her shoulders, trying for a certain humorous nonchalance. *Raging hormones, Memphis. The past three years of chastity are finally getting to you.* "You're getting horny, Memphis, my love."

Hurriedly, she finished the newspaper article from sixty years ago, noting that the last two people seen with Sadie on that night were Macauley Tate, early in the evening, and Amos Washington, shortly before midnight.

She skipped to the picture of Sadie Maynard. She'd saved it until last. It was different than the one her mother had given to her. The snapshot on her dresser in Manhattan was of a teenage Sadie, sitting in a porch swing, one foot tucked beneath her as she read a book.

Sadie had a short bob; heavy wing tips of hair swung out on her cheeks, and a soft wave of bangs covered half her forehead. Memphis studied her grandmother's eyes. Yes. She had inherited those almond-shaped eyes with the slight downward tilt. Her mother, Faith, called them "bedroom" eyes.

Caught in a moment of fun, Sadie's eyes were lit with laughter. Her lips, painted in a bowed 1920s style, were smiling. Were those dancing eyes a shield for secrets they couldn't reveal? Were the events leading up to the tragedy already in play when the picture was taken? Did Sadie always laugh so freely, or was she afraid? Did she already know a secret someone didn't want told? Old news photos were so unsatisfactory.

A cloud passed between the sun and the earth, and a shadow covered Memphis and the picture. Chilled by a shift in the wind and the coming twilight, she shuddered. She'd sat too long in the car wondering about her grandmother.

The day hadn't been totally hopeless. She'd obtained

the microfilm she needed. All she wanted now was to hold Katie in her arms. After all the blank stares she'd encountered today, the shrugged shoulders, turned backs, and cold receptions throughout the county, all she wanted was to feel Katie's loving innocence and complete acceptance.

She felt vulnerable here. None of her "big-city" expertise, or her exploits in Desert Storm and Bosnia had prepared her for the last two and a half years, and her reception here in Yancey was exposing raw nerves again. The last few years had brought her to her knees both literally and figuratively. All the brash self-confidence, pride in her work, and joy of living had been ripped out of her, dislodged by the bullet that had shattered her knee, and by Jake's desertion.

She'd survived because of Katie.

Her anger at Jake's exposing the family mystery without even bothering to ask her permission had been the first thing to call her back to action in the real world.

Perhaps she'd been precipitous in leaving the safe cocoon she'd created for herself and Katie in New York: the rare, but important photo shoots assigned by a nurturing editor who knew she needed quiet time until she fully recovered from her physical and emotional wounds, the cozy luncheons at intimate restaurants with good buddies, the fun of shopping with Margo who spent like a sailor on leave. Perhaps it was too soon to be without close friends and family nearby, and without a prescribed daily routine.

She sensed a menace here. Certainly there was a conspiracy to withhold information from her. People weren't openly hostile, but behind the facade of politeness there lurked a suspicious reserve.

Jake had said the book was due out the first of March. This was almost the end of October. She had less than five months to find out the truth and to prepare a counterview, a counterpunch. *God, help me, please.*

She looked at the worn Victorian house where her mother had grown up, raised by a stepmother who loved her dearly. Nelsey had placed large wooden tubs of golden mums on the wide porch that encircled half the house. Katie's tiny red tricycle sat in the yard, and clean white sheets flapped from a clothesline in the spacious backyard. A small smile and a feeling of warmth broke Memphis's grim mood. The place looked kind of homey. She was glad her editor had insisted she take time off. Maybe spending a few months here wouldn't be as bad as she thought.

As she got out of the car, she avoided looking at the dusky, dense green woods behind the house. She hadn't heard the chilling scream since the night of their arrival, so it must have been a bad dream.

§ 4 §

"*I* got there and he wouldn't talk to me, Nelsey. His horrid daughter stood on their porch barring my way like the National Guard protecting Fort Knox. Said I was a nosey Yankee, nobody wanted me in Yancey, and I should go back to New York where I belonged." Memphis practically quivered with indignation. "Thank you for getting me to the front door, but it didn't work. I'm back to where I started with Harvey Root."

The aroma in Memphis's kitchen was mouthwatering, but the room looked like a disaster area, decided Nelsey. Broken eggshells covered the bottom of the sink, potato peelings littered a cutting board, and onion skins papered the counter.

Nelsey finished tying Katie's shoe, untangled the shoulder straps on her red corduroy jumper, and set her on the kitchen floor.

"Minnie Jo's mission in life is worshipping her father." She thought for a moment. "Well, then I expect we'll have to be callin' Senator Lilibet. Only one I can think of who can get to the old man, loosen his tongue a bit. Every other body in town is scared to death of him. He holds mortgages and notes on about everything in Yancey, except for the property Cutter and his father own. And even though H. A. is retired and his grandson is now president of the bank, it's big H. A.

who still calls the shots. Senator Brady and her husband, Black, are the only people who seem to be able to talk any sense to him."

"I photographed Senator Brady a couple of times in Washington. Maybe that will help me get in to see her."

"You don't need special acquaintance to see Lilibet. She's available to everyone, anytime. I think she's due here this week. Today's Sunday, so we'll call her office tomorrow."

Nelsey winced as she watched Memphis's attempts to put a three-layer cake together. The uneven layers tilted like a child's teetering pile of blocks. Thin, anemic chocolate icing dripped off the plate and onto the counter. She resisted the urge to take over the job. Memphis had insisted she would make Nelsey's birthday cake, and Nelsey hadn't the heart to tell her that several other cakes would probably be delivered today. Nelsey usually forgot, or tried to forget her birthday, but unfortunately others always reminded her.

Leroy had told Memphis several days ago that today was Nelsey's birthday, so Memphis had planned an after-church celebration lunch for Nelsey, Katie, and herself.

Problem was, Memphis Maynard didn't know a baster from a ladle, lard from butter, or pole beans from snap beans. When Nelsey had offered to help her with the chicken she was frying, Memphis had made her sit at the table with a cup of coffee. So Nelsey had held her tongue and watched as Memphis dipped the raw chicken in a lumpy batter and then underfried it for thirty minutes. The dubious platter of chicken now sat proudly on the littered counter waiting for the rest of the meal to be prepared.

Memphis crossed the kitchen to check on potatoes boiling on top of the stove. Strands of her springy sun-streaked bronze hair had escaped from the knot she'd fastened on top of her head. They bounced with energy as she walked, but Nelsey noticed the slight limp that occurred when Memphis was tired.

"You out lookin' for that grave again yesterday?"

"Yes, how did you know?"

"Jest a guess. You limp when you're tired."

The metallic rattle of the rusty twister doorbell interrupted their conversation. Katie dropped the pan lids she played with and ran from the kitchen, heading toward the front of the house shrieking with excitement.

"Who on earth could that be?" asked Memphis. She wiped her hands on the skirt of the big white apron that Nelsey had tied around her.

"Uh, well, it's probably someone for me." Nelsey fingered the red rose on her "go-to-meetin'" hat, which sat on the table in front of her, and cleared her throat self-consciously. "I hate celebratin' my birthday, but everyone else seems to want to do it for me. My daughters can't come, so every year I get visitors. I put a note on my door this morning before I went to church tellin' anyone who was lookin' where I was."

"That's nice. We have plenty of chicken, and I'll just add a few potatoes to the potato salad."

The bell rattled again, and Katie was yelling "doe-bell, doe-bell."

Memphis started to untie her apron strings and head toward the front door, but Nelsey stood up and said, "Stay put. I'll go."

As she walked through the house to the front door, she prayed. *Please, Lord, let it be someone who won't mind raw chicken and soggy potato salad.* Katie was on her tiptoes trying to reach the doorknob. Nelsey picked her up and opened the door.

Cutter and Birdy stood on the porch grinning at her. Cutter carried a lush arrangement of robust gold and rust-colored mums, tied with a burgundy satin ribbon, and Birdy held a beautiful cake, iced with thick swirls of rich dark chocolate.

"Happy Birthday," they said in unison.

"Happy Birffday," crowed Katie back to them, and they all laughed.

"Oh, mercy, why do you all do this to me every year?" asked Nelsey, secretly pleased to death.

"Because we love you, and this is your seventieth and that certainly deserves celebrating," said Birdy. "Look, I put ten candles, one for every seven years."

Nelsey looked at Birdy's beautiful decorated cake and thought of the pitiful one sitting in the kitchen. There had been no way to avoid this. Memphis had worked so hard on the preparations, and would have been insulted had Nelsey turned down her invitation for a birthday lunch.

Well, Lord, I don't know what you have in mind here, but lead us on.

Cutter and Birdy followed Nelsey and Katie into the dining room.

"Birdy, put that pretty cake on the table there and look for plates and napkins in the corner cupboard. I'll find a vase for Cutter's flowers."

"I'll go with you," said Cutter.

"No, no, you stay here," Nelsey said, and she set Katie on the floor and headed quickly toward the kitchen. Cutter followed, as she was afraid he would. Cutter Tate had never in his whole life obeyed anyone.

Memphis, at work on the troublesome cake, turned as they entered. With white flour sprinkling her hair, a chocolate smear across her cheek, and mayonnaise globs on her apron, she looked like a teenager struggling eagerly but hopelessly through a home economics class.

"Who is it, Nelsey?" Brief splays of emotion—surprise, anger, then curiosity—etched themselves on Memphis's face when she saw Cutter. When she spoke, her tone was carefully neutral. "Oh, Cutter."

Her voice trailed off, and the spatula she held in her

hand dripped chocolate on the floor as she stared at him.

Nelsey heard the tiniest of sounds behind her and knew Cutter was struggling not to laugh. She used the heel of her shoe to step hard on his toe, warning him that he'd have her to deal with if he laughed at Memphis and the state of the kitchen.

"Cutter's brought some flowers, and Birdy Harless brought a cake."

Recovering quickly from either shock or embarrassment, or both—Nelsey couldn't tell—Memphis put the spatula in the bowl of icing and wiped her hands on her luckless apron.

"What lovely mums."

"Looks like you're getting ready for a party," said Cutter. "Hope you don't mind if we crash it for a while. Nelsey hates to be reminded of her advanced age, but we remind her every year."

"Umph," Nelsey grunted.

"No, absolutely not," said Memphis. "We have more than enough food. Please make yourself at home. Uh, Nelsey would you mind getting our company a Coke, or beer, or whatever they want, while I clean up this mess?"

From behind Cutter, Birdy's tiny voice piped up, "Why, honey, we'll all help. That'll make it more of a party."

Birdy squeezed eagerly around Cutter, who still stood in the doorway. Nelsey introduced Memphis and Birdy, and prayed Birdy would mind her fast tongue. Birdy was the kindest of souls, but she was flighty, and so straightforward that sometimes she didn't think before she spoke.

"Uh, well . . . please have a seat, I'll try to finish . . ."

Cutter interrupted, the smile in his voice even more pronounced. "We'll make ourselves at home. There are some pots boiling over on the stove."

Memphis ran to the stove and grabbed the handle of the pot holding the potatoes. She jerked her hand back, and muttered "dammit."

"Oh, you've burned yourself," said Birdy. She ran to inspect the damage to Memphis's hand while Nelsey, oven mitts on, removed the offending pans from the stove top.

"No, no, it's fine, really," insisted Memphis. "Just a bit red. Here, Nelsey, give me those eggs. I'll devil them if you will finish up the potato salad."

Cutter poured himself a cup of coffee and seated himself at the table. Katie stood studying him carefully with a solemn face, her tiny fists on his knees. He studied her back, waiting. Because of Birdy's big mouth, the whole town knew that Katie was Jake Bishop's daughter, and Nelsey, curious about Cutter's reaction to the child, watched them from the corner of her eye as she drained water from the potatoes.

Katie's rosy cupid mouth stretched into a grin as she decided this giant who'd invaded her kitchen was acceptable. Nelsey's heart almost burst with love as she saw Cutter return her grin. She wondered why she'd ever had an anxious thought. Cutter had always been great with children.

Birdy found a vase for the flowers and then elected to help Memphis shell the eggs. Nelsey could tell it made Memphis nervous.

"Birdy, you know what they say about too many cooks in the kitchen. Sit and rest yourself. Tell us what's goin' on that we don't know about." Usually people were trying to shut Birdy up, so Nelsey knew she would jump at the invitation to talk, about anything and everything.

"Well, let's see, did you know Tommy Tee and James Cady got fined again for hunting out of season? Don't know why they haven't learned by now. Same thing happens every year. But they're dumber than turkeys, so it's no wonder."

Memphis turned to stare at her. A dab of yellow egg yoke perched on the end of her nose. "You mean it's not hunting season yet?"

"Why no, honey, it sure isn't."

Memphis rubbed at the end of her nose with the back of her wrist, smearing the yoke across her cheek. Nelsey saw Cutter hide his amusement by bending to help Katie pick up an aluminum lid.

"Umm, that's strange," said Memphis, turning back to her eggs. "I've seen lights in the woods behind the house where they shouldn't be, and hunters were the only answer I could think of. But, I guess hunters wouldn't be out at night with lights, would they?"

Startled, Nelsey, preparing to strip the skin from a potato, lowered her knife carefully to the counter so she wouldn't nip herself.

Trying to keep her voice steady, she said, "No, they wouldn't. 'Bout what time of night do you see these lights?"

"After midnight. Started seeing them shortly after we got here. Probably kids out camping, don't you think?"

"Maybe," said Cutter thoughtfully.

"Anything unusual about these lights?" asked Nelsey

"Well, yes, now that you mention it. The color changes sometimes, like from a pale yellow to an iridescent blue . . . and then kind of floats away. Really, rather eerie."

"It's probably kids camping out and playing around before it gets too cold," said Cutter.

"Sure," said Birdy. "But, honey, if you ever get scared, you just call me and I'll come up and stay with you."

"No, I haven't been afraid, except for the first night we were here and I thought I heard someone screaming." She laughed self-consciously. "I was ready to go back to Manhattan, like they say, in a New York minute."

"You heard someone screaming?" asked Birdy, her voice rising two octaves. "Mercy, honey, I'd of run out of this old house fast as I could go." In a nervous whisper to Cutter, which could be clearly heard by Nelsey and Memphis, she said, "See, I told you Sadie's ghost . . ."

Cutter stopped her short. "That's enough, Birdy. Nelsey, I'm sure Memphis won't believe *me*, so you tell her that the supposed appearances of the ghost of her grandmother have never mentioned screams or lights."

Nelsey had never heard anything about screams, but all of her growing-up years she had heard tales of the lights that accompanied Sadie. But the tight lines in Memphis's face convinced her it was okay to tell a white lie, for the moment anyway.

"No, I never heard anything about any screaming or anything."

The lighthearted atmosphere in the kitchen had turned to one of fine-tuned tension and Nelsey felt like spanking Birdy.

"I never related the screams *or* the lights to my grandmother," said Memphis firmly, but politely.

Nelsey could tell Memphis was angry and holding it in check. She frantically searched for something to say to break the uneasy silence. Cutter scooped Katie up in his lap, then slid her down his leg to rest on his moccasin as he bounced her up and down in the air. Her happy laughter broke some of the tension and Nelsey sighed with relief.

"Memphis, do you want celery in this potato salad?" she asked, praying that Birdy would curb her tongue a while longer.

"If you think it needs it, yes. I'll get it for you."

Memphis crossed to the refrigerator, and Birdy said over Katie's laughter, "Oh, Memphis, you're limping. I hear you've been hiking. Have you sprained your ankle?"

Memphis grimaced, hid her face as she busied herself in the depths of the refrigerator, then straightened and returned to the counter, her back to Birdy and Cutter.

Nelsey's heart sank. *Oh, Lord, will you please shut Birdy up? I know she doesn't mean it, but she's sure causin' some trouble here on my birthday.*

"So, you've heard that I hike. Somehow I'm not surprised. Everyone seems to know everyone else's business around here."

"Oh, no, I didn't mean to be nosey, I just felt bad that you've obviously hurt yourself."

"Birdy, will you mind your own . . ."

"That's okay, Nelsey. I limp sometimes because I caught a stray bullet in my knee in Bosnia. I have a small titanium plate in there, and a couple of artificial joints, kind of like new ball bearings."

Cutter stopped joggling Katie for a moment. An expression of respect and concern lit his eyes and softened his mouth.

"Oh, you poor thing. That must have been awful," said Birdy.

Nelsey, who knew the whole story because Memphis had told her, thought to herself that Birdy couldn't imagine how awful.

The doorbell rang and Nelsey, thanking God, sent Birdy to answer it.

The rest of the afternoon brought more visitors, food, and a keg of beer.

Later, Nelsey looked around at the ten or twelve people in the parlor and was grateful for their presence. Her daughters, one in Oregon and one in Detroit, couldn't afford a trip to West Virginia, but always sent gifts and telephoned her. So every year, since the death of her two sons in Vietnam, between thirty to forty friends showed up for her birthday.

She was grateful that Memphis didn't know how large this party usually was. Half the people who came annually had stayed away today because they knew Nelsey was at the Maynard house. She knew when she got home there would be a rash of messages and gifts waiting for her, but they'd turned their backs on Memphis.

And, boy, will I give them a piece of my lip for staying away because of Memphis. She's sure showed she's not wantin' to hurt anyone, she just wants to find her grandmother's grave so she and her sister can put a marker on it and honor her memory. They're all thinkin' she's going to expose things that needn't be exposed. Well, so what? Maybe there are things that need exposin'.

Alcohol had uncorked any polite restraints anyone had had at being in the Maynard house. That bothered Nelsey, but those who had come were having such a good time celebrating her birthday for her that she hated to scold them for drinking a bit too much.

Leroy was here, and Cle Hutton with Sally Junior. Cle was drunker than a polecat. Sally Junior had him propped up in a chair. Billy Gus and Elva Hatfield were eating their way through the corn pudding and fried chicken that Elva had brought. Memphis's chicken still sat forlornly untouched. Nelsey scooped a few pieces from the plate and dropped them in her apron pocket so it would look as if some of the raw bird had been eaten.

Cutter had been more quiet than usual today, more of an observer than a participant, but he'd loosened up some and was telling Charity Brady and her boyfriend about the bear he'd spotted near her family's mountain cabin.

If there was any strain in the room, it existed

between Cutter and Memphis, which interested Nelsey. Considering Memphis's mission here, it was natural that they would be wary of one another, but this was more than wariness. Their ignoring each other must be obvious to everyone, not just Nelsey. Except for the few words they'd exchanged when Cutter had first arrived, they hadn't spoken once.

Katie tugged on Memphis's flared gray flannel skirt and her mother bent to pick her up. As she did so, the last of the day's sunbeams shone strong for a brief moment through the window and caught at the shiny silver mesh belt Memphis wore around her waist. Silver strips of light swiftly braided, corded, then arced across the room to encircle Cutter's shoulders. The nape of Nelsey's neck prickled with goose bumps. She closed her eyes, but opened them quickly to see if anyone else had noticed the strange play of dazzling light.

Nothing had changed. The woven silver cord, a shimmering but solid rainbow, still arced between Cutter and Memphis.

Nelsey accepted then that no one saw the phenomenon but her. It was the "sight." She'd inherited it from her grandmother, Granny Tucker. She didn't have moments of the "sight" often, like Granny had had, but enough to know this was important knowledge being given to her now.

Be danged if she knew what it meant. Filled with disquiet, Nelsey closed her eyes again. When she opened them the arc was gone.

She didn't want to think about the import of the silver cord, or Memphis's tale of the "lights in the woods." In fact, she wouldn't think about any of it, not now anyway.

Katie was squirming in Memphis's arms. Long since time for her to go to bed. Nelsey went to get the toddler.

In spite of her resolve not to think about the supernatural occurrences around Memphis, Nelsey shivered with apprehension and clutched Katie to her tightly as she carried her upstairs.

Their eyes had met and held earlier. Only tremendous willpower had forced Memphis to break the spell Cutter cast and look away.

It was late in the evening, most everyone had gone home. The few strays who remained were loose and easy now, as if they were accustomed to coming to the Maynard house for parties.

She congratulated herself on the qualified success of the party and tried to focus on Birdy. But Birdy's face and voice blurred as Memphis thought of the way Cutter's patched and faded jeans fit him snug around the buttocks, and the way he wore his aged leather moccasins with such grace.

Stop it, Memphis. Concentrate on what Birdy is saying.

Startled now, she realized she recalled every detail of what Cutter wore today, even the way the band of his collarless white shirt lay askew against his collarbone, exposing tanned skin. She remembered the field watch he wore around his powerful wrist, and a few bristly black hairs curling around the black nylon band. She remembered too much, but try as she might to push his broad-shouldered image out of her mind, it seemed branded, burned into her brain.

He laughed at something Charity Brady said and she couldn't stop from glancing in his direction.

He lounged lazily, his shoulder against a wall, and stared at her openly, without apology.

Cutter Tate swept away polite forms of interest, friendliness, or curiosity, and conveyed pure animal arousal. His misty gray eyes enclosed her, took her in and kept her prisoner in a time and space beyond this house or the mountains. She'd been looked at before, by many men in many countries, had traded flirtatious glances and even exchanged and accepted a few hot invitations, but never had she felt this dangerous, compelling excitement.

A quiver traveled slowly down her spine, then gathered speed and curled swiftly around her hips, embracing her seductively. It was as if Cutter Tate made love to her from where he stood, his fingers caressing her, coaxing her to want more of the deliciousness, as if he knew her body better than she. An invading heat honeycombed through her, begging entrance to her private parts. The urge to cry out was so strong that it frightened her, and she was able to disengage from his deepening gaze.

Shivering, Memphis tried her damnedest to concentrate on Birdy's words. The bunch of clackety bones she had become in the last three years, juiceless and empty of emotion, had just been spiked with a powerful elixir. The implications were not to her liking.

No, it was not possible that she could be so affected by the grandson of the man who had probably murdered her grandmother. Perhaps this commanding attraction was mere timing. She'd had no interest in men since Jake had walked out on her. Perhaps this unexpected awakening of her body was simply nature taking its course, a woman's body yearning for attention and satisfaction. But any man would be better than Cutter Tate. Even Jake Bishop.

With determined effort she brought her attention back to Birdy.

Memphis had lost track of the friendly woman's fast chatter, but now wished for her camera, wanting to capture every expression on Birdy Harless's face. Seldom did you see such animation. Birdy literally acted with her face, emoting every word, expression, or thought with a stretch of the mouth, quirk of the eyebrows, puff of the cheeks, or widening of her periwinkle eyes.

Birdy's eyes softened and took on a luster that could only indicate love, and Memphis tuned in to what she was saying.

". . . well, that's one of the reasons we call him 'Cutter,' you know, because he cut class constantly, he was only eleven or twelve years old, was always being hauled in by the truant officer, and well, he thought bein' called 'Cutter' was funny, so then when he'd sneak into Ruby's and play pool with the miners, he almost always won and they'd buy him drinks. He'd order a Cutty Sark because he thought it was grown-up and because that's what his grandfather used to drink and, honey, do you know those awful men used to get him drunk as a skunk. I'd let him hide in my garage till he got over bein' sick. . . ."

Birdy is in love with Cutter, loves him deeply, thought Memphis.

". . . 'course he was also always cuttin' through someone's backyard, too, usually with Sheriff Maynard chasin' him because he'd stolen someone's hubcaps or a case of beer from Ruby's, but everyone knew old Sheriff Maynard had it in for Cutter, hated him, he did, so . . ." Birdy stopped abruptly and put her tiny hand over her mouth, her eyes wide with horror.

"Oh, dear, I'm so sorry. I really am. I forgot the sheriff was your grandfather. Sometimes I get to talking so much that I . . ."

Intrigued as she was with this information, Memphis held her hand up to forestall more of the apology that kept spilling out of Birdy. "Please, don't worry about it. It's not important. I wasn't close to my grandfather, in fact I barely knew him. What is Cutter's real name?"

"Macauley, after his grandfather, but no one ever called him that either. It's always been either Mack or Cutter." Memphis had the feeling that Birdy knew everything there was to know about Mack "Cutter" Tate.

To her credit, Birdy then changed the subject to the church social next week. Memphis let the chatter wind in and out around her, smiling, nodding now and then, hoping the barrage of words would keep her from looking at Cutter again.

". . . so I think it's time for me and Cutter to say good-bye. He's leaving this afternoon on one of the mysterious jaunts he takes two or three times a year. He thinks I don't know, but I always know. Honey, he gets restless as a tiger and then just disappears and doesn't come back for days. Well, I know sometimes he's checkin' on that land they're trying to take away from him, which I don't blame him a bit. Other times, he just goes into the woods and stays and stays, sometimes meets up with Black Brady. Black taught him all about the woods when Cutter was a teenager. Anyway, I see him lookin' this way and well, here he comes."

Memphis didn't have to turn around. She felt him at her elbow. The heat of his body radiated about her and lit up again the sensations she'd fought to squelch earlier.

"Birdy, darlin', are you ready to go?" he asked.

"Sure. I'll find Nelsey so we can say good-bye."

No, Birdy, don't go. Stay here. Don't leave me alone with Cutter.

Birdy was gone and Cutter stood in front of her. She wanted to push him away and then run, like a dumb kid.

"Have you used your camera much since you've been here?" he asked politely.

"Yes, I have," she answered, and managed to look him straight in the eye without a single tingle. "I've taken a few great shots on my graveyard searches. Lots of mountain scenes."

"I've seen some of your work. It's beautiful. Very impressive."

His voice was warm, low and intimate as if they were the only two in the room, and for a moment they were. Despite her effort to stay focused, everyone else had faded away.

"Thank you. I'm not sure about the quality of the shots I've taken, but I set up a dark room in the basement and will be developing some film soon."

Sally Junior's voice broke his studied surveillance of Memphis's face. Memphis sighed with relief.

"Well, thanks so much Miz Maynard," said Sally Junior. "I'm sure Nelsey is happy you're livin' so close. I've got to get Daddy home. I've got a date I don't want to be late for."

Everyone began to take their leave, and Memphis was happy to see Nelsey take over, saying thanks and good-bye.

"What did Birdy mean when she told me Cutter Tate disappears sometimes?" Memphis asked Nelsey after everyone had gone and they were cleaning up.

"Birdy saw that, did she? Guess she and me always knows. Cutter gets down on himself once in a while, and he's got a fire that burns in his belly that needs puttin' out sometimes. Don't know what causes it, but I can guess. Anyway, he goes into the mountains, and I really don't know what he does. 'Cept when he comes back, he's himself again."

Memphis decided she didn't want to ask any more questions about Cutter Tate. She might be told some things that she didn't want to know.

Sally Hutton, Jr., called Sally Junior by everyone in Yancey, sat in a dimly lit booth at Carpozzoli's and waited for Jake Bishop. Carpozzoli's had been a Yancey fixture since the fifties when her parents, Sally Kay and Cle Hutton, were in high school. The Italian restaurant still served good hot dogs, chili, and pizza. Nostalgic music on the jukeboxes brought back memories to the older generation. Sally Junior thought it corny but Jake Bishop loved it. This was "their" place to meet.

She sat on the end of a cracked–red-Naugahyde seat of a booth, her crossed legs protruding out into the room. One leg swung furiously, the pointed toe of her three-inch-high–heeled lavender shoe kicking the air, the other heel tapping nervously on the floor. She took another drag from her cigarette and threw her chin up as she exhaled.

Tony Bennett's "San Francisco" came from one of the jukeboxes. In the rear, behind the counter of a large open kitchen, a young Italian man worked on a pizza.

"Hey, Nicky, thought you said you were getting a new box with some of *our* music on it," Sally Junior called to him.

"It's coming tomorrow. Got Alanis Morissette, and Trisha Yearwood, and some Hootie and the Blowfish stuff. My dad says I shouldn't have ordered it. Says we're the only pizza joint in West Virginia with three jukeboxes, but I say, so what. We'll be famous. Do you want mushrooms on this?"

"Yeah. Jake likes mushrooms."

"Your dad know you're dating Jake Bishop?"

"Oh, hell, Nicky, you know my daddy doesn't care what I do. Ol' Cle Hutton just sits and drinks all day and talks about how he should never have let Lilibet Brady go, should never have let her divorce him. But then he'll say how he misses my mama, Sally Kay. He only misses Mama because she drank with him. He's a mess. You should have seen him at Nelsey's party today. Embarrassed me to death." She extracted a gilt compact from her bulky shoulder bag, checked her teeth in the mirror, wet her lips with her tongue, then snapped it shut. "By six o'clock every night he's drunk as a skunk, and that run-down mausoleum of a house is gloomy as a tomb. I have parties in the basement rec room and he never even knows we're in the house."

"Yeah, but ol' Cle and big Harvey are expectin' you to marry H. A. the turd."

"Stop calling him 'the turd,' and I don't care what they expect. The Hutton family lost its respectability twenty years ago when my grandfather went to prison, so I'm no great catch. I'm just havin' fun."

"Yeah, but Jake Bishop is twelve years older than you and real sophisticated, a big city dude. What do you want with him?"

"Hey, I've been around, too, you know."

"You had two years of community college, worked in Charleston for a few years, went to Myrtle Beach one summer and that's about it. I don't think working at the bank qualifies you for a jet-setter. Besides, no one trusts Bishop. You're not telling him things, are you?"

"Hell, Nicky, I'm not telling him anything he can't read about already. H. A.'s grandfather, Harvey, was a minor player, and H. A. has never said anything to me. We never thought about any of this junk until Jake came to Yancey. Anyway, what's the big secret? Witnesses saw Amos, Sadie, and Macauley Tate together that night, and while Amos was in prison Tate visited him all the time. That's a fact. So one of them did it. If it was Tate, that poor old black man took the rap for him because that's the way it was then, and everyone in this dumb town shut up about it because they loved Macauley Tate and, as the old people say, 'we take care of our own.'"

"That's right, and don't you be forgettin' it either."

"Oh hell, Nicky, there's been other murders in this town. I don't know why everybody can't forget about this one. It's ancient history."

"'Cause the rest of them didn't involve the sheriff and the chairman of the city commission and the whole fucking town, that's why, and there's still families in this town that were affected by the gossip. And because the other murders don't have a ghost."

"Oh, that ghost stuff is bullshit. The hick mountain people start rumors like that." She jabbed her cigarette out in the ashtray, jerked a small tube from her bag, and sprayed her mouth with breath freshener. "Jake and me just have fun. He's a nice guy. He really is. If anyone in this hick town would take the time to get to know him, they'd find that out."

"I only know that if it was me, Sally Junior, I'd be damn careful about gettin' into bed with Jake Bishop, and I'd be even more careful about tellin' him anything. I sure wouldn't want old man Root, *or* Cutter Tate on the wrong side of me. Cutter seems real easy most of the time, but I've heard tales of him when he was younger, and you've seen him when he gets mad."

"Well, now, Nicky honey, there's a hunk I've always wanted to get into bed with, but Cutter thinks of me as a little girl."

"Cutter killed a man, you dork."

"So what? He was a kid. It was a barroom brawl, and the man attacked him."

"I'm tellin' you, you better be careful."

"Oh shit, Nicky, you're no fun. Don't worry. I can take care of myself."

The glass front door of the restaurant, which fronted on the town square, opened, and Jake Bishop breezed in. Sally Junior's face lit up, and Nicky Carpozzoli slung a new pizza in his big oven.

§ 5 §

Jake and his cameraman were parked beneath the shadowy branches of an oak tree on the shoulder of the highway about sixty yards from Ruby's Good Eats and Beer. Jake sat in the rear of a van belonging to the Charleston, West Virginia Fox affiliate, WTVC, listening to the voice-over he'd made earlier and checking his makeup.

"Many a good time has been had, and reputation ruined, at Ruby's Good Eats and Beer. For fifty years, Ruby's has been the place where rebellious Yancey high school students come to defy their parents, and where roaming husbands look for a one-night stand, and weary miners come for a game of pool and beer chased with illegal whiskey.

"I'm here in front of Ruby's Good Eats and Beer, the shanty roadhouse where, believe it or not, wealthy, privileged Cutter Tate spent most of his growing-up years. Cutter Tate is the grandson of Macauley Tate, who many people believe murdered Sadie Maynard sixty years ago in May on a lonely mountain road here in West Virginia. In answer to your demand for more on Cutter Tate, we come tonight to Ruby's."

"Christ, Pete," he said to his cameraman, "this new pancake stuff is sticky as hell and the wrong color for me. I look like a damned ghost. I told you to get me a darker shade."

"Hey, Jake, you want perfect, have it sent from New York. I'm doing my best. You look fine to me."

Jake ran his hand over his cheeks again, and leaned in close to the mirror examining himself minutely. He frowned.

"Damn! Is that a pimple? Great time to discover it."

"Get your pretty ass going, dude, let's get this over with. With all those hints and come-ons you gave last week, you've got every woman in America panting to find out more about Cutter Tate."

"Damn right I do. But we've got enough in the can for a month of time spots. This one won't air until right before Christmas. Prime time, my boy, prime time for the juiciest work we've done. "Did you get a shot of the building and the parking lot?"

"Sure did. The flashing orange-and-blue neon sign is going to look real good, and the parking lot with all the old pickups and the fancy four-by-fours sitting next to each other is good stuff. Sets the tone real good."

"Anyone see you?"

"Not that I know of, but you know the odds are that we're not gonna get out of there without causing trouble."

"We've got to get in and out before Ruby knows we're there. I've been there enough to know that she doesn't come down from her apartment until about nine o'clock. But if they get onto us, I've arranged with the sheriff's department to come running if he gets my prearranged beeper signal. The sheriff hates my guts, but he's cooperating with us because he's trying to get something on Ruby so they can shut her down."

"Think of everything, don't you?"

"You don't get where I am without covering all the angles."

Jake brushed his hair again, retied the leather thong

on his ponytail, ran his tongue over his teeth, then flashed a grin at himself in the mirror.

"You do look great, Jakey boy," he murmured. "Time to do battle with the local low-blood."

He jumped from the rear of the van and joined Pete.

"I'll go in and sit at the bar. It may take me awhile to find someone who will talk to me. They're friendly enough when Sally Junior is with me. When I'm by myself, they'd like to ignore me, but there are a couple of real talkative old guys who'd probably like nothing better than to be on national TV. When you get my beeper signal, come in and pan the place until you find me and whoever I'm talking to, then close in. If we get lucky, we'll get out before Ruby knows we're there."

"Sure you don't want to wait and get a shot of her?"

"Man, there is nothing I'd like better, but we'll be lucky to get out with a few interviews."

"If she shows, I'll give it a try."

Jake spoke into his mike, continuing the voice-over he'd started earlier. "It's Tuesday night, free drinks for ladies from six to seven. By midnight the music is louder, the smoke thicker, and the language coarser. Ruby Barnes doesn't want us here. In fact, she said she'd call in some of her tough guys to rough us up if we came into her place with a camera, so we're here without Ruby's knowledge."

He finished the voice-over, which would be edited and patched in later with cover shots, and tucked the small undercover mike apparatus into his jacket pocket.

"Let's go." They walked together along the shoulder until they reached Ruby's and stopped at the edge of the gravel parking lot. "Stay here until you get my signal."

"Hey, dude, it's cold enough to freeze my balls. Don't be too long."

Jake walked in and surveyed the place. A pall of

smoke hung in gray layers in the large room, and despite the acrid look and smell of it, Jake craved a cigarette. The usual crowd circled the pool table. A few clandestine lovers sucking face huddled in wooden booths along the wall, and three couples two-stepped around the scarred dance floor to Randy Travis's "The Truth Is Lying Next to You."

He zeroed in on the long bar along the side wall at the far end of the room.

A group of laughing women was there, taking advantage of the free beer on their way home from work. Several of them gave him "come-on" looks, but he ignored them. Claytie Moore, one of the garrulous old men he hoped would be here, sat nursing a beer by himself. Jake slid onto the orange-Naugahyde bar stool next to him.

"Kinda quiet tonight, eh, Claytie?"

"Oh, hey, Jake. Yeah, but things will liven up later."

"Can I buy you a drink?"

Claytie hesitated. Everyone knew that Ruby hated Jake, so Jake figured Claytie was weighing his loyalty to her against his need for another beer.

"Sure. Wouldn't mind a long-necked Bud. Thanks, Jake."

"Anytime. How're things going?"

"Oh, can't complain. My Social Security check come in last week."

"You get a miner's pension, too?"

"Yeah, it ain't much, but I ain't starvin'."

Jake led him along for a while, giving him a chance to relax, putting him off guard.

An arm slipped around Claytie's shoulder, and his pal Art Edwards sat on the empty stool on the other side of him.

He nodded to Jake, and said, "Howdy, Claytie. Wife still beatin' ya?" He wheezed a smoker's laugh, and coughed.

Good, thought Jake. *I'll get the two of them swapping stories and maybe find out some of what I need.*

Jake let the two of them talk for a while, then asked if he could buy both of them another Bud.

Claytie was feeling no pain. "Sure."

"Why not," said Art.

"Like I was saying to Claytie, kinda quiet in here tonight, don't you think, Art?"

"Yep, but it won't be for long."

"I haven't seen many fights in here, but I hear there used to be lots of them."

They both laughed. "Hell, yes. We seen some of the best of them, ain't we, Art?"

"That's for sure. Remember the time Tommy Tee bit Beantop's ear till it bled, and Ruby banged him over the head with a bar stool?"

This was going exactly the way Jake wanted it to. He slipped his hand beneath his jacket and flipped on the undercover mike. The place wasn't too noisy yet, so he should be able to pick up everything.

But just to make sure, "Hey will you two speak up some? I've got a cold and my ears are all foggy."

"Well, hell, Jake, you oughta drink some shine. Clear up that cold and them ears right away."

"Yeah. Now what were you saying about fights and stuff? Sounded like fun."

They went on for a while, having a good time trying to outdo each other with the fights they'd witnessed. Then, without any prompting, Jake hit paydirt. He felt it coming. He reached in his pocket, fumbled for his beeper, and signaled Pete to come in with the camera.

Jake kept them talking. Out of the corner of his eye, he watched Pete enter and take a slow sweep of the place with the small camcorder, then head in their direction. He came toward them and reached the bar just as Claytie came forth with Jake's story for the week. He laid the obscure little camera on the bar, focused it, and let it run. Claytie and Art were so drunk and enjoying their storytelling that they didn't notice the man filming the three of them from the angled L corner of the bar.

"Yeah, and the time Casey, Bud, and Billy jumped the MacDonald brothers because Harlan kept playin' 'Heartaches' on the jukebox? I thought they was going to kill each other. They was blood all over the place. That was when Cutter still worked for Ruby. Jesus God, you should have seen him clean the lot of them out of here. Threw all of them out the door like they was empty coal sacks."

They slapped each other on the back and laughed uproariously.

"I hear Cutter got in a few fights himself," said Jake.

"Christ, yes. He was a real hellion."

"Someone told me a man died because of Cutter."

"Oh, hell, it was self-defense."

"Yeah? What happened?"

"A man from over Possum Bottom way come in one night. Never been here before. I knew he was trouble right off," said Claytie. "Had too much to drink real quick. Kept slappin' girls on their butts, and cuttin' in on dancin' couples. Cutter tried to quiet him down, but he was havin' none of it."

"How old was Cutter?"

"Oh, about eighteen."

"Been in fights before, eh?"

"Fightin'est kid you ever saw. Nobody fooled with him. But he really ain't got a mean bone—"

Jake interrupted to head him off from any kind words about Cutter. "Cutter Tate was ready for bear that night, eh?"

"Yeah, but that was his job."

"What happened? How did he end up killing a man who was just out for some fun?"

"Well, I think Cutter would have got him out of here without much trouble if the man hadn't got fresh with Ruby. He grabbed Ruby, pulled her on the dance floor, then started rubbin' at her tits. That made Cutter mad. He yanked the dude by the elbow clear 'cross the floor, socked him a hard one on the chin, and the man fell and cracked his head on the edge of the bar. He was dead before he hit the floor. Cutter felt real bad about it, and—"

"How much time did he serve?"

"Just the six months Sheriff Maynard held him in county jail. Sheriff wanted to keep him there longer, but the grand jury said 'no.'"

"You mean he wasn't indicted?"

"Heck, no. Everyone who was in here that night testified that Cutter was protecting Ruby and acting in self-defense."

"Who started the fight? Who got the first lick in?"

"Well, Cutter did. But he had to. The SOB was maulin' Ruby."

"Wasn't it really a case of rich man's son getting away with murder? Didn't his father pull every string to get him off?"

Consternation began to gather on the faces of Claytie and Art.

"Well, sure, Bill Tate got the best lawyers for Cutter, not that Bill cared one damned bit. He's always hated his own son, but he didn't want a Tate in prison. No jury would have ever convicted Cutter, anyway."

"So the grandson of Macauley Tate shares the murderous traits of his grandfather."

"No, we didn't say that," protested Art.

Pete moved in for a close-up and the old men focused on him for the first time. Realizing what they'd done, what they'd said, and how Jake had tricked them, their faces showed dismay, then quick anger.

Art, the younger of the two, stood up and called out to the men at the pool table, "Billy, Bobby Lee, give us a hand here."

Pete and Jake turned to leave. Claytie, moving quickly for an elderly man, slipped off his stool and barred their way. Art pulled at Pete's camera, and Billy and Bobby Lee jammed Jake against the bar. Pete jerked away from Art, quickly stowed his camera out of harm's way on the floor under the bar, then swung around and jammed his fist in the man's chest. Jake got a couple of punches in Bobby Lee's face, and then got socked again by Billy.

The roadhouse had filled steadily while Jake had conned the two old men, and ever eager for a fight, a crowd gathered swiftly around the skirmish, yelling raucous encouragement to the locals. Claytie disappeared.

"Jimmy, boy, get him in the balls."

"Kill the fancy dude."

A bearded man with whiskey breath jerked Jake away from Billy and whapped him in the eye. Blood burst from Jake's eyebrow, flooded his eye, and poured down his cheek. He saw Pete land on the floor with two men pounding on him.

Jesus, are we going to get out of here alive?

Ruby's apartment over the bar was an eclectic mix of veneered-maple Early American furniture and fifties chrome and plastic. Recently she'd invested in a comfortable deep-cushioned leather recliner, which she sat in to watch television on her extra-large set. Next to the recliner sat an aluminum fold-up TV tray that held everything from nail polish remover and emery boards to cherry-flavored chapstick and a stack of crossword puzzle books. When Cutter visited she insisted that he sit in the recliner.

Cutter tried to have dinner with her once a week.

Sometimes they went over her taxes, or mortgage complications with Root's bank, or business problems with beer suppliers, and sometimes they just talked. Ruby wasn't the cook that Nelsey was. Her mashed potatoes had the consistency of glue and her meat loaf, despite huge chunks of onion, tasted like cardboard. But he enjoyed the time with her, and he knew it was the highlight of her week.

"I don't know why you take Root to lunch so dutifully. I know you don't like the old fart any better than I do."

"It was my turn, Ruby. The Rotarians are very serious about taking their older members out to lunch once a month," he said with a wry smile.

"Yeah, well, you ain't never loved the Rotarians that much, so knowing you I expect you got an ulterior motive."

"I do. I like knowing what the SOB is up to. Besides, he knew my grandfather."

"They was never friends, just acquaintances. His old man and Macauley liked to hunt together."

Cutter poured more ketchup on his meatloaf and grinned at her. "So, maybe I like hearing hunting stories from years ago."

"Ummph."

Ruby's moth-eaten cocker spaniel, Willie, stirred under the table. He licked at Cutter's ankle, gave a sigh, and then went back to sleep.

There had been a series of cocker spaniels through the years, right back to the one Cutter first remembered twenty-seven years ago. He'd been eleven years old and rooting in the garbage can behind Ruby's building when her dog, Patsy, growled at him. It was the dog's barking that brought Ruby to see what the problem was and her discovery of Cutter.

Cutter had long known that his father blamed him for his mother's desertion, and that his father hated him with a passion that defied civilized description. And now the town of Yancey was about to learn the nasty living conditions that young Cutter Tate endured.

It wasn't the first time his father had left him to fend for himself. At first, there were maids and gardeners who made sure Cutter had something to eat and clean clothes. But his father's journeys to Europe to beg his wife to return lasted longer and longer. Eventually, Bill Tate hated the sight of Yancey, too, and his business trips also turned into months away from home. He let the staff go, and told Cutter he was old enough to take care of himself. He always left money, but no matter how careful Cutter was, it never lasted until his father came back. Ashamed and embarrassed, at school and around town he covered his father's long absences with lies and excuses. The only work he could find at that age was bagging groceries at Kroger, which they let him do when one of the high school boys didn't show. After Ruby found him and began to feed him, things changed.

Today William Tate would have been arrested for child abuse and neglect, and an attempt was made to do so at the time, but Cutter ran away from every welfare worker that appeared, and his father's powerful attorneys made sure no complaint was ever filed.

It was then that the town took matters in its own hands and looked after Cutter the best they could.

Willie snored and Cutter laughed.

"Remember how Patsy snored so bad when she got old?"

"Lord God, yes. Used to scare me half to death in the middle of the night sometimes. You loved Patsy the best, didn't you?"

"Yeah, I guess I did. Loretta was fun, Willie's been a good dog, but Patsy was special."

"Saved you from that son-of-a-bitch Maynard the first time he beat you."

"Sure did. She caught him around the ankle and bit down so hard he started cussing." Cutter laughed. "We went around and around in circles, me trying to get away, the sheriff yelling, and that old dog holding on for dear life. Must have been comical for anyone watching. The sheriff finally had to stop beating me so he could shake Patsy off."

Ruby frowned. Her sin-weary eyes squinted, but peered keenly at him from a face corrugated by sixty years of late, late nights spent in smoke-dense rooms.

"Never could figure out why the sheriff hated you so, but it wasn't funny then, and it ain't now. I cleaned the blood offa you enough times to not remember it as funny."

But humorous was the only way Cutter could look at some of those bad times. And he knew why the sheriff hated him, but he couldn't tell anyone.

Something hard and implacable shifted within him.

For a black moment he experienced the hot hatred he'd felt as the sheriff had lashed him over the back with his hefty belt, or slapped him around the face so hard that once he'd broken his jaw, and another time his nose. He'd never said so because it would upset her, but not much had changed in Ruby's apartment since those early years, and being here brought it all back sometimes. This was where he'd usually run to escape, or to hide. Here, or Birdy's house. Nelsey still lived on the mountain then, and his best buddy, Tom Davis, lived in a mining camp three miles outside of town.

"Ah, well," he said, with mocking solemnity, "you got to learn to forgive, Ruby Barnes, or you'll piss off God."

Ruby raked irritable fingers through her blue-rinsed permed hair. "The hell you say. You know you've never forgiven Maynard, and I haven't either. I hope he's sitting on hot coals right next to the devil."

"God, me too." Cutter let go with a huge laugh, releasing the old feelings of hatred.

"Don't know how you can stand havin' that Maynard broad around. Thought you were datin' that Alison person from Charleston."

"I am. I was. I . . ." Alison had told him that she loved him, which made him uneasy with his growing attraction for Memphis. He'd never felt this way about any woman before.

He drank his coffee and didn't say anything.

"Why do you have that funny look on your face? You're not fallin' for the Maynard woman, are you?"

He laughed. "Hardly." But even as he said it, he knew Ruby wouldn't like what he was thinking.

"A worried look, that's what it is, a worried look. You worried?"

"Some. I know enough to suspect that it's dangerous for her here, but I can't tell her."

"That why you going to see Nelsey more often than usual?" Ruby had always been jealous of Nelsey.

"Maybe. Let's just say I want to keep an eye on Memphis Maynard."

He didn't say that even more than the sense of responsibility he felt toward Memphis, he was drawn to her like a standing stud to a mare in heat.

Restless at the thought of her, he got up from the kitchen chair and wandered into the living room. The murmur of voices and music from the jukebox filtered up though the floorboards from the bar below.

"Sit in the recliner. I'll do the dishes while you watch TV."

He knew Ruby wanted him to stay. "No, I'll sit and read until you go downstairs."

"Suit yourself."

She returned to the kitchen, and he inspected the bookcase that held his books. He and Ruby never liked the same TV programs so he'd created a small library for himself so he could read while she watched *Wheel of Fortune* or *Access Hollywood*.

He extracted Pat Conroy's *Beach Music* and settled himself in an easy chair near Ruby's recliner. It was his third reading of the book. Some people thought Conroy overwrote, but Cutter loved the lyrical flow of his phrases and the way his images awakened feelings you sensed you possessed but had never been able to touch before. The fact that Conroy could put them to words on paper was a miracle to Cutter. Rarely did he leave the book without wet eyes, but tonight even Conroy couldn't hold his attention.

Instead of words and images from the printed page, Memphis's face flashed on and off at him like the neon sign outside the window. First came the intentness with which she had listened to Birdy at Nelsey's party, then the dark green eyes focused so lovingly on Katie that they took his breath away. He smiled as he remembered the flour on her face and her surprise at seeing him, then the look of "so what, I can handle you, Cutter Tate." He hadn't been able to take his eyes off her as she'd moved quickly, yet gracefully, among her uninvited guests. She had charmed them all, including himself.

It was more than charm, however, that he felt at the moment. A memory of the way she impatiently brushed away an errant tendril of hair on her temple played at him then seized him in the groin. If a mere flick of her wrist could arouse him, he wondered what a kiss could do.

He stood up abruptly and tossed the book in his chair.

He paced the floor, wrestling with his feelings.

Aside from the lust, which he figured many men had felt for her, he wanted to understand this compelling need to know her as a person. It was almost as if this was someone he was supposed to know.

The muffled noise from the bar grew louder, interfering with his thoughts. He cocked his ear to listen.

Recognizing the sounds of a fight, he moved toward the door as someone began to pound on it.

"Ruby, come quick." He recognized Claytie's voice, and yanked open the door.

"Cutter, praise Jesus you're here."

"What's going on?" Cutter asked, as they ran down the back staircase.

"Jake Bishop and another dude started filmin' me and Art talkin' about fights in the bar. Bishop was puttin' words in our mouths that we never meant to say."

"About what?"

"About you and that man from Possum Bottom, makin' it sound like you and your grandpa were cut from the same cloth."

Cutter felt the old fury climbing and fought to control it. He had to stay cool if he was going to do any good here. They burst into a melee way beyond the fight scene Claytie had left moments before.

Someone had called the sheriff's office, which would make Ruby unhappy. She avoided calling the law whenever possible, and the regulars at the roadhouse knew that. The law enforcement establishment only complicated things and stuck their nose in where it didn't belong. The citizens of Yancey and Yancey County liked to settle affairs in their own way.

Brown-shirted deputies swarmed the room. Everyone in the place had gotten into the act. Women were smashing chairs over deputies' heads, pool players were using their sticks to poke and gouge at whomever they could find, and men at the bar were flinging their fists in all directions, hitting foe and friend alike. It had become an out-and-out free-for-all like Cutter hadn't seen in a long time.

"Keep Ruby upstairs," he yelled to Claytie. "I'll straighten this out."

But first he had to find Jake Bishop. He waded

through the ruckus, ducking fists, chairs, sticks, and booted kicks, looking for Jake and his cameraman.

He saw Jake disappearing through a rear door and ran to catch him, but tripped over two women who had turned on each other. They rolled around on the floor, pulling hair, biting, kicking, and screaming like mountain cats. Cutter cursed, pulled them apart, set them on their feet, and shoved them toward the door.

"Madge, Shirley, go home," he yelled above the din. "You've got kids waiting for you. Go home."

He caught up with Jake running through the rear parking lot toward the highway.

"Hold up, Bishop."

Jake stopped and turned around with a smart-ass grin on his face. One of his eyes was turning purple, and blood dripped off his chin. Cutter's urge to damage the other eye was monumental, but he held his anger in check.

"I don't know what you've been up to, Bishop, but I trust Claytie enough to know he's telling the truth. Where's your cameraman?"

Jake's grin widened and he moved in closer to Cutter, as if daring him to press too hard.

"Pete is long gone, Tate. You don't think I'd go to all this trouble and then let my precious film get confiscated, do you?"

Cutter grabbed him by the shirt and brought him close to his chest. Trembling with rage, he ached to pummel the man's handsome, grinning face.

"You've gone too far, Bishop. Don't be coming into Ruby's place, or intrude on the lives of *any* of my friends. Understand?"

"Why? You going to beat me up, or kill me? You've done it before. And if I were you, I wouldn't be manhandling me." His brows lifted, and he lowered his voice like a Shakespearean actor. "Who knows where a camera lurks in yon evil woods?"

Cutter let go of his shirt and shoved him away. Jake brushed himself off, as if he'd just been handled by the garbageman.

"I've kept that in mind," said Cutter. "I wouldn't put it past you to have a camera hidden somewhere. That's why I haven't rearranged your pretty face by now. You would love to get that on camera. You're pretty slick. The sheriff got here real quick. Don't suppose you had anything to do with that, did you?"

"Suck it up, Tate. You're not going to stop me. This book is going to expose your grandfather, the town of Yancey, and you."

Behind them, Ruby yelled out the upstairs window, "Leave the shithead be, Cutter. Gotta stop the fight before someone gets hurt bad."

"We're not finished, Bishop."

"I know. Another time, another place."

Cutter watched Jake disappear down the road, then turned his barely controlled anger toward the fight inside the roadhouse. Running to the rear of the building, he uncoiled a garden hose, turned it on full force, and yanked it through the back door.

Blasts of cold water soon cooled off heated tempers and drunken rages, and before long deputies, drinkers, pool players, and leftover women sat on the floor nursing sore jaws, slapping each other on the back, and laughing.

Memphis moved cautiously in the cool blackness, not yet comfortable with the location of her developer tank, stop bath, and fixer trays. She pried open the flat end of the cassette and gently pushed out the 35 mm film. This was the first film she'd processed in the darkroom she'd set up in the basement.

The old coal bin in the corner made an ideal work place. It had taken a lot of elbow grease to scrub away the encrusted coal dust, but after taping cardboard to the small ground-level casement window, she'd fashioned herself a light-secure room. The room was cold, damp, and still smelled of dirt and carbon, but she'd processed film in far worse places. This suited her just fine.

The scissors should be right in front of her. Yes. As she snipped off the tongue of film leader, she listened for sounds from the portable intercom. Nothing. The house, the night were silent. Katie slept peacefully upstairs. Memphis could hear a cough, a burp, or the slightest change in Katie's breathing through the intercom.

In the blackness, she reached for the wire-spiraled reel on the counter and found it. Fingering the reel, she found the grooves for which she was searching. Unwinding two inches of film, she inserted it directly into the core of the reel.

Wind sifted through the trees in the woods just beyond the basement window. Odd that she could hear the melancholy sound through the small locked window with its black shade. But she'd heard the same soft sibilation when she'd worked down here setting up the tiny room, and had decided it must be the wind in the trees. The trees were almost leafless now. It made sense that wind would make an unusual noise as it made passage through the naked branches, and then insinuated itself through the widening cracks edging the crumbling window frame.

She attached the film to the clip at the center of the reel and rested it on the counter in front of her. Holding it loosely by the edges, she began to wind the film onto the reel.

Strange, though, how much the wind sounded like a woman humming. The impression of a feminine voice humming was stronger than the first time she'd heard the sound. Almost like someone was in the room with her, right behind her in the blackness.

A chill skipped down her spine. She shuddered, then laughed at herself.

"Come on, scaredy-cat. Buck up."

Memphis made sure there were no kinks in the film as she rotated the reel and continued to wind. Processing was not her favorite job, but she trusted no one else with her film. Printing was much more fun. Printing the negatives was an adventure. She felt great satisfaction in seeing the results of her work. The excitement that came with discovering a perfect shot, maybe only one out of a hundred shots, lasted for days after the printing.

There it was again. Under her breath, she caught herself humming along with the wind's stricken hymn. Yes. The wind hummed a hymn.

Abruptly, she was gripped with the sensation that this wasn't the wind. Someone was humming. Someone was here with her in the darkroom. Icy perspiration beaded her forehead. Her hands trembled.

Careful, Memphis, you'll ruin your film. You're hearing the late October wind preparing for winter. There's no one in this house except you and Katie. Katie.

Of course. Katie must be crooning in her sleep. She bent down and put her ear to the intercom speaker. No. She heard the faint sound of Katie breathing.

The blackness swirled, swam, and eddied around her and then closed in, sealing her in a coffin of endless suffering, girdling her with keen heartache from which there seemed no escape. Choking with the powerful sensation, she coughed. The harsh coughs hurt her throat. Reality gave way to blurry, fuzzy images that meant nothing. She felt for the edge of the counter and found it. Leaning in, hips hard against the support, she grasped at her throat, trying to massage away the awful racking. Never had she felt such sadness. Her eyes burned and brimmed with tears.

What in God's name was happening to her?

The wind stopped. The abrupt silence brought an end to the fierce episode of grief that gripped her.

Get a handle, Memphis. Your imagination is working overtime.

With huge relief, she drew a shaky breath, then another, and wiped the tears from her eyes. Easing her body away from the support of the counter, she stood straight and breathed deeply again.

Hurrying now, she finished the winding task and reached for the cover of the developer tank. *The cover wasn't where it was supposed to be.* Her fingers stumbled over cold cracked Formica. Someone had moved the cover. She was always, always, always precise with the arrangement of her tanks, covers, tools, and chemicals. She had used the same patterns time after time everywhere she had ever set up a darkroom.

Nelsey. Maybe Nelsey had moved the cover. Impossible. Nelsey hadn't been around for two days, and she never came to the basement.

Go back over the same ground. It has to be there. Her unsteady fingers finally brushed the smooth square form she sought. Sighing with relief, she placed the reel of film in the tank with meticulous care, and secured the cover. It had been a long day. Her nerves were frayed. She would pour the developer in tomorrow.

Hurrying now, she stretched to find the cord to the overhead light, eager to make the smothering blackness disappear.

A strident metallic scratching made her jump, and she missed the cord. She recognized the front doorbell's idiosyncratic ringing. Who would be visiting at this time of night? Trick-or-treaters? No. This was Wednesday. Halloween was on Sunday. Grabbing upward again, she found the cord and yanked on the light.

A swift glance around the small enclosure told her what she already knew. No one shared the space with her. *Curse you, Margo, for all those ghost stories when we were kids.* Nervous laughter hiccuped from her as she left the darkroom and shut the door behind her.

Upstairs, the doorbell rang persistently. She ran across the cement basement floor and up the rickety wooden steps, desperate now for company, no matter who it was.

"Okay, okay, I'm coming," she called as she ran through the hall toward the door. No sounds from the bedroom upstairs. The doorbell hadn't wakened Katie.

A tallish shadow showed through the old-fashioned frosted glass of the door. The double bolt wouldn't give and she cursed under her breath, twisting the lock with frustration. Nelsey had thought it odd that Memphis locked her doors. "No one in Yancey locks their doors,"

Nelsey had said. "Wouldn't do no good anyway. We all know the ins and outs of everyone's house." But the ingrained habits of Manhattan living died hard. Memphis felt better with the door locked. She stopped struggling with the lock as she remembered the hostility she'd encountered since returning to Yancey. Did she want to open the door to a late-night visitor?

"It's me, babe. Take your time."

"Jake," she said, recognizing his voice. Finally, the lock gave and she opened the door.

"Hey, babe."

"What are you doing here? When I said you could spend time with Katie, I didn't mean you could just drop in anytime you felt like it. We agreed you were coming on Halloween."

Jake leaned against the doorjamb, perennially young in jeans, slim black boots, T-shirt, and jean jacket. He grinned at her, his perfect teeth gleaming in the darkness.

"Are you going to invite me in, or am I going to stand out here and freeze?"

"It's not that cold tonight, and you didn't answer my question."

"I have a present for Katie, and the hotel manager said I couldn't keep it in my room any longer." He straightened, and held a cloth-covered basket up for her to see.

"All right. Come in, but I can't wake up Katie. It's too late. You can leave your gift and come back to see her tomorrow." She was already regretting that she had told Jake he could visit Katie at all.

He followed her into the Early American–furnished living room and set his mysterious gift down on the faded multi–wine-colored braided rug. His discerning journalist's eye swept the room with interest. "Looks like the Maynards needed a good interior designer."

"Never mind your sarcasm, Jake. Forty years ago, this was a dream come true for my step-grandmother, Alma."

He moved near the fireplace and sat gingerly on a maple settee with orange-flowered lumpy cushions. "Well, at least the fireplace is a keeper," he said, admiring the intricately carved white wooden paneling in front of him.

"I'm so glad you approve," she said.

"Now who's being sarcastic?" He patted the cushion next to him. "Join me, Memphis. We have things to talk about."

"Yes, we do, Jake, but not now." She sat in a maple rocker next to the sofa. "I didn't invite you here tonight, so don't expect me to sit and visit with you. Just show me your gift for Katie and then leave."

"Not even going to offer me a cup of coffee, huh?" He took hold of the floor lamp that stood between them and swiveled the light so it shone on her face. "Just as I thought. I could tell by your voice that something was wrong. You're white as a sheet. What's the matter, beautiful?"

"Nothing, Jake. Take that light off me."

"No way. Not until you tell me what's going on. You look like you saw a ghost. You look like you did when that land mine exploded near you in Sarajevo killing Sparky Jones. Remember?"

"You don't forget losing a best friend," she said, hearing the hardness in her voice and not caring.

"See, you got even whiter when I mentioned the land mine. All those tiny Katherine Hepburn freckles that never show ordinarily spring out all over your face."

"I am just fine! I was in the basement developing film when you rang the doorbell. It startled me, and then I had to run up the steps and get to the door before you woke up Katie. That's why I look funny."

She switched the lamp back to its original position and stood up. "It's time for you to leave, Jake."

"Okay, okay. I'll stop bugging you. Sit down." He reached for the wicker basket and set it between them. "I really wanted to be with Katie when she first saw this, but I suppose Halloween will be soon enough."

Memphis knew better. She knew Jake had manufactured an excuse to visit late at night because he figured he would find her alone, but she said nothing. Still shaking inside from her experience in the darkroom, she knew now was not the time for a confrontation with Jake. In their years together, she'd always weakened and given in to anything he'd wanted. No more.

Jake removed the white cloth covering the basket, and Memphis caught her breath in delight. A chubby black kitten, curled in a ball, snoozed happily in the bottom of the basket.

"Ohhh, Jake, a kitten. You were always great with gifts." The moment the compliment was offered she wanted to snatch it back. Give Jake Bishop an inch and he would take a mile. "But Katie is too young for a kitten."

Taking umbrage, Jake said, "What do you mean? No kid is ever too young for a kitten."

"Katie isn't even two years old yet. Small children aren't good with pets. They love them too much. They hug and squeeze and poke. They don't mean to, but they hurt the kitten, and the kitten scratches them back."

"Yeah, well, my kid is smarter than that."

"Trust me, Jake. The kitten is inappropriate. We can't accept it." But she couldn't resist stroking the silky black fur. It was soft and warm against her fingers. At her touch, the kitten woke up and lifted its head to look at her with inquiring liquid brown eyes. "Male or female?"

"Female."

"How old?"

"Ten weeks. Just weaned from its mother."

"How long since it's eaten?"

"Uh, I don't remember."

"Jake, how could you forget something like that?"

Knowing it might be a fatal mistake, she reached for the kitten and placed it in her lap. A tiny rough red tongue licked her palm. The kitten stretched lazily, mewed plaintively, and then tried to climb her sweater. She put it on her shoulder beneath her ear and heard minute grumbling sounds coming from the kitten's tummy.

"She's hungry. I'll feed her before you take her back to wherever you got her."

Jake followed her into the kitchen and watched as Memphis warmed milk and poured it into a small bowl. She placed the kitten on the floor next to the bowl and it lapped hungrily. Jake settled himself in a ladderback chair.

"Don't get too comfortable. You're leaving as soon as the kitten has finished her milk."

"Let's talk, Memphis."

"I said all that I intend to say when we talked last week. You can see Katie once a week and on holidays, if you're around."

"I know, that's good. That's not what I want to talk about. This is not personal, it's professional."

Ah, ha, she thought, *now the real reason for his visit comes forth.*

"What is it?" she asked impatiently.

"The *Washington Post* called me yesterday. Actually, their religion editor called. The *Post* is doing a series on religious cults. They knew I was here working on the Sadie Maynard book, and called to ask if I would do them a favor and cover a snake-handling church in Grady, which is about thirty miles from here."

"And so?"

"They also said they knew you were here and want you to do the shoot."

"You told them I was here, didn't you, Jake?"

He held his hands up in protest. "I swear I didn't, Memphis. They said they needed the impact we would have on the whole series. The guy said a Bishop-Maynard byline sells newspapers like nothing else, anywhere, anytime. They also offered a hefty paycheck, and I know how you are with money." He folded his hands behind his head and tilted back in his chair. "In fact, I'd bet my bippie that you're broke right now."

She ignored his reference to her spendthrift habits. He was daring her. She'd always taken him up on his dares, and he knew it.

"The Bishop-Maynard byline days are over, Jake."

"They don't have to be, Memphis," he said softly.

The persuasive gentleness in his voice brought back sensual memories. She avoided his deep blue eyes by picking up the kitten and putting it in her lap. It purred contentedly and settled into the sag of her skirt.

"Think about it, Memphis," he continued. "This is the kind of story you love. It's got a persona all its own. It's got drama and the quirks of human nature that you love to uncover."

Memphis tried to ignore the stir of interest his words created. She hadn't worked on a story in three years.

"I can't, Jake. I'm concentrating on my grandmother's mystery. Spending time with Katie fills the rest of my time."

"This won't take more than a day, maybe two. Bonus benefit . . . there are several old cemeteries on the trip to Grady. You can stop and look for your grandmother's grave site. I've searched most of them, except for the mountain Cutter Tate owns, but I know you won't be happy until you've done it yourself."

"Did you say Cutter Tate owns a mountain?"

"Yep, and it was the first one I tried to explore, but he's got No Trespass signs all over it, and guards posted here and there."

"Why is he so protective? Doesn't that make you suspicious?"

"Has something to do with land his grandfather left to him, which Cutter claims his father illegally sold the mineral rights to. And sure it makes me suspicious as hell, but I haven't given up. That's one reason I haven't finished my book. Gotta go over Tate's land with a fine-tooth comb, and I will as soon as I figure out how."

Memphis hid her enormous interest in this bit of news, and her anger at the mention of *his* book, but Jake's offer became more tempting. The urge to be back in the thick of her profession tugged at her. Trying again to push away the old excitement of discovery and accomplishment, she picked up the sleeping kitten and took it to the back door.

"I'll think about it, Jake. In the meantime, Miss Priss here probably needs to do her business. After that, it's time for you to leave."

She stepped onto the back porch and put the kitten on the ground, keeping an eye on it while it relieved itself. When it was finished, the kitten looked around blindly in the darkness. Not yet old enough to see through the night as adult cats could, she sought comfort in the cold blackness, searching for the warmth of the lap that had cocooned her.

Memphis scooped her up and sat down on the stoop. Lonely and cold herself, she lifted the silky warm pod of life to her cheek and they purred together, comforting each other. The sky was starkly clear and beautiful tonight, the moon half-full. A harvest moon soon, she thought. Shadowy mountain peaks merged with the indigo sky. The dramatic view seemed famil-iar, and for a moment she was calmed and succored, as if she'd finally come home. Had Sadie ever sat on this back porch, arms resting on knees perhaps, gazing at the far peaks, dreaming of . . . what? What would Sadie dream of?

She shook herself, coming back to the present and the kitten's soft, contented purring. It was cold. Four strides across the porch would take her into the warm, lighted kitchen and Jake's company. But did Jake's company bring comfort or danger? Would she ever feel safe again, with anyone, anywhere?

When she thought of what had happened when she told Jake she was pregnant, she stopped talking, stopped revealing anymore of herself. The hurt was still too great. Jake had said that she'd made a mistake, that this wasn't the time to get pregnant, not in the midst of war. They had a job to do, and she had been irresponsible. Despite the rationality of his argument, she wanted the child with all of her heart. He had tried to hide his fear of this threat to his freedom, and his dread of responsibility, but she had seen it in his eyes and the selfish purse of his mouth.

Her anger at his abandonment still boiled in disbelief, still shook her to the core. But she'd let it rule her life and actions, had allowed it to spread insidiously into all of her life decisions.

Are you going to let your distrust of Jake, and men in general, rule the rest of your life? What a coward you've become.

She had loved her work. Had taken great pride in recording just the right moment, the right face, the right emotion, in capturing what others couldn't see.

This huge maternal hovering over Katie wasn't healthy, and she knew it. Wasn't good for Katie and wasn't good for Memphis. Memphis was learning to trust Nelsey, and Nelsey loved Katie as if she were her own grandchild. Last week, leaving Katie with Nelsey,

Memphis had spent two entire afternoons away from her child. The time was right for her to return to work, part-time, at least.

There was another consideration. Jake was right. She was broke. She had a small trust from her mother's estate, which kept her from starving. She'd had to pay the rent by doing layouts for food magazines without her byline. Her attempts to budget sent Margo into gales of laughter. Her flighty older sister was better at handling money than Memphis. Money had never been important to her, and her cavalier attitude toward bills and bank balances had resulted in some embarrassing situations. Stranded once in Paris, she'd had to hitch-hike to Nice. She smiled. One of her more delightful adventures.

Lately she'd become more adept with checks and accounts. She'd had to because of Katie, but she still hadn't caught the gist of the whole unpleasant proce-dure.

The kitten purred and licked her cheek. Memphis crooned and held the kitten closer, rubbing the warm-ness against her cool skin.

The click of the door behind her brought her out of her reverie.

Jake said, "Daydreaming again, Memphis? Some things never change. Come in. It's cold out there."

"Nightdreaming, Jake, not daydreaming." She stood up and passed him as he held the kitchen door open for her. "And things do change. I'll do the snake-handling story with you, but only on a professional basis. If you step over the line, I'll disappear so fast your head will spin."

His attempt to disguise the look of triumph that flitted briefly across his face failed. She knew him too well. "I mean it, Jake. I'm not the adoring woman I was three years ago."

"Maybe not, but you're still brilliant, beautiful, and

I'm willing to bet you're still as willing to act impulsively on your instincts. Your desire to get to the soul of a story is what makes your work so good, Memphis. I'm happy to be working with you again."

"It's just one story, Jake. We're *not* working together again. Time for you to leave. I have an early morning appointment with Senator Brady."

"Okay, I'll pick you up early Sunday morning to go to Grady."

"Sunday is Halloween, Jake. Katie doesn't understand much about it, but she knows she'll wear a fairy costume and she'll get some candy. We'll have to go another time."

"Look, the *Post* wants this story, like, yesterday. I promise I'll get you back here before dark."

Jake's promises ran like water through a sieve. "Tell you what, we'll go on Sunday if we take separate cars. That way I'll be sure to get back here on time."

Jake got a pained look on his face. "I don't like the arrangement, but if that's what it takes to get you to go, then sure."

Memphis was surprised he agreed so easily, but sighed with relief.

She looked pointedly at the big round tin clock on the wall. "Time to say goodnight, Jake."

"Uh, Memphis, could I just look at Katie before I leave? I promise I won't wake her up."

The sincere yearning in his eyes surprised her.

"Okay, but then you have to leave."

"What's the matter? Afraid of me, beautiful?" The familiar insinuating sensuousness came into his voice. Would he never give up?

"Hardly, Jake."

Minutes later they stood over Katie's crib. Memphis switched on a dim night-light near the bed.

She heard Jake's swift intake of breath as he stared down at his daughter, and again Memphis was surprised. A single beam of light from the hallway shone on Katie's blond hair.

"Oh, God, she has hair like mine," he whispered.

"Yes, and she has your blue eyes." Memphis adjusted Katie's covers. "Whoops, she's lost Opal Marie. She cries if she wakes up and can't find her."

"Opal Marie?"

"Her rag doll," whispered Memphis. "There she is."

She retrieved the doll from the floor and tucked it next to the sleeping child.

Jake grinned. "Where did you come up with that hick name? The name of one of your mountain relatives, or your overactive imagination?"

"My imagination, I guess. I just picked it out of the air. She's a cozy dolly, and Katie seemed to like the name. It's one of the first names she learned to say. Come on, Jake, it's time to go. If we stay here much longer we'll wake her up."

Downstairs, Jake said, "Memphis, it's too late for me to take the kitten back to the woman I got it from. Would you mind keeping it until I come to see Katie on Halloween?"

"Sure, Jake, but if you think I'm going to change my mind and let Katie keep it, you're wrong."

Senator Elizabeth Brady's Yancey office was in a wooded copse carved out of a secluded, but entirely accessible, cove within walking distance of Main Street. The one-story building had been built with concern and appreciation for the natural environment that surrounded it.

Memphis had a short wait in a large window-walled, light-filled square lobby filled with cushiony deep armchairs and sofas in neutral whites and beiges. Haydn's lilting Symphony no. 94 in G Major came from hidden speakers. Directly opposite the senator's office was the office of her husband, industrialist Black Brady.

The receptionist ushered Memphis into a blue-hued room furnished with antiques and tasteful West Virginia mountain crafts. While Senator Brady finished a phone call, Memphis studied the woman across the desk from her with unabashed admiration.

Sixtyish, Elizabeth "Lilibet" Brady had aged with grace. Many women grew androgynous in appearance as they grew older. Not Elizabeth Brady. This powerful senator was feminine and sensual without being fussy or phony.

Smiling at Memphis, she came around the desk and shook hands with her. "I'm so sorry. I hope you weren't waiting long."

"No, only about five minutes."

Settled before the fireplace with tea and cookies, Senator Brady said, "I'm sorry Black isn't here today. He's a great admirer of your work and was anxious to meet you. Now, what can I do for you? Nelsey said you needed help with Harvey Root?"

She explained why she was in Yancey and then said, "I'm sure Mr. Root could help. I'm not saying he's hiding anything on purpose, but perhaps he knows more than he realizes he knows. If I could pick his brain a bit, maybe I could come up with something."

"You're not going to give up on this, are you?"

"No, I'm not," said Memphis, and for some reason found herself telling Lilibet Brady things she wouldn't have told anyone else. She wondered if the woman affected everyone this way. "I feel as if my grandmother would want me to do this, in fact, I . . . can almost feel her encouraging me, talking to me. . . . Sometimes I even feel as if I've been summoned here. . . . Uh, sounds silly, doesn't it?"

"Not at all."

The senator placed her teacup on the butler's table between them and gave Memphis a long look. Memphis knew she was being read by an expert. She stayed silent during the scrutiny. Finally, Senator Brady spoke.

"There are things I think should stay buried, and some that shouldn't. I learned that the hard way." Trained at recording emotion on people's faces, Memphis saw the pain that passed briefly through Senator Brady's violet eyes. "In this instance, I'm going to help you. Because it was a local case, I took the time to review it when I was in law school, and I feel Amos Washington was sentenced unfairly."

"Thank you, Senator."

"There is a consideration, though, that concerns me greatly." The wise eyes narrowed slightly, and Memphis knew this woman could be as hard as nails when necessary. "Cutter Tate is a particular favorite of mine and Black's. Cutter was a rebellious child and teen. For good reason. Black took an interest in him, took him beneath his wing. He became like a second son. They spent a lot of time in the mountains together while my husband taught Cutter woodlore and survival skills, and other things Black is good at."

She smiled a soft, secret, loving smile then continued. "I'm hoping this investigation of yours won't hurt Cutter in any way. He's had enough pain in his life."

Memphis hesitated. "Senator Brady, I'll be honest with you. Much of the new evidence I've uncovered leads to Cutter's grandfather and Harvey Root. I can't promise you that Cutter won't be hurt. I only know that it's not fair my grandmother's real killer was never punished, and a poor black man spent the best part of his life in prison for something you and I both feel he didn't do."

"Yes."

The senator got up from her armchair and walked

over to a large mullioned window. She stood with her hands clasped behind her back and gazed into the barren woods, shorn now of leaves and life. Memphis watched the woman's shoulders move as if she'd sighed.

Finally, she returned to sit with Memphis and said, "I was thirty-two when Cutter's grandfather died. I was a young woman going through my own problems and upheavals. I didn't know him well, but remember him as a kindly old gentleman. Other than a few gambling junkets every year to Nevada, he had few vices. He seemed a sad, lonely man, but he always had time to do kind things for others. It would surprise me to find that he had anything to do with murder. However, in this case, I think the truth should out, no matter what, so I'll help you. I have only one request."

"Yes, ma'am?"

"If it looks as if you must expose Cutter's grandfather as a murderer, I would like for you to come to me first. Black will want to know."

"I will."

"Good." Senator Brady smiled. "Now we have to convince that old curmudgeon, Harvey Root, to give you an interview. I understand the whole town has given you the silent treatment."

"Yes, they have. I really do think there is a cover-up going on here."

"I hope not, Memphis. In any case, don't take it personally." She laughed. "Underneath all the gruffness and imposed silence hide a lot of very nice people. I don't know why Mr. Root is being so difficult, but the rest of them feel they're protecting a man they helped raise."

Memphis didn't share the senator's rosy view of her constituents.

"Senator Brady, there's one more thing. I'm searching for Sadie's burial site. I know that you and Mr.

Brady own Aracoma and Catawba Mountains. I also know that you've turned most of the land over to the Nature Conservancy, and that the public has free use and passage through the mountains as long as nothing is disturbed or destroyed. But Nelsey says no one knows those mountains like the Brady family, and there are far reaches never explored by anyone except you or your husband and children. I'm wondering if you have ever seen or found anyplace even faintly suggestive of a burial site?"

"Nothing I can recall right offhand, Memphis, but the possibilities are endless. Have you explored Aracoma and Catawba yet?"

"No."

"Please feel free to traipse to your heart's content. You won't find any mining damage on our mountains. They're peaceful and beautiful. If you should ever need a place to rest, there's a cabin we call Uncle East's. It's remote and few people find their way that far, but I'll draw you a map should you ever need shelter. You know Cutter knows these mountains as well as we do, and he owns a beautiful mountain called Macauley's Mountain. It lies beyond Aracoma and Catawba."

"So I've heard, but I've been told that he doesn't welcome visitors."

"That's true, but he has good reason. Maybe in your case, he'd make an exception."

"I don't think so, Senator Brady," Memphis said with a wry smile.

"Yes, I suppose you two are at cross-purposes, aren't you? What a shame. I think you'd like one another." She glanced at her watch. "I have another appointment right now, so I'll send the map to Uncle East's cabin over to you at the end of the day."

Senator Brady got to her feet, signaling the end of their conversation.

The senator offered her hand and Memphis took it.

"You head on over to the Roots'. By the time you get there, he'll be ready to talk to you. Good luck."

The Root house was a long narrow red-brick structure among other substantial homes on a quiet side street. The intrusive sounds of screeching coal tipples transporting coal from the mountain, and of railroad trains rattling through the small town, were muted in this enclave.

A short, ample-bosomed woman, Minnie Jo Dale, Harvey Root, Jr.'s daughter, greeted her. With a frown runneling her fat face, Minnie Jo ushered Memphis through a dim hallway to the rear. The house was immaculate, but smelled of yesterday's pot roast, and Minnie Jo's Charlie perfume. They entered a small library, which looked out on an even-smaller garden. The faded hoary garden had taken on a wintry look as had the faded hoary old man who sat and looked at it.

On the wall next to him hung a large ornately framed painting of the first Harvey Root, this old man's father, and the man who Memphis suspected shared some of Macauley Tate's guilt.

"My father has a guest coming to take him to lunch in an hour," said Minnie Jo Dale. Her sour face expressed disapproval at this whole episode. "He keeps to a strict schedule. I'll be back in forty-five minutes."

"Of course," said Memphis.

Minnie Jo Dale tucked the afghan closer about her father's lap, and said, "Remember, Father, you don't have to tell this woman a thing."

He grunted and waved her away.

As Minnie Jo marched stoically to the door, Memphis was reminded of stout Viking women going to battle. No wonder her husband, Dickie Dale, had gone out for a Dairy Queen twenty years ago and never returned. Memphis had gathered enough Yancey gossip to know that Minnie Jo had been so angry at her cowardly husband's desertion, she'd petitioned the court for a change of her son's name to that of his grandfather. So the child became Harvey Adler Root, the third. Forever after, the citizens of Yancey, amused at the soap opera proceedings, called the grandson H. A., the turd.

Memphis made herself comfortable in an armchair next to Harvey Root and pulled out her notebook and a small cassette recorder.

"Thank you for seeing me, Mr. Root."

He spoke without looking at her. "If Senator Lilibet wants me to talk to you, I'll talk to you. It won't do any good. I know nothing."

"We'll see. Sometimes just recalling events with someone else can jog a memory." She would soften him up, take him off guard by talking of things that might seem irrelevant. "What was Yancey like in those days? You were twenty years old and having a good time, I'm sure."

"Umph. Yancey was more civilized then. A few politically connected men controlled the town. Made living much simpler. Didn't have to deal with the riffraff you have to deal with today."

"Yes, I understand that there was a powerful group of men who ran the town in those days." The truth was that everything she read indicated the town and county were ruled by corrupt and ruthless men who would stop at nothing to stay in power, and Root's father had been at the head of the pack. But she couldn't say that to Root.

He shifted his concentration from the garden to her. His brown eyes, beneath beetling brows and watery with age, looked at her with contempt.

"You young people think you know it all. You don't understand that our forefathers intended only the intelligent landowners should rule. When we let women vote, and let all those foreigners into the country, that's when all the trouble started. That's when trouble started here, too. The coal companies started building those damned cheesy camps and importing Italian, Hungarian, and Polish miners. Cheap labor. We didn't mind the coloreds. They knew their place."

"I see. You mean people like Amos Washington."

"Amos was the best handyman in town. A good hunter, too. My father and Macauley Tate got their best game when Amos went hunting with them."

"Which brings to mind, Mr. Root, the old limousine your father used for foxhunting. Newspaper reports say the backseat had been removed and canvas tacked around the windows. Is that correct?"

"Yes. Father, Mac Tate, and other men used it to transport the carcasses they killed. Amos was the only one who could drive the damned cantankerous thing. He understood how to get it cranked up when it broke down."

"So Amos drove these men on their hunting trips?"

"Yes."

"Did anyone else ever drive the old car? It would seem to me that would be a challenge for a teenager. Did you ever drive the old car, Mr. Root?"

His heavy lids drooped lower, almost hiding his contemptuous gaze.

"No, Miss Maynard, I never drove the hunting car. I had my own Ford Roadster. I told you, no one could handle the car except Amos. Sheriff Maynard used it a time or two to transport prisoners, but he ran it into a ditch and swore he'd never drive it again."

"So when the blood in the back of the car was identified as human blood instead of animal, Amos became a suspect, as did your father because he owned the car, and Macauley Tate because he and Amos used it frequently."

The old man just stared at her, not answering.

Memphis continued. "This car was also supposedly

used to discreetly transport prominent men to meetings of a secret organization, which met in the old bank building on Cox Street. And that, in fact, your father and Macauley Tate were driven to a meeting in that car on the night of Sadie's murder. Is that true, Mr. Root?"

"I don't remember, Miss Maynard, if the car was used for such purposes. There were dirty things going on, though, and your grandmother was part of it all." His gravelly voice dripped with venom. "Your grandmother, Sadie Maynard, was a talented slut."

Memphis's heart drew up and shriveled with hatred for the aged, bitter man who sat before her. Suddenly nauseous, she swallowed the sour bile that rose in her throat, and poured herself a glass of water from the pitcher that sat on the table between them.

Don't let the bastard see that he's gotten to you. Take this, Memphis, and tuck it away with the rest of the hurts you've endured since you've been in Yancey.

"There's no need for you to insult my grandmother, Mr. Root. Let's stick to the reason I came to talk to you. What dirty things were going on?"

"A key club. Men with keys to a room where they had sex with willing women. I never attended, but one of my friends was allowed to go with his father. Men and women having sex, Miss Maynard. You're grandmother was an eager participant."

Shocked, Memphis paused briefly to compose herself.

"Do you have proof of this, Mr. Root?"

Her pause gave the old man time to put a lock on his slipping tongue. He clammed up, but his wintry look changed and his watery eyes inspected her with vivid lewdness.

"No, just rumors. At age twenty everything seemed dirty and intriguing to me."

She hadn't the stomach to pursue the line of questioning.

"Didn't your father own the building where Sadie was seen that night, and where he, Tate, and Washington were seen also? Wasn't it the old bank building?" she asked, battling to control her quaking voice.

"It was, and you know that he did. You've already checked the record of deed at the courthouse."

"Doesn't that indicate that he was involved with whatever was going on there?"

"It indicates nothing, Miss Maynard, and nothing was going on there. My father was president of the bank, the most respected man in town, as was and is my whole family."

"I'm sure." Time to change the line of questioning. "The trial records say that every second of Amos Washington's time was accounted for on the night my grandmother was murdered, until after midnight. Sadie's time of death was estimated at twelve midnight. They also say that the hunting knife that was used to slash her throat and mutilate her was owned by Macauley Tate, and that Mr. Tate could *not* account for his time that night. Why do you suppose Amos Washington was indicted instead of Macauley Tate?"

"I don't know, Miss Maynard. The murder and the trial were sensationalized throughout the state for two years, but I was a young man who soon lost interest." His pig eyes narrowed. "You do remember that though the knife belonged to Macauley Tate, it was found under Amos's bed, and the pistol used to shoot her was found in his drawer."

"Easy enough to frame Amos by placing the knife under his bed, and the gun in his drawer. Both belonged to Tate. There was other incriminating evidence against Macauley Tate. Your father was his best friend. Surely you heard something that would indicate why Tate wasn't indicted and Washington was."

"I heard nothing. Amos was seen driving the limo with Sadie in the passenger seat on Twenty-Two

Mountain that night. That's where her body was found, and that's good enough for me."

"Another witness says he saw Sadie with Macauley Tate shortly before midnight."

"Apparently the jury elected to believe Macauley Tate."

"You don't suppose the jury may have been tampered with, do you, Mr. Root?"

"Amos Washington was indicted because he was guilty. He acted guilty. My family and the Tate family shared Amos. He lived on the Tate estate, but sometimes, if he'd been working for us, he would spend the night here. Over our garage." Harvey Root shifted his gaze back to the garden outside the window. He lifted his palsied hand and pointed with a yellow-nailed finger to a garage at the end of the garden. "Make no mistake, he was guilty. Through my bedroom window, I saw Macauley Tate come to see him that night. They talked late into the night."

Memphis allowed herself a sliver of excitement. She'd known if she got Harvey Root talking long enough something would come out. This was fresh information. Information not forthcoming in trial transcripts. She was sure that his tale about sexual orgies was said intentionally to hurt her, but Macauley Tate's visit to Amos Washington the night of the murder sounded true.

"I see. Why do you think Macauley Tate would visit Amos Washington late at night?" She tried to make her tone conversational, casual. "Visiting a black man in the middle of the night certainly wasn't something a white man would do in the 1930s."

The old man's hand tightened on the arm of his chair. He knew he'd made a mistake. "You wouldn't understand the ways of men, Miss Maynard," he said coldly.

She decided to shake the old man up a bit. She'd

been too nice. Maybe making him angry would loosen his tongue.

"I haven't been able to find out how your father was exonerated of any connection to the crime, Mr. Root. I find that curious. After all, you say he was the most prominent man in town at the time and suspected of a heinous crime. Why was he not investigated further, yet suspicion follows the name of Macauley Tate to this day? Is there a possibility he paid someone off?"

His weak watery eyes narrowed to slits, and his fingers tightened on the chair until they grew red and white from the pressure. When he finally choked out his answer, his voice was tinny and shaking with tension as he tried to control his anger.

"It wasn't necessary to put it in the newspaper, Miss Maynard, because everyone in town already knew the highest power in this county cleared my father. On the steps of the courthouse just before the grand jury met, your grandfather, Sheriff James Maynard, put his arm around my father's shoulders and announced that they'd spent that evening together."

Memphis tried to hide her surprise, and quickly asked another question.

"I would think, since your father owned the newspaper, that it would have been on the front page."

"My grandfather was a modest man, and he hated having his picture taken. There was a small article written about it on a back section of the paper and that was it. However, it did make the front page of the Charleston papers."

Curiouser and curiouser. Her heart beat a little faster. The answers were all around her. She sensed it, felt it, but none of it had come together yet. There was a huge chunk missing.

"So that left two suspects, Tate and Washington?"

"Exactly. My father's name never came up again."

A knock on the door stopped her next question.

Minnie Jo opened the door and stuck her head in. "Father, Cutter's here to take you to lunch."

Cutter Tate, here, in the midst of her long-awaited interview with Harvey Root? This convenient interruption had clearly been planned. Furious at the continued glaring efforts to derail her investigation, Memphis gripped her pencil so hard that it snapped in her hand.

By the time Cutter Tate entered the library, Memphis was on her feet gathering her notes together and slinging her bag over her shoulder.

Cutter, tall and formidable, stood between her and the door. She should feel fear in the presence of these two men, one old and menacing, the other young, secretive, and powerful, but anger overrode any fear.

"Memphis. What are you doing here?" he asked, obviously pretending surprise.

"Hello, Cutter. I've been having a nice visit with Mr. Root. Thank you, Mr. Root. You've been very helpful. More than you know," she said sweetly.

Let Cutter Tate figure that one out. Let him wonder and worry about what Harvey Root had told her.

Memphis swept by Cutter, holding her anger in check until she left the house, and hating the involuntary catch of her breath at his closeness.

§ 7 §

"Praise JEE-zuss," hollered a frail elderly woman
kneeling on the bare cement floor.

"When I die, Jesus, let me die snakebit," ranted a
white-haired man in shirtsleeves standing at the pulpit.
He held two fistfuls of thick-bodied, squirming rattle-
snakes.

"Amen, amen, JEE-zuss," howled the wall-to-wall
crowd inside the gunmetal gray cinder-block building.
"JEEEE-zuss saves."

Memphis and Jake had walked into the religious
service thirty minutes ago, and though they'd been
expected, no one in the noisy sweating crowd seemed
to notice the strangers in their midst. Not even the
children, who had been placed to the rear of the room,
cast a glance their way. Everyone writhed, twisted,
danced, and prayed in their own manner, caught in an
ecstasy of primitive worship like nothing Memphis had
ever seen.

Jake made notes while Memphis snapped shot after
shot, fascinated, yet repelled by the snakes and the
people who handled them.

Her professional eye and lens caught the housewife
who triumphantly raised her arm above her head, a
plump snake curled in her palm, and a stout man with
two snakes rippling about his waist.

Her searching soul caught the everydayness of the

people who came here for release and healing. The black-lined eyes and wan, fissured faces of the men told of a lifetime working coal in warrened crannies and holes. The married women were worn, old before their time, their fingers gnarled, red, and rough like those of an old man. The younger married women, faint remnants of youth fading fast from their weary faces, were already shapeless in cheap polyester dresses. Eyes filled with resignation showed a sad acceptance of their slide into a hopeless future. Memphis knew employment and safety hazards had greatly improved in the mines in the last thirty years, but mining was still a rough way to make a living, a living that no one on the outside ever said thank you for.

The white-haired preacher wrapped two slithery glistening olive green snakes about his chest and raved, "Brothers and sisters, remember Mark, Chapter sixteen, Verse eighteen. Jesus says, 'They shall take up serpents; and if they drink any deadly thing, it shall not hurt them; they shall lay hands on the sick, and they shall recover.'"

"You better believe it, preacher!" shouted a man. His face a study in joyful hysteria, he drew his shirt over his perspiring head, ran to the front of the room, and dipped a hand into a wooden box to pull out a snake. The snake hissed and its head darted for the man's wrist. His hand trembling, he pinched it around the neck and twisted it around his wet chest. Memphis couldn't believe the viper didn't sink its dripping fangs into the plaster white skin. "Praise God. I *knooow* you love me. I have sinned, but I *knooow* you love me."

Seven or eight people handled snakes now, all at the front near the pulpit, while others writhed and danced in various states of delirium.

It was the last day of October, and though a nipping cold front numbed the tucked-away mountain cove where the humble church stood, the chill could not be felt in this one-room building that boasted neither furnace nor stove. Passion and faith rose with fervor from the believers' bodies and swathed the room in heated waves, steaming the smudged and dusty windows. Memphis imagined that if the rough gray walls could have perspired, they would have. Hot and getting hotter, she shed her heavy parka and looked for a place to store it.

"I wouldn't do that if I were you," Jake whispered in her ear. "Keep it with you, or you may find a snake curled up in your sleeve later."

He took the opportunity to nuzzle her ear, giving the lobe a nip of a kiss. She gave him a scathing look and moved away to deposit her jacket on a deserted folding chair.

A strong element of sensuousness enveloped the scene. It grew with each shout of triumphant faith, so in a way, Memphis couldn't blame Jake for his nuzzling. The dullness of a life of overdue bills, sickness, and fear of the future became lost as the room rocked with physicality, with the wild, careless, long-ago throes of primeval seduction.

She snapped frame after frame, losing herself in the frenzy of the crowd and its emotion. The panicky fear that had swept over her when they first entered the shouting, sweating crowd of snake holders, had faded to flitters of excitement and the challenge of capturing the right moments and feelings.

Jake put his hand on her shoulder, and directed her attention to a family near the front of the room. Gingerly, she moved through the crowd and closer to the family group. An ancient man, who must have been the grandfather, had reared his head back, and held a spitting, writhing snake at the entrance to his gaping mouth. Around his wrinkled neck hung two yellowed laminated three-inch-square photos. A woman in the family, long red hair streaked with gray and matted with sweat, spoke in tongues as she prayed with her hands open, palms up, to the heavens. The same yellowed photos hung on a beaded chain around her neck. Intrigued, Memphis tried to zoom in on the pictures, but found the angles awkward. Not satisfied with the shots she would get, she decided to try to interview the family later.

"Hallelujah, thank you JEE-zus," yelled a young man, slipping the strap of an electric Fender bass guitar over his head. He strummed a chord. A man with a fiddle, and another with a set of drums, joined him as they headed into a rockabilly "Reach Out and Touch the Lord." The faithful began to sing, the volume growing until the small perspiring space vibrated with the beat. Memphis felt the throb through the soles of her feet, and her heart tripped fast with excitement.

Knowing she could lose her professional eye for the story if she got carried away, Memphis worked to control her uneven breathing. She made her way back through the lost, but happy, worshippers to Jake, who had returned to the rear of the church. In a corner two teenagers, assigned to keep an eye on the younger children, groped one another with hot feverish hands. Breathless, she leaned against the wall and closed her eyes. Jake moved closer to her.

"Okay, beautiful?" he whispered in her ear.

Grateful for his presence for the moment, Memphis nodded "yes" and smiled. He put his arm around her waist, nudging her close to him. Her eyelids jerked open. She straightened, stepped away from him, and kicked him sharply on the shin.

Leaning against the wall, his legs crossed casually, her well-aimed kick hadn't bothered him. He laughed. "You miss the loving, don't you? We were good together, beautiful."

"You're as immature as the two hormonal kids in the

corner. Don't get your hopes up, Jake. It's not going to happen with us again."

"Yeah?" He pointed to the teenagers. "Those two hormonal puppies will be outside in the bushes together in no time. Don't you envy them? Seems to me I remember a few times we ripped off a quickie in the bushes. There's nothing better than a hot, fast fuck, lovey. I'll be around when you're ready."

"Disgusting as always. You promised me this was just a job, Jake. No hanky-panky. If you don't keep your hands off me, I'll destroy all my film and you won't have a story." She knew she wouldn't. Destroying her work was like sinning to her, but the bluff sounded good.

"Okay, I promise," he said, holding up his hands in a placating gesture, a shade of alarm in his voice.

She moved away from him to find a safer place to watch, but decided to go outside instead. The singing had become a chant that seemed to go on forever. She needed fresh cool air.

Standing on the wooden steps of the plain makeshift church, she hugged her waist with her arms and inhaled deep drafts of the sharp cold mountain air. The afternoon was growing grayer and colder as it drew on. Tonight was Halloween. She hoped the weather would be kind to the fun-seeking children, and wondered again if she should take Katie trick-or-treating. Katie had a costume, but she was a bit young, and Memphis worried about their reception at the doors of unfriendly Yancey people.

A skittish wind picked up and blew brittle brown leaves all about until a few settled around her feet.

Detecting movement out of the corner of her eye, she turned her head to see the two impatient teenagers slip from a side door of the church and run swiftly hand-in-hand into a nearby grove of trees. Jake had guessed right about them. She envied their youth, their unrestrained passion, and their disregard for consequences. For a fierce hot moment, she wished herself back to that age again, free of responsibility, and eager for all the promise that lay ahead. The wish was fleeting. The pain of getting from there to here had been too great, too savage, too destructive. No thank you, she thought. *I'll take today and be happy with it.*

The singing had finally stopped and the front door of the church opened. Jake motioned to her. Memphis climbed the steps to meet him at the top.

"They're taking a break. I think we can interview the pastor now, and maybe some others," he said.

They made their way to the front of the church, greeted by many friendly mountaineers along the way.

"Howdy. Glad to have ya."

"Hey," said one gaunt young man, shaking Jake's hand. "Come to see if the Lord loves ya, huh? Well, he does, brother, he does. Believe it!"

A gray-haired woman patted Memphis on the shoulder. "Hey, honey. Handsome man ya got thar. You be keepin' your eye on him now. God loves ya."

Pastor Ray Elkins greeted Jake with a bear hug, and bowed from the waist to Memphis. "Welcome to Grady Church of God. Don't know why a newspaper would want a story about us, but we're honored. Anytime we can git the word of the Lord out, we're happy to oblige."

"Thank you for letting us attend the service, Pastor Elkins," said Jake. "This is photographer Memphis Maynard. Do you mind if she takes a few pictures of you while we talk?"

"'Course not," said the pastor, and gave Memphis a sweet grin.

"Tell me about the snakes and why they're important to your services," said Jake.

"God uses them to let us know if we've been sinnin' or not. I'll go the longest time and not get bit, and I'll be thinkin' I'm a right good feller and I'm on the road to glory. But about the time I'm feelin' thataway, one of them vipers will bite just to remind me who's the Lord and who's the sinner. Son, I'll tell you, the last time it took lots of prayin' to save me. Jest ask Aurianne. This here's my wife, Aurianne."

The bent-over woman standing next to him said, "Praise the Lord, that's for sure. Doctors said Ray wouldn't last out the week, but we prayed night and day, and thar he stands afore ya."

While Jake and Ray Elkins talked, Memphis studied the man, and through the lens of her camera realized Ray Elkins was much older than she'd first thought. *Looks to be about eighty, but strong and healthy for his age.* Must be all that snake venom, she thought with irreverence, then shook her head to chastise herself. Professional that she was, Memphis always treated her subjects and their lives with respect.

Ray Elkins displayed his bare arms to Jake, pointing out snakebite scars. Memphis snapped a picture of the arms, and heard the old man say he was eighty-three years old.

"Were you a coal miner?" asked Jake.

"Sure was, for nigh onto forty years. But I did preachin' then, too. Weekdays, I'd mine. Sundays, I'd preach. Don't have any friends left from those days, or much family either, 'cept for Aurianne."

"You look healthy for your age," Memphis said. "That's unusual for a man who spent forty years in the mines." Especially one who handles lethal snakes on the weekends, she thought.

"Well, ma'am, I come from hearty stock. My Scotch-Irish grandfather lived to be ninety-five. An' I always got exercise and plenty of fresh air whenever I could. When I was younger, everytime the union went on strike, I dug graves to make ends meet. Gave us eatin' money and kept me in good shape."

Crouched to get Pastor Elkins's interesting face from a different angle, Memphis straightened up quickly. She and Jake exchanged glances.

"Dug graves, huh?" asked Jake casually. "Then you'd know a lot about graveyards around here. What about in Yancey? Know anything about graveyards over that way?"

"Sure, I lived on Twenty-Two Mountain for many a year."

"How long have you been digging graves?" asked Memphis, trying to keep the excitement from her voice.

"Oh, I dug for nigh onto forty year, until I was sixty and my shoulders gave out on me."

"Pastor Elkins, I'm looking for my grandmother's grave site. Maybe you can help me."

"Maybe so, though my memory ain't so good anymore. What was her name?"

"Sadie Maynard."

"No, cain't say as I remember ever buryin' anyone with that name. Say, ain't that the murdered woman from a long time ago? Seems like I . . . maybe there was . . ." Memphis watched his face carefully as she waited for him to sort through his memories. He scratched his head and closed his eyes. Finally, he opened them, and his honest blue gaze told her he remembered nothing. "No, cain't say as I recollect knowin' anything about whar she's buried."

Heavy disappointment filled Memphis.

"You must know most of the small cemeteries way back in the hills."

"Sure, I'd be happy to go with ya someday. I'll take you up roads and hollers only mountain people know about. I figure I've traveled most of them between here and Yancey."

"Is there anyone else here who might know anything back that far?"

"Old man Chafin over thar used to dig a few graves. He's older'n I am. Most of the Chafins still live over on Twenty-Two. If I'm able, I pick them up fer church on Sundays." Pastor Elkins indicated the family Memphis had taken pictures of earlier.

Memphis excused herself while Jake continued to interview the preacher.

Weak and frail now without his zealous faith to hold him erect, the perspiring patriarch of the Chafin family sat on a folding chair. The middle-aged red-haired woman fanned him with a cardboard fan picturing a vivid Jesus Christ on the cross. In a moment of Sunday school boredom, someone had blacked out Jesus' teeth, and penciled an irreverent mustache over his upper lip.

Memphis introduced herself, explaining that Pastor Elkins had suggested she speak with them.

"Sure. What can we do fer ya, honey?" asked the red-haired woman. Her face held vestiges of once fiery beauty, and intelligence blazed from her cornflower blue eyes. "Granpa can't talk much anymore, but maybe one of the rest of us can hep ya. I'm Vanta Lou, this here's my Aunt Mellie and my cousin, Willa Laid, and here's my brother, Robert."

"Nice to meet all of you," said Memphis. "I'm looking for my grandmother's grave site, which I'm sure is located somewhere between Yancey and Grady. I wondered if you knew about any out-of-the-way graves located in unusual places."

The Chafin family conferred quietly for a few minutes, even asking Grandpa if he could think of any such grave. While they talked, Memphis again noticed the photos hanging around the necks of Grandpa Chafin and Vanta Lou. On closer inspection, she realized the faded, sepia brown photos were of long-ago people.

Finally, Vanta Lou answered for all of them. She seemed to be the spokesman for the group. "No, ma'am. I'm terrible sorry, but we can't think of anything right offhand."

Memphis handed her business card to Vanta Lou. "Thank you anyway. If you do, would you please give me a call? I've written my Yancey phone number on the card."

"I'm sorry, Miz Maynard, but we don't have no phone."

"Well, if you remember something, the next time you come to Yancey, you could visit me."

"We don't come to town hardly a'tall. Jest afore Christmas and sometimes in summer. Whar do you live in Yancey?"

"Do you know Sheriff Maynard's house outside of town near Logan Creek?"

The old man grew agitated and grabbed his granddaughter's hand, shaking his head back and forth in wobbly fashion. "What's the trouble, Granpa?" she asked.

He held his finger in the air and shook it back and forth in a forbidding motion. "No," he said in a reedy but adamant voice. "Not the Maynard place. Place of ghosts and violence. No more spiriting."

Memphis smiled at the old man and waited for Vanta Lou to tell her grandfather he should know better, but she didn't. She looked at Memphis with a troubled frown. "Granpa says we can't go near your place. But we'd be mighty proud to have you visit us anytime."

"What does he mean when he says 'spiriting'?"

"He's afraid we'll get spirited away jest like his brother and sistern, my Uncle Clyde and my Aunt Opal Marie."

Thinking she'd misunderstood Vanta Lou, Memphis asked, "I'm sorry, but I don't understand. Who was spirited away? Who was Opal Marie?"

Vanta Lou pointed to the laminated photos around her neck. "A long time ago, Uncle Clyde and Aunt Opal

Marie were taken by the spirits. We wear these here pictures all the time, either around our necks or in a pocket to ward off the evil. The spirits know we're onto their tricks if we wear these."

Vanta Lou nodded to the rest of the family. In silence, her aunt and cousin extracted the same pictures from their peeling-black-plastic purses, and her brother pulled his from a shirt pocket. Solemnly, they showed them to Memphis, then replaced them from where they had come.

Gathering her shaken wits together, Memphis asked, "Why do you think the spirits took them?"

"They jest disappeared an' never come back. That's what happens when you been tryin' to fool the Lord, and Opal Marie had been misbehavin'. Granpa don't want us near the Maynard house because Opal Marie was seen near there the night she disappeared, and he's heard there be ghostly lights and sech around the house."

The outside door opened and the congregation began to drift back into the room. The guitarist softly strummed "The Old Rugged Cross," and Pastor Elkins announced it was time to renew worship. Their next break would be suppertime three hours from now.

Memphis, trying to absorb all this intriguing new information, glanced at her watch in frustration. She couldn't stay any longer. It had taken them ninety minutes to drive here. She wanted to be home to dress Katie in her fairy costume and get the candied apples ready for trick-or-treaters.

"Vanta Lou, I need to ask you more questions for my newspaper article. Would you please tell me how to find your house so I can visit you soon?"

"Sure. We'd be right proud if you came."

There followed directions that rambled from one dirt road to another, over two creeks and down one hollow, to a group of cabins in a thicket of mountain laurel.

Memphis wrote hurriedly because Pastor Elkins had started his preaching, and Grandpa Chafin was frowning at her. She'd sort the directions out later.

"Find out anything?" asked Jake

She'd be damned if she'd tell him that she'd seen and heard sounds at the house that others had seen, and which were probably the source of the Sadie ghost stories. Her practical mind fought with her believing heart. Was her grandmother trying to tell her something? And how could she tell Jake that Katie's doll had the same name of a young girl believed to have been taken away by "spirits" a long time ago, a name that had come to Memphis out of nowhere.

"Eh, no, not really."

Jake found her parka for her. She diligently inspected for snakes before she slipped it on. Outside, on the way to the Jeep, Memphis's hands shook as she zipped up her parka.

"Cold, babe?" inquired Jake.

"No. I'm fine."

This is stupid, Memphis. Nothing to be concerned about. Pure coincidence. There must be many people named Opal Marie. Means nothing.

In the Jeep, her arms felt like melting Jell-O and her hands shook so badly that inserting the key into the ignition took intense concentration. The sense that someone sat in the passenger seat next to her was so strong that she reached out to feel the seat and found nothing but space.

Regardless, as she made her way home to Yancey, she knew something or someone rode with her.

An inch from Cutter's nose, the bronze, cold, ungiving wall glared back at him. He cared to look neither down the sheer face of the mountain into the yawning abyss beneath him, nor up to the top of the perpendicular incline that was his destination.

Which was exactly how he felt about his life at the moment. Most people found it difficult to live in the present. Not Cutter. This last half hour of staring at the rock, of balancing on the piton, of cursing the crumbling handholds above his head, of meticulously planning his next move, held at bay the darkness of his younger years. A darkness that returned to plague him unannounced from time to time.

Memphis Maynard's mission in Yancey had caused the latest eruption of his carefully withheld, tamped-down emotions. She shouldn't be here.

Black had told him time and again not to climb by himself, but the complete absorption of thought involved was what he needed. His only competition was with himself. He had to think with his body, demanding the best of himself. He had to prove he could survive by himself, without anyone's help. If anything went wrong, the fault was his own, not in his gear or a climbing partner. Climbing required total commitment from his protesting muscles and nerves, and in seemingly dire situations, any reserves of character a man possessed.

Scaling a mountain was like a chess game, and it was beyond time for him to make his next move.

Decide or die, Cutter.

His swollen fingers were numb, and the pain in his calf muscles darted sharp into his buttocks. The only possible escape route was a small ledge twenty feet beneath him, but fifteen feet to his right. It required his clinging with one hand, and balancing on the piton with his foot, while he used his axe to fix another piton as far to his right as possible. It would take several such moves before he could fasten a rope to a piton and abseil safely down to the ledge. From there, with luck, he might find the crevasses or outcroppings he needed to reach the top.

Clenching his jaw, he ordered each stiff finger to

obey the messages from his mind. Finger by finger, he removed his hand from its questionable hold, then worked each digit gently until feeling returned. He gingerly extracted a piton from his side pack and reached for the faint crack he could see above his head and four feet to his right. Straining until his shoulder ached beyond endurance, he shoved the piton into the tiny crevasse. Then, left hand digging into its tenacious hold, and foot balancing precariously, he used his axe to drive the piton further into the iron mountain. From this he would fasten his rope to travel across and down to the ledge.

Three hours later, with light fading fast from the late October sky, he climbed atop the flat boulder that guarded the entrance to the glen the Brady family used for picnics. Black had told him that Elizabeth used to call it her "secret place."

Exhausted, he lay still, savoring his moment of triumph. He'd beaten the mountain again. For this short moment in time he'd fed whatever it was that drove him to take such fatalistic chances. Satisfied, for a moment.

Soon the cold wind turned his perspiration-soaked clothes to iced sacking. He got to his knees, crawled through a thick border of trees, and into the dark glen. Beautiful in the daytime, at night the glen was a place of mystery, and freezing cold in the winter.

Chilled and fatigued, he stood and made his way around the pretty pond to the far side and a path that led to Uncle East's cabin. Night was falling. His destination was an hour away. He'd need to move fast to make it there before the shadowy forest became impenetrable.

By the time he reached the cabin, Cutter couldn't see his hand in front of his face. The smell of wood smoke beckoned him and he knew Black was waiting for him.

Black Brady, his back to the door, was stoking the

fire when Cutter entered. He didn't turn at the sound of the door, and Cutter knew Black was angry by the hold of his shoulders.

"Climbed Baldface by yourself, didn't you?"

Cutter sank into a chair near the fireplace, and said, "Yep."

The legendary mountaineer—and wealthy industrialist—propped the poker against the log wall, and took a chair across from Cutter. Black, the only man except for his grandfather who had ever given a damn about him, crossed his arms on his chest and shook his head in wonder.

"You can't do it, my boy, you can't keep challenging Old Man Mountain and expect to get away with it. He'll only satisfy your demons for so long. Then he gets bored of fiddling with your challenges and takes over."

"Had to do it, Black. You'd never believe how much better I feel."

A smile broke Black's stern visage. He said, "Yes I would. Fought a few of those demons myself in the same manner. But, dammit, Cutter, I thought you'd gotten rid of most of those black times."

"Thought I had, too, until Jake Bishop and Memphis Maynard agitated the whole thing again."

"I saw the nasty piece he did on you at Ruby's. Dirty journalism. Is that what the climb was all about?"

"Had something to do with it. People in town are getting a little stiff with me. They don't like all the attention. Worried about other reporters coming in."

"You've never been concerned before about what others think. Don't let him bait you. I'm worried about you." Black studied Cutter, inspecting him as an adult bear would a cub.

"No, you're not. You're just jealous, old man. How long has it been since you've made a climb?"

They laughed, because they both knew Black was still capable of doing just about anything he'd taught the younger man to do. Sixty-five years old, Black Brady's handsome face was weathered, worn, and wise, his hair silvery white, but his well-tuned, lean, and muscular body had stood the test of time.

"The resurgence of this old story hasn't distracted you from the hearing next week, has it?"

"No, Black, no one is going to take my land from me. Grandfather wanted me to have it, and it's the only tangible thing I have left of his. I've fought long and hard for it, and I'm not about to let a bunch of bloodsuckers steal it now. Just wish you could be with me."

"I do, too, but I promised young Black that I'd meet him in Paris next week. You don't need me. There's no one better in a boardroom than you, Cutter. Your law school training has come in real handy. You'll slice up those corporation lawyers like you always do."

"Yeah, but I'm getting tired of the battle. I wish United Mining would just give up and let me enjoy my land. I want to give part of it to the Nature Conservancy, as you and Lilibet have, but I can't do anything until the title is free and clear and I'm sure they're not pulling coal out of Macauley's innards."

"You've held them off for fifteen years, you'll do it again." Black stood up and squeezed him on the shoulder. "How about a sandwich and a beer?"

"Beer first, sandwich later."

Cutter drank his beer while Black fixed him a pile of sandwiches.

An amber glow from the fire filled half the room in warmth, and the flickering yellow light from a kerosene lamp reflected off a mellowed-pine table. The only sounds were the wind outside and the light thud of Black's knife when it hit the cutting board as he sliced thick pieces of ham. The sturdy cabin had never been modernized with electricity or plumbing. Cutter knew the ham, mustard, and beer came from the natural springhouse snug in the hillside just behind the cabin. Black had probably carried the homemade bread in a backpack on his trek over from the Brady family's remote mountain retreat, Brady's Lair.

Even Cutter, who was almost a member of the family, had never been invited to Brady's Lair. But this cabin was haven to anyone who found it, though there weren't many who had. The cabin was almost as inaccessible as Brady's Lair. Black had shown him the way here when he was fourteen and he'd used it as a refuge ever since. Black's grandfather had built the cabin in 1910 and had lived here by himself until he died in 1966. As Cutter understood it, Uncle East, as he'd been called, would have been happy knowing the cabin was now a refuge for Brady family favorites, or the stray stranger who happened upon it.

They ate their sandwiches in silence.

Cutter wiped his mouth with a paper napkin, sighed, stretched his long legs in front of him, folded his hands across his stomach, leaned back in his chair, and closed his eyes. This, for a precious moment, was peace. Black remained quiet. He had an infinite capacity for silence, which Cutter was learning too. The words would come when they should, if words were needed.

Tonight they were. They came slowly, cautiously. Black already knew Cutter's story, knew of the cold indifference of his mother, and finally her complete desertion, knew of the beatings his father had given him after his grandfather's death, but Cutter hadn't shared his feelings for years.

"When I called last week, Elizabeth said you were in Zaire with young Black."

"Yep. We're part of a world hunger group trying to come up with a solution to their problems."

"You must be proud of young Black. He'll make a fine foreign diplomat someday."

"*Happy* for him is a better way to say it. I love him fiercely, but I take no blame or credit for my children. They are what they are. Pride lays an onus of unnecessary responsibility upon their shoulders."

"What do you mean?"

"A parent's pride feeds on a child's need to keep his parents happy. Fine, as long as the child is following his own path, as long as they are fulfilling their own destiny and not some notion of their parents."

Cutter chewed on that for a while.

"Must be nice to have someone love you that much."

"Feeling sorry for yourself tonight?"

In the fading glow of the embers, Black poured them both a snifter of Courvoisier.

"No. Nostalgic, maybe. Wishing I could go back just once to one of those Saturdays Grandpa and I fished at the lake on Macauley's Mountain. Wishing I could feel his encouraging hand on my shoulder as I struggled over my fifth-grade history homework. Wondering if maybe I imagined the deep love he felt for me, and wondering if through the years I conjured up a companionable relationship that didn't really exist. Maybe I wanted it so bad that I made it up."

Black was the only person he'd ever been able to talk to this way. Yes, Nelsey loved him and understood, and Ruby loved and protected him, and Birdy was a good friend, but only Black listened without judgment.

"You didn't make it up. Your grandfather passed on to you the gift of loving. You inherited it genetically, but more than that, through his great love for you. Never doubt it."

"And yet my father hated me and everyone around him. Did he learn nothing from Grandpa?"

"I think, to your grandfather's sorrow, your father never had a great capacity for love to begin with, and what he had turned bitter when he realized the woman he wanted to possess was a shallow, calculating fortune hunter. Unfortunately, he blamed a terrified ten-year-old boy for her desertion, and there was no one there to convince him otherwise."

"Thank God there were people like you and Nelsey who helped me through those years." He hesitated before bringing up something he'd wanted to discuss with Black before, but had never had the nerve. *Black won't ask questions. He would never invade my privacy.* With Black the thirty-eight-year-old man could be twenty again. "Black, how do you feel about secrets?"

"Depends on whose secret it is and what it is. If it's hurting people then it probably isn't worth keeping. Generally, however, a promise to keep a secret should be kept."

"Just about what I figured."

Again, Cutter hesitated before pursuing the conversation further. Though he suspected Black sensed the romantic nature Cutter hid, it was difficult to talk of these things. Everyone thought of him as rough and tough, but laid-back and amiable on a day-to-day basis, which was the way he wanted it.

Cutter sighed and took a satisfying swallow of brandy. He leaned forward, his elbows on his knees, and stared into the fire.

"Do you believe some people love more profoundly, more intensely, than others?"

"Yes, I do," said Black softly. Cutter saw him glance in the direction of his wife's photo, which sat on a shadowed bookcase nearby.

"You're lucky, Black."

"I'm blessed, but it didn't come easy. I had much to learn. The ability to love was there, but it took Elizabeth to teach me how to release it, and how to treasure love. Elizabeth was the miracle."

"Alison says she loves me."

"And how do you feel?" He felt the older man's incisive gaze as he waited for Cutter's answer.

"It doesn't feel right. There's pleasure there, and it's fun being with her. She's pretty and bright and kind. I believe her when she says she loves me, and I'm ready to get married. I'm ready for children. But do I love her enough? Am I being unfair to her?"

"Sounds like it to me, but I don't have to tell you that you'll *know* when you've found the person you want to spend the rest of your life with. There won't be any questioning, Cutter. You're on the right track when you say 'it doesn't feel right.'"

"Have you ever just touched someone and felt an immediate connection?"

"Yes." Cutter couldn't see Black's face, but he could hear the smile in his mentor's voice. "Have you?"

"Yeah." Black would never ask who, but Cutter wanted to tell him. "Memphis Maynard."

"I see. Interesting."

"What do you mean . . . interesting?"

Black said nothing for a long time, then said, "Considering your mutual backgrounds, there *is* a connection, of course, but this sounds as if you felt more than that."

"I did."

Again, Black was silent, then said softly, "Fate takes odd twists and turns to accomplish what it has in mind. In time you'll discover, either to your liking or disliking, the meaning of what you felt when you touched Memphis."

He stretched his arms above his head, yawning. "I'm ready to stack some z's. You?"

Black had decided the conversation had gone far enough for now, and Cutter knew it had, too. There were things a man could only learn for himself.

"Yep." He reached for a beautiful old quilt, which had been tossed across a willow twig bench near the fireplace. "I'll roll up out here."

Black laughed. "Giving the old man the bed, huh?"

Cutter, rolling up in the quilt, murmured sleepily, "Don't care, just want to sleep for two days."

Black's paternal squeeze on the shoulder was the last thing Cutter felt before he dozed off.

Katie, finger in mouth, stared at her image in the cheval glass mirror. Jake, the man she was introduced to an hour ago and who she would call "Uncle" for a while, stared at her too. Entranced with her every move, he watched as she picked up the top layer of pink-net tutu and stuck it in her mouth also.

"Won't that make her sick?" asked Jake anxiously.

"No," answered Memphis, who watched both of them with amusement, Katie seeing herself in costume for the first time, and Jake seeing his daughter awake for the first time.

The doorbell rang downstairs, and Memphis knew the first trick-or-treaters had arrived. Nelsey would answer the door, but Memphis didn't want Katie to miss a minute of Halloween fun.

"Okay, Katie, time to see if we have visitors."

"Uh, you suppose I could carry her downstairs?" asked Jake.

"Sure."

Jake picked her up gingerly, as if he was afraid she would break. Katie drew back and inspected him anxiously with her big blue eyes. Memphis could tell she was wondering if Jake was part of this strange new concept called Halloween.

"Twickortweet?" she asked Jake, then twisted and held her arms out to her mother, questioning the wisdom in letting this man carry her.

"It's all right, Katie."

Downstairs, they found Nelsey talking to Birdy.

"Hi, Memphis," said Birdy. "Hope you don't mind if I stay for a few minutes. Nelsey usually comes to my house for Halloween, because she never gets many trick-or-treaters out this way. My dad is taking care of treats at my house till I get back."

"I admit it. I'm a sucker for the kids," said Nelsey, a big smile on her face.

"But, Nelsey, you should have gone to Birdy's like you always do."

"No, you made the right decison about keepin' Katie here 'stead of going out, and I wanted to be with her. We'll have a few kids come. Some of the families who live on the edge of town, and maybe a few mountain children will come down. It's best this way. Don't want to get Katie too excited or scared."

"Right," stated Jake emphatically.

It was Nelsey's and Birdy's turn to stare at Jake, and Memphis struggled not to laugh at his sudden and uncharacteristic paternal behavior. He blushed crimson to the edge of his blond hairline, and hastily set Katie on the floor.

Katie made a beeline for the black kitten, Miss Priss, who she spotted curled in her basket near the sofa. To Memphis's dismay and delight, Katie and the kitten had bonded immediately, and the thought of returning it to Jake had disppeared.

The doorbell rang and the next hour was filled with giving out treats to wee ghosts and goblins, and Katie's oohs and ahhs.

At nine o'clock, Katie had fallen asleep on Memphis's lap, face smeared with orange candy, Miss Priss clutched in her arms.

"Whoo. It's been a long day," said Memphis. She took a sip of the hot apple cider Nelsey had made and laid her cheek atop Katie's curls.

"I'll carry Katie up to bed for you," offered Jake eagerly.

"No, you won't," said Nelsey. She glared at him, daring him to lay any claim to fatherhood at this point.

"Nobody gonna touch that child tonight but me. Memphis, you're tired. You stay put. I'm takin' her up."

"Okay, okay." Jake held his hands up in mock surrender. "I have to go anyway. Gotta few things to do before the night is over."

Memphis could imagine what they were. Sally Junior was probably waiting for him somewhere. *God, was she doing the right thing, allowing Jake access to Katie? Her heart said yes. Her brain said no.*

After asking if he could see Katie next weekend, Jake left.

"Well, I should say goodnight, too," said Birdy. But she didn't act like she was going to, thought Memphis. She sat there, her pointed chin resting in her little hand, her small face screwed up in a frown. "But I wanted to ask you something, Memphis, honey."

"Ask away."

She liked Birdy, and appreciated her offer of friendship in a town that still largely ignored her, but she was exhausted and sometimes Birdy's conversations turned into monologues on the gossip in Yancey, and the deplorable state of the world in general.

"Huh, well, I know you and Jake were out aways today, over toward Grady. Did you see Cutter, by any chance?"

Surprised, Memphis said, "No. Should we have?"

"Well, no, not really." Birdy coughed, attempting to hide her embarrassment. "It's just that, except for an evening at Ruby's, he's been gone ever since we were here for Nelsey's birthday, which is a bit unusual. Most of the time, when he disappears on these mountain treks, he's back in a couple of days."

Memphis wondered if this was the real reason Birdy had come tonight. Not because of Nelsey and the trick-or-treaters, but because she wanted to find out if Memphis had seen Cutter.

Birdy said her good-byes quickly after that.

Memphis sat wearily at the table, sipping on the cider, thankful for Miss Priss cuddled warmly in her lap where Nelsey had placed her, thankful for Nelsey upstairs with Katie, and thankful for a full and productive day. She was anxious to develop the pictures she'd taken at the church.

The doorbell rang. A late trick-or-treater.

In the vestibule, she picked up a tray of candied apples, and opened the door.

This was no child. The visitor was dressed all in black—black trousers, black loose shirt, and black ski mask, with hands held behind his back. Memphis couldn't tell whether the person was male or female.

Memphis presented the tray of apples and said, "Hi. I also have some Tootsie Rolls left, and maybe a few Snickers bars."

The mysterious person ignored her offering and whipped out an enlarged photo. Memphis recognized an old *Life* magazine cover photo of her and Jake. A skull and crossbones had been painted across the bottom. Beneath the skull and crossbones were the words, "LEAVE TOWN, BITCH, AND TAKE THE FUCKER WITH YOU!"

The visitor punched the bottom of the metal tray with his fist and flipped it hard into Memphis's face. The edge of the heavy tray cut into her forehead as the photo came sailing at her also. She staggered trying to find her balance, but fell.

Stunned, she lay on her side with caramel gummed in her hair, the wooden handle-stick of an apple poking her eye, and felt blood trickling down her temple.

For a breathtaking moment she knew her attacker had entered the house and stood over her. Trembling, she opened her eyes to look up at the masked figure. Vulnerable and shaken, Memphis felt waves of hot hatred coming at her.

She made a trembling snatch at the black mask, but the figure jerked back, and began to laugh maniacally.

Nelsey called, "Memphis? You okay?"

The intruder turned and ran, slamming the door behind him.

Sitting up, she did a slow burn. "No, I'm not okay. I'm angry. I'm mad as hell."

§8§

Memphis stood hidden in the middle of a wet rhodo-dendron thicket panting with exertion and alarm. The faint path she'd followed along the foot of Macauley's Mountain had faded hours ago. She'd climbed cautiously since then, feeling her way more than anything, finding no signs of a camouflaged burial site, and letting instinct lead her. She'd begun to realize the task of finding a single grave on one of these vast mountains was almost hopeless.

Right now she was more concerned with the men in the clearing in front of her. They would have heard her clumsy approach had not the tension among them been so palpable.

"Back off!" Cutter said grimly. "Back up until your sorry ass hits a tree. Now, stop. Don't move a muscle, don't even twitch an eyelid, or I'll nail you, you stealing sons of bitches."

Cutter, aiming a large, lethal-looking bow and arrow, confronted two men, one large and nervous, the other short and defiant. They wore elaborate, obviously recently store-bought, climbing clothes. Mud caked their shiny leather boots, and their stiff new khaki trousers looked bent instead of comfortably wrinkled. Hastily dropped surveying equipment lay at their feet. Cutter, on the other hand, looked perfectly at home in his rough-hewn mining tans, and battered, laced-up construction boots. An unzipped lightweight black windbreaker hung loose from his broad shoulders, flapping around in the quickening breeze. He wore no hard hat today. It looked to Memphis as if he'd interrupted the men in the midst of a surveying project.

The big man moved his hand toward a shirt pocket and Cutter released an arrow.

It whizzed close to the man's ear and dug into the tree behind him with a soft *thung*. He turned white, and his eyes grew wide with alarm.

The short man reached for a back pocket. Cutter's hand and arm moved so fast they were a blur of lethal motion. In one swift, sweetly harmonized action, he rearmed, aimed, and let go with an arrow that sliced into the dirt at the tip of the man's boot.

"I was only reaching for the papers that prove we're here legally," said the smaller man. "You may own the surface of this mountain, Tate, but your father sold off the mineral rights long ago. You're fighting a losing battle. You can't keep us away much longer, and you can't hold us off much longer today with only a bow and arrow."

"United Mining will never take another cut of coal out of this mountain." Cutter's back was to her so she couldn't see his face, but the anger and hatred in his voice shook Memphis to her core. "And I'll kill one of you with this bow and arrow before you take another step. Now which one of you wants to sacrifice himself? Go on, Hagar, try me."

Incredibly, Memphis knew he meant what he said, and she knew from the expressions on the faces of the men that they knew it, too.

She tried to take a breath, but found she couldn't breathe normally. Shallow, panting puffs, which sounded like bursts of thunder to her, came from her laboring lungs. *Don't be silly, Memphis. No one knows you're here. Calm yourself.* No one had seen her or heard her. She could quietly back away and find her way back down the mountain. But fear, curiosity, and a photojournalist's instinctive nose for news kept her frozen in place. She hadn't found any graves, but after all, hadn't she come here to discover *any* secrets Macauley's Mountain might hold, and hadn't she come as quickly as possible, hoping to beat Jake's planned trip?

She wasn't going to leave now.

Her head ached, and the stitches in her forehead itched like crazy. The bandage felt damp and loose. It had been a week since the mysterious trick-or-treater had attacked her, and she was no closer to determining who the black-costumed person was than she had been then. Fortunately, the cut had required only three stitches, which were to be removed next week. She still shook with fear everytime she opened her front door. Common sense told her she should leave, and she'd been tempted to, but stubbornness, and a deep desire to finish her mission here, had kept her in Yancey.

An early November rain, which had been a gentle drizzle an hour ago, had become a steady downpour. Though the down parka she wore kept the top half of her dry, her boots and jeans were soaking wet.

"Don't know why you're so hot over it all, anyway," said Hagar. "You're rich enough, and we're not ruining the surface of the land."

"You're violating what's mine."

Hagar stepped forward. Cutter's arrow zapped through his jacket sleeve, knocked him backwards, and nailed him to the tree. As Hagar struggled to free himself, the bigger man lunged at Cutter, and Cutter threw himself across the clearing to meet him full force. He pinned him to the ground, but the man caught him in a bear hug, and they rolled over and over on the rain-soaked grass toward Memphis. The man gouged Cutter in the eye with his thumb, and Memphis heard Cutter grunt with pain. In a rage now, Cutter shook him loose, threw him aside like culled crayfish, and stood up. The man rose up, his fist aimed at Cutter's chin, but Cutter kicked him in the groin, and chopped him on the back of the neck. The man fell limp at his feet.

Memphis shuddered. She had witnessed hideous violence in Bosnia, atrocities that still woke her up with nightmares. But this seemed different. A painful exposure of a private man's personal nightmare.

Hagar, still trying to free himself from the tree, shouted to Cutter. "You don't fight fair, Tate."

"Damn right, I don't."

"That how you killed that man at Ruby's?" he taunted.

"I learned how to survive at Ruby's," said Cutter, his voice chill and bitter, as he walked toward the man pinned to the tree.

Memphis, cold and shivering, wiped rain from her face, and strained to hear more of this interesting information. Jake had told her about Cutter's scrapes with the law when he was young, and she had found old newspaper accounts of the killing at Ruby's when Cutter was eighteen.

"Sure," sneered Hagar. "Had nothing to do with learning how to survive. Your old man's money got you out of trouble, Tate. You were nothing but an embarrassment for your father. Too bad old Sheriff Maynard isn't still alive. He'd make sure you gave us no more problems."

Again, the referral to her grandfather's strong feelings toward Cutter Tate. Birdy had mentioned it, too. Was it true? Why would her grandfather have a vendetta against Cutter? The questions mounting in her mind begged to be answered. Maybe Nelsey could answer some of them. But even Nelsey was closemouthed about some of the things Memphis asked her.

Cutter held Hagar's jacket collar in his fist, and jerked him up at the neck so that his toes dangled, barely brushing the ground, like a hanged man dancing futilely on the gallows. He pulled the arrow from the trunk of the tree, freeing him, and then shoved him back against the tree so hard that his head made a thudding sound when it hit the trunk. Hagar kicked at him and tried to sock him on the chin again, but Cutter laughed and shook him so hard that Hagar bit his tongue. Blood gushed out of his mouth, down his chin, and onto his glossy gray parka, leaving dark purple splotches.

He held his hands up in a gesture of surrender. "Okay, okay. We'll leave. But we'll be back. There's no way you're going to win this battle, Tate."

"I wouldn't bet on that, Hagar." He threw the man on the ground and said, "Now take your buddy and get out of here."

Memphis watched as Hagar, bloody and vanquished for the moment, crawled cautiously over to his friend and tried to revive him. "He's out for a while. You'll have to help me carry him to the truck."

"Sorry. You got yourself in here. You get yourself out. Drag him. It's only two miles to the dirt road you trespassed on. Oh, by the way, you'll need these." He tossed a bunch of keys onto the ground.

Hagar grabbed them, and stood up. Holding his partner's jacket collar, he began to pull him across the wet meadow toward the woods. His progress was slow, and Cutter stood with his arms across his chest, watching until the two men met the treeline. Hagar stopped and looked back.

"We'll be back, Tate. You know we will."

"Best if you didn't, Hagar, but if you do, I'll be waiting and I'll kill you."

The two men disappeared in the dense forest.

Memphis knew it was time for her to leave. She stepped backwards, and her weak knee gave way.

Dammit. Now was not the time to lose her mobility.

In her determination to climb and explore this mountain before Jake did, and in her hunger for fresh clues into Sadie's death, she'd ignored the insidious hints of discomfort in her knee. The climb had been steep, a challenge to her newfound mountain-climbing abilities, but she'd pushed on, disregarding the twinges of pain that came now and again from her bad knee. As she knelt now in the dripping brambles of the dark green thicket, she chastised herself for her stupidity. As determined as she was to get to the bottom of Sadie's story by herself, perhaps she'd pushed too hard.

Maybe she should have invited Jake to come with her. No, something within her insisted that this was her story, her personal search, and hers alone. Cutter Tate had his painful motivations, and for reasons she didn't quite understand, so did she.

She struggled to get to her feet, but the damned knee wouldn't cooperate. She looked around for a stout branch that she could hang onto while she pulled herself up. Once she could stand again, she was sure she could limp back the way she came. It might take her awhile, but she would make it. Thank God, Nelsey had said she would spend the night if Memphis was late in returning. It was going to be later than she'd planned.

There was no supportable branch in reachable distance. This was a gnarled, aged rhododendron thicket, and the strongest of its glistening moss green limbs were high above her head. She would wait until Cutter left the clearing, and then she would crawl out backwards.

"You can come out now, Memphis."

Her stomach rose to meet her banging heart. Cutter

stood in the center of the clearing, facing the thicket, his rugged face a study in grimness. His bow and quiver were slung across his shoulder, his thumbs shoved between his belt and his waist, and he stared in her direction.

Giving a mighty push of her thighs, she managed to half stand, half squat among the wet greenness, then fell backwards on her bottom, scraping her forehead as she went. A wrenching ripping in her knee told her she was in serious trouble.

"I would if I could," she yelled. "Unfortunately, I seem to be caught in the brambles."

She watched as he strode angrily toward the thicket. He parted the branches. They stared at one another, and her heart rose up and down like a roller coaster. What would he do? His dark hair lay plastered against his forehead, and his silver eyes blazed with violence and anger from his encounter with the two men. The anger she could handle, but the violence frightened her.

"I'm sorry," she said defiantly. "I came upon you accidentally, and when I realized what was happening, I thought it best to stay hidden. How did you know I was here?"

He relaxed a little. The violence began to fade from his eyes, but the anger was still there. "Your Joy, Memphis. Never wear perfume into the woods. A woodsman's, or an animal's, most sensitive organ is his nose."

"Something you learned from Black Brady, I suppose, and the bow and arrow, too."

"Yes."

"But you said nothing, gave no indication that you knew I was here."

"Frankly, once the situation heated up, I forgot you were here."

"I see," she said. Trying to buy herself some time to decide how to get out of the brush without asking for his help, she commented, "You've had some disparate teachers in your life, Ruby Barnes and Black Brady among them."

The breeze had turned into a brisk wind and the late afternoon grew colder. He zipped up his jacket and stuck a hand in the back pocket of his tans. Framed against the wet wind-tossed trees, and a grim gunmetal sky, he looked like a dark avenger come to take on the world and all of its sins—angry, defiant, just, and all-powerful.

"I had a disparate childhood." His jaw tightened as he continued to stare at her. "Get up. I'll show you the way out of here, and you can be on your way home."

Though she hated it, she knew that she would have to ask for his help. She closed her eyes, swallowed hard, then opened them.

"I swore I'd never ask anyone for help again, but it seems my knee won't cooperate. Sorry, but could you give me a hand?"

His hard, angry stare altered not a bit. He reached in, took hold of her extended hand, and yanked her upwards. Relieved to be on two feet again, she took two steps and stumbled out of the thicket.

"United Mining disarmed my guard and broke through the gates. You must have followed them in."

"I did no such thing."

"There's only one road to this point. Where did you leave your Jeep?"

"At the bottom of Aracoma."

"You took the transverse path from Aracoma to Macauley's? You hiked up here?" he asked in disbelief.

"Of course."

"Great. I wasn't planning on leaving yet, but I'll have to take you to the road. It's the easiest way down."

"Fine," she said shortly.

"Follow me."

He swung on his heel and headed to the treeline.

Memphis took one step and her knee collapsed beneath her. Panic set in as she knew beyond a doubt that she was helpless. She detested helplessness in anyone, but particularly in herself.

Shit, dammit, and every other dirty word I can think of. I'm not going to get home tonight without some help from the avenging angel.

The rain came in silver sheets now, and she could barely see his disappearing form.

"Cutter?"

He turned back and came toward her. When he reached her, he stared down at her as if she was an unwelcome rodent in his garden, an annoyance he didn't want to have to deal with.

"Just what I figured. You can't walk, can you?"

"No. Not at the moment, at least. I'm sorry if I'm an inconvenience, but I have to appeal to your better nature, if you have one, and ask you to take me down to my Jeep."

He scooped her up in his arms as if she was a child, and said, "Frankly, Madam, to paraphrase Rhett Butler, it wouldn't have made a damn bit of difference if you could walk or not. No one's getting off this mountain tonight, not even the two sleazebags who just left here. I knew that thirty minutes ago."

"Why not?" she asked. Her heart beat triple time now, and she tried to ignore the hard bulky mass of his arms as he held her against his body.

"Two reasons," he answered, and entered the thick forest. "The road is slippery with deep mud, treacherous by now. Hagar and his buddy are probably in a ditch somewhere. And secondly, this rain is only the prelude to a hell of a storm."

"But I have to get home. I've never spent the night away from Katie."

"There's a first time for everything." She felt his gaze center on her. She looked up to find his silver eyes gleaming at her like a cat's eyes caught peering through a window on a rainy evening, then dissolving into the darkening night. "Nelsey's there, isn't she?"

"Yes." She thought she saw relief fill his eyes, but the darkness closed in on them again.

"Then she'll be fine." He squeezed her good knee, then released it.

"Ouch. Stop that."

"Skinny."

"What?"

"Anyone ever tell you you're skinny? I'd have thought Nelsey's cooking would have put some meat on these bones by now."

"I do most of my own cooking."

"Oh, well, that explains it."

"My, my, quite the gentleman in town, but up here on the mountain you're an insulting boor." She thought she felt his chest heave with a chuckle. "Nelsey will worry if I don't get home tonight."

"Yes, she will. But Nelsey's a tough old bird. If she knows where you were headed, then she knows I'll watch out for you. *Does* she know where you were headed?"

"No."

"Did anyone? I'm surprised Jake Bishop isn't with you."

"Jake's out of town for the weekend."

The anger in his voice had been fading, had been turning to one of amusement, but she felt his body grow taut again, and heard the anger as he said, "So, you hightailed it up here without telling anyone, even your partner in spying, Jake Bishop. Didn't even stop to ask me if I minded. Sadie's grave must be mighty important to you, something you figure is worth sneaking out of town for, worth trespassing for."

"Jake is not my partner," she tried to say, but the wind took her words and flung them away.

Overhead, the branches of the bare November trees whipped around in gales of gathering wind and water. They were out of the woods now, and Cutter's stride lengthened as he walked faster.

"Where are we going?" she yelled, jouncing against him as he began to jog.

Either he ignored her, or he couldn't hear her, for there was no answer.

Lightning flashed, scissoring the blackness with brilliant light. The driving rain had soaked through her jacket, and felt like thousands of tiny needles hitting her face. She wanted to hide her face in his solid chest, but resisted the urge. *Remember who's carrying you, Memphis.* Small objects pelted her jacket, then more of them on her face and legs, as if the storm gods threw sharp gravel at them.

Hailstones.

Cutter clutched her closer, bringing her head into his shoulder, and she burrowed into his soaked jacket searching for warmth and shelter. She secured her hold around his neck, and he held her even closer, until her nose found the warm pulse in the hollow of his neck. Not caring now who carried her, she was grateful for the strong arms that held her, and the broad chest that shielded her from the rain.

As the tumult beat at them, deafening them, slashing, drowning them with its force, Memphis felt as if an omnipotent protector carried her through the maelstrom. He couldn't subdue the storm, but it would never vanquish him. Cutter existed within the fury as if he were a part of it, as if the storm had created him, a sovereign in his element. He seemed a willing participant in the battle, equal to the challenge and certain of victory.

Was he even aware that he carried cargo? Thunder bellowed and lightning sliced the sky, and as if in answer to her silent question, he crushed her tighter, protectively against him.

Her nose snug now in the hollow of his neck, her anxious heartbeat met his and slowed to match its strong, steady rhythm. Something loosened inside of her. The anesthesia she'd numbed herself with to endure the atrocities in Bosnia, and to survive Jake's desertion, loosened a bit around the edges. Never carried in the arms of a loving father, or a passionate lover, the feeling of being protected and cared for undid her. A poignant ache rocked her from her toes to the crown of her head, then faded away and left a spreading warmth in her chest.

Inexplicably, she felt tears form beneath her tightly shut eyelids. *God, Memphis, nothing to cry about.*

As she was about to examine this strange phenomenon, Cutter slowed and stopped in front of a shed of some sort, a large triangular shiny black shape in the furious night. He kicked the door open and carried her inside. He closed the door with his shoulder, shutting out the slashing storm, and most of the noise, and carried her swiftly through aisles and down pathways. Limbs and leaves brushed against her arms. Were they in a cave of some sort? Cutter would know every inch of his own mountain. The smell of healthy soil, pungent and earthy, and a floral scent, permeated the place. Obviously they were sheltered because the noise of the storm had abated and the howling wetness berated them no longer. But over his shoulder and overhead, she could still see lightning splitting the tumultuous night, and could hear the sound of hailstones against . . . glass.

Yes, glass.

He kicked open another door into a room that seemed much smaller, and placed her on a rough wood floor.

"Where, in God's name, are we?"

"A greenhouse," he said.

Through the dimness, she watched him walk away from her and rummage in a large wooden box. He tossed articles through the air and they landed softly on her. "At the risk of sounding like an oily, mustache-twirling roué, you'll have to get out of those wet clothes. Put on that flannel shirt and those old work pants of mine. Will you need help?"

"No. I may not be able to walk, but I can certainly dress myself," she said indignantly, trying to hide her embarrassment at being in this situation in the first place.

"Good. Would you prefer that I build a small fire before I excuse myself, or would you rather I leave now so you can change immediately?"

His mocking tone of formality irritated her.

"Build the fire." The driving rain had soaked through her jacket, and she was chilled to the bone. Quaking with cold, she yearned for heat and admittted she missed the warmth of his body shielding her.

In the dimness of the small room, she saw him bow from the waist as he said, "At your service, ma'am."

Why was he being so unpleasant? Maybe he was as embarrassed as she was. Cutter Tate? Never. She had a feeling that perhaps she'd invaded a sanctuary, a part of his life that he preferred to keep private. But it was more than that. There was a touch of nervousness in him, and a defensive anger.

She watched as he knelt and, with deft efficiency, built a fire in the small fireplace in front of her. It ignited quickly at the touch of a match. He extracted clothes for himself from the chest.

"I'll leave now so you can change."

With trembling fingers and chattering teeth, Memphis shed all of her soaked clothing and donned the dry shirt and pants he'd left for her. The soft flannel shirt felt like heaven against her skin. She rolled the long trousers up until they met her ankles, but she could have fit two more people inside the waist with her. She needed to find a piece of string, or rope, or a large safety pin, but the damned knee had immobilized her.

She eyed the big chest where he'd gotten the clothes, appraising the distance and the effort it would take to reach it.

Piece of cake.

She shucked the entangling pants and crawled across the floor, catching a few splinters as she went. At the box, she struggled to her knees, but was knocked back on her bottom at the excruciating pressure on her bad knee. She tried again, and this time pulled herself to her feet and leaned against the box so her knees wouldn't have to take her weight. She noticed an elaborate lock lying on the lid and knocked it onto the floor, then struggled to lift the heavy top. It gave and fell back against the wall with a small thump.

The light from the fire didn't reach this corner of the room, so she rummaged through the box in darkness, fingering articles questioningly—a shirt, pair of boots, cans of food probably—nothing to fasten trousers with. There were candles, a can opener, more clothes, a tool of some sort. Deep in a corner were some tied papers, letters maybe, a blanket. Nothing there. She tried the other side and found a bottle of pills, matches, more clothes, another blanket.

Dammit.

Leaning precariously, all her weight on one leg, she lost her balance and hit the floor again, cracking her head on the corner of the chest as she went down.

Cutter knocked on the door and then opened it as she tried to get to her feet again.

"I heard sounds, thought . . . what the hell are you doing in my chest?" he yelled. He was furious.

"I'm sorry," she said. "I was looking for something to tie around my waist."

"You were snooping. You can't resist investigating every nook and cranny, can you? Well, there's nothing here you would be interested in, so leave things alone."

He picked her up, carried her across the room, and deposited her rudely on a cot that sat next to the wall. She watched in amazement as he returned to the chest in two huge strides, slammed the top shut, then picked up the lock from the floor and fastened it shut. He retrieved the pants she'd left in front of the fire and threw them at her. She caught them in midair before they hit her in the face. Why was he so angry?

"Put them on and stay where you are! I'll be right back."

He left, leaving the door into the greenhouse open, and came back in seconds with a long piece of twine. He handed it to her.

"Now, put them on, and I'm not leaving this time."

She struggled to pull on the huge pants without exposing herself, while he stood in front of her, his arms folded stiffly across his chest, watching her every move. Finally, she slipped the twine through the loops and tied the waist about her. She glanced up at him, not sure what to say.

"I wasn't snooping, as you so rudely put it. I needed a belt."

Her voice shook with indignation and from the cold. Her head hurt and she was freezing. The warmth of the fire didn't reach the cot.

"Never mind. Are you cold?"

"Yes."

"Lie down. I'll pull the cot over to the fire and get blankets and brandy."

He left to rummage in the chest.

Remembering the bottle in the chest, she asked, "Do you have any aspirin, and a Band-Aid maybe?"

"Yes. Is your forehead hurting? Nelsey told me about the attack on Halloween. Didn't know we had such mean bastards in Yancey."

"Yes, well, if they think I'm going to be frightened away, they're wrong."

The past week she'd developed various theories as to who'd been behind the Halloween terrorist attack, and Cutter's name had surfaced more than once. But even with all the history and suspicion between them, she didn't think he would stoop to such tactics. If Cutter wanted to get rid of someone, he'd come right out and tell them, or pick them up by the shirt collar, as he had Hagar and his cohort, and throw them out.

He came back, handed her a tumbler of brandy, and watched as she sipped its honeyed warmth.

"Ummm. Burns all the way down and feels wonderful. As they say, nectar of the gods. Thank you."

He spread a blanket over her, then pulled the cot close to the fire.

In the flickering light from the fireplace, he knelt by her side to inspect her forehead, and his face creased with concern.

"Damn. You're bleeding."

"I knocked it on the edge of the chest just now."

He felt her bandage. "I should have checked this right away. It's wet from the rain, of course, and about to fall off. I was so angry. . . ."

He shut up, set his mouth firmly, and carefully peeled the wet dressing away from her tender skin. He dabbed at the trickle of blood that ran down her temple and leaned closer to see better, his face inches from hers. He smelled of woodsmoke, good, rich earth, and rain. The knot that formed in her belly whenever Cutter was around grew bigger and tighter. The beat of the rain swelled, but the silence around them drew taut, as if the small room waited for something.

With gentle fingers he lifted damp strands of hair that clung to her temples and combed them away from her face. His fingers fumbled briefly as he cleaned the wound with Mercurochrome, but he set his mouth harder and continued.

"Your stitches held, but barely." His voice was strained. "You should see the doctor tomorrow."

As he fastened clean white gauze and tape over the stitches, his gaze dropped to hers. The angry silver eyes had turned smoky with rich desire.

Memphis drew rigid trying to control her treacherous, trembling body. It shook not from cold, or anger, or indignation. It shook with a primeval craving for him to touch her in other places, for him to lower his mouth and kiss her, for him to caress her breasts and suck the nipples until they were hot and tender with love. He hovered over her for an infinite time. His heat radiated and warmed her in breathless waves, spreading deep within her until it settled in her groin. Her inner thighs quivered for his touch.

She ached with longing.

His fingers trailed down her cheek, and for a timeless moment traced her mouth. She reminded herself that these same hands had killed a man, but she didn't care. He lingered, and she knew he was fighting the moment as hard as she was, that portentous, wanting, decisive moment that hangs between a woman and a man from which there is no turning back.

No, she couldn't, she wasn't ready for this. This was the wrong man. He saw the decision in her eyes, and withdrew, his face suddenly a mask.

"There, that bandage will hold until you get to the

doctor," he said roughly. "Go to sleep. The storm should be moving out soon."

God, how she would love for him to massage her hurting knee, but she couldn't let him touch her again. The consequences would be more than she could resist.

Exhausted physically and emotionally, she found his suggestion that she sleep easier than she thought. Warmed by the brandy, and wrapped from head to toe in the soft blanket, she drifted in and out of slumber, dozing lazily while the storm raged about them. Cutter had rolled up in a blanket on the floor next to the cot.

A seismic clap of thunder woke her up, and she sat up in bed with a small cry as the ground quaked beneath them, and wind clattered the windows.

Cutter said, "It's okay. We're safe here."

He patted her back. She lay down again, but extracted a hand from the blanket and reached over the cot for his, a motion that seemed so natural that she didn't give it a thought. He held her hand loosely at first, as surprised as she was at her gesture, then his fingers closed firmly over hers. His hand was square, warm, the palm hard.

"Everything is shaking so, it feels like the mountain is as alarmed as we are."

"Yes, but he isn't," Cutter said quietly. "Old Man Mountain has endured, survived, created and re-created himself through thousands of centuries. I always try to remember that when things get rough."

She thought about that.

"You're not really alarmed, are you?" he asked.

"No, but it's awfully nice to be inside and safe here with you."

The last part of it slipped out easy, like treacherous silk. Safe? Safe with Cutter Tate? She'd better finish it and thank him.

"Thank you for taking such good care of me. I'm

accustomed to taking care of myself. Accepting help from others is always hard for me."

"You're welcome."

She watched in fascination as lightning flashed through the glass above them, and rain rolled in sheets down the slanted roof of the greenhouse. She loved the sensation of being in the midst of the maelstrom, yet not being touched by it. Mother Nature was putting on a dramatic performance for them.

Warm and lazy again, she talked on, as if the blanket and the brandy, and her hand in his, had loosened her tongue and her reserve.

"I'm not crazy about storms, though. Never have been. When we were children living in Memphis, Margo and I were by ourselves a lot because my mother worked two jobs. The worst storms always seemed to come when she was away and we were alone."

"Your mom worked two jobs?" Cutter chuckled. "I had the impression you were born with a silver spoon in your mouth."

"No, that came later. My father deserted us when I was a baby. When I was thirteen, my mother married our stepfather, Abe Lewis, who we adored. He whisked us out of Tennessee, off to Manhattan and a life of privileges that we enjoyed immensely and were grateful for, except then Margo and I were hardly ever alone. We found that we missed it."

"So storms never bothered you again, huh?"

She got the impression that he was encouraging her to talk, and she didn't mind. They were marooned here together. She could compare it to getting to know a fellow seatmate on a transatlantic flight, but it was more than that. It felt right. She glanced over the edge of the cot, and saw that he lay on his back with his arm behind his head watching the storm above them as she did.

"Not until I got to Bosnia."

"What happened there?"

As he waited for her answer, Cutter found it hard to believe that he'd brought Memphis here, and that she lay next to him sharing the excitement and the glory of the storm that raged around them. When she'd reached for his hand, he'd wondered if it was just for the comfort of another human's touch during the storm. He wondered what she would think if he revealed that storm-watching in his greenhouse was one of his favorite things to do, or that sometimes he was even idiot enough to lie out in the middle of his meadow and let all the furies beat down on him.

After his initial worry about getting her to safety, and then his anger at her intrusion into his trunk, he found the present time with her deeply peaceful. He loved hearing her voice, and marveled that her comfort level with him was such that she could tell him about her childhood.

He'd asked her about Bosnia, and he held his breath, waiting to see if she would continue their easy sharing.

She was quiet for a long time, and he knew she was thinking about what to tell him.

"I thought I could handle the horrors of war," she finally said. "Thought I was tough. I'd been through skirmishes in South Africa, and in Israel, and spent months in the desert during the Gulf War." She paused. "But I'd never seen children involved in war."

"Must have been bad."

"It almost destroyed me," she whispered.

He squeezed her hand.

"Sometimes they fought alongside the grown men, but most of the time they were trying to escape. They lay in the streets, bloody and blown apart like discarded remnant scraps from a butcher shop. Innocents. Initiated without their permission into the worst of man's inhumanity to man. I stopped to comfort a little girl once. Her leg was broken, her jaw was broken. Her mother and brother lay dead next to her. Land mines. I can't even imagine the pain she was in. I tried to find help for her, but no one was interested. They all hid behind walls sniping at each other. I carried her to a field hospital." She stopped, and he could tell she was finding it difficult to continue. "It wasn't unusual to stumble across a severed limb, a leg, or even a head, and realize it was part of a child. It all seemed so . . . so futile."

"It's okay. You don't have to say anymore. Psychiatrists tell us we should tell all, scrape our souls clean. I say, bullshit. Remembering is sometimes more painful than being there again."

"No, these are things that I want to write about, have made notes to do an article, or write a book." Her voice faded then returned stronger. "Maybe this night of nature's power has loosened my tongue for a reason."

He held her hand tighter, listening to her as thunder rumbled. The hailstones had stopped, and rain drummed steadily on the glass overhead.

"One day, I got caught in a storm, not as bad as this one, but similar, and I was alone. Jake had gone on ahead of me. I took cover in the empty shell of an apartment building. The rain came down in sheets. I heard someone whimpering, and noticed coppery water running into a puddle around the corner from where I sat. I found a little boy about five years old lying in a stream of dirty water, bleeding from the mouth. I took him into my shelter with me and held him in my arms. When it thundered or lightning flashed, he shuddered and clung to me. He was delirious, called me 'Maman,' over and over again. Died in my arms, and I didn't even know his name. I think of him now, every time it storms, the two of us alone together in the rain."

"Christ."

"Problem was, that to survive I had to numb myself, dry up. I developed a no-response mechanism that got me through the rest of my time there." In a small voice she said, "I found out I was pregnant with Katie while I was in the hospital with the knee. It was the beginning of a renewal, a promise that life does go on."

She stopped then, as if she'd come up against something she couldn't reveal, something that was even more painful than the rest.

"The best of times and the worst of times, eh?"

"Yes."

He probably shouldn't say it, but he said it anyway. "Evidently Jake felt differently."

"Yes," she replied, but she casually disengaged her hand from his, and changed the subject. "Cutter, is this your greenhouse?"

"Yes."

"Kind of strange, isn't it, building a greenhouse on a mountain in the middle of nowhere?"

"A bit." He cleared his throat, biding for time, then went forward hesitantly. "I . . . I use it to start new plantings. . . . United Mining has already destroyed some of my land. They dug so much coal from beneath part of the mountain that the surface began to sink. Sinkholes. Plants and trees were dying. So, I built this ten years ago. It's become a refuge of sorts."

"You've been fighting them that long?"

"Longer. Since I was twenty-one, read my grandfather's will, found out the mountain belonged to me, and then discovered that my father had illegally sold the mineral rights to United Mining. The will stated in clear terms that Macauley's Mountain was to remain untouched until I came of age and decided what I wanted to do with it. My father had had his stroke by then, and couldn't undo what he had done, even had he been willing to do so."

"Surely, he was tricked, or maybe thought he was doing what was best for you."

Suddenly, he questioned himself. Was he doing the right thing, telling Memphis of private emotions he'd shared with no one before? Something within him trusted her, and he went on, revealing parts of himself as easily as she had exposed some of herself to him.

"No. My father knew what he was doing. Not only is he greedy, but he hates me," he said, trying to keep the bitterness out of his voice.

"Why do you think he hates you?"

"I don't think it, I know it. He blames me for her desertion. My father has always been an intense but cold man, and very possessive. The only person he ever loved was my mother, if you can call it love. Unfortunately, she didn't love him. He met her when he was in Scotland one year."

He could still recall the delicate floral scent of his mother's expensive French perfume. He used to search for recent chairs she had sat in, and hide there quietly to inhale the fragrance of this beautiful creature who went in and out of his life so blithely. Her crystal laughter was heard only when she spoke over the phone to someone far distant over the sea.

"She was the daughter of a minor English nobleman, and much sought after . . . all the things my father thought were important in a woman. She married him for his money. He tried to control her, possess her completely, but my mother had other ideas. She spent most of her time in Europe spending his money."

The rain was lessening. Thunder rumbled in the distance. He paused for a moment, and stared into the black wetness, watching the rain roll silently down the slant of glass high above them.

"My mother should never have had children. When I was seven," he continued, "she told me I was conceived on one of her rare trips back to Yancey and that my father had raped her. She left soon after that. We never saw her again. My father tried everything to bring her back, short of kidnapping, but she lived with a powerful man who had more money than he, and as long as she stayed out of the United States he couldn't touch her. He blamed me. Said I should never have been born. Said she left because I was too much trouble."

"Oh, no, Cutter. It's hard to believe a father would be so cruel."

She turned on her side to look down at him. He chanced a glance at her, and regretted that last revelation. The pain he had opened up was reflected in the expression on her face. But he wanted her to know about his grandfather so he continued.

"It was my grandfather who took care of me, loved me, sheltered me, made me feel worthwhile and wanted. He died when I was ten."

He stopped again, and cleared his throat.

"I didn't exist for my father after that," he finally continued, soft and sad. "I ran wild and he didn't care. Ruby found me going through the garbage behind her bar one day. Took me in and fed me. My father began staying away for longer periods. He dismissed the cook, and the maid, and I was left in the house alone, so I went to Ruby's for food. She told Nelsey, and Nelsey would pull me off the street, or out of the woods, make me take a bath while she washed the clothes I had on."

He laughed bitterly. "By the time I was twelve, I'd become the town project. Birdy's mother helped me with my homework, her father taught me to drive. When Sheriff Maynard beat the shit out of me for something I'd done, Billy Gus and Elva found me in the woods and cleaned me up."

"My grandfather beat you?"

"More than once. He hated me as much as my father did."

"But why?"

"I don't know." But he did know. "And I think I've said too much. Let's forget it, okay?"

"Okay."

The rain had stopped while he talked, and slowly, slowly, the sky cleared, a bright star popping out here, and over there, and there. The storm had cleaned the night until it sparkled with glitter and grandeur. They watched in reverent silence as the firmament spread out before them in a frosty, glimmering, shimmering show of stardust and moonglow, as if they were being rewarded for fighting the storm so courageously and coming through untouched.

But had they come through untouched? Cutter knew they hadn't.

"By the way," she said sleepily, as she tugged the blanket up close around her chin and closed her eyes, "just for your information. I didn't put perfume on this morning. Ever seen pictures of me on the battlefield, Tate? I don't get all dolled up to go hiking."

He chuckled.

"Yeah, well, perfume lingers, Maynard," he said softly. "It's on your jacket."

His great desire to kiss her overwhelmed him.

And damn the consequences, he thought.

He sat up and leaned over her. She opened her eyes and looked into his. Slowly, he lowered his head and kissed her softly on the lips. The pink vulnerable softness trembled against his mouth, and the tremble transferred to him and ran down his spine to circle his hips and light his loins.

Yes, yes, God yes, how I want you, he thought. *But not now.* She was learning to trust him, and this time together has been too precious, too important, to push any further.

Almost groaning in frustration, he tucked the blanket closer around her chin, and gave her a chaste kiss on the cheek. She smiled sleepily at him, and he thought he saw relief in her eyes.

He resumed his monklike position on the floor in agony.

"Yeah, perfume lingers, Maynard," he whispered to himself.

§ 9 §

The attic, though dusty and dim, seemed a cozy place on a rainy day. The rain had continued through the week, washing away the last of fallen leaves, and bringing the chill edge of winter. This wasn't a storm. This was one of those humdrum, all-day, late-fall rains. Like obedient troops, the drops rolled steadily down the outside of the dusty dormer window.

Memphis returned a moldy book to a flimsy cardboard box, and stopped for a moment to watch the rain.

She looked back on her stormy night on the mountain with Cutter with mixed emotions. The next morning had brought a touch of embarrassment at the previous night's revelations, but they had parted with more tolerance for one another, and a mutual respect for what each had survived. The treacherous ride down the steep, slippery road at dawn in Cutter's Range Rover had been made in silence, a silence that acknowledged they each still held radically opposing goals, and a silence that recognized a growing intenseness in their physical and emotional attraction for each other.

Memphis ran a finger across her lips, remembering the difficulty she'd had in going to sleep after his soft, sensual kiss.

She forced herself to return to her work, and as she

shook out the folds of a dusty quilt, she thought of all the questions she'd wanted to ask him, but would probably never know the answers to. Was his mother still living? Did he always hunt with bow and arrows, and why? Where had he gone to school, and had he ever been in love? And why had her grandfather hated him? Cutter said he didn't know, but she was sure that he did.

Katie played on the floor next to the diamond-shaped window, a discarded purple-feathered hat teetering precariously on her head. She plunked the remaining strings of a battered banjo. At her side, Miss Priss rolled around in a crush of torn chiffon skirt the color of cherries. Occasionally, the fast-growing kitten batted at the loose strings that sprang from the banjo, and Katie giggled.

Memphis wished for her camera. The fair child with the purple hat, and the black kitten tumbling in the bright cherry skirt, were an enchanting affirmation of life amidst the ghostly memories the attic held. Downstairs, Nelsey, who'd become a welcome daily fixture, was making vegetable soup for dinner. The succulent aroma of tomatoes, onions, and beef broth drifted throughout the house. Through the open trapdoor, Memphis could hear her singing her favorite hymn, "There's room at the cross for me, there's room at the cross for you."

Yes. A good day for doing the job she'd been putting off since she arrived here. Repositories of the past, attics could be bad or good. So far, this one had been neutral, tending toward bad.

She sighed, fitted the top back on the box she'd been digging in, and sat back on her heels. Her knee gave a quick twinge to remind her to treat it with more respect. It hadn't fully recovered from the night on the mountain. Carefully, she lowered herself onto a small footstool, and surveyed the miscellany on the floor

around her. Most of it had belonged to her grandfather:
leather belts, white shirts yellowing with age, an old
holster sans gun, several framed community awards,
an empty piggy bank.

The belts brought a particularly fearful memory: her
grandfather threatening to whip her with a belt because she'd broken some glass canning jars on the
basement floor. Her mother had intervened, yanking
the belt out of his hands, telling him that he was never
to touch one of her children. And he never did after
that. From then on, if she or Margo were naughty, her
grandfather would stomp out of the house, slam the
door, and not come back for hours.

She lifted the lid of another box and found pictures,
and photograph albums. She pulled out a heavy
framed picture of her grandfather. He'd been a handsome man, in a frontier sort of way. He had a long jaw
and hawklike nose. A silvery blond mustache covered a
short upper lip. He'd tried to make up for a receding
hairline with long sideburns.

There were times when he made attempts to be a
good grandfather. After all, they were the only grand-
children he would ever have. She recalled his reading
books to them, and teaching them to swim in the lake.
She remembered his instructions to Faith to "dress up
the children because I'm taking them to town to show
them off."

Grandfather would take them into Yancey, all
cleaned up in cool, starchy sundresses and "mary-
janes," and walk them through town several times,
displaying them like trophies. He seldom introduced
them to anyone, and if he did, they never chatted for
long. Soon, they would be parading along again, Margo holding his hand on one side, she on the other. They
were never allowed to play with other children, so had
learned to amuse themselves in the numerous nooks
and crannies of this old house. Favorite times had been

when Faith took them out into the mountains to hike and explore.

Faith had told her that Grandfather had been a rigid man—arrogant, proud, and dedicated to maintaining his righteous reputation and stature in the community. When she was ten years old Memphis wouldn't have known how to describe his behavior, but she recognized now that her mother had been correct in her assessment.

She shoved the picture back into the box, and quickly sifted through the rest of them. Were there none of Sadie?

In the bottom, as if they'd been placed as far from discovery as possible, as if someone never wanted to see them again, were faded snapshots of Sadie and James Maynard when they were very young, probably first married. They stood on the running board of a long, open Ford Roadster. Sadie faced James and leaned into him, her chest against his arm, knee bent, toe pointing in the air behind her. She laughed. Her profile seemed teasing, wanting to pull something from him, daring. He faced the camera with a small smile and a stiff wave.

The sense of disquiet she'd had since first arriving in Yancey grew stronger. Disgusted with herself and the uncomfortable range of feelings she'd experienced the last two and a half months, she flung the pictures back into the box.

Katie giggled.

Memphis turned to see that Miss Priss had dragged the chiffon into Katie's lap. Katie had placed the purple hat on the kitten. The two of them were in a pull-and-tug game with the shoestring of a lady's boot, circa 1930.

Returning to her task, Memphis pried open the top of a rusty trunk. A faint lilac fragrance drifted into the musty attic air. Her heart skipped a beat. Sadie's things? Must be. Alma had always smelled of apples and furniture polish. She couldn't imagine Alma *ever* using a lilac cologne. She lifted a neatly folded pleated white shirtwaist and brought it to her nose. Oh, God, it smelled good. It was a fragrance Memphis would have worn, but they didn't make perfumes with romantic nuances like this anymore. Her Joy was the closest she could find.

"Perfume lingers." Cutter's voice echoed softly in her ear. She bit her lip to distract the flutter that played in her tummy.

A long brown wool skirt lay beneath, and beneath that more skirts and blouses, a blue gingham house-dress, an apron. In the middle were clothes from the twenties, short flapper shifts, and shoes with bows. Near the bottom, particular attention had been paid to wrapping tissue paper around a sequined sheath of ankle length, 1930s style. Memphis carefully undid the paper, and caught her breath in pure pleasure at the sight of the silvery shimmering ivory sequins. A dress to dance in, a dress to flirt in and laugh in and have a good time in. It looked brand new, as if it hadn't been worn much.

The pile next to her grew as she dug greedily, elated with her find. Close to the bottom she found another slim sheath, this one black, with beaded top, loose off-the-shoulder straps, and floating chiffon skirt. A sophisticate's dress, sexy and seductive, meant for se-cretive nights, and memories.

My, my Sadie. You must have been an interesting lady.

The bottom layer held books, trinkets, jewelry. She lifted a book of poetry from the dark depths of the trunk. Several pages were marked, corners pinched down. She opened it to one of the marked pages, and found a dried lily of the valley nestled in the crease.

Lest it should turn to dust at her touch, she was careful not to disturb the delicate flower. Reverently, barely breathing, she read the poem marked lovingly with the lily.

". . . I miss him in the weeping of the rain; I want him in the shrinking of the tide. . . ." Edna St. Vincent Millay.

Something wet fell on her hand, and another and another. God, how long had she been crying? The tears dripped steadily off her cheeks, onto her hands, and seeped through her fingers onto the pages. She did nothing to stem them, because with them came peace, the first peace she'd known in a long time. She didn't try to understand what was happening; she just accepted it.

Inside the front cover was an inscription, written in a strong hand. "For Sadie, my eternal love, the light that makes the sun shine and the moon glow, the light that makes it all worthwhile."

Nelsey's voice came from behind her, startling her out of her reverie.

"So, you found Sadie's things."

"Yes." Hastily, Memphis dashed away the tears, gently closed the book, and turned to face Nelsey, who stood with her hands tucked beneath her apron, an odd look on her face. "Did you know they were here?"

"To tell you the truth, I'd clean forgotten about them."

"This trunk was packed lovingly, by someone who cared a lot about her. It couldn't have been Alma. Alma never knew my grandmother. She met grandfather two years after Sadie died."

"That's the way the story goes."

"My mother couldn't have packed it. She was only three years old. And grandfather probably would have thrown most of this away."

"That's true."

"But you knew they were here. How did you know?"

Nelsey hesitated for a long time. She looked straight at Memphis, not hiding her struggle with conflicting decisions.

Finally she said, "My mother packed that trunk."

"What?" gasped Memphis. "Your mother knew Sadie? Then you must . . . of course, you would have been about ten years old. You knew Sadie."

"Not really. I knew Faith."

"But how, I mean, why haven't you told me?"

Nelsey sat on a wooden crate, squared her feet on the floor, and placed her hands on her knees

"At first, I thought you'd leave after a spell, and there wasn't any need to tell you. But you've stuck. I do believe you're here for the long run, so I got to likin' you and figured you deserved to know what I know, which ain't much. I've jest been waitin' till the time was right, and I guess this is the time."

"Please."

"We lived in a holler far up Ferrell Creek, hard to get to, but worth the trip to the women who brought their children to Mommy. To keep food in our mouths, she baby-sat children. Sadie had brought Faith several times, especially if she was going to be gone overnight. Mommy loved Sadie. Sadie was gay and sweet, and always took time to sit and talk before she left. Most of them women just dropped their kids off and hurried away. She brought excitement into my mother's life. I used to hide under the porch and listen to them talk."

The look of remembrance, of misty, far-off, and beloved times, filled Nelsey's nut brown eyes. Memphis knew Nelsey had gone back to Ferrell Creek, was there now under the porch, dirt under her bare feet, her mouth catching flies as she eavesdropped on her mother and Sadie Maynard, the sheriff's wife.

"Sadie would tell her what was happenin' in Yancey—the politics, the church goin's-on, and the gossip, and the parties. They would laugh and giggle, and I think Mommy felt like a girl again. Sometimes, though, Sadie would cry—husband troubles, she would say—and then they would whisper so I could hardly hear." Nelsey paused, then continued. "One night Sadie brought Faith real late. She was cryin'. She was in a big hurry and had no time to visit. I heard her say that she and James had a big fight, he'd hit her, and she wanted to get Faith out of the way of the trouble. Said she would probably be back for her in the morning, but if she wasn't, would we please take care of Faith 'til we heard from her again. Might be two or three days."

Nelsey stopped talking for a long time, and gazed out the attic window. Memphis, fascinated and hanging on every word, finally had to prompt her.

"Yes, and then?"

Nelsey folded her hands in her lap and set her mouth firm.

"We never saw or heard from her again."

"Was that the night she died?"

Nelsey nodded. "They found her body later that night."

Memphis heard Katie fussing, heard the kitten scatching at something, but couldn't take her eyes off Nelsey. "My God, you mean my mother was with you while her mother was being murdered?"

"Yep."

"Oh, Nelsey, I wish you'd told me sooner."

"Wouldn't have made no difference as to why you come here."

Reviewing Nelsey's story, Memphis decided that was true, and Nelsey had been typically mountaineer in her closemouthed behavior about personal things. Memphis decided she would have to forgive her. If she had known, she would have questioned Nelsey in detail about that last night. As it was, Nelsey had probably revealed all that she knew in a friendlier manner than if Memphis had had to question her.

"How long did you keep my mother?"

"The sheriff called late next mornin'. Wanted to know if Faith was with us, and we told him yes. He asked if we would mind keepin' her for a while. My mom said, 'No, that would be fine.' She loved Faith as much as she loved Sadie. Faith stayed with us for about two months, 'til he found a live-in baby-sitter here in town. 'Course then he married Alma about a year and a half later."

"When did your mother pack up Sadie's things?"

"She brought Faith here to the house. Me and my brothers come, too, and stayed for a few days while the new baby-sitter was learnin' about Faith. Mommy saw that nobody was takin' care of Sadie's things, nobody cared about them, so she packed them up herself . . . cryin' the whole time she did it." Nelsey stopped again, glancing out into the rainy afternoon. "She and my big brother carried the trunk up here. That's the last time I saw it 'til right now."

Katie let out a whoop of distress and they both jumped to see what had happened. Katie and the kitten had disappeared, but in a far corner a flurry of motion caught their attention. Jumping over boxes, skirting broken chairs, and lamps without shades, they reached the hapless two-year-old. She and the kitten had climbed onto an old bed whose springs had loosened long ago. The springs had held, but sank with her weight, and the thin mattress cocooned Katie in a deep cushioning hold that she couldn't climb out of. Miss Priss had clawed her way to the edge of the mattress, and balanced there with tail waving in the air, but Katie was caught.

Katie stopped crying when she saw Memphis and Nelsey laughing. Frowning, she held her arms up to be lifted. "Mama, Katie fall."

"I know, sweetheart, but you're okay." Memphis picked her up and hugged her, while Nelsey rubbed her soothingly on the back.

"I think it's time for some vegetable soup," said Nelsey.

"Righto."

Memphis glanced longingly at the trunk, but knew she would have to come back later to explore it more thoroughly. She also needed to think about all that Nelsey had told her.

Sally Junior screamed like a banshee, then muffled the sound in her damp pillow. Jake came with a mighty heave. He lay for a moment on her backside, then turned over to lay next to her on the sex-soaked sheets.

Jake flipped back the sheet, got out of bed, and went to the window. He parted the vertical blinds, saw that it was still raining, and pulled them back together. Then he climbed back into bed with Sally Junior.

"Good day for sex," he said. He thought of the lyrics of a Stills song from Crosby, Stills, and Nash: *If you can't be with the one you love, love the one you're with.*

Sally Junior sucked his earlobe, her sweet young breasts swinging tantalizingly close to his mouth as she squirmed around to get in the right position. He lifted his head to catch a nipple in his mouth, but she swung away, laughing, and settled to sit on his stomach. She reached behind her and caught hold of his swelling penis.

"Christ, go easy with that thing," he moaned. "It's had a lot of use this afternoon."

"You got that right. Ooh, Jake, baby-hunk, I'm sure happy you came to Yancey. You are just what I needed."

"And you're what I needed. You're the sweetest bit of ass this side of the Atlantic."

"You really think so?" She lay down on his chest, rubbed around a bit, then raised up to offer him a pink nipple. "Huh? Am I really the best you've had?"

"That you screamin', Sally Junior? You okay up there?" yelled her father.

"I'm just great, Daddy," she yelled back. "Have another drink."

"I'm not drinkin'. Too early in the afternoon."

"Where the hell is he?" whispered Jake.

"He's in the library, right under us."

"Christ!"

"It's okay. He's drunker than a skunk. In an hour he'll be passed out."

"Well, he seems to hear okay."

"Sally Junior! What the hell you doin' up there, girl?"

"I'm masterbatin', Daddy," she screamed. "What the hell you think I'm doin'? Leave me alone."

"Sally Junior, don't talk that way to your father."

"Shut up, Daddy. Have another Jack Daniel's."

"Jesus, Sally, you're kind of rough on your dad," said Jake.

"He deserves it. Hell, my Aunt Clarice won't even come home anymore. Can't stand to be around him. She stays in Paris all the time. This used to be her bedroom."

Jake looked at their reflections in the mirrored ceiling. Much of the bedroom was mirrored. The mirrors were set so that the bed and its occcupants could be seen from every angle.

"She the one who decorated this room?"

"Yes. The mirrors were here when I inherited it, but the colors and decorations are my own."

The first time he'd visited Sally Junior here, sneaking up the back stairs so as not to alert her father, Jake had almost gagged at the bright pink frilly floral prints on the bed and little boudoir chairs. Accustomed to the tacky room now, he was amused at the sophisticated mirror arrangement that so contrasted with the obvious girlishness of the rest of the room. The mirrors, of course, provided interesting sexual turn-ons.

"Your Aunt Clarice must be a fascinating woman."

"She is. Been married six times, but her marriage to this French count has lasted for ten years." Sally Junior sighed. "I'm planning on living a life just like hers. That's why I want you to take me with you when you go, Jake."

"Yeah, we'll talk about it later, honey. But I'm not leaving for a while. Have to keep finding material for those five-minute TV spots I'm doing. I think you've got a nice life right here, and interesting friends. Before we got into it so hot and heavy this afternoon, you were telling me about your friend Penny who does housework to earn money for college."

"Yeah, well, she's nice enough. God, Jake, can you believe it? We did it three times this afternoon." She snuggled up close to him, and swung a leg over his body, imprisoning him. "You're an animal."

And you're a little fucking machine. But I'm more interested in Penny right now.

He played with her hair, curling a blond strand around his finger, then tugged on it playfully. "Tell me more about what you do when I'm not around. Do you and Penny meet for lunch, or do you have a drink after work?"

"Well, you know I work at the bank, so my hours are more set than Penny's. But we do meet for a drink sometimes. Most of the time we go to Nicky's for a beer, but when we're feeling brave, we go to Ruby's. Daddy would die if he knew I went there."

"Yeah. It's pretty rough."

"That's what's so exciting about it. But Ruby watches out for us. Just like she did for my mom and dad. They used to sneak in there when they were in high school. Ruby is sooooo old."

"Must be about seventy-five, and looks older," said Jake, trying to be conversational. "Looks like she's been rode hard and hung up wet."

"What does that mean?"

"Never mind. So what do you and Penny talk about when you're out? Does she like doing housework for the Roots?"

"God, she hates it, but they pay her good, and Minnie Jo pretty much leaves her alone."

"Must be an interesting old house," he said, trying to generate more conversation about the Roots.

"I guess. Penny says the house is so stuffed with things that you have to be careful when you open a closet door. Something might fall out on you."

"Just think. If you married H. A. the turd, you'd inherit all that stuff. I imagine there are some valuable things there."

"Yeah, well that's true," she said, sounding interested for a moment. "But I'm not marrying him. I'm leaving with you, remember?"

"We'll see. Penny ever find anything valuable?"

"No," she giggled, "but she found something dirty."

"Dirty?"

"She was in Mr. Root's office, under a table polishing the feet. He came in and didn't see her there, and he doesn't hear too well. She said he unlocked the bottom drawer of his desk, and took out some pictures. Said he looked at them, was running his hands all over them, and giggling. By that time, she knew she'd better not reveal herself, so she stayed where she was. Said he got all excited and red in the face, was panting. Minnie Jo called him to supper, and he closed the drawer in a big hurry. He locked it, but left his keys on the desk. After he left, Penny opened the drawer." Sally Junior laughed. "Said they were dirty pictures of women. One of them was with Root when he was young, and another man, and they were doing things with naked women. Some were old pictures, from years ago, like from the 1930s. Others were recent, like from *Playboy.*"

"Wow. Who would have thought? Anything else in the drawer?"

"Yeah, she said there were some papers that looked like club records from a long time ago. Had lists and names on it that she didn't recognize. She was hoping there would be more dirty stuff."

"I see. Well, you never know about folks, do you? Do you suppose lewd old Root sits up late at night drooling over his pictures?"

Sally Junior laughed. "I doubt it, Jake. Penny says the Roots are asleep by nine-thirty every night."

Sounds good to me, thought Jake.

He put the keys in his pocket so he wouldn't forget them. He rummaged for the letters and found them right where he kept them. His hand closed over them with relief. He knew they were safe here, but every now and then he had to reassure himself.

Should I indulge myself and read them?

He knew them by heart by now, but always derived great pleasure in the reading of them, even though afterwards he was left with such sadness.

Yes, it's that kind of day.

He looked out into the steady rain; the naked black skeletal trees were glistening wet. The sparse green that remained drooped forlornly, waiting with dread for the coming winter. He poked the fire. It sprang up, brightening the room with warmth and cheer.

Settling into his chair, he reached for the snifter of

brandy at his side and gave it a swift twirl, then watched the rich amber liquid swirl lazily in its fragile glass bowl.

The rain drummed earnestly against the wide expanse of glass bringing back her recent presence here.

Yes, he would read them.

He opened the first page.

§10§

"Nelsey told me no one in Yancey locked their doors, but I didn't believe her," whispered Memphis.

"Shhh. Do you remember where Root's office is?" asked Jake.

"I was only inside the house once, but I think it's along the main hallway."

They were in the dim kitchen of the Root house. Memphis recognized the stale aroma of pot roast. *Must be Minnie Jo's favorite recipe.* A small green beam, illuminating the clock on the microwave, gave them enough light to make out the confines of the room. Jake bumped against a wooden chair, but caught it before it fell to the floor. He gripped his knee and cursed under his breath.

"My, how graceful."

"Shh, dammit. I knew I shouldn't have brought you."

"You're not fooling me for a second, Jake Bishop. You're using this as an excuse to spend time with me. You knew when you told me about Root's locked drawer with the naughty pictures from the 1930s that I would insist on coming with you. I'm going to make sure you don't keep anything from me."

"Okay, okay, just be quiet and watch where you're going."

There seemed to be two doors to choose from; Memphis favored the door to the right. Guiding Jake by the elbow, she pointed to the door, and they made their way carefully through the kitchen.

The door swung open onto what Memphis sensed was the long hall she had described, but it was pitch black. She stood for a moment, letting her vision adjust to the darkness, then, leading the way, she groped along the wall. Memphis had laughed when Jake had insisted that they both wear all-black clothing, like cat burglars. Now she was glad. For ease of movement, she'd had to leave her bulky jacket in the Jeep, so her long black tights and black turtleneck sweater felt good in the chilly house.

If she had guessed correctly, Root's office must be right next to the small library where she'd interviewed him. She motioned for Jake to stay where he was, and felt for the door closest to them. She opened it and knew immediately it was the library. The smell of cigar smoke hung heavy in the air. In the fireplace, a fading red ember dropped with a small hiss from the grate onto the cinders. From the corner came the dull ticktock of the grandfather clock.

Memphis felt out of place, and guilty, guilty, guilty. They were trespassing in the worst possible way. These were the sights, sounds, smells, and the inner sanctum of someone's life. This was a personal haven, which no one should ever enter except the owner. Trespassing on Cutter's land had been different. That was mountain land, and hadn't seemed so personal. This, this was wrong. She felt it to the core of her being. Anything accomplished in such a manner could only bring dire results. She took a deep breath and fought off her sense of doom.

I hate doing this, but if no one's going to cooperate or help me, then I'll have to resort to snooping.

She closed the door gently, and motioned to Jake to follow her. Feeling her way along the wall with Jake right behind her, she found the next door. Upstairs, a night-light went on in the hall. Its faint glow reflected on the wall of the stairwell. She froze, trying to melt into the shadows. Jake's body went stiff with apprehension. The flush of a water closet echoed loudly in the quiet. Her heart banged against her ribs as panic and fresh guilt swept through Memphis.

No, this has to be done.

Footsteps padded softly, a door closed, the night-light went off, and all was still again. They stayed where they were for five minutes. Finally, Jake nudged Memphis forward.

She felt for the next door, found the handle, and opened the door. It squeaked, and she held her breath. No sounds from upstairs.

Sally Junior had told Jake there were no windows in the office, so Memphis switched on her flashlight and swung it around the room. Yes. There was a desk, swivel chair, file cabinets, and the big mahogany table Penny polished. She pulled Jake inside, and they shut the door. Jake turned on his flashlight, too.

"Okay. So far so good. Now to get the infamous drawer open," said Jake. "You look through the desk for the keys, and I'll search the files."

Hoping by some minor miracle it might be unlocked like the kitchen door, Memphis pulled at the lower right-hand drawer. Locked tight. Quickly, she searched the other drawers in the desk. Harvey Root was a neat man. Everything was organized, every paper in place, every pencil, pen, and paper clip had a designated niche. No keys. With precise prudence, she replaced every item to its original resting place.

"Nothing here. You find anything?" she whispered.

Jake finished his search of the files, and said, "No. I'll have to pick the lock."

"Oh, great."

"Not to worry. I consulted a burglar friend." Jake held up a slender pointed tool. The lethal-looking polished steel instrument glinted in the beam of the flashlight.

"What is it?"

"A bodkin, used for piercing leather. He said it will do the trick."

They knelt next to the drawer. Memphis aimed her light while Jake jiggled at the lock. His first attempts failed. Memphis found she was holding her breath as he worked at the stubborn lock.

"Maybe if you jab at it hard, it will force it open."

"No," said Jake irritably. "My burglar buddy said if you find the right position and give a quick twist, the lock should give easily. He said these old-fashioned drawer locks are easy."

He slipped the tool in again, worked it carefully, and the lock gave with a light snap. He gave her a big grin

The latest issue of *Playboy* lay on top. Stacked underneath the magazine were black-and-white "nudie" photos of women from the thirties and forties in all stages of undress and suggestive poses.

"Hmmmm. I don't think Root would miss a few of these, do you?" asked Jake.

"Jake!"

They removed the magazine and the photos and found letters bound with a rubber band, and financial statements. Memphis spread the financial papers flat on the desk and took pictures of them. She also took shots of a few of the lewd photos, and a yellowed, torn sheet of paper that looked like a list of names. Jake replaced them in the drawer as she finished them, one by one.

The squeak of a floorboard cracked loud in the deep stillness of the house. They froze in place and switched off their flashlights. Another creak. Jake stopped untying the string around the letters, and they both listened. Another creak, closer and louder. Someone was coming down the stairs.

"Be right back, Daddy. I'll have your milk warmed in no time."

Minnie Jo, obviously on her way to the kitchen, was in the hall right outside the office door. The restless, nocturnal habits, typical of a man of eighty, had gotten her out of bed in the middle of the night. From the way she spoke, this was not an unusual occurrence. Memphis mentally cursed Sally Junior and her friend, Penny. Then she blamed herself. She should have thought of this. The Roots might be in bed asleep at nine-thirty, but that didn't mean they slept soundly until daylight.

Muscles tensed, jaws clenched, scarcely breathing, she listened. Jake placed a hand on her arm, both cautioning and reassuring her. The kitchen door opened with a swinging swish and a soft thud as Minnie Jo shoved it until it locked in an open position. She turned on a light, and its illumination traveled down the dark hallway and spilled beneath the office door. Memphis took a step backwards, as if to escape the unwelcome glow. Jake shook his head, indicating she shouldn't move, and held her arm so tight that it hurt. The viselike grip on her arm and the bulk of Minnie Jo in the kitchen barring any escape made her feel like a trapped animal. She fought her wild inclination to make a dash for the front door.

With each sound from the kitchen, Memphis imagined Minnie Jo pouring milk into a pan, placing it on the stove . . . or, no, maybe she was pouring the milk into a mug and heating it in the microwave. Memphis just wished she would be done with it so they could be out of here. Minnie Jo was humming, now she was singing "Slow Boat to China." *Oh, God, Minnie Jo, you're slow, so slow. And you're off-key.* Memphis had to pee, and her nose itched. Why did your nose always itch when you were hiding? *Well, you can scratch your nose, dummy. Minnie Jo's not here in the room with you.* No, but Memphis felt like she was. She scratched the tickle, then had to sneeze. She squeezed her nostrils to hold the threatening eruption.

Finally, the light went out, the kitchen door swished closed, and Minnie Jo walked by their door and made her lumbersome way up the stairs.

Memphis grabbed the letters Jake had been holding, knelt and put them carefully in place, replaced the *Playboy* magazine, and shut the drawer.

"What are you doing?" hissed Jake.

"We're leaving now. We've got what we need."

"Those letters might contain something we should know."

"Penny said he was salivating over the magazine and the pictures. I'm sure the letters are just treasures from an old flame. I'm getting out of here. Now. And you're coming with me. If you don't come with me, I'll call the sheriff when I leave and tell him I saw you entering the Root house in the middle of the night."

"Okay. Sometimes you can be a real bitch."

Minutes later, they were in the alley behind the Root home. Memphis breathed an immense sigh of relief and leaned shakily against a convenient wall of the Roots' garage. She took a deep breath, trying to calm herself. The air had a bite of early winter and smelled of coal smoke. Grit and grime beneath her shoes reminded her she was in town, and not on the hillside where her house stood and where she wished she was right this minute.

"We should never have done this, Jake."

"You're wrong, Memphis. Sometimes the end does justify the means."

She doubted it, and was just happy the whole smarmy episode was behind them. Their shoes made gritty, grinding sounds as they slipped along the shadowy alley corridor that led to the lit street ahead. It was only a short-block long, but seemed like a mile. As they were about to emerge into the light, a figure lurched up from the sidewalk and confronted them. Memphis gasped.

"Relax," whispered Jake. "It's only Shine McCoy."

"Hey, what'ch-all doin' there? Caught you, didn't I?" He slid down the wall he'd been leaning against and sat slumped on the sidewalk. He leered up at them. "Hee, hee, I knowed what you been doin'. Been back thar gettin' some pussy, ain't you, bud?"

"Yeah," whispered Jake. "Shhh, don't tell anyone, eh, Shine?"

"Hell, no, buddy. I won't tell no one." He winked at them. "Hey, you s'pose you could help me home? I kinda can't make it tonight."

He tried to sing "Show Me the Way to Go Home," but dissolved into helpless giggles.

"Shh, Shine, shh. You don't want to wake anyone, do you?" whispered Jake.

"No, I shore don't want to do that," Shine whispered back. "The sheriff's mad at me anyway. Says I'm a disgrace to the town of Yancey. But, hell, I don't see it that way. I jest do in public what most people do behind closed doors."

"Yeah, yeah, Shine," said Jake, humoring him.

"Do you know where he lives?" asked Memphis.

"Yeah, and I better take him. If I don't, he might meet someone else and tell them he saw us. This way, I can tuck him in all safe and secure. Call me when you get the film developed."

"I will."

"Hey, who's the purty lady?" Shine asked loudly. "You sure gotcha a humdinger thar, pal. She any good at neckin'?"

"Shhh, be quiet," implored Memphis.

"Well, she be real persnickety, don't she, Jake?" he said, even louder. "Comes out of the alley with you, then gets real prissy."

Down the alley came the sound of a window sliding open. They had awakened someone. Memphis's stomach dropped to her toes.

"Hey, you come home with me, honey. We'll take off all that black stuff you got on, and I'll show you a good time."

"Hey, what's going on out there? Who you talkin' to, Shine?" yelled a man. "Go on home and sleep it off, or I'll get the sheriff after you."

"See, Shine, I told you," whispered Jake. "If you aren't quiet, you're going to wake up in jail in the morning."

"Yeah, okay, I'll be good. You takin' me home, buddy? If you take me home, I'll invite you for Thanksgiving dinner. My sister in Pig Corner is a good cook, and she won't mind."

"Yeah, sure. Come on, Shine, let's go." Jake hoisted the man up and propped his shoulder under Shine's armpit. "But that reminds me, Memphis. Thanks for inviting me for Thanksgiving dinner. Uh, you're not going to cook, are you?"

"Why? Something wrong with my cooking?"

"I've had better."

"Thanks a lot," she whispered. "You'll be happy to know that Nelsey will be the cook. She usually goes to Cutter's house for Thanksgiving, but she said she would spend the day with us if she could invite Cutter and his father, and if she could do the cooking."

"Cutter Tate will be there? I don't think I like that very much, Memphis."

Memphis didn't like it much either, but Nelsey had become so important in her and Katie's lives that Memphis had had no choice.

"Well, it really isn't any of your business, is it, Jake? If you want to see Katie, it will be on my terms. See you then."

Memphis passed Nelsey's house on the way up the hill. Except for a yellow porch light, the place was dark, quiet, and peaceful looking. Katie was spending the night there. Memphis had told Nelsey that she and Jake had things to talk about concerning Katie, and that she wasn't sure how involved the discussion would get. She hated lying to Nelsey, and she was sure that Nelsey thought Memphis and Jake were "shacking up" in a hotel room somewhere.

Disturbed by familiar feelings of camaraderie she and Jake had shared this evening, she turned off the ignition and sat for a moment, keys in hand. Entering the Root home had brought back memories of similar adventures and escapades. Buoyed by the excitement, they inevitably had made love afterwards. She and Jake had not always been circumspect in their gathering of information for a story. They had resorted to some methods Memphis looked back on with shame, but she'd been young then, and Jake had been her God.

Thank heavens all that had changed. She saw Jake for what he really was, a charming but shallow opportunist. He was Katie's father, however, and he seemed to have a sincere interest in her, so she had to be fair and allow him into their lives. But only on her terms.

Invading the Root house had made her feel terrible, but she had to find some answers soon. It was the frustrating feeling that the answer lay right in front of her that drove her.

So be it. I'll do what I have to do to discover who murdered Sadie, and why.

Hating what Nelsey must think of her, and feeling guilty about sneaking into the Root house, she realized she wouldn't be able to sleep right away. She was too keyed up. She got out of the Jeep and walked toward the porch, still deep in thought. A light breeze blew, chilling the back of her neck, and she hunched into her collar.

Then it came. Floating and riding the drift of the breeze.

Stopped in her tracks, she listened intently. This was not her imagination or a trick of the wind. A woman hummed a tune that sounded like a hymn. But sound carried in freakish ways in the mountains. In fact, the brief breeze that had brought the haunting sound had died down, and the night was still. From behind the house came an odd illumination. The lights again, she thought. A chill ran down her spine, as if someone had traced an ice cube straight down her back. She shivered and huddled closer into her jacket.

Don't look at the light. Move, Memphis. Get into the house. This weird mountain phenomena will disappear once you're safe in bed.

In her bedroom, the humming stopped, but she paced back and forth. She wasn't focused enough to start developing the footage she'd taken at Root's house. Besides, it was probably much too cold in the basement. She put on a nightgown and her favorite red flannel robe, and went to the kitchen to make hot chocolate.

It seemed odd being here without Katie, or Nelsey, who sometimes spent the night now. She had never been in the house by herself. It had a middle-of-the-night stillness, just like the Root house, only this had become a familiar stillness. The random sounds were friendly ones, not something to be frightened of. She realized that she'd become accustomed to the shaky old house, had even begun to think of it as home.

Studiously ignoring the lights that might be in the woods behind her, and the humming she'd heard, she sat at the scarred pine table and wrapped her hands around the warm mug of cocoa. She reminded herself that the abrasive squeak she'd just heard was an errant limb of the vast oak tree against the far side of the house, assured herself that the friendly rumble in the basement was the water heater. A faint click and muffled rush announced the onset of the oil heater and the warm air it would soon be sending through the chilled house, a convenience her grandfather had installed just before his death ten years ago. Mighty welcome now, she thought.

A rough, wet lick on her ankle startled her. She looked under the table to find Miss Priss at her feet, batting at the hem of her robe.

"Oh, hello, little one. I'm not alone after all, am I? I thought you were with Nelsey and Katie." She picked up the kitten, brushed it against her cheek, and settled it in her lap. "How nice to have some company."

She finished her cocoa while Miss Priss slept in her lap. The kitten was getting leggy. Her charcoal paws drooped gracefully over Memphis's thighs. Soothing herself with strokes of the satiny coat, Memphis soon began to lose her edginess, but knew she couldn't sleep yet. Too many memories chased her, and too many yearnings to be shoved away and forgotten.

When she went to toss the remainder of her cocoa, she tried to avoid looking out the black void of window just above the sink that faced the woods behind the house. But no one could have ignored the play of light that cavorted in the depth of the hard-angled trees. A gold light hovered about a tall evergreen, then wove itself around a winter-bared oak. Suddenly, it swirled away, then rushed back to settle near the tree line, finally becoming a misty glow of pearly white, then a brilliant blue.

The misty glow, the uneven flow from tree to tree, and the heights the lights rose to were almost other-worldly. *Okay, admit it. They are otherworldly, and so is*

*the humming. I could call Nelsey. Nelsey said to call her
if I ever saw the lights again, but I would wake Katie.*

And for some reason she couldn't clarify, perhaps
because she was growing accustomed to them, the
lights and the sounds didn't seem life threatening.

Miss Priss, who'd jumped from her arms onto the
counter, arched her back and hissed, and her fur
ridged like a porcupine's quills. Memphis took the stiff-
legged kitten into her arms to soothe her, but Miss
Priss scratched her wrist and leaped to the floor. The
humming came now, soft and sad this time. She was
sure it was a hymn.

"Relax," she said out loud. Her voice, if somewhat
shaky, sounded good to her, normal on this peculiar
night. "This will all be a great story to tell when you get
back to Manhattan."

The light floated hesitantly, almost as if it couldn't
make up its mind what to do next. Then it faded to a
faint bluish white and retreated slowly into the trees.
Memphis shivered. The sense of disquiet she'd had
since she'd arrived in Yancey hung heavy about her
now. When was the last time she'd felt any peace?

The attic. The attic was musty, dusty, and dim, but
she'd been happy there for a while. Why? Sadie's trunk.
With relief, she remembered the promise she'd made to
return to the attic for a more thorough search of
Sadie's trunk. A perfect excuse to avoid a lonely,
sleepless night. She retrieved Miss Priss from behind
the pantry door and headed upstairs to the attic.

Sadie's trunk was as she'd left it, top open and three-
quarters empty. On the floor next to it were a few
favorite dresses, stacked books, and jewelry and trinkets in a discarded shoe box , all to be taken downstairs
for better perusal. Memphis deposited the kitten on an
overstuffed square pillow covered with faded needle-
point.

The bare lightbulb dangling over her head did little

to chase away the shadows in the corners of the attic, and even less to brighten the recesses of the large trunk. Anticipating the problem, Memphis had brought a kerosene lamp. She pulled a tall wooden stool next to the trunk, placed the lamp on it, and put a match to the wick.

Amber light sprang in wavery, flickering life, dancing here and there around vague forms in dim, forgotten spaces, illuminating some, cloaking others. It transformed a dressmaker's form into a knight wearing a suit of armor, and a basketball on top of a cooler into a bonneted lady. A snow sled she hadn't noticed before jumped out in sharp clarity, as did a lovely tapestry hanging on a far wall.

She bent over the edge of the trunk and searched the bottom layer for memorabilia she might have missed. The light scent of lavender was familiar and comforting. Faith's baby clothes filled the bottom of the chest. A ragged much loved pink teddy bear hugged one corner. She pulled out a garish-orange stuffed pig. A cardboard tag hanging from its ear said "State Fair, 1935." What state fair, she wondered, where? Who had gone, who had won this funny, tacky pig for his fair maiden? She tried to picture her stern grandfather pitching balls at a bull's-eye to win a pig for Sadie. Well, everyone was young once.

A flat round black disc caught her attention. She lifted it from the depths of the trunk and discovered it was a scratched, much used phonograph record. The label read "I Remember You." Obviously a song her grandparents had enjoyed, perhaps dancing to it on private evenings by themselves. She wished for a phonograph player so she could hear the poignant romantic melody as they had heard it.

Finding nothing more of interest in the trunk, she turned to the clothes she'd set aside. She'd planned on taking the two evening dresses downstairs to try on later, but couldn't resist the lure of the shimmering ivory sequined dress. Would it fit? Eagerly, she took off her nightgown and robe, laid them across the pillow next to the sleeping kitten, and slipped the silvery sheath over her head. It fit as if it had been made for her. At first the silk lining was cold against her, but soon warmed sensually to her skin. Excited now, she searched the trunk for shoes to match, and there they were. Silver slippers tied with ivory satin bows. The shoes were tight in the toes, but she didn't care.

Sorry now that Nelsey, or Katie, or Margo, or someone wasn't here to see her dressed as Sadie, she searched for a mirror. She took the kerosene lamp to a cheval mirror in the corner.

Memphis was startled at the slim, excited young woman from the pre–World War II era who stared back at her. She drew her hair on top of her head, and tried to imagine what it would look like short and wavy, as Sadie would have worn it. The amber light danced and flickered, and for a singular moment Memphis was Sadie, ready to go dancing with her newest beau, wondering what the evening would bring, wondering if he would think she was beautiful and if he would try to steal a kiss.

But the image soon flickered and faded as the long night began to tell on her. She yawned, and sat on the floor next to the trunk to go through the stack of books.

She set aside the book of poetry to read later, and looked through the volumes her grandmother must have kept as favorites: several mysteries by Dashiell Hammett, some works by Dos Passos, collections of poetry by Robert Frost, Erskine Caldwell's *God's Little Acre*, John Steinbeck's *Tortilla Flat*, Fitzgerald's *Tender is the Night*. A varied reading list. If she'd had to judge her grandmother by her taste in reading, Memphis would have said Sadie had good taste, was imaginative and romantic, and had a touch of naughtiness in her.

She ran her fingers lovingly over *Tender is the Night*. How comforting to know that Sadie loved this story as much as Memphis did. Unable to resist, Memphis opened the Fitzgerald novel. Happy with the dress, and happy with the book, she relaxed and lay on the floor, head on the pillow with Miss Priss, and read.

Her eyelids drooped, and she dozed.

Soon, she dreamed of a flirtatious young woman in a silvery dress tossing her head and doing the Lindy, of a lovely woman enjoying a picnic with a man by a stream, of the same woman hiking, turning her head to laugh at something the man behind her had said. The man was misty, in the shadows, but he was big, strong in his silence, and deeply in love with the woman. They made passionate, earth-shaking love on a jade green mountainside. Afterwards, the woman cried for an unknown reason, and the man held her in his arms, and leaves on the trees quivered in fear for the safety of this love that was so deep, so durable, so passionate.

A rough lick on her cheek woke her up. Miss Priss purred into her ear, and Memphis purred, too. She was still lost in the midst of the strange, emotional, realistic dream. The shared happiness, aching sadness, and wild passion had touched her deeply. She closed her eyes, willing herself to find the man and the moments again. But she couldn't.

Between her thighs, beneath the soft silk lining of the sequined party dress, she felt curling warmth and wetness. A misty feeling of relief and peace filled her entire body. She had been there, she had climaxed. Her sexual liason with the mysterious man left her loose, satisfied, fulfilled, and complete.

"You're crazy, Memphis Maynard," she whispered.

But there was no way she could deny the plain fact that she was wet and creamy in the most intimate manner, and warmly and sensuously happy in the way only a satisfied and thoroughly loved woman can be.

She smiled.

"Well, one thing is for sure, Miss Priss. I would certainly like to meet him again."

Wanting the moment to last forever, she luxuriated in the delicious feeling for a while, putting the kitten on her chest to stroke. Forgotten were the lights, the humming, the guilt from the invasion of Root's home, the search for Sadie's grave, and the mysterious circumstances of her death. For a time Memphis relived her dream.

But soon, the splintery wood floor felt hard, and the air cold. She gathered the kitten in her arms, and headed toward her bedroom, taking with her the beaded black dress and the book of poetry with the inscription.

§11§

Nelsey surveyed the Thanksgiving table with pride. The pride wasn't for herself, but for Memphis. The woman might not know how to cook, or sew, or iron, but she sure could set a beautiful table and arrange flowers.

Memphis had discovered the heavy cream-colored damask cloth in the attic. *Probably belonged to Sadie, because, forgive me, Lord, Alma was a good soul, but she never had a smidgen of good taste.*

Margo, Memphis's sister, had sent the weighty silverware, which had belonged to Faith, and had then got herself on a plane in Texas and come to visit for the holidays. Colorful bouquets of dwarf black-eyed Susans, which Margo had flown in at Memphis's request from her favorite Manhatten flower shop, were tied with royal blue twine, set in twig baskets, and placed at each setting.

Peals of laughter came from the kitchen. Nelsey drank in the sound, like cool water to a thirsty old woman. *Amazing, Lord, what love and laughter will do for a shabby house that maybe holds a few tired ghosts.*

"Nelsey, come see what Katie's done," called Memphis.

In the kitchen, Nelsey joined the laughter of the sisters as they watched Katie and Miss Priss lick candied frosting from a big bowl Nelsey had set aside for Memphis to wash. The toddler stood on a chair next to the table while the black kitten teetered on the edge of the ironstone bowl. The white sticky stuff clung to the kitten's black fur in fat tufts, and was smeared all over Katie's face.

"Lordy, it's nice to hear some laughter in this house," she said. "You two always have such a good time together?"

"We pretty much had to entertain one another when we were young," Margo said, and smiled. She put an arm around her sister's shoulder and gave her a quick hug. "And we made sure we had a good time."

"We were only twenty when Mom died, and she'd always told us to watch out for one another," said Memphis. "She became almost paranoid about our safety, and our stepfather aided and abetted her."

"So when the nannies got too smothering, or the car that picked us up from school was late, we usually sneaked off and got into some kind of trouble."

They exchanged mischievous looks and laughed again.

"Poor Mom, if she'd known I was going to end up dodging bullets on battlefields, she'd have had a fit," said Memphis.

Margo had the same slender, fine-boned build that Memphis did. They looked like sisters, except Margo was a brunette. Her hair was straight, and without the wave that made tendrils curl helter-skelter about Memphis's face. Margo's was arranged in an elaborate toffee-twisted sort of figure eight, and fastened with what looked to Nelsey like cherry red, Chinese knitting needles. She wore a red turtleneck sweater, and a matching swirling ankle-length jersey skirt. Margo moved about in theatrical strides, dramatic in every gesture and intonation, where Memphis moved with a more natural gliding grace. Both of them burned with vibrant energy that almost singed the air.

The three of them went to work cleaning up Katie and the kitten, Katie giggling all the while, and Miss Priss struggling to escape. Nelsey hoped her questions sounded casual.

"So, Faith was overprotective, was she?" asked Nelsey. "I remember you girls weren't allowed much freedom when you were here as kids. They pretty much kept you tethered, but I always figured that was your grandfather's doin'."

"It was," said Margo, with a frown. "Mom was never like that until after the last summer we spent here. Great God, after that she treated us like two virginal princesses in an ivory tower."

Margo nudged Memphis in the side and started laughing again.

"Remember the time she caught you in the elevator making out with Mr. Smedly?"

Memphis joined her in uproarious laughter.

"Who was Mr. Smedly?"

"Our piano teacher. He was only twenty-five, and Memphis was fifteen. Mom grounded her for a month, and we got a new piano teacher, ancient Professor Carruth. He smelled like mothballs and Bengay."

"Why do you suppose Faith was so protective?" Nelsey asked, probing gently.

Nelsey could see that Margo's visit was lifting Memphis's mood. Memphis was like the wind. You couldn't hold her mood in your hand and be sure it would be there tomorrow. Yesterday, after her night with Jake Bishop, Nelsey thought sourly, she'd whistled all day long, happy as a lark. *Ummph. Should have been tired, 'cause I know she didn't get in till two in the morning. Heard her car go by.* But this morning, she'd come up from her darkroom with a strained face, pale freckles standing out that Nelsey had never seen before, and a pinched look around her mouth.

Margo had arrived soon after that, though, so any

attempt to discover why Memphis looked so desolate disappeared. Nelsey was glad Margo had erased most of the tenseness Memphis had carried with her all morning. All that remained were fragile, almost disappearing, gold freckles, and faint circles beneath her eyes.

Memphis took Katie upstairs to give her a bath. Margo washed dishes, while Nelsey basted the turkey. A companionable silence held them for a while, but Nelsey could tell Margo wanted to talk. She waited.

Nelsey was putting the finishing touches to a gingerbread man and placing it flat on top of a pumpkin pie, when Margo spoke.

"Memphis told me about what happened Halloween night. I've been worried about her ever since. What do you think of the whole thing?"

"Why, I think jest exactly what you think. What would any person think? Obviously someone is trying to scare her into leaving Yancey."

"Anything else happen?"

Nelsey hesitated. She hadn't told Memphis about the sheets. Hadn't planned to until after the holiday. But maybe she should tell someone.

"Yep, Monday afternoon. But I'd rest better if you didn't tell Memphis till tomorrow. I want her to have a good day." Margo stood looking at her, drying her hands on a worn dishtowel. "When Memphis and Katie were grocery shopping, I went to take the clean sheets off the line. They were splattered with mud and something that looked like blood. Was probably ketchup or something. I'da thought it was a kid's joke, but a message was spelled out in blood red on one of the sheets. Said 'leave, nosey bitch.'"

"Great God, Nelsey, don't you think these incidents should be reported to the authorities?"

"Memphis said she didn't want anyone to know about Halloween, so I don't expect she'll be wantin' anyone to know about this either. Don't think it would do much good anyway."

"Do you have any idea who might be behind any of this?"

"Nope." *But I do. Jest not much use in speculatin' until there's more proof. Don't want to set a cat among the pigeons.*

"Do you think this Cutter Tate might be involved?"

"No. By the way, he'll be here this afternoon with his friend, Alison, so I 'spect you'll want to mind your manners."

Taken aback by Nelsey's tartness, Margo frowned. "I beg your pardon. I'm always polite unless I see something I don't like. Cutter Tate's family was definitely involved in this Sadie mess that Memphis is so obsessed with, so I just find it a trifle odd that he's spending Thanksgiving here."

"Cutter's like a son to me," Nelsey said defensively. "I invited him, and he asked if Alison could come because she told him she was going to be alone."

"Well, it certainly should be a fascinating dinner party. Cutter Tate, his girlfriend, his father, and Jake Bishop, who is positively my least favorite person on the face of the earth."

Nelsey said nothing. She turned her back and resumed her pie decorating.

Soon she felt Margo's hands on her shoulders and a swift kiss on her cheek. "Sorry, Nelsey. I shouldn't be so bitchy. I should be thanking you for caring so much about Memphis and Katie. But I worry about them."

"You don't bother me none. I understand that you worry about them, but they are jest fine." *I'm worried too, but darned if I'm going to tell Margo that. She can't do nothing about anything anyway, and might make things worse if she was to run to the sheriff.*

The telephone rang. It was Cutter saying that his father was ill, and could he please bring Birdy instead?

Her family had gone to their cabin on the lake for the day. Nelsey assured him that was just fine, and hung up.

Well, Lord, here we go again. You sure got an odd sense of humor.

At twilight, they'd all gathered around the table, and at first Nelsey thought it might turn into one of the best Thanksgivings she'd ever had. Though it had been a soapstone day outside, all grim and dreary, the dining room looked festive and cheery. Lordy, everything smelled good, too. The roasted turkey with chestnuts, the cinnamon aroma of pumpkin pie, and the brown-sugar sweetness of potato pie filled the house. A crackling fire burned in the small fireplace, and Alma's cheap chandelier from Sears did itself proud, reflecting flickering candlelight from the beautiful table.

But as she surveyed their guests, she decided if not one of the best, it was certainly going to be one of the more interesting days she'd ever experienced. Pretty Alison seemed to be the only one oblivious to the currents of emotion circling the table.

Memphis, trying to disguise the unease that Nelsey sensed stewed within her, sat at one end of the table, and Nelsey at the other. To Nelsey's right sat Birdy, pert and bright, and not good at hiding the worshipful glances she cast Cutter's way. A jealous Jake, who, Nelsey surmised, felt he should be the only rooster at this hens' party, sat in the middle between Birdy and Katie. If looks could kill, Jake's would have shot down Cutter Tate long ago. A curious, observant, and protective Margo sat at Memphis's right.

It was Cutter who worried, yet fascinated, Nelsey. There was about him a smooth, almost deadly calmness. Though polite, and quietly charming, Nelsey recognized the physical hints that betrayed the storm raging beneath his surface: the arching quirk in one dark eyebrow, the muscle in his jaw that locked then loosened, the way the color of his eyes changed to the gray of a March sky. Cutter was mad as hell. The more caustic Jake got, the quieter and angrier Cutter got. Everytime he looked Memphis's way, his fingers tightened on his knife.

Margo made a silly toast and they all lifted their wine goblets. Cutter's goblet seemed to catch fire with the reflection from the chandelier, and the dazzling light arced silver and gold between him and Memphis, circling their heads round and round with crowns of dizzying color. Nelsey knew that, again, she was the only one who saw the brief phenomenon.

Oh, Lordy, not again. This is no trick of the sun. It's dark out.

Her goblet slipped from her hand, missed the platter of carved turkey, but soaked the tablecloth instead.

"Heavens above," she said, "you'd think I could drink water without spilling it."

Alison started to rise out of her seat. "It's not much, Mrs. Kinzer. I'll get something to wipe it up."

"No, but thank you, Alison. You sit still. I know jest where things are in the kitchen. Y'all go ahead eatin'. I'll be right back."

The tension about the table was such that Nelsey knew if she took a deep breath the suction might cause the room to fall in on itself. She hurried into the kitchen so she could breathe with some relief.

Cutter's palm hurt with the pressure he exerted on his knife handle. *Relax. Don't let this cocky son of a bitch across the table get to you.* He loosened his death grip on the knife and, with deliberate calm, laid the knife beside his plate. *What's the problem anyway, Cutter? You should be enjoying yourself.* The atmosphere was certainly perfect—cheerful fire, delicious meal, beautiful women, and good conversation.

Ahh, but beneath the conversation, and behind all

the holiday trappings there lay a mounting tension. He knew he was to blame for part of it, but could do nothing to stop himself.

Alison, pretty, sweet, and even funny at times, sat at his side, but he couldn't keep his eyes off Memphis at the end of the table, and he felt guilty as hell. Alison had called to invite him to dinner in Charleston, and he'd told her of his commitment to Nelsey. Feeling as though he owed her a return invitation, Cutter had invited her to Yancey, but knew now that it had been a mistake. He fought to pay attention to Alison's light patter, disciplined himself to be polite and attentive, but his eyes inevitably returned to the woman who lit up the room.

Memphis, wearing an ivory sequined dress, which she explained had belonged to Sadie, looked devastatingly beautiful. Despite faint half-moons of lavender beneath her eyes, and a breathless quality in her speaking, all of which indicated either weariness or stress, she kept the conversation lively and sparkling. Margo Maynard contributed to the joking, and they played straight man to each other's wisecracks. They would have made a great stand-up sister act.

"Memphis, honey, you look so gorgeous in your grandmother's dress," said Birdy. "What fun you are to wear such a thing! Why it makes me feel good just looking at you."

"Thank you, Birdy. That's exactly why I wore it. I needed cheering up, and I've been fascinated by this dress and another one I found in Sadie's trunk."

"You used to cheer up real easy after we'd finished a good story, or a glass of good wine, and sometimes even a jog around the park would do it," Jake said, and winked at her. "'Course there's no park here, or good wine, either."

Cutter hated the possessive familiar tone Jake used

with Memphis. And his continual doting attention to Katie grated on his nerves.

"I'm sure Memphis has found places to run in Yancey, and I'm also sure we can locate some excellent wine somewhere around," said Margo dryly. "I for one, at this time, would like to thank Cutter for supplying this delightful Chilean red."

"You're welcome." He had said little during the evening, not trusting himself to be civil. "My grandfather kept a superior wine cellar. But this is a recent addition that I added myself."

"Remember the time we rode the camel in Egypt?" asked Jake of Margo and Memphis, excluding the rest of them with his reminder of times the Maynard sisters had spent only with him. "And Margo fell off, and neither of us knew how to get the stupid animal to kneel so we could get off, or help her get back on?"

Cutter smiled while they all laughed, but felt his jaw tighten. He tried to relax. *Jake Bishop acts as if he belongs here. I'll be damned if he does.* His only consolation was that Margo seemed irritated with Jake, too.

"But, Memphis," said Birdy, harping back to the dress, "don't you think it's simply amazing that it fits you so well, almost as if it had been made for you?"

"Yeah, we really should get a picture of you," Jake said. He reached to wipe mashed potatoes off Katie's face, and Cutter wanted to smash *his* face.

Katie is Jake's daughter. Give it up, Cutter. You knew Jake Bishop was going to be here. He shouldn't have come, and he shouldn't have brought Alison, but he couldn't disappoint Nelsey. *Admit it, Cutter. You came because you wanted to be near Memphis again.*

"No, I don't need a picture, I just feel good in the dress, and I thought Katie and Margo would get a kick out of it."

"Mama pretty," said Katie. Jake smiled indulgently,

patted her on the back, and winked again at Memphis, implying a relationship that Cutter had assumed was over.

"You have a serious eye problem, Jake. Have you seen a doctor about that twitch?" asked Margo, sarcasm dripping.

Cutter erupted in laughter, and Jake shot him a look of pure venom.

Nelsey returned to the table, and Cutter got up to pull her chair out for her.

"Quite the Southern gentleman, eh, Tate?" remarked Jake. "Surprising, considering you were practically raised at Ruby's Good Eats and Beer."

Cutter's hand gripped the back of Nelsey's chair with such force that his knuckles cracked. Enraged at the man's lack of civility at a holiday gathering, Cutter said bitterly, "That was a slimy bit of work you did at Ruby's that night, Jake. Ruby doesn't deserve your rabid interest. If I'd known you were going to be here, and if it weren't for Nelsey, I'd . . ."

Nelsey stopped him. Turning on the pretense of settling her sweater about her shoulders, she placed a swift hand on his fist to calm him down. Birdy, too, caught the swiftness of his rage, and chimed in to change the subject.

"Hey, Jake, Shine McCoy's telling everybody in town that you rescued him real late the other night, and that you had some beautiful angel with you. Is that true?"

"Yeah, well, he was really soused, and he needed someone to take him home. I just happened to be handy."

"Sounds more interesting than that," teased Birdy. "Come on, give us the real skinny. You having a secret affair with someone?"

"You know me, Birdy, a girl in every port. No, seriously, Shine imagined the beautiful woman part."

"Don't think so," Birdy persisted. "Shine said she was

dressed all in black like a cat burglar, and the street-light lit up her hair like sun dancing off water. Didn't know ol' Shine was such a poet. What were you doing out so late, and with a beautiful woman to boot?"

With a pang, Cutter remembered the starlight shining on Memphis's hair in the aftermath of the storm. Knowing she couldn't see him watching her that night, he had drunk in the wonder of light glinting hither-thither about the fine bronze tendrils.

Jake squirmed in his seat, but said sharply, "Shine is a drunk, Birdy. He's lying about the woman. Could we just drop it, please?"

"Come on, Jake," said Cutter lazily, playing with the trapped mouse. "Satisfy our curiosity. Who was the lady, and what is there to do so late at night in a one-stop town like Yancey?"

He suddenly knew the woman must have been Memphis, and he regretted the question the second he asked it. He didn't want to hear the answer.

"It's none of your business what I was doing, and there was no woman. Believe me, Tate."

"I wouldn't believe you if your tongue were notarized."

A freezing silence held everyone for infinite seconds. Cutter knew he was behaving abominably and would catch hell from Nelsey later, but he watched with pleasure as Jake Bishop struggled to maintain his cool. Jake's face turned pink. He bent his head. Tucking his chin into his neck, he reached for the band that fastened his blond ponytail, pretending that it needed adjusting. That done, and in control, he looked at Cutter and smiled complacently.

"Touché, Tate. Now if you don't mind, let's drop the subject. If there *were* a woman, you wouldn't want me to sully her reputation, would you?"

Cutter had to give it to him. Jake Bishop was a worthy adversary. This man was no fool. Far from it.

But now Cutter knew for certain that the woman had been Memphis. He burned with jealousy. This was no time for his dangerous temper to take over. He would examine his feelings about Memphis later.

But he couldn't resist a final jab. "Didn't know you possessed such chivalry, Bishop." For Nelsey's sake, to save Memphis embarrassment, and to salvage the rest of the party, he continued mildly, "Good for you."

A flurry of polite conversation followed the cold exchange of words between the two men. They all commented on the spiced apples and brandied peaches. Alison asked for Nelsey's popover recipe, and Margo said she'd never had such tasty turkey.

"Great God above, Nelsey, everything is divinely scrumptious. It's been ages since I had a home-cooked meal," said Margo. "Maybe I'll come and live with you and Memphis for a while. I could use some fattening up."

Cutter smiled, remembering his comment to Memphis about *her* skinniness. He caught her eye, she smiled, and he knew she remembered. She'd been so light in his arms that demon night, as if all the fury, all the intensity she generated had hollowed her out inside. But then, when he'd held her tighter to him to shield her from the storm, her soft, warm, moist mouth had pressed against his neck, and he knew the fire within her still burned.

He took his time smiling at her, not trying to hide his pleasure of the memory. She dropped her gaze, adjusting the napkin in her lap, but as if she couldn't resist either, quickly glanced up and their eyes held again. Katie fussed for more turkey. Memphis tore her gaze away from him, but he knew she remembered the sensual kiss they'd shared, and that she'd felt the powerful undercurrent flowing between them that night on the mountain. Today, it was still there and even more powerful, so much so that he wondered that others around the table couldn't feel the sensation.

Damn. Was he falling in love with the woman? No. He wanted her to leave Yancey. Too much history, too much water over the dam.

Alison touched his arm and whispered, "Cutter, are you all right? You look a bit pale. I know Jake Bishop is hard to take, but I've seen you handle worse."

He patted her hand. "No, I'm fine, Alison. You've just noticed my summer tan has faded."

"Oh, Alison, honey, what a silly ninny I am. I forgot to ask how you placed in the Kanawha Valley Horse Show last week," said Birdy, staring pointedly at Alison's hand on Cutter's arm.

Alison took her hand away, and he could have cursed Birdy's nosiness. Sometimes she overdid the protective sister role. Alison was a warm, demonstrative woman whom he liked very much. He wished Birdy would stop judging who was, and who wasn't, good company for him.

Memphis asked to be excused. "It's my turn to do kitchen duty. I'll serve dessert."

Jake practically knocked his chair over in his hurry to get up. "I'll help you."

"I don't need help."

"Sure you do. It'll be like old times."

"We never spent any time in a kitchen."

"Yeah, well, we'll make up for it now," he said, following her with a lecherous grin.

Cutter's jaws ached with the effort to keep his mouth shut. He clenched them tighter, enduring the pain, and forced himself to sit still. He would follow them into the kitchen after a decent interval. No way was he going to let them stay in there alone.

In the kitchen, Memphis searched for a knife to cut the pie.

If she kept busy she might recover from the embarrassing jealousy she felt at the sight of Alison sitting so cozily next to Cutter. She'd been shocked at the uncovering of her unwelcome jealousy. After all, she had no claims on Cutter and certainly didn't want any. Or did she? Her lips tingled at the memory of his mouth moving tenderly over hers that night in the glass house.

Oh God, Memphis, stop this.

Keeping busy would also help her forget for a while what she'd discovered in the darkroom this morning, and the ghostly humming of the wind that had plagued her again while she was there. She stopped for a minute to listen, but there was no wind. The night was quiet. There had been no wind this morning, and no wind this evening.

Going to the darkroom had become an act of courage.

Jake came in and stood close behind her, practically breathing down her neck.

"Go away, Jake. You came to spend Thanksgiving with Katie, not me."

"Those Hepburn freckles are popping out all over. What's got you so upset?"

"Could be you and your abominable behavior."

"No, you were stretched like a rubber band when I got here earlier. Nelsey said you were in the darkroom early this morning. Did you develop the film?"

Memphis said nothing, and focused on the pies.

"Come on, beautiful, what happened this morning?"

"Nothing, Jake. Your imagination is running overtime."

"You processed the film, didn't you?"

"Yes," she said reluctantly. "Everything but the financial records."

"Well, come on, give."

"Nothing interesting."

Memphis trembled inside, but managed to keep her

hands steady. She knew she'd have to tell Jake eventually. He held her shoulders firmly and turned her to face him.

"You're lying."

She shook herself free, and said, "Okay, there was something. But I want to discuss it with Margo first."

"That bad, eh? Memphis, when I let you come with me on that excursion into Root's house it was with the understanding that we would exchange information from now on. My editor is begging me for the last few chapters of the book."

"I didn't promise to exchange information on everything."

He grabbed her shoulders again, and Memphis knew he wanted to shake her.

"Look here, babe, you know better than to play games with me. This is a professional partnership we have going here."

She struggled to get free, but he held her tighter. "Number one, it's not a partnership of any kind, and number two, it's personal on my part, Jake, not professional. Big difference."

"What did you find, Memphis?"

"Let me go. This is not the time or place. Everyone will be wondering where we are."

"I'm wondering if you still taste the same." He pulled her closer and kissed her.

"Stop it, Jake. Let me go," she hissed.

"Tell me what you found, or I'll kiss you again."

Anger drove away the panic she'd felt building. "I'll tell you when I'm damned good and ready. Now let me go or I'll scream."

"You won't scream because you don't want anyone to know what's happening in here."

He kissed her again, this time so hard that the ridges of his teeth cut into her lip. She was so damned mad that all she wanted to do was knee him in the balls.

She lifted her knee, but he anticipated her action and barred it with his leg.

"I'll call Nelsey," she said softly, breathing into his face inches from hers. "I'll tell her I need help."

"Try it. I'll kiss you again. You used to love making love in out-of-the-way places."

His fingers bit deeper into her shoulders. He forced her closer, bending his head for another kiss.

"Let me go!"

"Let her go, Bishop," said Cutter, quietly.

They both jumped, startled by his presence in the kitchen, but Jake didn't release her. Memphis wondered how long Cutter had been there, and how much he'd heard.

Jake turned his head to stare insolently at Cutter, who leaned casually against the door frame.

"She's the mother of my daughter, Tate. I don't think she minds a kiss or two. This is none of your business."

"I've just made it my business. It's quite obvious that Memphis isn't interested in your kitchen lust."

There emanated from Cutter the feel of a lion about to leap on its prey, yet he leaned against the wall with his hands in his pockets, a lazy smile on his face, and a look of lethal stillness in his silver eyes. He intrigued Memphis, but frightened her. Everything about him signaled imminent danger. She wrenched herself free of Jake's hold.

"He's right, I'm not the least interested," she said to Jake, "and thank you, but I don't need rescuing, Cutter. I can take care of myself."

Cutter walked toward them, hands still in his pockets, and Memphis wondered if he hid clenched fists. Jake turned to confront him. The two of them faced each other, giving no ground. She could have cut the thick tension in the kitchen with the cake knife in her hand. She dropped it hastily on the counter.

"Stay the hell out of our lives, Tate," Jake ground out between clenched teeth.

"You stay the hell out of my life, and I'll stay out of yours," said Cutter, his voice lethal in its softness.

"Sorry, Cutter Tate, your life was destined to become grist for the mill when your grandfather murdered Sadie Maynard." Memphis saw muscles in Cutter's jaws bunch and knot, then smooth out. Jake continued relentlessly. "It didn't help when your father tossed you to the mercy of the town, and then cheated you out of Macauley's Mountain. Jesus, come to think of it, your life would make a great novel. Poor, unloved, rebellious rich kid, grandson of a murderer, comes home to do good deeds for town that cared for him, and to reclaim battered mountain land, but nobody really cared. Yeah, I think I'll write it someday. Make a mint."

"Jake! Stop this."

"I don't need rescuing either, Memphis," said Cutter, his voice a whisper, his eyes a deadly flat chrome color. He stood an inch taller than Jake, his form big, but pared lean and hard, hunched forward, his hands out of his pockets and fisted. But Jake gave not an inch. "Leave us, please."

"I won't leave." Frightened by the hate she felt emanating from Jake, and the violence about to erupt from Cutter, she tried to stay calm. "You're acting like children. The two of you have been sniping at one another all evening. If you *have* to fight, then go hurt each other somewhere else, not in my house, not around Katie."

At the mention of Katie, they both caved in a little. Cutter's shoulders relaxed, and Jake backed up a step.

"Where's that pie, Memphis? Do you need . . . ?" Nelsey had entered the kitchen, and quickly surmised the situation. In a grim voice, she said, "Don't know what's going on here, but you young men get holt of yourselves. Cutter, go outside. Take a fast walk around the house. Jake, never thought I'd say this to you of all people, but Katie needs tendin' to."

Cutter banged out of the house, and Jake went into the dining room.

"You okay?" Nelsey asked.

"Yes," said Memphis, with a sigh, "but I have a feeling that what just happened isn't finished."

"You're right. Knowing Cutter, it isn't."

Memphis spread the photos on her bed. Margo stared at them in shock. The black-and-white photographs from sixty years ago seemed grossly out of place in the homey bedroom. Women in various stages of undress and vulgar poses smiled at the camera. In others, naked men and women cavorted in sexual positions, seemingly unaware of the camera that caught them. A single head shot of their grandmother, which didn't seem to belong with the others, was part of the display spread on Memphis's bed.

The house was quiet, Katie asleep in the next room, Nelsey gone home. The fading aroma of cinnamon and turkey were the only reminders of the holiday. The two sisters had sequestered themselves in Memphis's room for a midnight chat.

"Great Christ, Memphis. This is disgusting. *Our* grandmother? A member of a secret sex organization? I simply refuse to believe it."

"I don't think she was, but unfortunately it confirms things Root told me that I chose to dismiss as an old man's dirty meanderings. Look at the tint of the photo, and the window behind her. Her picture was taken in a different location than the others. I think her picture here was meant to *imply* that she was a part of the lusty parties, or that Root, or whomever was the original owner of these photos, had a secret thing going for Sadie, and included this shot with the stack of nudies.

From what I can tell of detail in the background of the others, it looks like this party was held in the board-room of the old Root Bank Building."

"How do you know?"

"It's only used now for community meetings and such. I picked Nelsey up there one day. Her quilting group meets there once a month." She picked up one of the pictures. "See all this ornate molding around the ceiling, and the huge chandelier? That would have been very unusual and elaborate in a small town like this. I'm sure there wouldn't have been another room like this within a hundred miles. The newspaper gossip says Sadie was in the Root building on the night of the murder."

Margo studied the photos, frowning.

"Most of the men are older, except for this young man. He's in several of the pictures. Looks almost wild with sexual delirium."

"Yes. The spoiled twenty-year-old son of a wealthy man. Harvey Root, Jr. The owner of these pictures. The disgusting old man who keeps these locked in his desk drawer, and who told me that he'd only heard of the key club, but never attended. But this is the picture that disturbs me most."

She handed Margo a shot of a man whose back was to the camera. He sat in a chair fondling the breasts of a naked buxom woman who straddled his lap.

"Why is this one any different than the others?"

"Do you see the large mole on the back of his neck?"

"Yes."

"Look familiar?"

"Well . . . kind of."

Memphis produced the picture of Sheriff James Maynard she'd found in the attic. "This profile shot of Grandfather shows the mole."

"Great Christ, do you think he took part in this party?"

"Obviously he did. But I don't think it was a one-time party. One of the newspaper articles that I found mentioned rumors of a secret sex club that met twice monthly. Supposedly many prominent men were involved."

"But, Memphis, that means the highest law official in the county knew of and participated in the whole disgusting thing."

"Exactly."

"But why wasn't it played up more? I mean, this could have been a scandal of huge proportions."

"Because some member of the Root family ordered the newspaper to kill it, not pursue the story."

"Ordered?"

"Yes, ordered. Just like Cutter Tate ordered the editor of the newspaper to let me see the microfilm. Everyone in this town listens to two people. Cutter Tate and Harvey Root."

"Why?"

"Most of them are really fond of Cutter, but aside from that, I've discovered he's a powerful man. His grandfather left him a lot of land, and through the years he's bought up more and has established small manufacturing companies throughout the mountains. Something Black Brady has encouraged him to do. They both believe small business and manufacturing companies are the only salvation for these poor mining communities. He owns half the town. Root owns the other half, and the hospital, and the electric company, and the bank . . . and the newspaper."

"What do you think this has to do with Grandmother's murder?"

Her hand trembling, she handed Margo shots of two of the yellowing papers she'd photographed. One was a note, the other held a list.

"The list is names of women. Noted next to each name is a particular talent they were known for, such as dancing with veils, or foreplay. A couple of the last names I recognize from families who still live here. Nice, ordinary people. Look at the bottom of the list."

"Grandmother's name has been added. You can tell because the typewriter print is different. It's bolder than the rest."

"Exactly. As if it had been added in haste, or as an afterthought. And speaking of haste, I was so nervous about being in Root's house illegally that I didn't get the whole thing in focus. Look closer, down in the corner, and you can see what looks like the beginning of a list of male names, probably members of the club. I can see several names clearly. James McKay, Joe Franklin, Orville something."

Margo said, "Doesn't look like you were out of focus. Looks like it was a partially torn list, attached to the other. The rest of it's missing."

Memphis handed her the other print. "Read the note."

"'Sadie, Amos and I will pick you up behind the Root Building.' It's signed 'Mac.' My God, this indicates that Macauley Tate and Amos Washington were both involved in some way. So maybe Washington wasn't as innocent as you think."

"Maybe, or maybe it's just what I need to prove Tate's guilt. Thing is, we don't know when the note was written. It may have been written months before the murder, but it does mean that Tate and Washington were engaged in some sort of dealings with Grandmother."

"Aside from the nauseating fact that Root loves to get off on the loathsome treasures kept in his locked drawer, why would he keep the other things? The list and the note?"

"Blackmail. He had to have been blackmailing someone, and from the looks of it, probably our own grandfather. And maybe Macauley Tate. More and more, I find Tate the most likely murderer, and yet something is missing."

"I don't like any of this, Mem. It scares me to death. It's a shame you can't trust Cutter more than you do. I'll have to admit that he shivers me timbers, not because he seems evil, but because he's deliciously tempting. I'd beg him to put his shoes under my bed in a second. I don't know Root, but he sounds evil."

"He's evil, I sense it, I know it." She hesitated. "I haven't made up my mind about Cutter, but I know they're friends because Cutter takes him to lunch."

"You're up against too much, kiddo, and I can't stay here to help. I have to be in Houston on Sunday. Please, go home. Go back to Manhattan. As I said, all of this scares me, and is it worth it?"

"Yes. I came here with my wings broken, cowed by life and a bit frightened, pissed at Jake for telling my story, and with some sense of wanting justice for Grandmother and for Amos Washington. Also, I think my survival instinct told me to get off my butt, and move, get out of the shell I'd built around Katie and me, and the Sadie investigation was an excuse to do so. But now, I'm angry and getting angrier. I'm going to get to the bottom of this, no matter what."

Margo stared at her, her eyes filled with apprehension. "Oh, God, Memmie, I love you so much. You're all I have. Please be careful."

"Oh, turn off the drama, Margo. I'll be fine. My biggest concern is making sure Jake doesn't see these. It would make his book even juicier. I've got to get to the bottom of this before the book comes out."

§12§

Memphis and Margo piled their plates high with more turkey casserole and tuna noodle supreme. They plied Katie with green Jell-O filled with carrot slivers. The sisters, accustomed to the reserve of Episcopal churches, found this Saturday-After-Thanksgiving Social at Nelsey's Church of God a welcome change.

"Margo, I don't think I can eat another bite of this."

"Stuff it down," ordered Margo, "and go back for more. Whoever brought it will love you. I'm determined you'll make a friend or two. That's why I jumped at the invitation from Nelsey."

"I'm not going to turn the community my way by coming to one social and eating someone's tuna supreme."

"No, but it's a beginning. It's been fun so far, hasn't it?"

"Yes, it has." Memphis laughed. "I particularly liked when everyone turned to stare at your belting rendition of 'Old Rugged Cross.'"

Margo stuck her tongue out at Memphis. "It's the only way I know to sing."

"Oh, wonderful. Look who just came in."

Minnie Jo Dale pushed her father's wheelchair between the crowded tables.

"Who is it?" asked Margo.

"Harvey Root and his daughter, Minnie Jo Dale."

Margo glared at them, then grinned. "Dirty old man. He looks like an old bullfrog, and she looks like frog daughter who got kissed by the pig prince."

Nelsey came to take Katie to play with a group of children in the next room. As she wiped Jell-O from Katie's face, Memphis asked her, "Is Harvey Root a member of the church?"

"Nope. Harvey's an Episcopalian, but he attends everything that goes on in Yancey. Gets an invitation to everything and always goes. Some say it's because he hates Minnie Jo's cookin'. I say it's to keep an eye on everyone. Y'all be sure and have some of Elva's pound cake. Best thing here."

She hoisted Katie in her arms and left.

Margo went to get the cake, and Memphis watched Harvey and Minnie Jo as they moved among the crowd.

They were approaching her. The resentment she held toward the old man threatened to erupt in a ridiculous urge to scream at him. *Nerves. Why am I so nervous? Because, in spite of my bravado, I'm scared of him.* Harvey held up his hand, a sign for Minnie Jo to stop pushing the chair.

Memphis thought, *He might have the body of a frog, but he's got pig eyes.*

"Hello, Mr. Root."

"Hello, Miss Maynard. I see you haven't left town yet. Didn't know you were here for such a long stay."

"I didn't either, but I've grown to like it so much, I may stay permanently. I do own a home here, you know." *One of the few he doesn't hold a mortgage on. That ought to give him something to think about.*

"Yes. Sheriff Maynard's house. Things okay out there?"

"Of course, why wouldn't they be?"

"Someone told me they saw lights there in the woods where they shouldn't be."

Her heart stopped for a moment, then beat hurriedly on. Her house sat on ten acres, two miles from town. Had Nelsey told him about the lights, or has someone been hanging around the house near the woods at night? How else would Harvey Root know about the lights? Nelsey was closemouthed about all things. So Harvey Root must have someone spying on her, or he had ordered the light show himself.

"I have no idea what you're talking about."

His pig eyes, watery with age, narrowed.

"Those lights scare your daughter, Miss Maynard?"

"There are no lights."

"Hummph! Mothers today care nothing for their children. In my time, mothers took their children out of harm's way. Your mother wouldn't have stayed in a house with such things going on."

A stupid urge to hit him almost overwhelmed her and her hand fisted in anger. *Don't hit him, Memphis. He's threatening you, and he wants you to make a scene.*

She calmed herself, and didn't respond to his challenge.

"Excuse me, Mr. Root, Minnie Jo, I see my sister beckoning me." She couldn't wait to get away from them.

As she turned to leave, she heard him say, "Faith was a wiser woman than you."

Why did he persist in talking about her mother? God, what a hateful old man.

Margo handed her a plate stacked with pound cake, and said, "I can tell you're upset. We'll talk later."

Memphis watched Harvey and Minnie Jo as they moved ponderously through the room. They were either given a wide berth, or were approached with obsequiousness. They stopped at a table. Several women hurried about making space for them, and others went to get food for them from the potluck table. How odd, she thought, that around the Root table hung a stillness, while the rest of the room bustled with noise and activity. It was as if they carried with them a permanent pall of gloom.

Nelsey appeared at her side, and they watched as Harvey held up his hand and ordered everyone at the table to lower their heads in prayer.

"But everyone said grace before he got here," said Memphis.

Nelsey grimaced. "Harvey's a sanctimonious, condescending old man. One of those people who loves Jesus and hates everyone else."

Alison had passed the dilapidated shack many times on her way into Yancey, but had never been inside. After hearing Jake's taunt of Cutter during Thanksgiving dinner, she'd told Cutter she wanted to visit Ruby's before she went back to Charleston.

Cutter watched her face as they stood just inside the door. He tried to imagine the place as she would see it from her perspective.

It was Saturday night, but it was early so the place was fairly quiet. By midnight the music would be louder, the smoke thicker, and the language coarser. Eighty-year-old Ruby Barnes sat at the far end of the bar in the darker recesses of the place. A cigarette hung from her thin cracked lips, the smoke curling about her ancient face. He knew she had seen them when they first entered, and watched them intently.

Alison focused on the pool table. A young woman in stiletto heels, legs long and shapely, denim skirt short and tight, played an old miner. Everytime she made a shot she twitched her butt, and the circle of spectators laughed and nudged each other. But the scrappy old miner, intent on winning, knew he was up against an experienced player, and took care with each shot. Cutter wondered if Alison recognized Sally Junior, one of his neighbors.

"She's gonna beat the shit out of you, Claytie," one of the spectators yelled. Sally Junior winked at the cackling man.

"I'm starving. Would you like something to eat?" Cutter asked.

"Sure. A salad would be wonderful."

"Sorry. I'm afraid it will have to be something the short-order cook can do. Spec does a great job with hamburgers, or western omelets." He remembered then how assiduously she watched her weight, and wished he'd never mentioned food.

"Well, sure, why not. I haven't had a hamburger in years." *Good for you, Alison. You're a good sport.*

On their way to the bar, they passed booths filled with underage students. A boy blatantly massaged his girlfriend's breast as they French-kissed and groaned with agony over their newfound ecstasy. Alison's face pinkened, and her step quickened. On the small dance floor several couples danced dreamily to the Platters' "The Great Pretender." Red, green, and yellow canned lights played on their shuffling figures.

At the bar, Cutter indicated Alison should sit on one of the orange-Naugahyde chrome-trimmed stools.

"Hey, Spec," he yelled, and slapped the bar. "How about two hamburgers with everything?"

"Comin' right up, Cutter," yelled Spec from the short-order kitchen window.

"You grew up here, Cutter, in this place? I can't imagine it. I can't imagine anyone growing up here."

"Did I grow up here? Not entirely. I had semesters at several boarding schools, from which I was eventually thrown out and shipped home. Ruby or Nelsey took up the slack when I needed someone."

"Did you sleep here?"

"Sometimes. Ruby has a nice apartment upstairs. When I got older, I helped around the place, sweeping floors, doing dishes, tending bar, bouncing trouble-

makers." He laughed. "Ruby taught me how to iron.
One night after I'd thrown out a loudmouthed boozer
at three A.M., we ironed the clothes I took away to
college."

"Is Ruby here?"

"Yes." He knew Ruby wasn't ready to greet this
girlfriend of his. She was still estimating the worthi-
ness of Alison. She would make herself known when
she was ready. A spark flared at the end of the bar, as
Ruby lit another cigarette, but Alison didn't notice.
"She'll be along in a minute."

A splintered wooden sign hung askew behind the
bar. Orange hand-painted letters said "NO PEDDLIN',
NO POLITIKIN', NO PREACHIN'."

"Did Ruby paint the sign?"

"No, her dad did. He started the bar."

"Hey, Spec," yelled a patron at the bar, "I need a shot
of Wild Turkey."

"You'll have to wait 'til I finish Cutter's hamburgers."

"I thought the place had a beer-and-wine license
only," said Alison.

"It does."

"Doesn't she get in trouble?"

"Ruby's been in jail numerous times, but continues
to run the place as she pleases, law or not." Alison's
forehead creased in concern. "It's okay. We won't be
raided. The sheriff had her in jail last month, and will
probably leave her alone until next year."

"Hey, Spec, how about my Wild Turkey?"

A voice, indistinguishable as male or female, rusty
from age and whiskey, came from the end of the bar.
"I'll get it for you, Billy."

Ruby, dressed in jeans and a loose plaid flannel shirt,
emerged from the shadows, and went behind the bar.

"Who is that?" whispered Alison.

"That's Ruby."

Alison watched with great interest the arthritic yet

efficient movements of the old woman as she worked behind the bar.

Ruby gave Billy his Wild Turkey and then made her way to where Cutter and Alison sat. Her skid-marked face was immutable. Cutter knew that behind the unreadable face were wise thoughts and hard opinions reflecting a life with many heartaches. She ignored Alison.

He waited for her to speak first. She removed the dangling cigarette from her lips and stubbed it out in an ashtray.

"Thought you'd be up on Macauley's today, or finishing at Cat Teeth. You usually waste no time gettin' out of town the weekend after Thanksgiving."

"I have company this weekend. Alison's on her way back to Charleston, but she wanted to stop in and meet you." He introduced them.

"I see." She focused her sin-weary eyes on Alison. "Why would that be, missy?"

"I like to meet all of Cutter's friends. I've been told that you were kind to him when he was growing up."

"Kind, eh? That what you think? I suppose you could call it that. I'd say it was more like feeding a starving cat. Nothin' kind about it. Somethin' you just do."

Alison didn't quite know how to handle this blunt-talking woman, but she made a stab at it.

"Well, the young rebel turned into a nice man, didn't he?"

"Hah! Don't know him very well, do you, missy?"

"Well, I thought I did."

Alison grew more uncomfortable by the minute. None of her well-honed social graces would work here. Cutter frowned and wished Ruby would let up a bit, but he knew she was testing Alison in her own way and there was nothing he could do about it.

"You ever been around him when his back's to the wall? He's a mean son of a bitch."

"Don't you think any of us are when we're backed into a corner?" Alison, attempting a banal discussion with Ruby, was on losing ground. Ruby didn't *discuss* anything.

"Hey, will you two stop talking about me like I wasn't here?" he said, and forced a chuckle. "What am I, stale beer?"

Ruby had lost interest in Alison and said to Cutter, "Need some of your lawyer advice. Harvey's going after my mortgage again."

"Okay. I'll come by Monday and we'll talk. Wish you'd let me do what I suggested before."

"No." She placed her knobby hand over his, and he knew she wanted to give him a hug, but would show no affection in front of Alison. "Don't want that kind of help. I take care of myself, Cutter, boy. You know that."

She'd forgotten Alison, which meant that she had taken her measure and Alison had come up wanting, for the moment anyway.

"Hey, Ruby, turn on the TV. West Virginia–Syracuse game's on," yelled Billy.

"Hell, no, I want to watch the Florida–Florida State game," someone else yelled.

"Ain't no Florida game, Hank. Played last week." Ruby reached beneath the counter, flipped a switch, and behind the bar a big-screen TV came on.

Sally Junior settled herself on the stool next to Cutter.

"Hey, Ruby."

"Sally Junior, your dad had his lunch yet?"

"'Course he has. Don't be so snotty, Ruby."

Ruby lit another cigarette, and narrowed her eyes at Sally Junior.

"And don't you be talkin' to me that way. You may be twenty-five, but you're still a brat to me." Ruby drew deep on her cigarette. "Plenty of times you been here gettin' drunk and rubbin' your twat against some man—Jake Bishop lately—and your dad's been home with nobody to fix for him. It's your business, but you take care of Cle before you come here or I'll lock the door against you."

"Okay, okay." Sally Junior arched her body to reach for one of Ruby's cigarettes, rubbing her breasts seductively across Cutter's arm in the process. "Hi, Cutter. Heard the latest in Memphis Maynard's dumb investigation?"

"No."

Sally Junior lit her cigarette, tossed her hair back, and huffed the smoke toward the ceiling.

"Well, Nick said Memphis, her sister Margo, and Katie came in for pizza. While he was serving them he heard Memphis say that she was going to try and find the Chafin place on Twenty-Two. Said the Chafins had told her they might be able to show her a grave site or two near Chigger Holler."

"Well, I hope she finds their place," he said, trying not to reveal his immense interest in this information. "But I doubt it. Hell, I can hardly find it, and I know these mountains better than most."

"She and her husband ought to pay a mind to what they know best instead of messin' around in Yancey," said Ruby.

"Jake was never her husband," said Cutter shortly. Ruby looked at him oddly. "When is Memphis going to Twenty-Two?"

"Nick said she mentioned going tomorrow. She's waiting till her sister leaves, and she wanted to go before Jake got back from LA. Nick said she's kind of dumb because with the weather like it is, you never know when it's going to snow. But I think I'd be more worried about the mountain people that live back in those hollows. Hell, my daddy says some of them haven't come out of there in years and would shoot you soon as look at you."

Ruby slid their hamburgers across the glass-topped bar. Alison acted as if she wasn't quite sure what to do with it. Cutter lifted the top of her bun and poured mustard and ketchup over the meat patty, onions, and pickle.

"There you go."

She smiled at him, lifted the hamburger to take a dainty bite, and swallowed with effort.

Ruby observed all of this sourly, while Sally Junior hid a smirk and leaned over to flick an ash in the ashtray, taking advantage of the moment to rub her breasts across Cutter's arm again.

"Ain't got much of an appetite, do you?" asked Ruby of Alison. "Don't you like hamburgers?"

"I, uh . . . haven't had one since I was a teenager."

Cutter smiled at Alison as he prepared his own hamburger. "She's full of turkey and sweet potatoes. It's me that's hungry. She's just keeping me company while I eat. Right, Alison?"

Alison smiled wanly, trying to choke down another bite.

Respect for Alison began to dawn in Ruby's eyes, but his mind was elsewhere.

Damn Memphis. She said she could take care of herself, but she's going into territory, traditions, and behavior that she has no knowledge or understanding of.

Pretending to concentrate on his food, he ignored the hurried football play-by-play of the television broadcaster, the music from the dance floor, and the clack of the pool balls as they racked up another game. His mind was on Memphis.

He believed that she was tough, that she *could* take care of herself. He knew her well enough now to realize that if he hadn't been there that stormy night on Macauley Mountain she would have crawled off the mountain by herself, or found shelter of some kind.

But there was a sort of wounded vulnerability beneath all her toughness. His strong urge to be with Memphis, and to watch out for her, both irritated him and intrigued him. Why couldn't he just let her muddle through until she realized there was no mystery here? Then she would pack up and leave and he could relax.

Later, as he stood in Ruby's parking lot and waved good-bye to Alison, he still wrestled with his self-imposed dilemma. The area Memphis would be going into was not safe. Strangers had been known to disappear. He would go after *anyone* who went into Chigger Hollow by themselves, male or female. Most people had enough sense not to go alone.

"Maybe I'll call her tonight and talk her out of it," he muttered to himself.

No. Nelsey probably already told her not to go. Forget it. Go to the greenhouse and forget Memphis and Chigger Hollow.

§13§

Memphis stomped on the brake and jolted to a stop. Before her rushed a broad creek strewn with large boulders. She'd driven through several creeks on the trip up Twenty-Two to Chigger Hollow, and the Jeep had performed well, but this was no ordinary creek. This was almost a river. She'd figured that sooner or later she would have to leave the Jeep and walk. The dirt road had faded into a trail with potholes, and then into nothing more than a path, but she'd stayed with the Jeep as long as possible because of its warmth and protection. Tree branches had gouged its sides, and she dreaded inspecting the damage she'd inflicted on her trusty vehicle.

"Well, Memphis, ol' girl, guess this is it. Time for leg power. Wonder how the Chafins get across this creek? Must be a bridge somewhere."

Dreading the icy air, she zipped her parka up close to her chin, fastened the hood snug around her ears, and climbed out. She walked along the creek bank several yards in each direction but found nothing. Returning to the Jeep, she donned her backpack, which Nelsey had packed with a sandwich, an apple, and a thermos of hot coffee. Nelsey had made plain her opinion of Memphis's trip to the Chafins'.

"Shouldn't be doin' this. A damn fool notion. Old

man Chafin's as mean as they come. He'd as soon rip your gut with a huntin' knife as look at you."

"Why, he seemed like a nice man when I met him at the church," Memphis had replied, amused at Nelsey's fussing over her.

"That's 'cause he was at church. Besides, what kind of people are they, who worship snakes? Never have trusted them people."

"His granddaughter, Vanta Lou, was friendly. She gave me the directions to get there."

"Vanta Lou's a good person, the only decent one," grumbled Nelsy under her breath. "That's another thing. You'll probably get lost."

"Have a little faith, Nelsey."

Nelsey had sighed. "Guess I'll have to. I can see I'm not going to talk you out of it, so all I can do is pray."

Memphis drew the hastily written directions from her pocket, and the map she'd made for herself, and spread them on the hood of the car. The creek in front of her must be Up Run. Had Vanta Lou said anything about a bridge? She seemed to recall something about a raft. She couldn't remember, but there had to be a way, and she would find it. If this was Up Run, then it looked like she had one, maybe two hours of hiking ahead of her.

After a thorough search Memphis found a log raft tied and partially hidden beneath the drapes of an evergreen tree on the far bank of the creek. It was attached to a frayed rope and a pulley, which would bring it to her side. Looking around, she could see why the Chafins crossed here. This part of the creek was relatively free of boulders. It was a safe crossing if the water was calm. She eyed the rushing creek and the larger boulders downstream with trepidation.

Nothing to do but give it a try, Memphis. You've come this far. Can't stop now.

Several mighty tugs brought the raft to her. She climbed tentatively aboard, then grabbed the pole and jammed it into the creek bed. With her weight added, the raft gave a sluggish swing and headed down the creek despite its attachment to the fragile rope rigging. She grasped the pole and pulled with all of her might toward the opposite side. Slowly, the wildly swinging raft came around. Another pull, and she neared the center of the creek. Every pull practically wrenched her arms from her shoulders, but she ignored the pain, knowing this was the only chance she had of finding the Chafins. Two more pulls and she'd reached the creek bank.

She secured the raft to its mother tree and set off up a beckoning ravine.

The sun had burned away the early morning mist that she'd traveled through in the Jeep. The day was stinging cold and clear, with a vivid blue sky. Though winter had scalped the branches and hardened the root-gnarled ground, there was a dignified beauty in the starkness of the mountain landscape. Memphis stopped to rest on the fallen, rotting stump of a once mighty chestnut. She rummaged in her backpack and found the camera she'd stuck in at the last minute.

For a while she got lost in the joy of shooting nearby scenes, hoping to capture wonders cached by the remote forest and viewed by few human eyes: an evergreen split asunder by lightning, still living and green on one side, but brown and dead on the other; a large gray rabbit scurrying into the shelter of a mountain laurel; and the remains of a long-deserted lonely campfire circled with stones.

She reveled in the complete stillness, a quiet so deep she could hear herself breathe. Almost too still, she thought.

A bird song she didn't recognize sounded plaintively

in the barren forest. She listened for another call. It came, but sounded strange, off-key; the interval between notes seemed wrong. Packing the camera away, she shook off the feeling that she was being watched. After all, this wasn't the dense forest of summer. Except for patches of evergreens spotted here and there, there were shafts of light and space between the tall bare trees, and she could see the sky. There couldn't be anyone hiding, watching, tracking her. Could there?

Imagining things again, Memphis. This isn't the dark-room, or the ominous woods behind the house. This is an open forest.

Thirty minutes later she arrived at a rope bridge suspended over a deep gully. She deposited her backpack on the ground and sat on a flat boulder to contemplate this challenge. Massaging her aching knee, she tried to absorb the beauty of the rocky gully, but knowing she was going to have to cross the swaying bridge interfered with her appreciation.

In the distance, dogs bayed and she thought she heard a human voice. She checked her map and found her position not far from the Chafin place, which gave her the courage to attack the frail-looking bridge.

Knowing she would need every bit of hand dexterity, she removed with regret her warm, bulky gloves. Panic hit her halfway across the unsteady structure. She stopped, closed her eyes, and gripped the slippery handhold with all of her might. *Focus, Memphis, focus.* She opened her eyes, and, never daring to look down, hand by hand, step by step, finished her trip across the bridge. With a huge sigh of relief she arrived at the other side, stepped onto solid ground, and tried to forget that she would have to go back the same way she had come.

A lumpy young man, in filthy overalls and flannel shirt, emerged from the trees before her. Startled at his sudden appearance, she stood and stared for a moment, but finally recognized Vanta Lou's brother, Robert.

"Hello, Robert."

" 'Lo."

With a twist of his hand, he indicated she should follow him.

The baying of dogs grew louder as they walked.

The odor of dog excrement and pig slop almost made her gag as they entered a large clearing. A humble house on stilts, sagging and weathered gray with age, stood in the center. To the left were the stubbled remains of last summer's vegetable garden, and to the right sat a dilapidated chicken house surrounded by skinny chickens pecking irritably at the frozen yard. At the rear she saw a hog enclosed in a large pigpen. But dominating the scene, and deafening to the ear, were the brown-and-white coonhounds.

Reared up on hind legs, three dogs yelped wildly at a caged raccoon suspended ten feet high from a pole. Slobber flew from their yapping jaws, spotting the dirt-caked overalls of several men encircling them. Grandpa Chafin held a stopwatch and clicked it now and then. The helpless raccoon seemed frozen in place in his small prison

"What are they doing? Why doesn't someone let the raccoon down?" asked Memphis.

Robert didn't answer, just plodded past the men and toward the house. One of them, a big hulk of a man, gave her a toothless grin and ran a lustful look over her. The rest of them ignored her. Memphis saw Vanta Lou waving to her from the porch, three children clinging to her legs.

Vanta Lou wiped her hands on her apron and shyly shook hands with Memphis. "Pay the men no mind. They'll be done soon. They's trainin' some young howlers. Come in. I got tea all ready fer ya."

Inside of the house was one large central room, which held a small kitchen area, beds lined against bare walls, and table and chairs before a fireplace. Three doors led to smaller rooms around the living area. Closed tight against the winter, the house held cooking odors from several days; bacon, beans, turnips, and the musty smell of bedding that begged for a long-needed wash. Denim curtains at the windows, and a red-and-white patchwork quilt on a wall showed Vanta Lou's attempts to bring color and cheer to the dreary place.

Vanta Lou seated her before the fire. Memphis shivered with cold and exhaustion, but soon relaxed in the warmth of Vanta Lou's friendly welcome.

"You jest drink that chamomile now, and you'll be warmin' up real fast like. Couldn't decide whether you'd want vegetable soup or bean, so heated both. I hardly ever have company so it was right excitin' when I heerd you was comin'."

"I thought you told me that you didn't have a telephone."

"Oh, no, ma'am, we don't."

"How did you know I was coming?"

"Oh, we've known since before you hit Up Run. We have our own way of communicatin'. Through bird-calls, and sech. Word travels fast around here."

That explained her feeling of being watched, thought Memphis.

Two boys, who looked about eight and ten, hung on their mother's chair, and a toddler sat in her lap. They were silent, each of them with a finger in their mouth, their pale-blue eyes wide at the sight of the stranger in their midst. The little girl in Vanta Lou's lap looked to be Katie's age.

"What is your name?" asked Memphis.

"Take your finger out of your mouth and answer the lady." The child shook her head shyly. "Her name is

Opal Marie, and this here's Bobby, and this 'un's Elmurry."

"You named the young one after your great-aunt?"

"Yes. Wanted to honor her memory." She fingered the photograph hanging from her neck. "The spirits like it."

Memphis wondered again at the odd mixture of religious beliefs these people held. It seemed to be fundamental Bible-Christian faith mixed with Early American Indian spiritual beliefs, and a few ancient druid doctrines thrown in for good measure.

Thinking of her adventurous trek up here, she asked, "How do you get around without a car or truck?"

"We walk most places. That's why we only get to Yancey about twice a year. Wish we could get thar more often. The young'uns need milk, but I don't have no way of gettin' it."

Memphis made a mental note to get milk to these children somehow.

"But you couldn't possibly walk all the way to Grady to church."

"Oh, no, ma'am. We walk to the road and Preacher Elkins picks us up—when he remembers. Sometimes we wait for hours and then walk back home."

"He forgets to pick you up?"

"Yes'um. Preacher Elkins don't remember so good. Thinks he does, but he don't. Fact is, about the only thing he knows from day to day is his preachin' and the Bible. He remembers that he was a miner, and that he dug some graves, but that's about it. Aurianne is his third wife, but he thinks she's been with him from the beginning. He don't even remember burying his other two."

So maybe the grave-digging preacher did have knowledge of Sadie Maynard's burial site, but couldn't remember. A squiggle of excitement stirred in Memphis. This innocently given bit of information made the trip to Chigger Hollow worthwhile.

Grandpa Chafin came in, glowered at Memphis, and sat down in a rocker near the fire. He lit a clay pipe and stared into the fire.

"Git me some coffee, Vanta Lou," he said.

"Yes sir."

Vanta Lou stood Opal Marie on her feet and hurried to get a mug of coffee. She gave her grandfather his coffee, and then placed a steaming bowl of bean soup in front of Memphis. A fatty chunk of sideback resting in the center of the thin liquid repelled Memphis, but she forced herself to taste the soup. She didn't want to insult Vanta Lou's eager hospitality. She found the soup surprisingly tasty. The children joined her at the table now. Memphis watched as they dipped crusty chunks of stale bread into the broth, and then she copied them. Good hardy fare for a brisk December day.

"Granpa, Miz Maynard has come to find her grandmother's buryin' place. You got any notion of whar it might be?"

The old man said nothing for a long time.

"Granpa?" Vanta Lou prompted him.

"Cain't say as I recall no graves in Chigger Holler, 'ceptin' our own. Wouldn't tell her if I did. Ain't right to be disturbin' the dead. Best if she leaves soon as she eats her soup."

"Shame, Granpa. The good book says you be kind to yer neighbors."

"Ain't bein' rude. Bein' smart. Harlan is bringin' a box of snakes up the trail for takin' to church on Sunday. The vipers know if thar's a stranger around."

Vanta Lou got a worried look on her face. She explained to Memphis, "Harlan's my husband. Sometimes he finds snakes for Preacher Elkins. Preacher pays him good money for them." She turned to her grandfather. "It's not good, Harlan bringin' the snakes. You know they don't like bein' disturbed in the winter. They'll bite quick as anything."

Grandpa Chafin glared at his granddaughter. "You ain't strong in the faith, Vanta Lou. Ask the good Lord for forgiveness or he'll punish you."

A strained silence fell as Vanta Lou busied herself wiping the mouths of the children and Memphis finished her soup and bread. Grandpa Chafin fell asleep in his rocking chair.

Vanta Lou whispered to Memphis, "I know a cove down the mountain that's got funny-lookin' spots in the earth. I never felt right in the place. I'll take you thar after I get the little one to her nap."

Half an hour later, with Vanta Lou's two older children trailing them, the two women made their way into a secluded cove guarded by giant oaks and thick evergreens. Memphis inspected the spots mentioned by Vanta Lou, but decided with great disappointment that they were only odd fossil formations formed hundreds of years ago by some unknown animal.

"Wish I could be of more help, Miz Maynard, but I got to hurry back to the house. Granpa ain't no good at watchin' the baby if she should wake up."

"I understand."

Though disappointed, Memphis considered her trip a success. She had discovered that Preacher Elkins *might* have information that he just couldn't recall, and Vanta Lou, lonely for company, had enjoyed her visit.

As they made their way back to the house, Vanta Lou chatted eagerly, asking questions about what Memphis had seen on television lately, and had she ever been to a movie. They discussed the raising of children, and Vanta Lou said she wished her children could go to a real school. She told Memphis how she had walked five miles each way to school until eighth grade. That's why she was the only one in the family who could read. But that one-room school existed no longer. Vanta Lou would have to teach her children what little she knew.

Memphis decided to include paper, pencils, and books with the milk delivery. She snapped pictures of the children as they walked.

The house was in view now. A man, who must be Vanta Lou's husband, Harlan, worked in the pigpen, feeding the hog. In a far corner of the yard Robert fed the dogs. Nobody paid attention to the toddler who played alone on the porch. Opal Marie sat next to a wooden box and played with a brownish pink snake.

The snake wasn't happy. It jerked and writhed in the child's small hand, and Opal Marie laughed at its movements. Memphis heard Vanta Lou's quick intake of air, and her own breath caught in her throat.

"Ohh, no. Jesus, no. Opal Marie don't know about faith yet. The snake'll git her." She raised her voice. "Harlan, look to Opal Marie."

He couldn't hear her. "Robert, Robert, get to Opal Marie," she screamed.

Robert dropped his pan of scraps. He picked up an axe next to the woodpile and ran toward the porch. Running as fast as they could, Memphis and Vanta Lou watched in horror as the snake sank its fangs into the baby's leg. Robert reached the porch, and with a quick motion belying his seemingly slow-wittedness, he chopped the head off the snake.

As they ran, the scene unreeled in slow motion now to Memphis, as if time had stopped and wanted to be rewound again. She could only imagine the horror Vanta Lou must be feeling.

Grandpa Chafin emerged from the house, rubbing sleep from his eyes. As Memphis and Vanta Lou climbed the steps, Robert kicked the snake into the yard, and Grandpa Chafin picked up a sobbing Opal Marie. Harlan climbed the steps in two leaps to inspect the punctures near his daughter's ankle.

"Give her to me, Granpa," said Vanta Lou.

"No. I told you the stranger would cause trouble." He gripped the child to him and glared at Memphis. "Leave here, now! Iffn' you don't, I'll make sure you don't ever make no trouble fer anyone else no more."

"Granpa, Miz Maynard's bein' here did nothin'. Now give me the baby. I gotta tend to her," she said anxiously. "Harlan, I think I saw some rattlesnake plantain down by the creek. Run see if you can pull some, and Robert, find the kerosene."

"Anything I can do to help?" asked Memphis.

"Salt, I need salt. Elmurry, show Miz Maynard where the salt be. Granpa, give her to me. We'll take her into the house."

"Harlan, you stay put. You, too, Robert," said the old man, as he held the screaming, squirming child. "Me and God will heal this infant."

Memphis said to Vanta Lou, "The one thing I *do* know is that she has to be quiet so the venom won't travel to her heart so quickly, and you should tie a cloth above the wound, probably around her calf."

"Granpa, please, Granpa, jest let me hold her and rock her, an' it won't hurt to put some plaintain on it, and some kerosene and salt. It'll draw the poison."

The three men stared at Vanta Lou without moving, but from the corner of her eye, Memphis saw eight-year-old Bobby run toward the creek. Elmurry emerged from the house with a box of salt and a small bottle of kerosene and handed them to his mother. Memphis whipped off the silk scarf around her neck and reached to tie it around Opal Marie's leg, but the old man backed away. The child had grown quieter and her skin had taken on a bluish sheen.

"She's gettin' better already. Harlan, Robert, start yer prayin'. Stranger, you git. Vanta Lou, I'll let you rock her soon as the stranger leaves. I need to cast the demon out of this young'un."

Memphis wanted to stay, but she knew her presence agitated the situation so she turned to leave with great reluctance. She saw panic hit Vanta Lou's face for a moment, and then a look of decision.

"Stay put, Miz Maynard."

The mother walked quickly into the house and returned with a twelve-gauge Remington shotgun. Her mouth set with determination, she aimed the gun at the three men.

"I saw you load this gun with double-ought yesterday, Granpa, and you know I know how to use it real good, an' I have a feelin' Miz Maynard does, too. I heerd she's been in the wars. You hand Opal Marie to Miz Maynard, or I'll shoot your head off."

"Now looky here, Vanta Lou honey, there be no need for this," said Harlan.

"You shet up, Harlan. I'll hit you next, and then Robert."

Memphis could tell by the purple flush of Harlan's face that Vanta Lou shouldn't have talked to her husband that way. If he hadn't been on Grandpa Chafin's side, he sure was now.

Her mind raced to keep up with the dangerous situation. The child was obviously in need of professional medical care. As a mother, Vanta Lou instinctively knew that. Though Memphis shook with fear inwardly at the implications of what might happen here, outwardly she stayed calm. Vanta Lou and Opal Marie needed help.

A deadly silence followed as they all took stock of one another, the men and the sick baby on one side, the mother and her newfound friend on the other.

"Give Miz Maynard the baby, Granpa. If you don't, she kin catch her real quick as your head comes tumblin' off."

Everyone heard the fierce determination in her voice.

Grandpa Chafin, a look of utter hatred gleaming from his eyes, gave the child to Memphis. She placed the limp form on the slatted wood porch and swiftly knotted her scarf above the wound.

Bobby, out of breath and pale, had arrived with the rattlesnake plantain.

"Bobby, you rub some of that on your sistern's ankle," ordered Vanta Lou. "Elmurry, pull my hanky from my pocket, pour it with kerosene and salt, and tie it round her hurt."

The boys did as she ordered. Harlan made a move toward them, but Vanta Lou jerked the shotgun at him and he stepped back.

"Miz Maynard, pick her up. We're goin' to tek her to a doctor."

Grandpa Chafin, his eyes red with hate, shook a trembling finger at her. "You're a terrible sinner, Granddaughter. You'll burn in hell."

"If it'll save my baby, I don't keer, Granpa. I'm prayin'. I been prayin' ever since I seen the devil bite her. Sometimes *God* needs help, especially if it's a baby who don't know about faith, and I'm prayin' we reach the doctor in time." Never taking her eyes off the three angry men, Vanta Lou said, "You tek her and run ahead, Miz Maynard. I'll be right behind."

Memphis lifted the feverish child in her arms and ran toward the forest path that led to the suspended bridge. Behind her a blast from the shotgun shattered the remote mountain stillness. Fear pumped her heart and her legs, and her feet flew over the frozen ground.

* * *

Cutter puttered around the greenhouse. He knew he was "puttering," but he didn't care. It took his mind from other concerns.

He liked these early-winter weeks in his glassed enclosure on Macauley's Mountain. He could almost feel the rows of plants and seedlings hungrily soaking up the sunlight and the bright blueness that shone through the glass. Cutter liked to call it "mountain blue." Later, in February and March, he would ache to work outside with his land again, but for now the ground was too frozen to work with, so he spent his extra time here with the seedlings he would plant in the spring.

The glass had beaded with moisture from the warmth of the inside air. He inhaled the satisfying scent of rich, fertile earth, and the sweet aroma of a hosta lily that he'd nursed way past its prime. Gently, he dug up its bulb and hid it away in the burlap sack he used for storing bulbs.

The work at Cat Teeth was almost completed. One of his cleanup crews was finishing up the last of the earth camouflaging they could do before winter set in. He would inspect it later, but he had complete faith in them. Cat Teeth was the final job his company would do before next spring. His environmental cleanup firm, Tate's Environment Clean-Up—TEC, as it was known and incorporated—had become a hugely successful endeavor. He'd come back to Yancey to practice general law, with an emphasis on environmental concerns, but before he knew it his anger over the mistreatment of his own land and others had resulted in the formation of TEC.

His clients were varied: the state government, private mine owners who wanted no trouble with the EPA, and local communities anxious to repair the damage left by previous generations of mine owners. Pleased at the response to the services his company offered, he had soon become immersed in his mission and the work itself. For the last five years, he'd formed a satisfying pattern of directing TEC from April through November. December, January, February, and March were spent in his small law office on the square in Yancey, with stolen moments here on Macauley's, or at Uncle East's cabin on Catawba.

As he tucked the burlap bulb sack away for the winter, the velvet green of a partridgeberry plant caught his eye. He stopped for a moment to smooth a rich green leaf with his thumb. The green of Memphis's eyes. The plant was a creeper. He would plant it under some acid-loving shrubs next spring. Perhaps it would attract more birds. Early American Indian women had used its red, edible, berrylike fruit as an aid during childbirth. A chuckle escaped him as he thought of Memphis's indignation if he compared the green of her eyes to that of a partridgeberry creeper.

The smile faded as he finally succumbed to the worry he'd stemmed all morning. The thought of Memphis journeying alone across Up Run and into Chigger Hollow shook him to his boots. He knew little violence occurred in the back hollows anymore, but that was only because there wasn't much for the original mountain dwellers to get riled up about. Memphis had the questionable ability to stir up anything for the least of reasons. Disturbing a grave on land the Chafins or MacDonalds considered sacred would certainly be cause for trouble.

The Chafins were fairly safe these days, but their MacDonald cousins in the next cove were an ugly bunch to deal with. Vanta Lou Chafin was married to her cousin, Harlan MacDonald.

The anxiety he'd held in check since Sally Junior had mentioned Memphis's planned trip crawled around in his belly like the earthworms he'd just put in an empty coffee can. He couldn't stand it any longer and was overcome with a sense of urgency.

He scrubbed his hands clean, threw on his parka, and ran for the Range Rover. As he slipped the four-wheel drive into gear, the two-way radio crackled. He flipped the receiving switch and heard Nelsey's voice.

"Cutter, you there? Been lookin' for you everywhere."

"I'm on Macauley's."

"Good, then you're not far from Twenty-Two. Memphis has gone lookin' for the Chafins, and I can't help but be worried about her. Got any ideas?"

"Yeah. I'm already on my way."

"Thank you. She'll be mad you come after her, but I think it's for the best."

"I'll call you later."

Halfway up Twenty-Two, almost to Up Run Creek, Cutter screeched around a curve and met Memphis's Jeep tearing down the rutted dirt road. Her Jeep skidded to a stop, and he slammed on the brakes of his Range Rover. Memphis laid on the horn, motioning wildly out her window for him to move, get out of the way. The barrel of a shotgun emerged from the passenger window, and it looked as if the rear window had been shot out.

What in God's name had she gotten herself into now?

He got out of the Range Rover, heart in throat, and walked toward the Jeep with his hands over his head.

"Memphis, it's me."

Now he could see Memphis at the wheel, and Vanta Lou Chafin in the passenger seat. Their faces were white with strain. Vanta Lou kept the shotgun aimed at Cutter's chest, never wavering for a moment.

He heard Memphis say, "It's okay, Vanta Lou. Put the gun down."

When he reached Memphis's window, he saw that she gripped the steering wheel so tightly that her fingers were striped red and white. The two women, and a young boy in the backseat, were breathing heavily as if they had run a long way. The boy's face was paper white. He held an obviously ill child in his arms.

"Cutter, move your Rover. We've got to get this child to a doctor."

"What happened, Memphis?"

Vanta Lou said breathlessly, "Mister, if you ain't goin' to help us, then git out of our way, or I'll cut you down like I did Granpa. My baby here is snakebit."

"What kind of snake?"

"Copperhead."

"Is someone following you?"

"They were. They ain't now."

From where he stood, he could see blotchy marks under the baby's skin, which he knew wasn't good. Time was a critical factor now. She seemed too quiet, probably in shock. He made a quick decision.

"Vanta Lou, put the gun down. Get in the backseat and take that nasty-looking rag off the wound." He pulled his penknife from his pocket and tossed it to her. "Make an incision right above the fang marks, then suck the blood a few times and spit it out quick. It'll help some. Memphis, move over. I'll back the Range Rover into the bushes and be right back."

"I can take care of this," she said defiantly, a wild look in her eyes.

He realized then that Memphis was in shock, too.

"I know you can," he said calmly. "But I have resources you don't have."

"Tell me," she demanded, still defiant, as if Vanta Lou and the baby were her sole responsibility and be damned if she'd let anyone interfere with their salvation.

"My hangar is twenty minutes from here. I can have

the baby at the poison control center in Charleston forty-five minutes from now."

Wisdom overtook her sense of responsibility.

"Okay, let's go," she said.

He ran for the Range Rover, thanking the sense of urgency that had brought him here.

§ 14 §

Cutter spoke quietly into the phone.

"No word on the baby's condition yet. I'll call you as soon as we know anything."

"Is it bad?" asked Nelsey.

"It's not good. The doctor told me she has a twenty percent chance of making it."

"Lordy."

"Send Leroy up Chigger Hollow to see how bad Grandpa Chafin is hurt, and to make sure the other boy, Elmurry, is okay."

"They're not goin' to be wantin' help."

"I know, but Vanta Lou shot her grandfather in the leg, and she's worried about him."

"You think Leroy should take the sheriff?"

"No. This is a family matter, and having the sheriff there will make it worse. They're comfortable with Leroy. He can handle Harlan and the other MacDonalds should they be there."

"How's Vanta Lou, and Memphis?" asked Nelsey.

"They've tried to get Vanta Lou into the emergency room waiting area, but she won't go. Sits on a bench next to the alcove where they're working on the baby, holding Bobby, praying. They've never flown before, or been in a hospital, or even been out of Yancey for that matter. Scared to death. Won't look at or talk to anyone but Memphis."

"And Memphis?"

He glanced out of the phone booth. Though he kept a close eye on Vanta Lou and Bobby, making sure they were well taken care of, he always knew where Memphis was. His mind and body honed in on her presence automatically, like a homing pigeon. She leaned against a far wall, away from the action in the busy corridor, her back to them, her shoulders hunched. The red of her jacket made a hot splotch against the clinical lime green wall.

"She's okay. She's in some sort of shock herself. The emotional impact of the last two hours just hit her, I think."

"She's not as tough as she puts on."

"I know. But she sure came through for Vanta Lou and the kids. If it hadn't been for Memphis, I don't think the baby would have made it."

"I do believe you had something to do with that too," Nelsey said dryly. "Take care of her."

"Exactly what I plan on doing."

They said good-bye, and his eyes found Memphis again.

Her shoulders were shaking. She was crying, and his reaction shocked him. It was as if someone had sliced him from head to toe, yanked his organs free, and exposed his tough but bleeding hide for all to see. He placed the receiver back on its cradle and emerged from the cubicle.

He knew instinctively she would resent his intrusion, that she would resent his discovery of her vulnerability, but he didn't care. He only knew he had to comfort her, had to take away some of the hurt. He stood behind her, sensing her fragility, which was like that of a frightened fawn.

"Memphis?"

She didn't turn around or acknowledge his presence. He looped his arms about her bowed shoulders and

without speech or preamble pressured her carefully
back toward him.

She stiffened, but soon leaned against his chest with
what sounded like a sigh of relief. The crown of her
head fit neatly beneath his chin.

Memphis's hair felt like strands of fine silk against
his face. The antiseptic smells around him evaporated
as he surreptitiously buried his nose in her hair and
inhaled the light scent of her: a breath of her Joy
mingled with a touch of the woodsmoke she must have
picked up from the Chafin cabin. He delighted in the
feel of her against him. The length and width of her fit
him perfectly.

"Would my handkerchief do, or would you prefer a
Kleenex from the nurses' center?" he asked softly.

"I don't know what you're talking about. I'm not
crying."

He turned her around to face him. She glared at him,
her eyes filling and brimming over with tears even as
she denied them.

"It's okay, you know. You're allowed."

"I never cry."

"Seems like 'never' just happened."

He took his handkerchief, a gift from Nelsey every
Christmas, from his pocket and gently blotted her face
dry. Beneath the wetness lay the faint freckles that
seemed to pop out when she was upset. He wanted to
kiss each and every one of them, but knew she wouldn't
permit that. After he'd dried her tears, he gathered her
to his chest and tucked her head beneath his chin. She
kind of sighed into him, as if she was willing to let go
for this one moment.

"I'm sorry," she said into his chest. "This isn't like
me. I've been shot at before, but I've never seen such
hatred directed at someone's own flesh and blood.
Grandpa Chafin and Harlan acted like they really
wanted to kill Vanta Lou. They chased us. Vanta Lou

shot at them. Harlan was shooting at us. Running with Opal Marie's limp body in my arms, with gunfire all around me, flashed me back to Sarajevo . . . and I almost lost it. I don't know how we got to the Jeep in one piece. It was surreal, like a scene from a grade-B movie."

"The Chafins and MacDonalds have always been rabid in their religious beliefs. Vanta Lou broke an even stricter law though. She disobeyed the men in the family, and that's worse than not obeying God."

She shuddered.

It was then that Cutter knew he was lost, lost in the paradoxes of Memphis Maynard: her fragility versus her strength, her vulnerability versus her courage, her wild intensity versus her gentleness. She intrigued him beyond measure and he knew he had to have her, had to explore every part of the slender body in his arms, had to delve into the beautiful soul he glimpsed within. If he could have his way, he would lift her in his arms right now and race as fast as he could to a remote part of the earth where no one existed but the two of them. He didn't know if this was love because he didn't know what love was, but he didn't care. Whatever it was, no one else had ever entranced him so. No other woman had ever filled him with so much longing, a longing to *know* her as the Bible implied, and a longing to search the depths of her secret joys, fears, and dreams.

Her breath came in short bursts, and she shifted her weight from one leg to the other. He remembered then that she had run a long way on a weak knee carrying a toddler. He set her away from him, but held tight to her shoulders.

"Look at me," he demanded. "Does your knee hurt?"

He saw the pain lining her eyes, and the whiteness about her mouth.

"Yes, I guess it does. I forgot about it." She shrugged off his hands.

"You need medical attention, too."

"I don't. I'm fine." She stepped away from him with resolution, and he knew she'd recovered her equilibrium. There would be no more coddling of Memphis Maynard this evening. "I want to see how Vanta Lou and Bobby are doing. They're probably hungry."

"I brought them sandwiches, coffee, and some milk. The food is sitting on the bench untouched. They don't want anything. They're praying."

She studied him curiously. "You sound as if you don't believe in praying."

He shrugged, trying to keep the bitterness out of his reply, but not quite succeeding. "Like Huckleberry Finn, I prayed once and nothing ever came of it."

"Sometimes heaven answers prayers in odd ways."

"And maybe God is a fool's notion made up by those who need a safety net."

"Don't we all need a safety net sometimes?"

"Look around you. Has God helped any of these hurting people?"

"I can't believe you've spent so much time with Nelsey and not been influenced by her faith."

"Nelsey tried, but by the time she got to me I'd been pretty well indoctrinated with . . . hate." How had he gotten into such a personal and revealing conversation with her? Few people knew how he felt about religion. If he wasn't careful he'd end up spilling his guts to her, something he detested in others. "I see the doctor heading Vanta Lou's way. Let's see how the baby's doing."

Vanta Lou had risen from the bench, still clutching Bobby. Cutter put an arm around the fearful mother. She almost bobbed in reverence to the authority figure in white who stood in front of her.

"Your child is going to be all right, Mrs. MacDonald. We were able to inject enough serum to prevent any permanent damage, but just in the nick of time. A few more minutes and it would have been too late."

Vanta Lou grabbed his hand and kissed it. The young doctor blushed bright red. "Kin I take Opal Marie home now, Doctor?"

"No, ma'am. She'll have to stay for a few days. We'll have to monitor her progress, make sure the venom didn't affect her heart."

Vanta Lou chewed her bottom lip, and looked worriedly at Bobby.

"Doctor, I don't have no money. Don't have money to pay you or to stay anywhar."

"Don't worry about a place to stay, Mrs. MacDonald. You can stay right here in the hospital with the baby. We'll fix a place for you."

Gladness flooded her face and she squeezed Bobby to her side. "What about my young'un here?"

"Well, uh . . . the rules . . . children aren't allowed. . . ," the doctor floundered.

Cutter said, "Don't worry, Vanta Lou, we'll make sure Bobby is looked after."

"But how will I pay these people?"

"Don't worry about that. We'll talk about it later."

"Don't want no charity, Mr. Tate."

"I know you don't, but all you need to think about right now is Opal Marie. Let your neighbors be neighborly. Let us help you for the time being. You just do what the doctor tells you."

"I'll get a hotel room and stay here with Bobby," said Memphis.

Cutter knew how much Memphis hated being away from Katie. Her offer was magnanimous.

A nurse approached them. "Mr. Tate, a phone call for you."

Cutter left Vanta Lou and Bobby in Memphis's care and went to the nurses' station. Birdy's anxious voice chimed in his ear.

"Cutter, I declare, you'd think you'd let a body know what's going on."

"I didn't think I had to give you my schedule everyday, Birdy, love," he replied, amused, but at the same time irritated.

"Don't be sarcastic, Macauley 'Cutter' Tate," she replied indignantly. "If I hadn't come to visit Nelsey, I'd never have known what happened to that poor baby."

Cutter wondered when Birdy had ever cared about the Chafins or MacDonalds before, or even knew them.

"Let me speak to Nelsey."

He updated her on the situation.

"Sounds fine, but I wonder if Memphis forgot she promised to take Katie to a Christmas party tomorrow. Katie's been talkin' about Santa Claus all day. How about if I send Birdy to take care of Bobby?"

"Good idea. What would I do without you, beautiful?"

"Oh, hush." There was a pause, then she said, "I love you, Cutter."

"I know you do. Thank you." He'd never been able to tell Nelsey, Ruby, or anyone else in Yancey how he felt about them. He wished that he could, but the words always lodged in his throat. He never knew what to say.

Memphis, Vanta Lou, and Bobby were sitting on the bench again. Memphis held Vanta Lou's hand as they talked.

"Birdy Harless is coming to stay with Bobby, Vanta Lou," said Cutter.

"Oh, Mr. Tate, I don't know how to thank you." Her worn, once-lovely face, lit with gratitude. "You and Miz Maynard saved my baby's life, and I'll pray fer you every blessed day."

"The look on your face is thanks enough for me," said Cutter.

"Me, too," said Memphis, "but Cutter, there's no need for Birdy to come. I'm already here."

"Did you forget about the party you promised to take Katie to?"

"No, but I thought Bobby needed me more," she said, a stricken look in her eyes. "Nelsey can take her."

"I thought you wouldn't mind if Birdy came to watch Bobby. It's already been arranged."

"Thank you, Cutter."

"You need to be with your young'un, Miz Maynard. Don't know who this Birdy person is, but if she's friend to Mr. Tate then I know she's safe."

The doctor came to escort Vanta Lou and Bobby in to visit Opal Marie.

Cutter glanced at his watch. "Birdy should be here in about an hour. We'll stay until she comes, then head home. I wish you'd have that knee looked at while we're waiting."

"No, but I could use some Advil."

At Cutter's request, a nurse soon arrived with the painkiller. Memphis swallowed it, and sank back on the bench with her eyes closed. Cutter drank black coffee and sat beside her, aching to gather her in his arms and soothe away all the hurt and weariness. But he knew the intimate moment that had occurred between them previously had been an anomaly. He'd caught her at a vulnerable time.

There will be other moments, he promised himself. Not moments of weakness, but a time when she would come to him willingly. *Someday, Memphis Maynard, someday.*

Memphis relaxed into the hypnotic state the steady drone of the airplane induced. Her desire to resume the light doze she'd enjoyed on the hospital bench was gone. The night was too beautiful to miss.

Cutter had explained that the Beechcraft Staggerwing they flew in, one of three of his vintage collection, had been designed to waft 1930s executives about the countryside, and was the Learjet of its day. The cockpit was small but comfortable.

In complete contradiction to the traumatic day she'd gone through, the night was still and hushed. Faint lights glowed on the instrument panel, otherwise the only illumination came from the myriad of distant stars spread like brilliant diamond chips against dark blue velvet. A light snow had fallen in the hours since they'd left Yancey, and beneath them swoops of alabaster hills and valley lay in blue-white serenity.

Spellbound, Memphis felt suspended in a state of wonder. The surrounding blackness was protective and private, creating a sense of oneness with the universe and the man sitting next to her. Cutter hadn't spoken since they'd taken off. She knew without asking that he, too, floated in mystical awe of the night. She understood his love of flying. The grandeur of the hushed, reverent blackness drew them together, two kindred souls in a complete state of mergence with one another and the universe.

Cutter reached over, took her hand, and brought it to rest on his thigh. Smiling in the darkness, she welcomed the firm warm hand covering hers. Remembering his holding her hand during the storm, she knew that had been for reassurance, while this was a recognition of an ancient linkage too primal to be described.

Despite her initial reluctance to be drawn into such a feeling of intimacy with Cutter, the pull, the enchantment of the night was irresistible. She'd given in to it as soon as they were aloft. The luminous stars, so close, yet so far, beckoned them onward, urging them to leave behind all those matters that waited beneath them on the earth. Profound bliss, which Memphis instinctively knew occurred rarely in a lifetime, filled her, and she floated with the sensation. She wanted it to go on forever, wanted to fly on forever, never touching land, never coming back. She knew this magic night would be an integral part of her soul, always.

Gradually, though, Cutter's strong male presence intruded on her reverie, and her feelings of peace began to erode.

He must have worked in his greenhouse this morning, because a whiff of fertile earth reached her, probably from his boots, and then she breathed in the clean smell of fresh-laundered shirt. Somewhere during their journey together through this long emotional day, Cutter had made time to change shirts. Her nostrils quivered like a mare in heat catching the scent of her stallion. His hand on hers, which at first had made her feel secure and given her a sense of sharing the night, now sent tremors through her arm. Through the rough fabric of his khakis the sculpted lines of his sinewy thigh muscles heated her palm. Every time he moved his foot or leg to work a pedal, his muscles bunched and rippled, and the soft, supple, inner portion of her thighs tingled with each of his movements. She thought about removing her hand from his, but didn't want him to know the spell was broken and she'd lost her composure. Her blood raced unreasonably, and butterflies danced crazily in her stomach. She sat very still, willing these intrusive physical sensations to disappear. But her nostrils flared as she caught the aroma of his musky aftershave, and the tingling in the soft flesh of her thighs moved up into the private center of her, moistening, warming, and betraying her.

She was lit with wanting, stretched with sexual tension, and it embarrassed her. In such a small, intimate space, Cutter must sense what was happening. She slipped her hand from beneath his and folded it primly with the other in her lap.

From the corner of her eye, she saw Cutter smile.

"We'll be landing soon," he said, breaking the silence.

"Leroy put flares out for us. Look, you can see them in the distance."

The flat top of Cat Teeth, which Memphis now knew Cutter owned and used for a landing strip, lay ahead of them. Tiny blinking lights formed a rectangular landing pattern.

Five minutes later they were down, and Leroy was helping her out of the plane. The wind blew sharp and bitter cold, nearly knocking her off her feet, and she marveled at Cutter's skill in landing the plane in the stiff breeze. The jacket she'd donned early this morning was inadequate for the winter blast. Old Man Winter had arrived with the snow and decided to settle in.

"Everything okay up at the Chafins', Leroy?" Cutter asked, raising his voice over the wind.

"Yeah, Granpa and Harlan are mad as hell, but they'll be thinkin' better by the time Vanta Lou gits back thar. Granpa's got some double-ought in his shin. Aunt Gracie MacDonald took right good keer of it. He won't be able to walk for a few weeks, but he'll be fine."

"Good."

Jimmy, the eager young man who lived near the hangar and took care of Cutter's planes, came into view.

"Hey, Jimmy. Just taxi it into the hangar and we'll clean her up in the morning."

"Yes, sir."

Cutter took Memphis by the elbow. "Your Jeep is parked over here. I'll drive you home."

"That's not necessary. Didn't Leroy bring your Range Rover down from Chigger Hollow?"

"Yes, but I don't want you driving down the mountain in the dark. Leroy says the roads haven't been cleared yet."

She bristled at his commanding tone but recognized the wisdom in his decision. She hadn't driven on snow-packed roads in a long time. She nodded her head, but shook her elbow from his grasp and went on ahead of him.

Halfway across the wind-driven, snow-covered field, her knee gave way. Her body lurched wildly as she struggled to regain her balance. Cutter grabbed her jacket from behind to hold her erect, and then swung her around to catch her close.

"You okay?" he asked.

"I'm fine."

"I don't think so. Your knee must hurt like hell, and you're shivering."

She tried to pull away from him, but he opened his roomy lush leather jacket and drew her inside, enclosing her safely within. For a second, she thought about beating on his chest and demanding he let her go, but then gave into the delicious sensations his heat created. *How wonderful you feel, Cutter Tate. How beautifully, wonderfully safe and strong. A haven, perhaps, or more, a place to get lost in and stay lost. A place to run away to and enjoy with abandon.*

He stroked her hair, and she looked up at him. They studied each other, incapable of looking away. Memphis wanted to say something to break the spell he was weaving, but didn't trust her voice to come out evenly.

Bending his head, Cutter kissed her with breathtaking lightness on the mouth. She trembled, rooted to the spot, afraid to move for fear she would collapse. He kissed the tip of her nose, then his strong, sensual mouth moved hungrily over her lips.

He lifted his mouth from hers, brushed her hair gently away from her face, and slowly placed a series of downy kisses from the corner of her mouth to her temple, on her brow, into her hair, then her eyes. The touch of his lips on her skin ignited shocks of sensation throughout her body. He found her mouth again, and she marveled at the warm sweetness of his tongue and the stirring passion it created. Voluntarily, she lifted her arms and put them around his neck as if it was the most natural action in the world. In a mesmerizing trance, she felt lost in a heaven similar to the one they had shared in the sky.

He took his mouth from hers and held her tight against him, pressing her face into his chest. Lowering his chin, he buried his face in her hair and rocked her back and forth. A faint groan escaped from deep within him. He kept her close with one strong arm, and cradling her head with his other hand, kissed her again. Deeply this time. Deep and rich and demanding. His firm mouth took command of hers, moving about, insistently asking for a response. To Memphis's amazement her lips opened generously as his tongue entered her warmness to explore, then tenderly caress.

The frozen core within her that kept at bay all the hurt and danger in the world began to melt. The thaw rippled slowly, languorously through her veins and then into her stomach to throb there restlessly. Breaking forth, the ripple became a river, and the grand sensuality ran free in her limbs, her breasts, and her heart. With giddy delight, her body trembled with passion and a swift hot wanting. She'd been kissed a thousand times, but never with Cutter's seductive confidence and searing sexual rawness. Never had the touch of lips and the hard curve of an arm plumbed the depths of her and created such profound desire.

At length, he released her, but she had to hold onto him for support. Her fingers unfisted his shirt, and her palms smoothed illicitly along the strong, healthy cordage of his ribs and chest muscles. She found them firm and reassuring, but it seemed a delectable map she'd explored before. Her lips burned to touch his bare skin and suck the dark-brown nipples she knew were there. Afraid of this sudden knowledge and hard wanting, she grabbed hold of his shirt again and looked up to find him gazing at her in wonder.

Returning to earth and the reality of the dark, cold night around them, they stood and breathlessly explored the face of the other.

"Well, well," he said softly, "what have we here? The beginning or the end of something? I like it, whatever it is."

The chill wind hitting her face brought Memphis into focus. The situation was impossible. She suspected this man's family of evil, of committing murder against one of her own. And though at times she felt she'd known Cutter forever, she really knew little about him except for what lay on the surface.

"Cutter, this isn't a good idea." Almost choking on her words, hating them, she tried to pull away from him, but he held her fast. "There's too much history between us, too many questions unanswered."

"What we're feeling just now isn't history, or questions, or answers. What we're feeling is happening now."

"What we're feeling is full-blown lust."

A fleeting smile caught his lips. "Memphis, what if I told you that I *know* Grandfather didn't murder Sadie?"

"I would say, because you loved him dearly, that is what you want to believe."

"So you're going to let this obsession of yours come between us?"

"It isn't an obsession, Cutter. It's a quest for the truth. And it will always stand between us, a barrier I can't scale even if you can."

Something hard and implacable crossed his face, and he released her abruptly.

"You're wrong, but that's your problem, and I'll let you solve it. Trust shouldn't have to be earned. Trust should just be there."

He's wrong, thought Memphis bitterly, *but he'll have to learn that for himself.*

Memphis wakened terrified from the fog of a dream too dim to remember. The scream again, but by this time she knew it wasn't herself screaming, and it wasn't coming from the woods. It was a recurring nightmare, and though she almost expected its appearance now and again, she could never rid herself of the abject terror it generated. It had come the first night she was in Yancey, and several times since. In the dream, she heard someone screaming, someone she was trying to help, but she couldn't get to them in time. In time for what, she asked herself?

The whistle of the coal freight lumbering through the middle of the night sounded in the distance, and seemed to signal that all was well.

Too weary to think about it all now, she nosed into her pillow and sank back into sleep. Her last thoughts were of Cutter's lips against her temple.

Katie wakened her in the morning, tumbling all over her bed like a puppy. Miss Priss soon joined their hugging and loving, jumping from Memphis to Katie and back with carefree abandon.

"Where was you, Mommy?" asked Katie, who was beginning to make whole sentences. "We s'pose a go to a party today."

She giggled as Miss Priss licked her ear.

"I was with a sick little girl about your age, and then I was flying in an airplane."

Katie's eyes widened at these pieces of information. "Little girl sick?"

"Yes, but she's fine now." Memphis hugged her then tucked her beneath the blankets, wincing at the ache yesterday's adventure had left in her knee. "And you and I are going to a party today. Are you ready to tell Santa Claus what you want for Christmas?"

Katie, not quite sure what all of this Santa Claus stuff meant, nodded cautiously.

Nelsey called from downstairs to tell them breakfast was ready.

Later, she helped Nelsey clean up the kitchen, then busied herself with phone calls to New York concerning a coming exhibit of her work at the Museum of Modern Art. She called Charleston to see how Opal Marie was doing. Birdy told her that Vanta Lou, Opal Marie, and Bobby Chafin were doing fine. Cutter had visited the hospital early that morning. He had convinced Vanta Lou that she and the children should stay there a few more days and give Grandpa Chafin time to cool off.

Plans to develop more pictures today evaporated. She found it more and more difficult to go into the darkroom. The damp cold had become a seeping chill that stayed with her hours after she left the place, and she continued to feel as if she wasn't alone in the small black space.

The emotions of yesterday still haunted her. She remembered with gratitude Cutter's quick response to the emergency, and the way he'd taken over with calmness and certainty, but not bossiness. His tenderness with Vanta Lou and the children had impressed her and shown her a side of him she'd never seen before. At the hospital, her inclination to fold into his protective arms on a permanent basis had seemed natural. Very natural. She had to admit that being in Cutter Tate's arms on a permanent basis no longer seemed so strange.

But this bothered her, and she was restless.

She wanted to forget about the Chafins for a while, and she particularly wanted to forget about Cutter's searing kiss and the tempestuous way she had responded. A strong physical sense of Cutter stayed with her. Just thinking of his mouth, the way his bottom lip dipped a bit at the corners, and the urge to kiss the crease in his chin, made her blood run fast and hot.

She needed to be busy, and Katie's party at the church wasn't until this afternoon.

"Nelsey, do we have the makings for a Christmas fruitcake?"

"Yes, I was plannin' on doin' some bakin' tomorrow. You want to help me?"

"No, I know I'm not the greatest cook in the world, but fruitcake is one of my specialties. I'm going to make one this morning."

Nelsey looked at her with major skepticism.

"You sure about this?"

"Honest. It was the one thing Faith let us help her with. She said nothing tasted as good as a West Virginia fruitcake, and that we should know how to make one. Margo and I got pretty good at it."

"Okay, but if you need any help, jest ask."

Nelsey showed her where everything was, and Memphis started to work, happy for something to do that didn't involve Sadie, or Cutter Tate.

She chopped and sliced candied pineapples, cherries, and citron, then measured out raisins and currants, humming as she worked. Katie played with Tupperware lids beneath the kitchen table. Miss Priss curled up in the winter sunlight on the windowsill, a ball of shiny black against the snowscape outside. Nelsey looked out of sorts hanging around watching nervously, so Memphis assigned her to beat the eggs and grate orange and lemon rind. Memphis sifted flour, sugar, cinnamon, and nutmeg together, humming louder as she went.

"Didn't know you knew any hymns," said Nelsey, looking at her in an odd way. "Where did you hear that one?"

"What do you mean?"

"That tune you're hummin'."

Memphis looked at her questioningly. "I've been humming a hymn?"

Nelsey hummed a few bars of the song Memphis kept hearing on the wind.

"I must have been doing it unconsciously. It has a name?"

"Sure. 'What a Friend We Have in Jesus.'" Then she sang a few bars. "'What a friend we have in Jesus, all our sins and griefs to bear. What a privilege to carry everything to God in prayer.'"

Weak in the knees, Memphis sank into a chair. "I didn't know it had a name and words."

"What's the matter? You're white as a sheet."

"Nelsey, I would have told you only I was afraid you would think I was crazy. I've been hearing that tune ever since I arrived in Yancey. At first I thought it was a trick of the wind, but then I started hearing it in the house, particularly in the darkroom. I finally decided it was just a peculiar way the wind was sifting through the valleys before it reached us here on the hill. Then I thought I must be dreaming, like the scream I told you about that I hear sometimes, but the scream and the song never come at the same time."

Nelsey's face had turned pale now and she sat in the chair next to Memphis.

"Wish you'd told me these things sooner." She grimaced. "Some things you should know. One of the stories told about the buryin' of Sadie Maynard says that the men diggin' her grave heard a woman hummin' that hymn. As far as the darkroom is concerned, another rumor has it that Sadie was found murdered here in the basement of the house and carried to Twenty-Two Mountain later."

"Oh, God, Nelsey, am I being haunted by my own grandmother?" she whispered. "I don't believe in ghosts, but some strange things have been happening."

"Like what?" asked Nelsey tensely.

"When I'm in the darkroom I always feel as if someone is in there with me."

"Does the presence feel good or bad?"

"Neither good or bad, but I get these intense feelings of incredible sadness. I can barely breathe sometimes, and have to finish my work quickly and get out of there. Nelsey, wouldn't I know if it was my grandmother?"

"A person would think so." Nelsey's mouth pinched with concern. "I don't think this presence means you harm."

"Then you don't think I'm imagining things?"

"No. I think the poor soul, whoever they are, is trying to tell you something. Next time it happens, you come git me. Tell me again about the scream."

"I don't like it, but I'm not so worried about that anymore. At first I thought it was real, that it was me screaming in my sleep, or someone in the woods behind the house. Now I realize it's a nightmare. In the nightmare, I hear someone scream, and I'm trying to help them but can't get to them. It usually wakes me up about midnight. I know because I always hear the whistle of the coal freight going through Yancey."

Nelsey reached to grip the edge of the table, and a long pause ensued.

"There's no train goin' through at midnight."

"But there must be. I hear it."

"No, we don't dig enough coal anymore." Nelsey's hand shook as she hooked a hank of her white hair behind her ear. "There hasn't been a freight, or any kind of train, at midnight since I was a young'un."

§15§

The day before Christmas was vivid blue and sunny, but keenly cold. The crisp-edged scent of expected snow charged the air.

Cutter had arrived unexpectedly on her doorstep early that morning.

She hadn't seen him since that cold breezy night on top of Cat Teeth. The feel of his kiss still raged in her blood. The crook of his hard arm enclosing her, the rich aroma of his lush leather jacket, and his warm breath stirring her hair lived with her through every night and awakened her every morning.

"Come on. Dress warm. We're going to find and chop down the perfect Christmas tree. Katie will have an old-fashioned West Virginia Christmas, one she'll never forget."

She'd fought down the effect of his closeness, the urge to reach out and brush her fingers across his fresh-shaven winter-touched face. "I can't, we can't. I have a lot to do before Santa Claus comes. I was going to buy a tree off a lot like I always do."

"That's what they do in New York. This is Yancey. Come on, I dare you."

"Did Nelsey put you up to this?" she'd asked suspiciously.

"Maybe, maybe not. What difference does it make?"

"Well, come on in. I can't leave you standing out

there freezing. I can at least fix you a hot breakfast. Nelsey isn't here yet."

"Didn't know you knew how to fry an egg," he'd said and smiled.

She'd laughed. "I don't. But scrambled eggs are easy."

They'd had fun in the kitchen. Cutter microwaved bacon and teased her about her lack of cooking skills while she scrambled the eggs. Weaving in and around their legs, Katie played with Miss Priss.

He'd seemed so at home in the house and made her feel so relaxed that she finally agreed to his tree-finding adventure.

Now an excited Katie, looking like a Christmas elf in her puffy red jacket and pointy hat, rode high on Cutter's shoulders. He seemed just as excited. They were heading toward the section of forest behind the house that held so many evergreens. He'd ignored Memphis's reluctance and her suggestions that they go elsewhere. How could she tell him that she had never been in the woods directly behind the house, and that she avoided them at all costs?

"Look at Katie's nose. It's as red as her hat."

Cutter frowned. "Do you think it's too cold for her?"

His concern for Katie touched her. "She'll be okay for a while."

"It won't take us long. If we can't find one, we'll chalk it up to a good try and buy one in town."

"I'm surprised you didn't stop by and pick up Nelsey first. She would have loved this."

"I did, but she said she had decorating to do at her church, and that we should go ahead without her. I'm glad. I like having the two of you all to myself."

His soft words generated in Memphis strong feelings of the warmth and joy of "family," which had its birth in the kitchen earlier. For a moment she let herself revel in the richness of love and caring that Cutter seemed to emanate. Though greatly loved as a child, she'd never ever experienced this feeling of belonging, of comfort, of rightness.

Jake said he didn't expect them to be a family, but Memphis knew better. He'd completely fallen for Katie, and had easily insinuated himself into their holiday plans. Their search for Sadie's grave had been curtailed by the winter weather, so Jake had time on his hands. He appeared at all hours of the day and night, making himself at home in a kitchen chair while she and Nelsey made lunch or dinner, or arriving just in time to gallantly offer to drive them into town for groceries, or to watch his favorite television show. It annoyed Memphis, but Katie had a right to know her, father.

It didn't take a rocket scientist for her to recognize the blatant difference in her feelings about Jake's presence in their lives, and Cutter's.

They passed through the first tree line. Memphis felt silly, but tightened her grip on the axe she carried. She shivered and fell a step or two behind Cutter and Katie.

Katie's happy chatter about birds and squirrels disrupted the peace of the quiet place. Memphis soon realized, despite the chatter, that the woods were tranquil and serene. To her chagrin, there was nothing to suggest the fear the night lights created in her, and there were no clues as to the source of the mysterious lights. In fact, there was nothing the least bit sinister. She felt nothing, saw nothing, sensed nothing that would cause her to believe this beautiful place held evil. Maybe Cutter's powerful presence challenged and exorcised the wraiths and demons Memphis had imagined lived here.

The once menacing trees seemed simply guardians of an innocent, ancient forest land, and to her great and final delight, she remembered they belonged to her. When the weather was nice in spring she and Katie would return and have a picnic.

They spotted and rejected several trees. Until finally, Cutter found an almost perfect eight-foot-high blue spruce.

"How about this one? Looks perfect for Princess Memphis and her Winter Fairy, Katie."

"I love it. Yes," said Memphis.

Cutter deposited Katie on the ground, and she and Memphis gathered pinecones while he chopped down the tree. Cutter worked up a good sweat and removed his parka, leaving only a T-shirt. She kept her eyes on Katie and the search for pinecones to avoid the sight of his arm muscles as they swelled, rolled, and receded smoothly with every movement. The thought of those arms around her, holding her, loving her, caressing her, warmed her in no time.

They dragged the tree back to the house, found Nelsey there, and spent the rest of the morning decorating the tree.

When Cutter left at noon, Memphis couldn't believe how much she missed him.

Candle flames danced and guttered in the reverent hush of the sanctuary, catching, now and then, the rich burgundy colors from the stained-glass windows. Margo had arrived in Yancey this afternoon and stood close beside Memphis at the Christmas Eve service of the Episcopal Church of the Good Shepherd. For once, though she missed Katie and Nelsey, she was glad they were at home. She needed this quiet time of worship and reflection. It was a time to give in and let God have his way. Time to give herself, if only for a short while, to the wisdom of the ages, to the wisdom that had perhaps brought her here.

Had God or the fates brought her to Yancey, or had it been her own stubbornness, and her anger at Jake?

Memphis didn't know, and right now it didn't seem all that important. What was important was that she and Katie and Cutter had shared a wonderful day and Margo had arrived safe and sound, and that a beautiful, decorated tree awaited her at home. She liked spending Christmas Eve in this charming old stone church in this small mining town in the mountains. She knew there were people here this evening who didn't like her, and maybe even a few who meant her harm, but she felt at home. This had been Sadie's church.

Sadie Maynard had been president of the Altar Guild here. Her name and the two years of her Guild presidency were listed on a plaque at the rear of the sanctuary. She had spent many an hour creating floral arrangements for the chancel and the sanctuary, and had women friends who respected and loved her. The same newspaper articles that had hinted unfairly that the murder victim was a woman of shady virtue had quoted ladies in the community who said that Sadie Maynard would never have done anything immoral. Despite differing testimony in following articles from various male leaders of the town, the women had continued to defend Sadie.

So someone had loved Sadie, someone had cared for her, thought Memphis defiantly. Her eyes ached with unshed tears, and yet she had gained a modicum of happiness knowing intuitively that this church had given Sadie peace at a time when she needed it.

The young minister's sincere, but droning, voice led them in solemn prayer.

A memory brushed its wings against her forehead, then threaded its way cautiously through misty eaves and cubbyholes in her mind, and soon the flame of her candle journeyed her across time.

The minister's face turned aged and grizzled, and his shirt collar looked high and starched stiff. The date posted on the hymn board was December 24, 1935. She stood in this church on another Christmas Eve and longed for the touch of a man she loved desperately. Her heart brimmed with love and hope. An elbow gouged rudely into her ribs. She didn't flinch at the pain, but smiled bravely at the frowning, annoyed, heavyset man who stood next to her. He could never hurt her again, not where it really counted.

Hot wax dripped on Memphis's hand. She jumped, almost dropping her candle. She glanced around, startled to find herself here. Where had she been? Shaken, she reached over and squeezed Margo's hand to make sure her sister was real. Margo looked at her strangely. Memphis didn't blame her. She certainly felt strange.

"Amen," said the minister.

"Are you okay?" whispered Margo.

"Yes."

And she was. For some odd reason the memory she'd just relived had restored her bruised faith in herself and in her grandmother's story, as if the memory had been sent to her on purpose. There was not a doubt in her mind that the brief moment in another age had been real. She'd worn a blue velvet dress, and the man beside her had worn a striped black wool suit. The church had been too hot and his suit was soaked with perspiration at the armpits. The rankness of his sweat still stung her nostrils.

Wait a minute, Memphis Maynard. Are you out of your mind? Stop this craziness.

A tear rolled down her cheek, and she shook it off impatiently. *Where had that come from?* Somewhere, deep down, she knew she wasn't crazy, and the feeling of love and hope rose again.

People were stirring, gathering their purses and coats, donning gloves. The service was over. The choir, which had just finished singing "Oh Come, All Ye Faithful," switched to a secular "Silver Bells."

Directly in front of them, Cle Hutton wrapped an expensive cashmere scarf, which had seen better days, around his neck, and turned to greet them. It was the first time Memphis had seen him sober. The once vitally handsome man, ravaged by alcoholism, seemed lonely.

"Merry Christmas," he said. "I can't think of a better gift than to see the beautiful Maynard sisters on Christmas Eve."

His brilliant blue eyes, red-lined and watery weak, raked over Margo with the expertise of a connoisseur.

"Merry Christmas to you, Mr. Hutton," they replied in unison, then glanced at one another and laughed. It wasn't the first time they'd spoken together like trained seals.

"Don't call me Mr. Hutton. My name is Cle. You probably already have plans, but would you like to drop by Hutton House and have a Christmas brandy with me?"

"Thank you for the invitation, but my Katie is waiting for us, and Santa Claus has some work to do. You're welcome to come and have a drink with us," said Memphis.

"Maybe I will," he said, eyeing Margo again. "Have to see what Sally Junior's plans are. She was supposed to be here tonight. Don't know where she is."

He smiled at them as he prepared to leave his pew. Then his smile faded and his eyes, eager at their invitation, turned bleak with sadness. Cle Hutton stared hungrily at someone, and Memphis looked to see who had caught his attention.

Senator Elizabeth Brady, his first wife, came down the center aisle with Black Brady, greeting friends along the way. Radiant in a wine red suit, her silvery hair swept back in its natural style, Elizabeth Brady saw Cle as he neared the end of his pew.

Memphis heard her say, "Merry Christmas, Cle. Everything all right with you?"

"Fine, Lilibet, fine," he replied with a note of bravado. Black Brady said nothing. Cle avoided his implacable gaze, and waited for the illustrious pair to move on before he exited his pew.

Memphis was stunned with the abject need in Cle Hutton's eyes, the unashamed admittance that, though he could never have her, after all these years he still loved Elizabeth Brady, and would forever. Memphis didn't know their story, but she hoped that she would never feel the misery that Cle Hutton tried to drink away every day.

Margo nudged her forward, and they began to make their way to the aisle, but Memphis stopped short in surprise. Cutter hadn't mentioned that he would be here this evening.

He came up the aisle toward them, pushing his father's wheelchair, with Birdy clinging to his arm. People spoke to him and he returned their holiday greetings warmly, but his eyes sorted through the crowd until he found her. An enigmatic smile formed on his lips, then vanished. He nodded, but didn't wait for a response. He bowed his head, listening to something Birdy said to him. It was as if he'd just wanted some confirmation of her presence. She was relieved that he ignored her. She didn't think she could face those disturbing eyes of his tonight.

Margo said, "Cutter's father looks like a carved marble figure that someone imprisoned in a wheelchair and forgot about."

"Oh, William Tate is definitely not forgotten about. He's given the best of care."

Memphis eyed the immobile old man. Margo was right. William Tate's skin was the whitish translucent blue of a longtime invalid. She wondered if he lived in silent, agonizing fury at his inability to communicate.

She hoped he did, hoped he lived in hell. Just punishment for the man's sins. On the other hand, if he could talk, or write, or blink an eyelash he probably could answer many of Memphis's questions.

"Cutter's good to bring him tonight," continued Margo.

"He hates his father. I'm really surprised he brought him."

"Sense of responsibility, I suppose," said Margo, then looked at her thoughtfully. "How do you know Cutter hates his father?"

"Oh, well, I . . ." She wasn't ready to tell Margo about the intimate, revealing conversations she and Cutter had shared, or his startling sexual effect on her. "Well, his father is universally disliked for a myriad of brilliant and cruel business transactions. And I've told you how the town kind of raised Cutter while his father ignored him. I think he's lucky to have a son like Cutter looking after him."

Margo gave her another thoughtful look. She started to say something, but they were pushed along by the crowd and her words were lost. Actually, Memphis herself was surprised at the strength of her feelings on Cutter's behalf, but she couldn't shove away the power of those feelings, which had prompted an automatic and fierce defense.

Outside, oversize snowflakes flurried softly, melting as they landed on coats and hats, not yet sticking to the ground. Bells from the tower chimed in tinkling silver accompaniment with the choir inside the church. Lamplight shone on the parishioners as they milled about greeting one another, or gathered in small groups to chat. Unwilling to give anyone the opportunity to snub them, Memphis thought it best to move quickly toward the Jeep.

She was pleasantly surprised when some of Nelsey's friends nodded and waved, and Billy Gus and Elva came over to say hello. Mitchell, who owned the hardware store, yelled, "Merry Christmas, Memphis." Every day something broke in the old house, and she'd spent a lot of time in his store the last few months. Raymond Gene, manager of the garage where she had the Jeep serviced, patted her on the back as he passed, and said, "Have a nice Christmas, Miz Maynard." Her heart glowed at the friendliness, and Margo beamed at the attention paid to her pariah of a sister.

"Ahhhh. I see you've made a few friends in Yancey, Miss Maynard," said a gravely voice.

Harvey Root, with Minnie Dale at his side, and his grandson, Harvey "the turd," pushing his wheelchair, gave her a thin smile.

"Yes, it looks as if I have, Mr. Root."

"This your sister?"

Memphis introduced him to Margo.

"Weren't you here Thanksgiving, Miss Maynard?"

"Yes, I was," replied Margo. "You have a good memory, Mr. Root."

"I don't miss much, and I never forget a beautiful woman, especially Maynard women. Where's your daughter, Memphis?"

"I thought the service too serious for a child, so Katie's at home with Nelsey."

"I see. Katie Maynard. Another generation of Maynard women. Is she as beautiful as you two are, and your mother, and grandmother were?"

Memphis hesitated, a hive of apprehensive bees beginning to buzz in her tummy. Should she acknowledge the compliment, or cut him off at the pass? He was going to make a malevolent point of some kind. She felt it coming.

"Katie looks like the rest of us," she said coolly, and turned to leave.

"You Maynard women just seem to keep arriving through the years. Umph. Stubborn genes. Too bad, too bad. Women like you are too attractive for your own good."

"Time to go, Father," Minnie Dale said nervously, and motioned for her son to push on.

Memphis hurried toward the Jeep, Margo following her. "What's that dirty old man talking about? What did he mean about Katie?" asked Margo angrily.

"Hey, Memphis, hey, hey. Don't be in such a hurry." Birdy chirped through the darkening night. "Give us a chance to say Merry Christmas."

Birdy rushed toward them, a bright smile on her heart-shaped face. *She looks happy tonight,* thought Memphis. *I wonder if the man with her has anything to do with that?* Cutter walked behind Birdy, an indulgent smile on his rugged face. His father evidently waited for them in the long dark limousine that sat at the curb.

"Hi, Birdy, happy Christmas to you, too," said Memphis.

"Margo, I read that you'll be touring in *Ragtime*. Gosh, I wish it would come to Charleston or Huntington so we could see it. Right, Cutter?"

"Right," he replied, but he focused on Memphis and frowned.

Birdy introduced them to a friend, and the two women peppered Margo with questions about the new Broadway hit.

Cutter took Memphis by the elbow and stepped her away from the chatting threesome. The firm warmth of his hand seemed to melt through the fabric of her coat, and her knees went as flimsy soft as the snow that fell around them. "What's the matter with you? When I left you this morning you and Katy-did were singing and dancing around the tree. Now you're white as a sheet. What's wrong?"

Through the dancing snowflakes in the wavery yellow glow of the streetlights, his silver eyes caught hers and held them, demanding an answer.

"Nothing's wrong. What are you doing here? Thought you didn't believe in this sort of thing?"

"I don't. People playing mind games with someone they call God. But it's a happy time of year when people are good to each other for a change. Birdy likes it when I bring her to church for special occasions. My father needed the fresh air, and his nurse needed a break." His grip on her arm tightened. "But I don't want to talk about me. Tell me what's upset you."

"I'm supposed to hate you, be afraid of you," she found herself whispering weakly, shocked at her disclosure. He bent his head close to hear her. "God, it's true, I don't trust you . . . yet . . . but it's Harvey Root I'm afraid of."

His grip had changed to a soothing motion up and down her arm, finally stopping to rest on her shoulder as if to assure her that, no matter what, everything would be all right.

"What did he do?" he asked roughly. His hand tightened, and he took hold of both shoulders and drew her closer to him. "Has he threatened you in any way?"

"Not really. It's all innuendo, and talking oddly about Katie. Oh, forget it. I'm sorry I said anything." Embarrassed now, and afraid of what the churchgoers around them might be reading into this, she tugged at a shoulder, but he held firm. "Let me go."

"No." He leaned even closer and said huskily into her ear, "Don't you know that I'd like to bring you into my arms right now? Hold you tight against me, and feel those exquisite bones heat to my touch. Kiss you until your knees buckle, until you're breathing fast and hard."

"Stop this. No." His sensual words in her ear sent delicious tremors to dangerous places. She shook at her arm, but he wouldn't let go. "This is crazy. People are looking at us."

"Let them look. After Jake's sleaze interview from

Ruby's that aired last night on *American Notebook*, they'll think we're having another disagreement. Besides, they know I don't give a damn what they think of me."

But he raised his head, and slowly, as if by chance, barely brushed her cheek with his in passing. He looked hard at her, then released her and slipped his hands into the pockets of his overcoat as if he had a need to control them.

"But I do care what they think of you," he continued. "Don't be afraid of Harvey. He's an old man. He gets confused sometimes, and he's getting senile. However, promise you'll tell me if he says anything else to you. I'll take care of it."

She lifted her chin. "I'm sorry about Jake's innuendoes on television. Remember, though Jake and I have shared some information, we are not working together. And I'm sorry I said anything about Root. I'm embarrassed. I can take care of myself, remember?"

He gave her a lazy grin. "Right. Superwoman. Well, it's nice to know you're not afraid of me, even if you don't trust me."

"Well, Margo, will you look at these two. Cozy as anything." Birdy caught possessive hold of Cutter's arm, and chattered on. "Memphis, I am *so* impressed. Margo tells me the Museum of Modern Art is exhibiting your work next month. Are you going to Manhattan for the presentation?"

"I don't know. Haven't decided yet. I'd probably have to leave Katie here, which I don't want to do." She wanted to go home, get away from Cutter's disturbing presence. "Have a nice holiday tomorrow. Let's go, Mar."

But rush as fast as she could to the Jeep, she couldn't escape Cutter's blistering gaze on the back of her neck.

What on earth had ever possessed her to say she wasn't afraid of him? Just the sight of him shook her to her toes. But was it fright, or something else? That whispered conversation with him had slipped out as naturally as the sun rose every morning. Never in a million years would she have imagined confiding in him like she had.

They arrived home to find Katie waving to them from the living-room window, and the house twinkling with red and green lights. The front door held a huge balsam wreath Nelsey and Memphis had created. Crumpled within a curve of its big red bow was a note for Memphis.

It said: *"Miz Maynerd, sory we missed you. We cum to Yancy to see the Christmas lights, like we do once a year. Granpa aint mad at me anymore. Cum see me when you kin. Pastor Elkins is sick an not havin church fer now but tol me sumthin I think mite hep you. Opal Marie's jest fine. Heve a Godly Christmas. Vanta Lou"*

Jake stared at the mirrored ceiling, his hands folded behind his head on the pillow. The disheveled blond hair that lay across his bare chest shone like pale gold in the dimness. He wished for a brief, fierce moment that the color of the hair was vibrant bronze and the woman Memphis instead of Sally Junior, but then chastised himself for being such a cad.

The mirror caught a small Christmas tree in the corner, decorated with garish orange and purple lights that blinked on and off. Sally Junior thought it "chic."

He started to play with the bleached-blond curls, but then checked his movement. He'd grown fond of this naive hick of a girl, but he didn't want to wake her right now. He had too much on his mind.

The spot he did with Claytie and Art at Ruby's had aired last night. His producer had called today and reported the interview had created a sensation, and *American Notebook* had its highest Nielson ratings ever. Booksellers were already clamoring for the book.

Here in Yancey, no one would speak to him. He didn't care. He'd be out of here in a month or two, and take Memphis and Katie with him.

On his visit to Katie yesterday he had uncovered a veritable treasure trove of information. Nelsey had been absent at church. While Memphis had taken Katie upstairs for a nap, he'd sneaked into her cellar darkroom. The prints he'd seen from sixty years ago of obvious sex favor parties had stuck with him all day. The "key club" parties had been hinted at or alluded to by several old geezers at Ruby's, but he'd never been able to verify anything.

A sexual scandal attached to the whole mystery would make his book even better.

The whole scenario was so obvious to him. He couldn't understand why Memphis didn't see it also.

This, of course, was the motive for Sadie Maynard's murder. Memphis, he was sure, had chosen not to believe what was before her very eyes. Regardless of what she wanted to believe, Sadie's name on the list indicated she had been a member. She was probably a newer member and that's why her name looked as if it had been added.

The important part of what Memphis had discovered was not the names of the women, but the partial list of men's names. Someone had torn the rest of it away. Who had done that, and did the list still exist? The way he figured it was that Macauley Tate, and others, knew someone had the list and got nervous about it. Maybe Sadie had gotten angry with someone and threatened to disclose the existence of the club and all its members. Someone had to silence her and Tate had either been elected, or had volunteered, to do the dirty deed.

Why couldn't Memphis see that, he asked himself. Of course, it would be difficult to admit that your grandmother was a downright whore. He'd half promised that he wouldn't besmirch her grandmother's name anymore, but he'd told his publishers and the host of *American Notebook*, Monty Montgomery, that he had a sizzling spot to air right before the book's release. He decided he'd get around the promise to Memphis with hints and innuendoes until he could convince her of the truth.

He sighed. It wasn't going to be easy. She'd become more obsessed with the so-called mystery, and had taken avenues of investigation he'd never imagined she would.

He yawned, and wished she would forget about the stupid grave site thing. It really wasn't important anymore. They had already proven that someone had gone to an immense amount of effort to conceal Sadie's grave, which meant whoever it was had something to hide. The brutality of the crime was probably the reason for the hidden grave.

Newspaper reports said the viewing of the casket, which was closed, only lasted one night. Both were unusual. Sixty years ago caskets were always open for three or four evenings of viewing, and funerals lasted all day. Sadie was the wife of a popular sheriff, and under normal circumstances the occasion would have taken on the importance of a state funeral. Sheriff Maynard had to have seen the body; not only was he the sheriff, but she was his wife. He must have been so devastated by her condition, and so brokenhearted at her death that he'd rushed the ceremonial arrangements. The lily-white town fathers, afraid someone would want the casket opened, thus revealing the savageness of their crime or the discovery of something they wanted to conceal, had probably encouraged the sheriff's hurried arrangements.

Sally Junior trailed a finger across his shoulder blade.

"Awake?" he asked and brushed the hair away from her face.

"Yeah. Merry Christmas, Jake." She giggled. "Did you get me a gift? I got you something."

"Honey, you just gave me the best present I'll get for Christmas."

She giggled again, and snuggled as close as she could. "Oh, shoot, baby-hunk, you're just saying that to make me feel good."

"No, I mean it. You were good when I arrived in Yancey, and now you're even better."

"Yeah, well, it's all those things you've taught me."

Jake smiled to himself. It was true. The next man to sample Sally Junior's talents would wonder how she'd picked up such sexual sophistication in the small town of Yancey.

"You're a fast learner." He nuzzled her breast and caught it with his mouth.

"No, wait a minute, Jake. I want to give you your present."

"Okay, and there's one for you in my coat pocket over there on the chair." Thank God, he'd remembered to pick something up before he came over here tonight.

She shrieked with excitement, and ran to extract a small rectangular box from his coat pocket, then ran to get a box from beneath her gaudy tree. Her big naked breasts bobbed heavily with all the movement, and she plopped back on the bed next to him.

"You open yours first," she said.

He knew she was dying to open hers, so he said, "No, you go first."

"Okay." She ripped the paper off the box and squealed when she saw the silver box from Justice Brother's Jewelers. "Oh, Jesus, baby-hunk, from Justice Brother's!"

"It's nothing important, Sally J. Just something I thought would look good on you."

She opened it and squeezed her hand across her mouth so she wouldn't squeal again, and looked at him with adoring eyes. Taking her hand from her mouth, she gave him a beautiful smile and he felt guilt from hell. It meant so little to him and so much to her. The piece was not of good quality, nothing to compare in cost or looks with others he'd bought in London, Paris, and Rome. She removed the diamond tennis bracelet from its box.

"Oh, Jesus, Jake. Daddy gave me some teensy tiny diamond studs when I was sixteen. I never thought I'd have anything like this. Thank you."

She jumped from the bed and ran to her dressing table mirror to put on the bracelet.

"You open yours," she insisted as she fiddled with the clasp.

The red cashmere sweater he pulled from the box was in good taste, and probably set her back a pretty penny, but it was something Jake wouldn't wear in a thousand years. His taste ran more to black turtlenecks, leather jackets, and jeans, but he hadn't the heart to tell her. He couldn't exchange it either. Everyone in town would know in fifteen minutes, and so would she.

"Hey, this is great. Just what I wanted. I'll wear it in New York next week." He would give it to his gay photographer friend, Paul.

Her face fell, and she walked slowly back to the bed, the diamond bracelet sparkling on her arm. "Oh, honeydunk, you're going to New York next week?"

"The producer, and my publishers, want to meet with me to discuss the last part of the project."

"Shoot, I thought you'd be here to take me to the New Year's Eve dance at the club."

"Sorry, babe. Can't do it."

She pouted, her lower lip trembling, then sighed. "Okay. Guess I'll have to go with Harvey, like I always do."

* * *

He settled into his deep armchair by the fire. The house uttered an occasional hiss, click, or sputter. Except for the distant melodic caroling of a church youth group, the town slumbered about him. The only illumination to read his letters by were the white lights of the Christmas tree, which twinkled in the corner of the dark library, and the cheerful glow of the fire in front of him.

He'd retrieved them from his trunk on the mountain, afraid they weren't safe there anymore. He handled them carefully, lovingly. The yellowed sheets of paper had been read and reread so often through the years they were fragile, and the script, faded.

He sipped his brandy, savoring the mellow richness before he swallowed, then sat the crystal snifter on the table next to him. Leaving the letters with the strong, boxy handwriting to one side for the moment, he lifted one of the letters with the feminine handwriting closer to his eyes so he could read better. Tracing the spidery handwriting with a loving finger, he read the words in almost reverent awe.

". . . tease not our ghosts with slander, pause not there to say that love is false and soon grows cold, but pass in silence the mute grave of two who lived and died believing love was true." Edna St. Vincent Millay, of course.

He lifted his brandy snifter and made a toast.

"Merry Christmas to you, wherever you are." He'd made the same toast in the same manner on many a Christmas Eve, but for the first time instead of melancholy, he felt a smile gentle his lips.

§16§

The broken glass crackled beneath his boot heel. With each step he took, Cutter's fury grew. Every crushing, splintering sound ripped into his gut like shrapnel. Macauley's Mountain breathed eerily quiet today, stunned by the knowledge that a sacrilege had been committed.

Seedling trays, once filled with rich earth and courageous green shoots, now lay empty and strewn on the floor. The lifeless shoots were brown and shrunken. His carefully stored bulbs, put away in safe dark places to sleep for the winter, had been tossed about as if someone had played ball with them. They were shriveled dry. Spotty patches of snow partially covered once protected orange hawkweed beds.

The greenhouse had been leveled to the ground and was open to the elements. Wildlife had picked through anything edible. Two brown rabbits sat on the edge of the carnage, quivering with the hope of stealing any tender shoots that remained.

A trail of chalky fertilizer roped in and around broken pots and plants and led to the door of his sleeping quarters. He dreaded seeing the damage they had done in there. His hand shook as he grasped the knob and opened the door. The room was intact except for the chalky substance they'd tossed about. Evidently they'd been in too much of a hurry to care about this room. The trunk was still locked. The cot was untouched, the stack of firewood neat, his chair and kerosene lamp in place. He would leave this until last. Cutter closed the door on the room and turned to begin an extensive cleanup job.

The intense physical labor did little to assuage his anger. It wasn't difficult to figure out who had wrought the destruction and why. He knew this was the work of United Mining scum even before he found a battered ballpoint pen with the UM emblem on it.

The construction of the greenhouse had been a labor of love for him. He and his grandfather had camped here for a week every summer, and Cutter had never forgotten the meadow and the intricate ways of reaching it. As he'd grown older, he'd returned as often as he could. He'd begun building the greenhouse in his early twenties, all by hand and no labor brought in to help. This had been his retreat, his private place. No one knew of its existence except Black, Nelsey, and Ruby, and then, by chance or fate, Memphis. Memphis didn't know that she was the only person he'd ever brought here.

This flat protected meadow near the top of Macauley's had been his hiding place since his grandfather's death, the place he'd escaped to when his father pretended he didn't exist, and when Sheriff Maynard beat him almost senseless. It had been here that Black Brady had found him after a three-day search. It was here that Black had begun to teach the twelve-year-old boy the ways of the mountains, of wildlife, and folklore, and survival.

Macauley's Mountain had saved and nurtured Macauley "Cutter" Tate. He'd built the greenhouse to give back some of what United Mining had destroyed.

The icy air affected him not at all as he worked steadily through the day. With thick gloves, shovel, rake, and wheelbarrow he gathered piles of shards and splinters. When dusk came and the task was only a quarter done, he grudgingly accepted that he couldn't finish the gut-wrenching job in one day.

He pulled off his gloves, wiped the perspiration from his face, and stood, fists on waist, to survey the havoc.

What a stupid, stupid waste. If they think this is going to run me off, they're wrong. They've made a big mistake.

His inclination was to spend the night and start in again tomorrow, but he needed special equipment. He would have to go down into Yancey for supplies. Besides, he could use a good stiff drink, maybe more than one.

The tires of his Range Rover spit and spun as he pulled furiously away from the piles of glass and dead plants.

Memphis's cheery whistle came out rather shaky, but she kept whistling and humming. The darkroom didn't seem so menacing if she hummed. The sadness didn't come at her so hard and strong. In fact, it seemed like the presence with her enjoyed the humming, singing, and whistling. She knew for certain that something visited her in the darkroom, and each time she forced herself to enter the space, the presence became less frightening.

Having the safelight on helped some, too. Its dim filtered light assisted her in making sure she wasn't fogging the printing paper.

"What a friend we have in Jesus, all our sins and griefs to . . ."

"Go away, whoever you are. Please go away," she whispered shakily into the dark. "I can't help you."

With her tongs, she lifted the last sheet from the stop bath tray, letting it drain for a few seconds into the solution, then put it into the fixer tray. She agitated the prints for a few minutes and then with huge relief turned on the light over her head. Her sense of sadness and desertion left, and whistling this time with sincerity, she transferred the photographs to a washer tray and rinsed them thoroughly.

The pictures of Vanta Lou's children were some of her best. She would call Manhattan tomorrow and ask her agent, Harrison Telly, if he could have them included in the exhibit at MoMA.

Yesterday she had delivered milk in thermos jugs, and pencils, pads of paper, crayons, and books to Up Run Creek. There had been no sign of Vanta Lou, and any attempt to cross the creek would have been pure folly. It rushed high and furious with lethal chunks of ice. She'd tucked a note for Vanta Lou in one of the books, telling her she'd come to visit as soon as the creek was crossable, and left her delivery in the protective crook of the large evergreen that held the raft's pulley system.

As she hung the photos from Thanksgiving and Christmas on a line to dry, her professional eye caught certain prints that delighted her. The Christmas shots were great, but the ones taken around the Thanksgiving table intrigued her the most. Margo had taken a few Memphis had been unaware of.

She laughed at a picture of Katie smearing mashed potatoes on Jake's face, and marveled at the sense of shared mischief Katie and Jake portrayed. Worldly Jake Bishop had fallen under his small daughter's spell.

There was a picture of Alison laughing, one hand patting Cutter's cheek lovingly and the other draped possessively over his shoulder. Cutter smiled back at Alison with affection. A shaft of pure jealousy shot through her, shocking her with its intensity. Not liking the feeling, her eyes sped past the couple. In the same shot, and probably not meant to be caught by Margo's lens, was Birdy, her eyes filled with desperate love as she looked at Cutter and Alison.

Something about the picture disturbed Memphis, something more than jealousy, so she hurried on to the next one.

The shot was another one of Cutter, only this time he looked in Memphis's direction. There was a hard set to his jaw, and blazing purpose in his eyes. She shivered. Whatever he wanted he would get. She'd photographed enough people to trust in the characterizations caught by the camera. Had Margo seen this in Cutter and snapped the picture as a warning to Memphis? Memphis acknowledged that the charge of lusting tension between the two of them had blurred or removed her innate fear of Cutter. She'd told him that she didn't fear him anymore, but that she couldn't trust him. Should she still be afraid of this man of many colors? Cutter seemed a peaceful man on the surface, but in this picture Memphis saw controlled anger beneath the calmness.

The next photo was of Memphis laughing at a smiling Katie. Who was standing behind them in the picture? Must be an odd reflection from the window behind them, or the lighting from the chandelier. Margo knew nothing about lighting or angles. She just shot as the mood took her.

No. This was not an accident of light or reflection. Someone stood behind her. A wavery image of a female dressed in white took stronger form as she stared at it.

Double exposure. Had to be a double exposure. But that was impossible. No one at the dinner party looked like the woman in white, nor were there any pictures taken during Thanksgiving or Christmas that could be remotely related to the tenuous figure who stood behind her.

She removed the print from the clothesline and spread it carefully on the counter to study it inch by inch. She found no explanation for the mysterious figure. Maybe when it dried completely, the apparition would disappear. She busied herself with other prints and work, whistling and humming with dogged determination, but when she returned to the dried photo, the figure remained, clearer than ever.

Gathering up the dry photographs, Memphis took them upstairs to share with Nelsey, who wouldn't come to the basement.

Nelsey said, "Humph. You must have done somethin' wrong when you was developin' the pictures." But her trembling hands as she held the print betrayed her fear at what she was seeing.

"I've gone over every procedure I can think of. There is no commonsense answer for this," said Memphis. Then she almost whispered as she asked, "What is it, Nelsey? Is there a ghost near me in the picture? Maybe this is who visits me in the darkroom."

Nelsey didn't answer. She held the photograph at arms length in front of her, as if she were farsighted, then rubbed her eyes with a knuckle and brought it close-up to examine it minutely.

"Nelsey?"

"Well, I know my eyes are okay because I jest had cataracts removed last year." She looked up, and the fear in her eyes worried Memphis. "Let me keep it for a while, study it. Anymore in there like this 'un?"

Memphis went through the pile of newly printed work she'd brought from the darkroom. They found another one, which looked like the image had just begun to form but had not completely materialized.

"I'll keep this 'un too." Nelsey spotted another print and held Memphis's shuffling hand still so she could look at it. "What are these?"

"Oh, how did they get in this pile?" She blushed. "I didn't mean for anyone to see these except me and Margo."

Nelsey held up the black-and-white pictures: one of a group of women cavorting topless and wearing only hose and garter belts, the other of Sheriff Maynard with the naked woman on his lap.

She paled for a moment, disgust crowding her eyes, then looked at Memphis with sorrow in her honest blue gaze. "It don't take much to recognize the back of Sheriff Maynard's neck. Didn't see him much as a young'un, but after I moved into the house down the hill, I saw him now and agin. What are these?"

Memphis explained there was strong evidence indicating a scandalous sex club existed during the mid-thirties in Yancey, involving prominent members of the community, including her grandfather. She thought blackmail might be involved, and that it might have something to do with Sadie's murder.

"You been carryin' this load, too? You should have told me. Don't remember anything about this, though. 'Course Mommy would have kept gossip like this from us." She thought a minute. "But you know who might be able to help you with this trash? Ruby Barnes at the roadhouse the other side of town."

"How?"

"Ruby would have been about twenty years old then, maybe older. The roadhouse was new and the center of a lot of illegal stuff, like sellin' stolen hooch and moonshine and sech. I know that much because Mommy used to go and drag my brothers out of there by the ear. I used to hear them whisperin' about 'hot Ruby,' and the 'big bosses' in Yancey meetin' there to party."

"I visited Ruby's soon after I arrived here. She wouldn't give me the time of day. In fact, everybody in the place turned their backs when I walked in. I don't know how Jake got that interview I saw the other night. If they don't like me, they'd hate Jake even worse."

"Didn't say nothin' to you, but I watched *American Notebook* that night, too." Her face darkened. "None of my business, but I never liked Jake, even if he is Katie's father. If there was a hatin' bone in my body, I'd hate him now, after what he tried to say about Cutter."

Memphis thought the piece had been scurrilous, too, dirty journalism at its lowest ebb. She didn't want to discredit Cutter, she just wanted to prove it was his grandfather who'd murdered Sadie and gotten away with it. Although lately, some of the puzzle pieces indicated others may have been involved.

"I'm surprised Ruby let Jake in in the first place."

"Sally Junior, that's how. She'd been takin' him out there, and they kinda got used to him. But he caused a fight the night he did that interview, about a month ago, and they haven't let him in since. They might be a mite friendlier to you now, since you've been to church with me, and been helping the Chafins and all."

"Good. I'll go right now. Thanks, Nelsey. Can you stay a while longer?"

"Sure, I'll spend the night if you want, but don't you think it's kinda late to be going to Ruby's by yourself? Why don't you wait till someone can go with you?"

"Who? Jake? I don't want him to find out about these pictures, and they're never going to let him back in there anyway. I'm feeling close to the solution to all of this, and Jake is the last person I want around me. I've got to find my answers before his book comes out. Margo's not here, and Birdy wouldn't be seen within a mile of the place. I'll be fine. In fact, I might even have a beer or two."

"Ummph. Be careful drivin' home."

"I'll have a Guinness, please."

"We don't sell German beer."

She started to explain that Guinness wasn't a German beer, but then decided that wasn't such a good idea.

"Then how about a Miller Lite?" she asked with her most charming smile.

The bartender didn't respond, but turned away to get her beer.

Memphis sat at the short angular end of the L-shaped bar. She had a view of the length of the bar and the room. The man waited on several other customers, never glancing in her direction. She wasn't surprised the beer was slow in coming. At the door she'd been practically frisked. A man and a woman kept watch, and everyone who entered was asked if they carried a camera or tape recorder. If it was someone they were unfamiliar with, like Memphis, pockets were emptied and purses searched.

Thanks a lot, Jake. You sure haven't made things any easier.

Ruby's was a certified dive, but she could tell it was clean and well run. Christmas and New Year's Eve decorations had been cleared away. Ashtrays on the bar were emptied quickly, shelves of wine held no dust, and the shining chrome beer pullers were beaded with sweating moisture, as were the lids of the coolers.

The unfriendly barkeep finally set her beer in front of her with a thump. Some of the golden liquid slopped onto the polished wooden bar. It pooled and filled the carved, dated initials of lovers who'd defaced the surface in 1948.

"Not very polite of you, Spec. Wipe it up for the lady." A woman, who Memphis assumed could only be Ruby Barnes, appeared and stood beside the bartender. A cigarette dangled from the corner of her dry crinkled lips. Blue smoke wreathed her head like smoke around a chimney. "You slummin', Miz Maynard?"

"Hardly, Mrs. Barnes. And I don't have a television camera with me, or a tape recorder. Nelsey said you might be able to answer some questions for me."

"I see. Questions about how much bulge Cutter's got in his jockey shorts?"

Spec snickered as he wiped up the beer.

Memphis's anger flared, but knew she had to stay cool or she'd never make it to first base. This woman's maternal protection of Cutter was even more fierce than Nelsey's.

"Now who's being rude, Mrs. Barnes?"

A spark of respect briefly lit the woman's eyes. She blew smoke from the side of her mouth, then removed the cigarette with thumb and forefinger and stubbed it out in an ashtray.

"Women have always been crazy over Cutter, and since that SOB Bishop started his TV stuff, they've been comin' in here like cats in heat. You here to sniff out what all them other curious, sex-hungry broads come for? Want to find out how Cutter Tate killed a man? Want to see where he spent his teen years? Then you can go home and fantasize what it would be like to screw him, eh?"

"No, that isn't why I came," said Memphis, holding her temper with effort. "I was hoping you could tell me about the men who frequented this place during the year my grandmother died, maybe give me an idea of any gossip or parties you may have known about."

"That was a long time ago. I have trouble recallin' yesterday. Just what is it you think I might know?"

Memphis hesitated. Should she show this hard-bitten crone the pictures of sexual orgies from 1936? *You've come this far, Memphis, you might as well go for broke.*

"Nelsey said this place was the center of action back then. She said she remembers her brothers talking about the town's high and mighties gathering here to party."

"I expect they did."

"I have evidence proving a sexual organization existed at the time, a place where prominent men, and a few of the prominent women in town, gathered to exchange physical favors. Do you remember anything about that?"

Ruby pulled another cigarette from a pack of Luckies that lay on the bar. She lit the filterless cancer stick, blew smoke lazily toward Memphis, then picked loose tobacco from her lip.

"You askin' if I took part in them parties?"

"No." She wouldn't let this outrageous old woman goad her into a confrontation. "I asked a simple question that has nothing to do with you. If the men gathered here, then they might have done some talking about things like that."

An elderly man climbed onto the stool next to Memphis.

"Howdy, Ruby."

"Howdy, Claytie." Ruby smiled, and Memphis saw that she wasn't completely without warmth. "Want your usual?"

"Yep."

"Spec, a Bud for Claytie."

Memphis considered her next move. Showing the embarrassing photos to Ruby would have been bad enough, but now the old man would see them, too.

"Ruby, do you have a place where we can talk in private?"

"No. You got something to ask me, you ask me here."

Okay, go for broke, Memphis. Now is not the time to get sensitive and prudish.

She pulled the photos from her bag and handed them to Ruby, leaving the one of her grandfather, and the one of Root, in the envelope.

"Do any of these people look familiar to you?"

Ruby squinted at the pictures, then fished reading glasses from the pocket of her plaid flannel shirt. Her gaze sharpened, and she gave Memphis a quick look before she continued through the pile.

"Yeah, I knew some of these people. They're all dead now so they can't help you. But maybe Claytie can." Before Memphis could stop her, Ruby handed the damnable pictures to the old man.

Memphis gasped and grabbed at them. She retrieved the major portion, but the old man had tightened his grip when she grabbed and he retained a few.

"I didn't intend for the whole bar to see these, Ruby," she said coldly. "Please give me the pictures, Claytie."

He didn't hear her, and stared at one of the pictures as if in a trance.

"Sweet Jesus," he whispered.

"What's the matter?" asked Ruby.

"It's my Opal Marie."

"What did you say?" asked Memphis.

"My Opal Marie." His hand shook as he held the picture so the two women could see, and he pointed to one of the women in the background. She was younger than the others, and an expression of fearful uncertainty haunted her unsmiling face. "I never thought I'd see her pretty face again."

"Who is the girl?" Memphis asked, but she already knew.

"Opal Marie Chafin, the girl I wanted to marry."

"Claytie, keep your mouth shut. You don't have to tell her anything."

"But I want to, Ruby. I ain't talked about my pretty girl in years. Don't have nothin' to do with the Maynard case anyway."

"Why didn't you marry her, and what happened to her?" asked Memphis.

Claytie looked at Memphis for the first time, his rheumy eyes big and sad.

"She thought she wanted someone else, one of the

rich guys here in town. Now I know where they was goin' that night."

"What night?"

"She was here with him the night your grandmother was murdered. They were havin' a big time, drinkin' and dancin'. I asked if I could take her home later. She said no because they was goin' to a party. I knew he wasn't treatin' her right, knew he only wanted her for screwin', but she couldn't see it that way."

Memphis breathed as deeply as she could, but her next question still came out nervous and shaky.

"How do you know it was the night Sadie died?"

"Easy for me to remember because Opal Marie walked out of here that night and I never saw her again."

"Who did she walk out with?"

"Harvey Root, Jr., of course, the spoiled brat who was leadin' her on. He give her all kind of gifts and things."

"Claytie, you've said enough," said Ruby.

Long lost in his memories of yesteryear, Claytie ignored her.

"Why did you never see her again?"

"She just disappeared. She only come to town sometimes 'cause it was hard for her to get here. I used to ride my horse up to see her, or she'd get a ride with one of the miners comin' to town. When she didn't appear the next week, I went lookin'. Her family said the spirits must have took her 'cause she was doin' evil things in town, and when they sent her brother to search for her, he never come back either."

"Didn't you do anything to try and find her?"

"Sure, I did. I went to the sheriff, but he was so torn up about Sadie's murder that he said he couldn't do much. He sent men to search for Opal and her brother, but they never found nothin'. I looked around myself and asked some questions, even got up the nerve to ask Harvey Root if he'd seen her, but everybody was so shook up about Sadie and all the talk goin' on about who killed her, that nobody had any time to look for a lil' mountain girl."

"What did Harvey Root have to say?"

"Said that her brother had come lookin' for her, and the last he seen of her they was walkin' down the road toward Twenty-Two."

Memphis held her breath. "What do you think happened to her?"

After all these years, a hard-fought sob almost strangled his reply.

"It was springtime. The creeks was high, some of them flooding. I remember Maynard's Creek looked like a river runnin' fast, and Up Run, near the Chafin place was swollen bad." He swallowed hard. "I think they got drowned tryin' to cross Up Run, and her ignorant people didn't think to look for them 'til it was too late. Later that summer, they found a big-man's body near the mouth of the creek. Said it was Opal Marie's brother. Never did find her."

The three of them were quiet for a moment, Claytie thinking of his lost love, Ruby looking at him with sympathy, and Memphis's mind racing with all the possibilities Claytie's story presented. From the jukebox in the background twanged the hard thump of Johnny Paycheck singing "Take this Job and Shove It."

Memphis took Claytie's hand and squeezed it. "Thank you for telling me. I'm sorry you lost her."

"She was somethin', she was. Real innocent, and a real looker." He smiled. "A few years later I met my Jean and married her, but I never forgot Opal Marie."

"Claytie, if you don't mind, you won't tell anyone else about our conversation, or the pictures, will you?"

"Hell, no. Ain't nobody ever been interested anyway.

At first I tried talkin' about it, but nobody ever wanted to hear about it 'cause they was more interested in the Sadie Maynard case."

A tired, smoky voice spoke from behind them.

"You do as Memphis asks, Claytie, or no more free beer."

Memphis didn't have to turn to know it was Cutter who stood close behind her. As if her body had waited for its cue, a tingle coursed up her spine, settled in her breasts, and stiffened her nipples until they ached.

Claytie twisted his head to see Cutter and looked hurt. "You don't have to bribe me, Cutter. I like this here lady."

"Good, so do I."

She heard the smile in his voice, but was afraid to turn around. He stood so close she smelled wood-smoke, and the tang of winter on him. It would be so easy to turn and go right into his arms. The strong urge cartwheeled her stomach.

A big smile broke Ruby's grim countenance when he first spoke, but was replaced with a look of concern.

"What the hell happened to you? You're bleedin' like a stuck pig."

Memphis whirled her stool around to face him.

"Just surface cuts. Nothing to worry about."

Nicks and scrapes were evident even through his heavy five o'clock shadow. Tiny rivulets of blood had dripped and dried in the stubble. An ear oozed blood from a cut. There were numerous deep cuts on both his hands, and he'd put Band-Aids on some of them. He looked exhausted, weary to the bone.

Memphis took his hands in hers, and turned them palms up. They were in worse shape than the rest of him.

"Cutter, what have you been doing? Your hands need attention."

His gaze met hers and held. "Why didn't you tell me

you wanted to come here? I would have brought you," he asked, disregarding her concern about his hands.

"I, ah, really never . . . there was no need until a few hours ago. Please, let's get your hands taken care of."

"Right." He took charge then, as he had with the Chafin baby, as she suspected he did in most places and situations. "Ruby, grab me a fifth of Chivas Regal and let's go upstairs. Memphis is coming, too."

Cutter told them about the destruction of the nursery.

The two women watched him carefully, their faces expressing shocked indignation. Memphis stood next to the table listening intently.

Ruby grabbed the back of a kitchen chair, her face white. Cutter held her by the elbow and felt the lightness of her weight as he helped her lower herself weakly into the wooden chair. Sometimes he forgot how old she was, and how personally she took any offense to Cutter.

"Okay?" he asked.

She waved him off. "Of course, but pour me a jigger of that stuff, too."

He sat down beside her and did as she asked. He threw back two jiggers of Scotch, neat, himself, then settled down to nurse and savor a tumblerful.

The whiskey warmed him, but Memphis's presence heated him even more. The surprise of finding her sitting at the bar with Ruby and Claytie had lifted his spirits considerably. Everything seemed doable again, and the leveled hothouse didn't drag at him as it had when he drove down the mountain. His fury still rose off him like a fever, but his depression had disappeared.

Ruby glanced up at Memphis. "Well, don't just stand there like an idiot. You wanted to see to his hands. Bathroom's at the end of the hall. You'll find antiseptic and bandages in the medicine cabinet."

Cutter knew that Ruby must really be weak in the knees. If she had felt well she would never have allowed anyone to touch him except herself.

"Yes, ma'am," said Memphis, and disappeared down the hall.

"Those GD sons of bitches," swore Ruby. "You goin' to let 'em get away with that?"

"No. But I'm going to bring an end to it once and for all. I'm tired of all the bullshit, lawyers' fees and foot-dragging. It's something I should have done years ago, but I hired other attorneys and followed their advice, because I was afraid I was too emotionally involved to do a proper job. I'm going to represent myself. Going to force a confrontation with United Mining's attorneys. I'll file a lawsuit challenging the validity of the damned document granting them mineral rights, and also demand to see any records of financial arrangements or money changing hands during the transaction."

"Thought a lawsuit like that had already been filed."

"It has, but their attorneys keep stalling mine. I've had it. No more."

"About time, boy. I've been waiting for you to get mad enough. Just sorry it took the wrecking of your greenhouse to do it. When you going?"

"I've already made arrangements to go to New York next week."

"Good."

He narrowed his eyes and looked at her hard. "I heard a little of the conversation between Memphis and Claytie. Were you mean to her?"

"Mean as shit. Threw about everything I could her way. Rudeness, meanness, insults. I was a real bitch."

Cutter cleared his throat and frowned.

"It's okay, son." She squeezed his arm. "She took it all without a whimper. Never broke, never backed off. I'll behave from now on. I like her. She's a tough cookie, and on top of that a real lady. You got something special for her?"

He had never been able to lie to Ruby. "Yeah, I think I do."

Memphis came back with first-aid supplies, silencing them.

Ruby said, "Well, Memphis, I've had plenty times cleanin' this man up. It's your turn. Besides, I expect you know a thing or two about nursin'. If you two don't mind, think I'll be going to bed."

Cutter stood to help her out of her chair, but she rebuffed him. "I'm fine. Leave me be. Sit down and get them hands looked to."

Ruby left. With a big sigh Cutter sat down again. He leaned back against the ladder-back chair and sprawled his legs out in front of him, relaxing for the first time since he'd discovered the destruction early this morning. Memphis knelt between his knees on the floor in front of him, placing the first-aid supplies next to her.

They said nothing as she took one of his hands and carefully cleansed it with Bactine. She searched diligently for glass splinters and extracted them with tweezers. He watched her bent head with the joy of a kid on the first day of summer vacation. It seemed so right for her to be here with him.

She raised her head to look at him. "Am I hurting you?"

"No."

"Didn't you have gloves?"

Was that tenderness in her voice? The same tenderness he heard when she spoke to Katie?

"Yeah. Didn't do much good, did they?"

"There are so many of them. This may take a while."

"That's okay with me. In fact, I hope it takes all night. I have you all to myself, Maynard."

She blushed. "Cutter, I wish I could tell you how sorry I am about what happened to the nursery."

"You are telling me, right now. With every splinter you remove you're telling me."

She caught at her bottom lip, then released it, and a faint pink tinge lined her cheekbones.

She went back to her work, and he leaned forward, elbows on knees, to inhale the fragrance of her Joy and the fresh scent of her hair.

"Hold still."

He smiled and, closing his eyes, buried his nose in her hair near the crown of her head. He could have stayed there forever.

The muted thump of the jukebox downstairs, the tick of Ruby's grandfather clock, and the snoring of Willie, the cocker spaniel, were the only sounds to be heard in the quiet kitchen. The contented silence filled Cutter with a peace he'd never felt before.

"Cutter, give me your other hand."

"Look at me."

She kept her head bowed and worked busily on his other hand.

"Look at me," he demanded.

Finally, she raised her head.

He kissed her softly on the forehead, then placed a finger under her chin and tilted it up so he could reach her mouth.

He took a moment to read her face, and found her eyes glowing, her lips rosy with tenderness. He kissed her then, as gently as he could. She responded with a subtle drawing in of his tongue through the supple portal of her mouth.

He'd meant to only kiss her, to play a bit with her mouth, to place small kisses on the fragile bones of her cheeks, but when their tongues met, the gentleness flamed to full-fledged wanting. His cock gorged swiftly, and he pressed her tight against him between his legs.

She gave to him easily, dropping the cloth she held, and the tweezers, and put her arms around his waist.

The kiss grew until Cutter ached with wanting her. She moaned and the sound sent his senses reeling and made his erection so rock hard that it hurt worse than his hands.

A nudge at his ankle and a sharp bark startled them.

Willie needed to go outside. They pulled away from each other laughing, lingering to place a few kisses here and there.

"Cutter," she said softly, "I wanted that as much as you did, but I don't think . . ."

He kissed the tip of her nose, interrupting her. "Stop. I don't care what you think. I know you still don't trust me. Someday that won't make any difference."

Uncertainty filled her eyes, and he hated it.

He smiled and said, "But right now, I have to let the damned dog out."

On his return, he found her at the kitchen table going through the photos Claytie had held at the bar. At his request, she reluctantly showed him the lewd pictures from 1936, including the ones of Harvey Root and her grandfather. He recognized immediately that the threat he'd suspected hung over Memphis was real.

He lifted her to her feet and held her close in his arms, wanting to keep her with him all night.

She must have wanted the same thing because she murmured into his chest, "I have to go home. Nelsey didn't like me coming here, and Katie will be upset if I'm not there in the morning."

"I know. I wasn't going to keep you. . . . Not this time anyway." He smiled into her hair, but sobered quickly. "I'll follow you home."

She stepped away from him. "Why in heaven's name would you do that? I got here safely. I'm sure I'll get home in one piece."

"Indulge me."

"Oh, okay," she said with reluctance.

"Memphis, promise me you'll be careful from now on." He wanted to tell her why, but knew he couldn't.

She looked at him strangely.

"Sure. I'm always careful," she said, then laughed.

They both knew she had a tendency to enter where angels feared to tread.

§17§

Cutter emerged from the boardroom feeling victorious, but knew the battle wasn't over. It had taken all morning and the better part of the afternoon, but he'd obtained a restraining order that would keep the United Mining thugs off Macauley's Mountain for a few months. It would give him time to dig around for financial and legal records, which he was certain existed, showing that his father had sold the mineral rights illegally.

Simon Harkey, CEO of United Mining, followed him out of the luxuriously appointed boardroom.

"Congratulations," said the man. Cutter shook Harkey's extended hand politely, but dropped it as soon as civilly possible. "I had no idea our local boys down there were creating such havoc."

Like hell, you didn't.

"My deepest apologies," the man continued. "I notice one of your hands is bandaged. We didn't discuss the handling of any hospital expenses, but we'd be happy to pay any costs incurred."

Cutter glanced at the white gauze that swathed his left palm, and smiled. "It was well taken care of."

"Good. I'm sure we'll get all of this smoothed out in no time. You're a hell of an attorney, Tate. You can come to work for me anytime."

And sell my soul in the process, thought Cutter.

"No thanks," said Cutter. "You wouldn't be happy with me for long."

Harkey laughed. "Join me for a drink? We'll talk about it."

"Again, no thank you." He eyed the man coldly. "Mr. Harkey, I was young and naive when this battle began. You and your board jerked me around for years. No more. You've got my back against the wall, and I don't like that. The gloves are off, and I'm not playing gentleman anymore. By this time next year, my land will belong to me free and clear, of that you can be damned sure."

"Cutter, why don't you give up? You can't keep up this legal stalling for much longer."

"Fuck off, Harkey. Have someone bring my coat, please."

Minutes later, he pushed through the ornate building's revolving door and emerged onto Wall Street. The winter wind whistled through the narrow canyon of sky-reaching buildings, and he hunched into his trench coat. Unlike the winds of Macauley's Mountain, which blew leaves and the scent of ice and snow, the city wind carried gum wrappers, pages of old newspapers, and eye-irritating grit.

The northern city's day was already darkening into dusk.

He lowered his head against the wind and headed out into the street to hail a taxi.

"Museum of Modern Art," he told the driver.

Drawn like a boy to a puddle of water, he'd had this destination in the back of his mind since early morning. Despite the sharpness of wit he'd had to maintain, remembering all the finite points of law he needed to outsmart United Mining's legal eagles, he'd known this was where he would head at the end of the day.

He'd read the announcement of a week-long exhibit of Memphis Maynard's work in the *New Yorker* as he'd had his breakfast this morning. Then he remembered Birdy had mentioned the showing after church on Christmas Eve. He'd been so preoccupied and concerned at the time with Memphis's fear of Harvey Root that he'd forgotten all about it.

On the drive uptown, he wondered if Memphis was here in the city. Birdy had asked Memphis if she was going to New York for the showing, and Memphis had said she hated leaving Katie. He was sure she hadn't come.

MoMA, at four o'clock in the middle of the week on a late January day, was not busy. Cutter took his time, lingering for a while to admire the Stieglitz collection, and then stopped to study Ansel Adams's extraordinary sensitivity to the land, his sense of timing in catching light that fell on a perfect place at a perfect moment. He studied Henri Cartier-Bresson, the godfather of photojournalism, and wondered if Memphis admired the man's work as much as he did.

He was saving the best for last, but finally, his heart beating fast with anticipation, he entered the stark white-walled room that held Memphis's photography. Two other photographers' works were being presented, and he made a pretense of looking at them, always conscious of the collection on the wall behind him.

Unable to resist any longer, he turned to view what he'd longed to see since early this morning. As he did a swift overview of the display, he remembered that she was young to have her work shown at MoMA. This was an honor usually bestowed on older, more critically acclaimed artists, yet she'd never said a word to anyone in Yancey except Birdy, who had asked.

Most of the display was divided into her time in Bosnia, and the follow-up series she'd done on Margaret Bourke-White's 1930 Depression families. There looked to be some newer shots off to one side. He'd look at those last.

Immediately, one was caught with her sense of the moment, and an acute judgment of what had been important in capturing a visual of the vanishing instant.

He had seen the Depression series at the library in Yancey, so he studied the shots from Bosnia. Four grieving women clustered around the body of a young girl: the girl's left hand still held a rifle; her right, outflung, in a puddle of blood. The girl's face was hidden by matted blood-soaked hair, but the naked agony and disbelief in the faces of the women was alive in the black-and-white print. He felt their grief in his gut, and this was Memphis's gift—a brilliant understanding of her craft, informed by compassion.

He moved on, touched again and again by her finely tuned instincts in catching the pathos or joy of the human drama. Her fear, her joy, her uncertainty reached out and touched her subjects with cutting honesty and empathy.

Three pictures hung by themselves. Captivated by them, and what Memphis had recorded, Cutter sat on a nearby stone bench to feast his eyes.

The shots of the two Chafin boys, Elmurry and Bobby, were obviously taken in the woods. Their ragged, tufted haircuts were plainly etched against a background of winter-peeled trees and stark sky. Elmurry's mouth was ajar as he seemed to be listening to someone not in the picture, and Bobby focused in the same direction. What caught the viewer was the hungry eyes in the gaunt faces. Hungry for what, the viewer wanted to know—food, attention, knowledge?

The answers were in a picture of a smiling Vanta Lou as she looked at her children with so much love that waves of warmth swept the viewer. The hunger in the eyes of the spindly mountain boys was not for love, but for food and knowledge. Memphis had a divinatory genius for seeing and capturing important moments of the soul.

He sensed that her work reflected Memphis's inner self.

Cutter sat for a long time. He wanted the pictures of the Chafins, wanted to be able to look at them anytime he pleased. He wondered if any of the pictures on exhibit were for sale. Finally, hating to leave, but needing information, he got up from the bench. He located a guide who told him he would probably have to deal with Memphis's agent. The guide gave him directions to the department that dealt with acquisitions and sales.

His conversation with the agent was succinct and successful.

"Yes," said Harrison Telly, "Memphis hates to give up any of her work, but she would part with those. They were added as an afterthought. She didn't send them to be sold, but she needs the . . ."

The agent shut up quickly.

"Needs the money?" asked Cutter.

"Well, eh, no, not really." Harrison Telly gave an embarrassed laugh, knowing he'd given out personal information about a client, and at the same time put himself in an awkward position in negotiating a good deal. "But, hell, we all like to make money, don't we?"

"How much do you want for the three of them?"

Harrison Telly was quiet for a minute. Cutter imagined him frantically searching for a price. Should he go high and chance losing the sale, or should he go low, thus guaranteeing Memphis some profit?

Cutter let him squirm.

Telly went low. Memphis must really need the money.

"Two thousand a piece. Six thousand."

"You should be ashamed of yourself, Telly. The photographs are worth a hell of a lot more. Someday they will hang with Stieglitz, Adams, and White. I'll give thirty thousand for the three of them, on one condition."

"Yeah, what's that?"

Cutter heard the suppressed excitement in the man's voice. He'd just made a nice little commission, and Memphis would think he was a brilliant agent.

"On the condition that Memphis Maynard never know the name of the buyer."

"You got it. It's a deal."

"One more thing. I have to leave in the morning, and I want to take them back with me. I'll have my bank transfer funds to your account immediately if you can have the photographs delivered to suite 1411 at the St. Regis this evening."

"Yes, sir."

He wanted to see them one more time, and made his way back to the photography gallery. A blond-haired man in a long black leather coat sat on the stone bench that Cutter had vacated a while ago. Jake Bishop. Cutter stepped back and stood to the rear of the room. Bishop studied the photos as Cutter had. He stood, walked closer to them, eyed them critically, tilted his head this way and that, then returned to his seat. Cutter couldn't see his face, and he didn't want to. He already knew from the intense angle of Jake's body, and from his complete absorption that Jake Bishop loved Memphis.

Irrational fear shook Cutter.

Did Jake Bishop have enough love, and did he have enough influence and power over Memphis to bring her back to him? The questions he asked himself disturbed him more than he cared to admit, and he wanted Jake Bishop out of sight and mind. He exited the room rapidly.

To his surprise and consternation, he saw Memphis advancing quickly through the mingling crowd. If she saw him she might guess he was the buyer of the pictures. She hadn't spotted him, so he ducked into an adjacent exhibit area and watched her pass.

The Yancey Memphis had been discarded. This was a New York Memphis wearing a long slim black cashmere coat, a burgundy silk scarf folded smartly between lapels, black boots, and smart black leather shoulder bag. Her tawny, sun-touched hair had been tamed and slicked smoothly back into a sophisticated chignon. A large tortoise comb fastened it tight. She walked briskly, weaving her way with big-city ease through the light crowd, carrying a small Saks shopping bag.

She seemed to belong here. Her energy, her intensity matched that of the huge monolith that she made home. But then he thought of her in Yancey and her fascination with the storm they'd watched on the mountain, and he remembered that magical night in the cockpit of the plane and the stillness of her body, the reflection of the stars in her eyes. Part of Memphis belonged to the mountains, too. She might not know it, but he did.

At the moment though, she was actually safer here in New York than she was in Yancey, and he wished Katie was here also. He remembered with apprehension the incriminating 1936 pictures of Harvey Root and her grandfather that she'd shown him. The possible harm to Memphis and Katie that they suggested lived with him every day. He'd taken steps to protect them but worried that his actions wouldn't be enough.

She entered the alcove where her work was displayed, and he hesitated, fighting with himself. Finally he gave into the temptation to step around the corner and see her again. He wanted to see her with her work, see how she reacted to the way the photographs were displayed, wanted to see if she watched any viewers for their reactions.

It didn't take him long to find out why Memphis was at MoMA today. Disappointment hit him like a jackhammer slamming him on the chest. She'd come to meet Jake, of course.

Cutter walked swiftly away.

"Jake, I didn't expect to see you here."

"Didn't expect to see you either."

He would never admit that his dream had just come true. She stood before him, and the vibrant sight of her made him more determined than ever to have her back.

"Why are you here?"

"To pay my respects, of course, to my stellar student. I think you've surpassed me, Memphis."

"Thank you. But you didn't come to New York to see my exhibit."

"No, I came because my publisher wanted a heart-to-heart about a publication date. The first of March, no question. It's ready to go."

He could tell by the strained look on her face that she wasn't happy with the information.

"How do you think Katie's going to feel about her father when she grows up and finds he's written a scurrilous book about her great-grandmother?"

"Ah, so we're going to try a little emotional blackmail, are we? I wouldn't worry. There won't be much in it about the rumors of sex orgies. If I could find the pictures I heard exist, then I'd put more emphasis on that. You sure there weren't any dirty pictures in the snaps you took?"

"A few, but nothing of any significance. No one we knew, or anything to indicate they had anything to do with the case."

She said it without a trace of guilt on her face or in her voice. Great little actress.

"Right, so I'm focusing on Macauley Tate. On a hunch, I looked through earlier editions of the *Yancey Record* and found pictures of social events with Macauley Tate in the background eyeing Sadie Maynard with more-than-normal interest. Because of the witnesses who saw Amos, Tate, and Sadie together several times that week, and twice on the night of the murder, and because the weapons used belonged to Tate and were found in Amos's room, I think Tate hired Amos to kill Sadie."

"What was the motive?"

There was skepticism in her voice and Jake didn't like it. In the beginning, she'd been more than ready to prove that Macauley Tate was the murderer. Had Cutter Tate influenced her in any way?

"Blackmail, of course. I'm sure Sadie knew something the big boys didn't want her to know, maybe something she found out because she was the sheriff's wife, and they assigned Tate and Amos to take care of her." He thought of the incomplete list of names he'd found in Memphis's stack of photos. "I intend to dig that out this week."

"You're determined to make my grandmother look bad in all of this, aren't you?"

He'd pushed her too far. He could tell by the flash of her eyes and the tiny freckles that popped out on her face that she was angry as hell.

"Sorry, beautiful. It's the way I make a living. Don't take it personally. Look, let's go have a drink, talk about old times."

"No, thank you. I'm meeting old friends for cocktails at the St. Regis. I have a package to drop off there."

"I'll join you." Better to be with her in a crowd than not at all.

"No, Jake. You're Katie's father, and for that I'll be forever grateful, but we're history. Please accept that."

"Where are you staying? Maybe we can get together later in the week."

"I'm staying at Margo's because my apartment is sublet for another six weeks, but I'll only be here another day or two, and I'll be busy." She glanced at her watch. "I have to go."

"So do I," he lied. He would have preferred to sit and view the exhibit a while longer, but there was no way he would let Memphis walk away from him. "Be seein' ya, kid."

He left, seething.

Memphis left MoMA holding a borrowed umbrella in one hand and the carefully wrapped Chafin prints in the other. A small shopping bag, which held her shoes for the evening, hung from her wrist. The folding umbrella was scant protection in the icy sleet, which came from all directions. She wasn't dressed for it. When she'd left Margo's apartment earlier in the afternoon, the wind was cold and stiff, but the sun had been shining. She should have recognized the signs of an incoming front.

Ah, well, she wasn't important, but the prints were. She hugged them close to her side.

She hated to sell them, but she needed the money. The money she'd made from the *Washington Post* spread on Reverend Roy Elkins's snake-handling church in Grady had lasted long enough to take care of Christmas expenses. This sale was manna from heaven.

Her irritation at Jake's assumption that she would drop everything and have a drink with him was still with her. Her anger at the conclusions he'd drawn about her grandmother ate at her. Even if Jake couldn't find proof that her grandmother was blackmailing someone, he would certainly hint at it, and also tie in the lurid rumors of sexual wrongdoings.

The in-depth article she was writing for *Vanity Fair*, the nucleus for her own book about her grandmother, was almost finished. But she wanted to be sure of her facts before she released it for publication.

The walk up Fifth Avenue from MoMA to the hotel wasn't far, but she was getting soaked. She tried to wave down a taxi, but it was rush hour during bad weather. Available taxis were as scarce as Knick fans at a Bulls-Heat game.

Now she wished she'd gone along with the original plan Harrison Telly had arranged with MoMA, which was to have a courier deliver the Chafin originals. Memphis had said that was silly since she was going there anyway. Even if she hadn't arranged to meet friends there, the hotel was on her way home.

"Just drop them off at the desk," Harrison had insisted over the phone. "I didn't get the name of the buyer, but she said she'd pick them up from the concierge."

"Why didn't you get the name?" Memphis had asked.

"Listen, the lady had a cashier's check deposited to my trust account. That was good enough for me."

"Frankly, Harrison, I'm disappointed in you. It would have been nice to know on whose wall my Chafin boys and Vanta Lou are going to be hanging."

"Yeah, you're right. I goofed, won't happen again, but look, you're thirty thou richer," he'd said.

She lowered the umbrella, ducked into a shop, and tucked her package under her coat. Securing it with the pressure of her arm, she stepped out into the sleet again, managed to raise the umbrella once more, and wound her way through the crowded street to the hotel.

❦18❦

In the small, elegant, and understated lobby of the St. Regis, Memphis removed her damp coat and retrieved the package from under her arm. A slip of paper attached to the back of the thick envelope, which she hadn't noticed before, fluttered to the floor. She stooped to pick it up, read it, and realized it was the address of the St. Regis with a room number on it, obviously intended for the courier service.

She made her way back to the bar, glanced around the bar with its "old club" atmosphere, and saw that none of her friends had arrived yet. Perfect. Her curiosity was killing her. She would slip up to Suite 1411, make the delivery, and say thank you. By the time she got back down, Bebe and Jonesy would be there.

In the elevator, she tried to smooth her hair back into some sort of order. The wind and sleet had just about destroyed the neat chignon she'd worked on earlier in the day. She tucked some loose strands into the figure eight, and turned her attention to her dress.

On impulse she'd brought with her from Yancey Sadie's black 1930s slim sheath, the lovely, romantic dress she'd found in the attic. She'd worn it tonight, knowing they were going to the Monkey Bar for dinner later in the evening. Anyone with common sense would have worn a nice warm black wool dress, but no one had ever accused her of being practical. She shivered now—the dampness from her trek in the weather was still with her—but she would never regret wearing the delectable vintage dress. It was timeless.

The fragile gossamer black chiffon cap sleeves just cupped the curve of her shoulder and melted into a soft dangerous scoop of beaded bodice. The skirt skimmed her hips and dropped into a filmy float close to her ankles. The dress caressed her skin, making her feel free, alluring, and impudent. In the Saks bag, wrapped in protective tissue, were the dainty black crepe de chine dancing pumps that belonged to Sadie, too.

It was fun to be all dressed up with somewhere to go. The last time she'd felt so festive was when she'd worn the other Sadie dress on Thanksgiving. She enjoyed being in Manhattan again, renewing friendships she'd neglected for three years, fueling herself on the energetic pace of the city and all it had to offer.

The elevator stopped, the door opened on a mirrored foyer, and she stepped out. She laughed at her reflection. Oh, super, Memphis, the boots look great with the dress. She thought about sitting in a convenient mauve brocade armchair to remove her wet boots so she could change into the shoes. But the boots would never fit into the small bag, and she would have to carry the awkward boots and her coat. Forget it, Memphis. This person who bought the photos isn't interested in what you look like. They just want their purchase delivered safely.

Directly in front of her was the door to Suite 1411. She rang the bell.

A man's voice yelled, "Hold on a minute."

She shifted her coat from one arm to the other and waited.

The door opened, and it took a brief moment for it to register that Cutter Tate stood before her.

They stared at each other.

Shock crossed his face, then concern, then annoyance. He frowned, his dark, craggy eyebrows coming together in one straight line.

"Cutter! What are you doing here?" But the minute she asked the inane question, she had the answer. "You bought the Chafin prints."

"Yes, and I'd get another agent if I were you. He wasn't supposed to tell you."

She was still struggling with the fact that he was here, in front of her, every long hard-muscled bit of him, glaring at her now as if she'd done something wrong. Anger surged through her. His deception was obvious, and she almost turned to leave. But the anger lowered to a simmer, and finally changed to reluctant interest.

He looked different somehow. Obviously, he'd been dressing to go out. He looked freshly showered, a fragrant soap scent drifted from him. His dark hair was wet, combed back neat. An immaculate dress shirt, loose and unbuttoned, lay gleaming white against his tanned skin. A navy- and wine-striped tie was draped around his neck, needing to be tied.

She tried to keep from staring at the triangular patch of crisp black hair that covered his chest from his nipples to his waist, then disappeared into the band of his charcoal trousers.

The anger she felt at his deception began to melt away at the shock of seeing him, and his decided effect on her physical senses. *Dammit!*

"I'm forgetting my manners. Come in."

"No, no, I can't. I'm meeting friends downstairs." She handed him the package. "That's why I brought the prints instead of the courier."

His eyes traveled the length of her, and her body responded like a delicate Stradivarius tuned to the finest nuance.

"But you're obviously damp and cold. Please come in and have a brandy with me. Since you now know that I'm the buyer, we should at least toast the sale."

He's right.

"But it looks as if you were dressing to go out."

He glanced down at himself as if he'd forgotten his state of half-dress, and then looked at her with a smile, "I was, but that can wait a while."

"Okay, sure. A brandy sounds good."

He stood aside and she stepped into the sumptuous suite, glancing around her with appreciation. The St. Regis had recently gone through updating and redecorating. This lovely salon was done in hushed tones of sandy whites and muted plums. Plush carpet, the color of eggshell, stretched forever. The windows were draped in sea-green brocade and filmy gauze, arranged tastefully so that a magical glimpse of the city's lights was revealed in a gap of the layers.

"How lovely," she said.

"Yes. This is my first trip since they redid the interior. This is the suite my grandfather always stayed in. I came here frequently as a child. They're good enough to let me have the same rooms every time I come. Here, give me your coat, and sit down."

"I really can't stay long. They'll be waiting."

"Right. But we have to toast the Chafin photographs, so I'll pour our brandies, and they can warm while I finish dressing."

He handed her a snifter of brandy and walked into the bedroom. She caught a glimpse of a white terry cloth bathrobe flung carelessly in a boudoir chair, a pair of leather slippers on the floor nearby, and his suit jacket lying on the bed. She had a crazy desire to saunter into the room, and watch him as he buttoned his shirt and did his tie.

Oh, God, Memphis, stop this.

She glanced around the lovely salon again. Why did it feel so right to be here with him? Lush groups of fresh flowers sat on every credenza, and a graceful, creative arrangement in ivory and lavender graced the low glass coffee table. The round table sat in front of a nonfunctioning fireplace, which was masked by a large pale-green–and–ivory oriental fan.

Cutter's briefcase rested on the desk, a half-full cup of coffee next to it. From hidden speakers came the smooth seductive voice of Dinah Washington singing "What a Difference a Day Makes." But the song seemed wrong. It should be "I Remember You," an old Johnny Mercer tune.

Now what on earth made me think that?

To break the spell of the suite, the music, and the personal items of Cutter's that sat around, she called out to him, "Did you instruct Harrison not to tell me you were the buyer?"

"Yes, does that bother you?"

She wiggled her toes in the damp boots, dying to remove them.

"Yes, it does. Why are you in New York anyway, and why didn't you want me to know you were the buyer?"

"I came to battle with United Mining, and I didn't want you to know I bought the prints because I was afraid you wouldn't accept the sale." Startled, she realized he'd come back into the room and stood right behind her, shirt buttoned halfway now, but tie still hanging loose.

"Despite the shock of finding you here, and discovering you're the buyer, I'm happy to know that you think they are worth . . ."

"Stop chattering, Memphis. You're not a chatterer. Boots bothering you?"

"Well, yes, but I might as well leave them on. I have to go out into weather again."

She knew she should leave right now. Her brain told her to say good-bye, but her heart and traitorous body insisted she stay.

He took the snifter from her hand, rolled it around a few times between his palms, and handed it back to her. "Drink this while I get your boots off."

"No, I really have to . . ."

"Yes."

He knelt in front of her and took the heel of one boot and pulled. It slipped off easily, and he tugged at the other one until it came off, too. "Your feet are cold."

He held both feet firmly in his hands warming them, and Memphis thought she'd never felt anything so comforting. The damp toes of her black hose seemed to dry in no time as he knelt in front of her, holding her feet quietly and looked at her with searching, smoky eyes.

"Relax, Memphis, I'm not going to ravish you, although I'd like to."

She laughed, but she knew her face tinged pink because that's exactly what she was thinking, and thought she really wouldn't mind if he did ravish her.

He concentrated on one foot, and massaged with slow, circular movements, his thumb tracing around each toe, then traveled lazily along the sole and up to her ankle. His thumb and forefinger circled her ankle, while he rotated her foot with his other hand. Her skin tingled, every nerve ending from her toes to her thighs leaping expectantly. The muscles in her calves melted into jelly.

"My grandfather always said a real lady had delicate ankles. You would have passed his test."

He moved to the other foot, and she finally relaxed back into the chair and closed her eyes.

"Cutter, this is wonderful, and I could sit here forever, but I have friends waiting."

"You can't put your wet boots back on."

Her eyes popped open. She remembered her shoes and sat up.

"Right. I have shoes somewhere." Where had she placed the Saks bag?

"In here?" he asked, lifting the bag from the floor next to her chair.

"Yes."

He pulled the shoes from the bag, and slipped them on her feet.

"They look like dancing shoes."

"I think they were."

"Then we'll put them to good use."

Dinah Washington's "I Remember You" drifted through the room, and he pulled her to her feet.

"My grandfather's favorite song," he said.

All thoughts of Yancey, murders, unwelcome visitors, greedy mine owners, and unsolved mysteries dissolved. Memphis felt they were in a neutral time zone of their own with no problems or conflicts. Cocooned and protected by the lovely room, the scent of the flowers, and the romantic music, everything vanished but the two of them. High above the city, the muted sounds of traffic disappeared and they were alone, completely and inexorably alone.

She drifted into his arms easily, and laid her head on his shoulder as he led her in slow twirls around the room. He was a good dancer, meeting the rhythm with effortless grace. She turned her head and snuggled it into his neck so she could inhale his aftershave and feel the warmth of his skin. The fine cotton of his shirt felt like soft silk next to her cheek.

He placed her hand around his waist, and reached up to undo her hair. The pins came out at his deft touch and her hair tumbled free around her face and onto his shoulder.

"That's better," he whispered in her ear. "Have I told you that you're beautiful?"

She shook her head, at this point really not caring, just happy to be here in his arms.

He took the tip of her ear between his lips for a moment, wetting it, then releasing it with lazy languor.

She took a deep breath and felt everything change, yet remain the same.

In a space between heartbeats, the song was still "I Remember You," but the sound was tinny and came from a radio. The furniture became jade velvet settees and pink flowery chairs. The fireplace had a fire that crackled merrily, warming a room chilled by a winter storm outside the heavy-draped windows. They danced on an exotic topaz-and-burgundy oriental rug. Her cheek rested on a shoulder clothed in a heavy suit jacket, smooth and expensive.

The hard arm that circled her crushed her breasts close to his chest, and nothing existed for her except the man who held her. The knot in her belly tightened, and she shook from the tension.

He'd insisted that she not wear lingerie beneath her new black frock. It moved sensually about her hips. He'd gone with her to buy the dress and the shoes. She'd never be able to wear them in Yancey, but he'd promised they would escape to New York or somewhere as often as possible. How could anyone be as happy as she was?

"Never be afraid again, Sadie. I love you," his husky voice whispered in her ear. "Our love will keep you safe."

She lifted her head to say "I'm not afraid when I'm with you," and found herself in Cutter's arms, but feeling the same deep, deep desire she'd felt in the dream she'd just had, and the dream she'd had in the attic when she wore the silvery Sadie dress.

"Good," Cutter said, his breath uneven against her temple. "There's no reason for you to ever be afraid when you're with me. Look at me."

His eyes asked her a question and evidently he found what he wanted because he scooped her up in his arms and carried her into the bedroom.

He placed her gently on the bed. "Turn over."

She obeyed him, and he began to unbutton her dress. With every undone tiny loop he kissed her bare back. Her heart leaped each time his lips touched her skin.

When he was finished he spread his kisses all over her exposed back, and she was gone, melting into oblivion.

"Turn over and sit up."

He slipped one cap sleeve off her shoulder and placed butterfly kisses from there across her shoulder blade and up into her ear, then traveled with the soft kisses down to the cleft of her breasts. He pulled the bodice of her dress down to her waist, and she sat before him, her breasts exposed and vulnerable, in full view.

He took a deep breath and closed his eyes for a moment. When he opened them, they were so fevered with wanting she thought she would catch fire from their heat.

"Please stand up," he asked huskily. "I want to watch you take off the rest of it."

She stood and the slippery chiffon fell about her ankles. She stepped out of it, her heart in her throat, and sat on the edge of the bed to remove her panty hose. She unrolled them slowly, amazed at her brazenness, but knowing he enjoyed every movement.

He undressed as he watched her with hungry eyes.

He pulled her to her feet and his eyes again traveled the length of her. "You're even lovelier than I imagined."

Evidently there would be no shyness between them

because Memphis reveled in his survey of her body, and drank in every hard-muscled ripple and sharp angle of his long lean body. Her heart leapt and hammered in her throat at the sight of his thick, rigid erection.

He reached to cup one breast in his palm, then brought her to him and kissed her, and soon they were submerged in the depths of a rich, soul-satisfying kiss beyond any Memphis had ever known. She was drowning in Cutter, immersed in his scent, his feel, his touch. His hot, bulging penis branded her belly, and she yearned impatiently for the feel of its ridged length inside of her.

They fell back onto the bed, and Cutter lay on his side next to her. His fingers traced the line of her trembling belly, and she shuddered, arching as he gripped her curly mound of hair, then ran his finger lazily over her sweet center. He played with the softness there as his tongue played with the taut tips of her nipples. A whimper escaped her and she saw him smile before she closed her eyes in sweet agony.

His mouth closed over one taut breast, while his fingers sought and found the sweetest place of all. Gently, teasingly, he stroked her hard little nubbin. Treating her almost virginal, he tenderly fingered the hot moistness between her legs, then as if he was savoring, he explored each crevice and nook of the creamy privateness.

Memphis shook now with wanting, feeling like a cat in heat, aching until she was embarrassed, dry, thirsty, hot with wanting.

"Oh, God, please, Cutter."

"Not yet," he said huskily, as he switched breasts.

She moaned, and his stomach tightened against her side, his penis grew fevered and calloused.

He levered himself over her, his knees holding her tight, and ran a rough tongue down the length of her, from the hollow of her throat to the top of her mound, then drove two fingers deep into her wetness. He pleasured her, pushing in and out with masterful strokes, teasing, soothing, teasing, stroking, teasing, until she cried out, and he smiled.

She closed her eyes. Tears coursed down her cheeks, into her ears, and off her jaws, onto her shoulder blades. Never, ever, in her entire life had she ever wanted anything as badly as she wanted Cutter Tate inside of her, filling her emptiness, satisfying, feeding this awful, sweet agony.

He spread her legs wide and slid his hips into the cradle of her thighs. For a moment he settled the length of him against her. They fit, hands, hips, chest, everything drawn to its assigned place as if they had been there before, as if she'd been created just for him.

He raised himself and placed the thick head of his shaft against her. Supporting himself on one strong arm, he took her chin in his other hand and said, "Open your eyes and look at me."

Their gazes locked as he pushed into her. *Oh, Jesus God.*

He moved lazily, slowly, enjoying the inside of her, but gradually his thrusts grew harder and deeper, and he never took his eyes from hers. Then she saw his eyes begin to glaze over with a primal wanting beyond understanding, carrying them toward an overwhelming peak of passion. Unable to focus anymore, she closed her eyes and let the growing tide sweep her along.

Cutter invaded her up to his hilt, groaning now with every deep thrust. No man had ever possessed her before, but Cutter did. And she wanted his possession, wanted the complete freedom of giving over, of belonging to this other soul, as he belonged to her. Savage pleasure exploded throughout her entire being.

They went at each other wildly, as if it was the first

time for both of them. The tension that had mounted in the previous months fed their savageness. He drove mindlessly into her, and she arched to meet him, banging against his hips, wanting more and more of this delicious primeval liberation. Her fingernails dug into his shoulders. Her inner muscles clasped his shaft spasmodically, again and again, caressing, giving, taking. She screamed with release, and soared over the top and into oblivion. He pulled out almost to his tip, then arched back, driving into her for the final plunge.

"Jesus," he roared, as he came. His hot liquid shot into her, spilled onto her thighs, and ran down to her boneless knees.

He collapsed on top of her with a moan, and she softly caressed the fevered skin on his broad back. Even in her euphoric state, she wished vaguely that he could stay there forever, attach himself to her like a barnacle and stay.

He rolled off, lay on his side, and brought her softly to him, kissing every part of her body he could reach. She did the same, wanting the wanting to never stop, wanting the bliss to never stop.

He cupped her into his body, buttocks against his penis, back against his chest, and she reveled in the feel of his crisp hairs against her skin. They didn't speak for a long time.

"Thank you," he eventually murmured into her ear, sending fresh shock waves to her already fragile nerve endings.

She smiled. "And I thank you," she said.

Cutter continued to brush his lips against her shoulder and caress her breasts. She felt cherished and precious, something she'd never felt before.

"I knew it would be this way, Memphis."

She cried then, huge tears rolling down her face and onto her neck. Any other man would have fallen asleep by now, or asked her why she was crying, but he didn't.

Cutter turned her around to him, and brought her close to his chest to kiss her tears away and embrace her, and let her know that he understood the depths of her emotion.

His soothing hand soon dried her tears and she snuggled close into his chest, letting the crisp hair tickle her nose.

"We just made wild, crazy love and there are heaps of things I don't know about you, Cutter Tate."

"I think we just proved words aren't necessary between us, but I'm ready for questions." She heard the smile in his voice.

There was a long comfortable pause, as she gathered her wits, and tried to remember all of the things she'd wondered about him. He waited, nuzzling her ear, hugging her close.

Finally, she whispered shyly, "Well, you must have gone to school somewhere."

"Never finished high school. Nelsey made me take the GED. At the time I wanted to get as far away from Yancey as possible, so I ended up at Stanford. Went to law school at Georgetown."

"Why do you hunt with bow and arrow?"

"There's no electricity at the greenhouse or Uncle East's cabin, so there's no way to freeze food. Uncle East's cabin has an ice house where the Bradys' store things, and I have an auxiliary generator, but I only use it to pump water for my plants. I'm not crazy about hunting, so I only hunt when I'm on the mountain for extended stays and need game to eat. A bow and arrow is more sporting than a gun."

"Why did my grandfather hate you so?"

His body tightened, his heart skipped several beats, and his breath against her cheek stopped for seconds, and she wished immediately that she hadn't asked.

He drew a deep breath and said, "I'm not sure, but I think it had something to do with Sadie's death and my grandfather. Sheriff Maynard took his anger out on me."

"I'm sorry, Cutter. Do you think . . . ?"

He tipped her head up, found her mouth, and kissed her hard, then chuckled. "How long is this list of questions? Are all skinny photojournalists so curious? No more questions. Not tonight, anyway."

Memphis began to explore his chest, something she'd been wanting to do since their first kiss on the airfield. She traced each hard-muscled contour, then kissed each dark-brown nipple. With huge delight, she slipped her hand down below the triangular patch of hair on his chest and found the thick tangle that covered his full testicles. He caught her hand at that point.

"No, if you touch me like that again, we'll have another wild scene. Let's make this one slow and easy. I want to get to know your body, too."

He hugged her to him, rocking her back and forth, and she covered his shoulder with small kisses.

Eventually, all this kissing and hugging led to languorous lovemaking, and they savored each other again and again until they were exhausted.

"Spend the night with me," he said.

"Oh, my God." She sat straight up. "Bebe and Jonesy!"

The clock showed midnight. He laughed uproariously, and said, "I think they've probably given up and gone home by now."

"Right." She snuggled up close to him, and closed her eyes, and yawned. "I'll stay if I can have breakfast in bed."

"Anything, Miss Scarlett, anything."

Just before sleep caught her, she remembered and asked, "Cutter, when we were dancing, did you feel as if we'd been transported in time? I felt like we'd danced before in the very same room, here in the hotel, only everything was different, like we were in a dream, but it really happened."

He grew still, and didn't answer for a while. She thought he'd gone to sleep, but finally he pulled her close and said, "Sweetheart, when I'm with you I always feel as if I'm in a dream."

§19§

"Law offices of Macauley Tate," chirped Birdy into the telephone.

The door between his office and Birdy's reception area was always open unless he had clients with him.

Cutter chuckled. Birdy loved sounding officious, but try as she might, she still just sounded like Birdy.

A fire snapped cheerily in the fireplace of his office. He revolved his leather desk chair so he could watch the snow falling steadily outside the large mullioned windows. He was comfortable here. Birdy had done a nice job of decorating the small suite of offices. Books lined most of the wall space from floor to ceiling, and cushy tobacco-leather sofas and chairs sat against one wall and in front of his desk. A tasteful wine-and-navy oriental rug squared an area of polished dark walnut floor.

Birdy kept the place running when he was working in the field with TEC, Inc., which was most of June through November, but she loved it when Cutter turned complete lawyer the rest of the year.

He found it difficult keeping his mind on the papers in front of him this afternoon. Memphis would come home today. They had wanted to spend the weekend together in Manhattan, but he had to return to Yancey because of a court case involving Ruby. Memphis stayed in the big city to attend a party given in her honor.

"Cutter," said Birdy from behind him, "where did those pictures come from? I didn't hang them."

He twirled his chair around and looked at the Chafin pictures in a prominent place right over the most impressive sofa in the office.

"Nope. I did. Great, aren't they?"

Birdy advanced closer to the pictures, and peered at them carefully, squinching up her nose as she inspected.

"Why, that's the Chafin woman and her boys."

"Sure is."

"Well, now, Cutter, it's none of my business, but I have to tell you that I don't think they belong here. After all, I had a certain look and feeling in mind when I decorated these offices and I just don't think these fit at all."

"You know I love everything you've done, Birdy, but you're right, in this case it *is* none of your business. They are staying right there."

"Well, mercy, Cutter. If it's that important to you, I guess I can put up with them. Where did you get them, anyway?"

"New York."

"But what would pictures of the Chafins be doing in New York?" She stopped tapping her impatient foot and grew still, her eyes widening as she looked at the offending photos. Her neck stiffened. "Memphis! The exhibit. You bought them from the exhibit."

"If you must know, Birdy, yes." To forestall further questions, he said, "Please bring Ruby's file to me, pronto."

"Thought you resolved the suit against Ruby in court this morning."

"I did. Just tying up loose ends." He noticed the sheaf of papers in her hand. "Are those messages for me?"

She gave the photographs one last distasteful look and turned on her secretary face.

"Yes. Pork Winthrop says he's tired of sitting in jail waiting for somone to bail him out. Wants you to come and get him this minute. Mary Faye called to say she'll be in on Friday for the changes to her will. Billy Gus says Jimmy is still encroaching on his driveway, no matter what you told him, and he's going to call the sheriff again if you don't keep Jimmy in line. Hank called and said to tell you his crew's finished cleaning up the greenhouse mess, and sealed up your storage room until spring." She raised her eyebrows curiously. "What greenhouse?"

"A friend's," he answered curtly. "What else do you have, Birdy?"

"The governor said for you to call him, and Nelsey called to say the flowers were beautiful, but some florist called from New York to say that they couldn't find the orchids you wanted. Why did you send Nelsey flowers? Has she been sick?"

He bypassed the questions about Nelsey. "When did the governor call?"

"Just five minutes ago."

He wiped his hand over his face, trying to hide his irritation. "Birdy, you should have let me talk to some of these people. Did any of them ask to speak with me?"

"Yes. Nelsey, and the governor, but you were busy."

"I'm never too busy to talk to Nelsey, or Governor Hatfield." He sighed, and held out his hand for the messages. "Okay, give me a chance to answer a few of these, then we'll work together on the Cavendish case."

"Okay. If Nelsey's sick, I'd better go see her this afternoon."

"Nelsey isn't sick," Cutter replied curtly.

"Oh, then it must be Katie's birthday."

"Birdy, need I remind you that a personal assistant is just that. . . . They keep their employer's business and personal affairs to themselves, and they don't ask questions. Understood?"

"Certainly," she said, then sniffed and minced primly out of the office.

An hour later, caught up with his work and not ready to research the big case he had coming up next month, Cutter threw down his pen and got up from his chair to pace restlessly.

His memories of the magic night with Memphis jumped from delight to guilt. He'd been wrestling with his conscience since he'd awakened the next morning with her in his arms.

He could still feel her slim, sleep-warm body snug against his chest, like a snail safe in its shell. The faint scent of Joy, which always lingered about her, had whet his appetite, and an immediate longing to enter her again, to fill himself again and again of Memphis— her fire, her gentleness, her compassion, her passion. He'd kissed her on the temple. She woke up and they made slow, lazy, early-morning love.

He smiled now, almost laughing aloud at the memory of all the questions she'd asked him while they held each other beneath the covers and waited for breakfast to be delivered.

"Is your mother still living?"

"No, she died ten years ago." An explanation followed of his mother's death from lung cancer in Scotland.

"Why do you still take coal from the mountains?"

"I finish projects already begun. I'd do it for free, but the state pays TEC, Inc. to clear it, then put it back in shape, and our people need work. We need more small clean industry in the area like Black Brady's television component and computer plants. I own several small factories that produce similar products, but I'm not an industrialist. I enjoy the environmental stuff, and being a small-town lawyer."

They peppered each other with questions and talk and personal disclosures, before, during, and after breakfast, until Cutter had to leave to get his flight back to West Virginia.

He was glad his heart was hidden for it was so illuminated, so leaping with promise and hope like he'd never felt before, that he imagined the glow would be blinding.

Then he was pierced with guilt. He knew she didn't trust him, and she had good reason.

How could he have made love to Memphis when he withheld from her that which she wanted the most?

His resolve to tell her would fade soon after it surfaced. Afraid she would never forgive him, and that he would never hold her in his arms again, he had decided not to tell her. But the guilt soon overtook him again and drove him crazy, and he promised himself for the eighteenth time to tell her.

He seesawed between joy and guilt.

He braced his arms, leaning on the windowsill with his hands, and stared at the drifting snow in indecisive agony. Tell her and lose her, or not tell her and try to hide his deception—which would eventually ruin their developing relationship?

"Grandfather, if there are such things as spirits, or angels or such, and you're around anywhere, I need your help," he whispered to the snow, and his warm breath frosted the cold glass.

Nelsey stopped to rest a minute, breathing hard. Pulling Katie on the sled through the deep snow had been tougher than she thought. *Getting old, Nelsey Kinzer. Your heart's still in it, but the body's beginning to go.* The delight on Katie's face, however, was worth any discomfort. Nelsey eyed the hill longingly. What fun it would be to make a run down the hill with Katie, but she knew that would be the height of foolishness. Katie would have to wait for her mama to take her down the hill.

Memphis had arrived home just an hour ago, and was in the attic searching for old valentines Margo had spotted there on her last visit.

They stopped at the front steps, and Nelsey helped a bundled-up Katie off the sled.

"Come on, young'un, I'm going to help you make your first snowman."

"Frosty no man?" inquired Katie hopefully.

"Yep, with coal eyes, carrot nose, and all."

"Yea-a-a-h," yelled Katie, clapping her mittened hands.

As they rolled big snowballs, Nelsey thought with discomfort of the mistake she'd made this morning.

When the flowers for Memphis from Cutter began to arrive, it hadn't been difficult for Nelsey to figure out what had happened while they were in New York. Secretly, she was pleased to death, and she supposed it had been inevitable, but knowing both of them as she did, and knowing the particular concerns they each carried, she could see problems down the road.

Lord, I know you're busy, but we need help here. It sure would be nice if you could figure out how to fix all this mix-up.

When the florist in Manhattan had called to say the special orchids Cutter had ordered weren't available, Nelsey thought Cutter should know. Unfortunately when she had called his office, Birdy had answered to say he was in court. Nelsey had called again later, and still not able to get through Birdy to Cutter, she'd left the message, hoping Birdy would get the impression the flowers had been for Nelsey.

Unless Cutter could come up with a good excuse, Birdy would have it all over town that Cutter had sent Memphis flowers. Hard to tell what damn fool reason she would give, or what she would imply. But Cutter and Memphis would be real unhappy if people were nibbin' into their personal lives. Too many people knew too much about them as it was.

In the attic, Memphis searched until she found the box of old-fashioned valentines Margo wanted. She carried them over to the window for better light, and wiped a clear spot on its foggy surface. Below her, Nelsey and Katie were placing a carrot on their snowman for a nose. The orange carrot and Katie's bright blue snowsuit were vivid against the white snow.

She sighed with pleasure at an unfamiliar sense of homecoming, something she'd never experienced before.

She smiled to herself. New York had been wonderful, in more ways than one, but even before fate had placed her and Cutter together, she'd begun to miss Yancey. Not just Katie, Nelsey, and the warm curl of Miss Priss around her feet, but Yancey and the mountains themselves: the quiet of the early morning, the sweet sounds of the twilight bells from the Church of the Good Shepherd when the breeze blew them toward Maynard Creek, the light kiss of the mist on her cheek when she climbed high enough on Macauley Mountain, and yes, even the faint clatter of the coal tipple as coal cars traveled down the mountain from the mine.

The baskets, bouquets, and vases of flowers that awaited her on her return home helped her remember the cherished feelings in Cutter's arms. She hadn't needed flowers to know that their night together had been as special for Cutter as it had been for her, but his thoughtfulness touched her deeply. She remembered their question-and-answer session, and the talk they'd had about politics and religious philosophy. Cutter had almost missed his plane. She also remembered with embarrassment the questions she'd been afraid to ask. Had he ever been in love, and with whom?

Come on, Memphis, back to the task at hand. You're acting like a dizzy schoolgirl with a crush on the captain of the football team.

She rustled around in the box looking for the lacy valentines Margo wanted. She found one, but then dropped it back in the box as the battle of confusing feelings that had plagued her for the last three days returned.

On the one hand, the night with Cutter had almost engulfed her with its completeness. Their powerful coming together had exposed parts of her that cried for release and expression. His passion, his masterful yet gentle handling of her body and her soul, had struck right through her nerve center to her heart.

On the other hand, following swiftly on the heels of these staggering emotions, were confusion and guilt. How could she have given herself so completely and so willingly to a man she didn't trust, a man whose veins carried the same blood as the man who must have murdered Sadie? She bounced back and forth from elation to confusion, wrestling with feelings she didn't want to deal with, not yet anyway.

Don't worry about it right now. Try to separate the two feelings. Dear God, for a little while, let me live in this world of bliss.

She rummaged in the box again, anxious to finish this favor for Margo so she could join Nelsey and Katie. A puffy satin heart caught her eye and she lifted it to the light. Neat. Margo should love this one. They didn't make valentines like this anymore. Real lace edged the heart, and seed pearls spelled the words "You Are Love." The heart opened to fine linen paper. Protected by the thickness of the heart, the sheet of paper had barely aged through the years. A strong hand had written portions of an Edna St. Vincent Millay sonnet, which Memphis recognized as one of her favorites.

Love me or love me not, you have no voice
In this, which is my portion to the end.
....

I do desire your kiss upon my mouth;
They have not craved a cup of water more
That bleach upon the deserts of the south;
Here might you bless me; what you cannot do
Is bow me down, who have been loved by you.

A chill ran down her spine and tears filled her eyes. Someone who loved to the fullest had chosen to send this to his beloved.

At the bottom, it was signed: To Sadie from M. Maybe M stood for Maynard. But why would anyone use the initial of their last name to sign a valentine?

Another chill coursed through her, and her tears dried. This card was not sent by her grandfather to her grandmother. Perhaps it was a card received by Sadie before she met James Maynard, when she was a teenager maybe, or maybe it was a secret admirer whom Sadie didn't know.

Instinct told her, however, that this was a valentine from a secret lover. Why else would it be signed with an initial? She looked hurriedly through the rest of the valentines, but there were no more from M. Memphis's hand shook as she reread the lovely card. The implications were horrendous. Could this have anything to do with Sadie's murder? Her heart stood still as she realized that M. *could* stand for Macauley Tate. Of course. A crime of passion. He had murdered her because he couldn't have her.

No. No. No.

All along, she'd wanted to prove Macauley Tate the killer. But not anymore, not after her explosive emotional discovery of Cutter.

No. There were a thousand other possibilities. Don't

jump to irrational conclusions. A single initial on an undated card meant nothing. Absolutely nothing.

The sound of Katie's laughter floated up from below, and she glanced down to see Katie and Nelsey making snow angels. She wanted to be down there with them, not here in the attic imagining terrible thoughts that might affect the rest of her life. She placed the rest of the cards back into the box, but set the puffy heart aside to look at later. She would send Margo the whole box.

Downstairs, she shrugged into her down jacket, stuffed her jeans into snow boots, and ran out to join Nelsey and Katie.

Yancey was having an especially wet winter. Snow came almost every other week, leaving little chance for a good street clearing. This afternoon the snow was still fresh, clean, and glistening white, not yet coated with black coal grime.

Nelsey sat on the steps for a well-deserved rest, and watched as Memphis and Katie made snow angels. Soon Katie wanted another ride on the sled.

"Okay, babe, let's go," said Memphis.

"She wants to go down the hill, but I thought I'd let you have that pleasure," said Nelsey.

"Katie, you're a child whose heart beats like your mom's. I've been dying to tackle that hill ever since it started snowing."

Memphis placed Katie on the sled in front of her, wedged between her thighs, and anchored her feet on the guide bars. Nelsey gave them a push. It took a few tugs on the rope to get them going properly, and a moment to remember how to use her feet on the guide bars that kept the runners headed in the right direction. Finally they were ripping down the hill headed toward Leroy's at the bottom. The speed and the wind against her face exhilarated Memphis, freeing her for a while from the apprehension the valentine had created, but she worried about Katie. She could only hope the child wasn't afraid, and was enjoying the swift descent as much as she was.

They zipped past Leroy's, slowed, and coasted to the middle of the bridge. Katie was so quiet, Memphis got off the sled quickly and knelt in the snow to look at her. A wide grin spread across Katie's pink-cheeked face, and her blue eyes sparkled with happiness.

"Again, Mommy, again."

Memphis laughed with delight, gave her a quick hug, and turned the sled to begin the trudge back up the hill.

"Yeah, well, you got it easy, kid. Now comes the hard part for Mom."

A quiet peace lay here in the valley. Traffic on the road across the bridge was light and slow. The swift flow and gurgle of Maynard Creek had been silenced by the dense slab of ice that capped the broad waterway. Most of Leroy's regulars must be snowed in at home. The only vehicle parked near the store was a battered old dark blue pickup with a rifle racked in the rearview window.

The truck was not one she had noticed at Leroy's before, but it looked vaguely familiar. Wasn't it the same truck she'd found parked right next to hers in town on several occasions recently? If it was, so what?

She tucked her chin into her collar and climbed the hill.

For the next half an hour she and Katie whizzed happily down the hill. When the sun began its descent, the shadows grew long, and the wind against their faces became sharp instead of exhilarating.

Memphis drew the sled toward Nelsey, who waited for them on the front steps.

"I think we've had enough. Got any of your scrumptious soup waiting for us?"

"Sure do. It's been simmerin' all day. Let's use the back door. I want to store the sled in the shed back there."

"Okay."

Nelsey went ahead. Memphis followed slowly, her legs and arms tired now, her knee aching.

"Memphis. Stay where you are." Nelsey's quavering voice stopped her in her tracks. "Turn around and go back in the front door."

"What's the matter?"

"All right, you can come, but leave Katie on the sled."

Memphis walked around the corner of the house and bumped into Nelsey who stood stock-still, staring at the back porch.

Hanging eye-level from a thin wire attached to a roof beam was Miss Priss. Her lovely sleek black body hung twisting languidly in the light wind. The wire wrapped around her neck had taken the life from her, and her once-proud little head rested at a macabre angle.

The End of her plumed tail had been nipped off and scarlet spots of blood spotched the white snow beneath her.

Memphis shivered with cold and with anger, and glared at the bare spot at her feet. Clearing the snow had been easy, but digging a hole in the frozen earth was proving almost impossible.

She had chosen a burial place for Miss Priss beneath the large oak at the corner of the house. The cat had loved to sit in the window and watch sunbeams climb the bare branches of the tree.

She made another stab at the frozen crust with the shovel. The shock of the galvanized steel shovel against the unyielding surface sent shock waves to her shoulder. The pain almost sent her to her knees, but she persevered, disregarding the pitiful spoonful of earth she'd managed to scoop out. Night was closing in quickly, but she didn't care, and for once she wasn't afraid of the dark woods that sat close by.

Dear God, who would do something like this?

There hadn't been any scare tactics used against her since Thanksgiving week when someone had written "leave nosey bitch" on the sheets hanging from the line. But despite the friends she'd made in Yancey, someone obviously still wanted her to leave.

"Oh, sweet Miss Priss, I'm so sorry you were hurt because of me. You should have lived a nice long life of warm kitchens, sunny windowsills, good catfish, and welcoming laps of love."

She struck at the earth again, and couldn't stop the painful grunt that came from her chest.

Strong leather-clad arms wrapped her from behind, and capable hands grasped the handle of the shovel, halting her next vicious stab at the icy crust.

"Nelsey called me," Cutter whispered warm against her cheek.

She whipped around and let the tears come, crying into his chest.

"Why, why, Cutter? I don't understand how someone could be so cruel," she got out between sobs.

"I don't either, sweetheart."

He held her tight while she cried in anger, in fear, in frustration, and in sorrow. Finally, weak with spent emotion, she stopped and he rocked her in his arms.

She wiggled out of his embrace and tried to see his face in the dark. She found the stony set of his jaw, and drew a gentle finger along it.

"I'm okay now. Give me the shovel."

"I'll do this in the morning. Come in and eat some of Nelsey's soup."

"No. I won't leave her out here like this."

"It's too dark, and you'll need a pickax, not a shovel."

"Then let's look for a pickax."

He sighed and brushed his warm knuckles against

her cold cheek. "You're determined to do this, aren't you?"

"Yes."

"Okay, but only if we can find a pickax, and you'll let me do it."

She agreed, and after questioning Nelsey, they discovered a pick in the shed. Memphis stood close by Cutter's side, holding a lantern for him, as he dug the hole. Miss Priss went to her resting place in a large felt-lined cigar box that Memphis had found in the attic.

Later, at the kitchen table, Cutter sat hunched over a cup of steaming hot coffee. Katie was asleep, and Nelsey, who was spending the night, slept in the room next to Katie's. Memphis busied herself heating soup left for them on the stove, finding biscuits and butter in the refrigerator, and making a salad.

"Sit down. I need to talk to you," said Cutter.

Memphis didn't like the tone of his voice. It made her nervous.

"Just a minute. The salad's almost ready."

"It can wait. Sit down."

"Really, Cutter. What's the problem?"

She sat across the table from him, wiping her hands dry on a paper towel. One glance at his hardened jaw, and the craggy eyebrows drawn taut, made her more nervous.

"I want you to leave Yancey."

"What?"

"You heard me."

"Why?"

"You know why. Someone here wants to do you harm. At first it was just dirty words on sheets, and a mean Halloween prank, but the incidents are getting vicious. I want you and Katie out of harm's way."

"There's no circumstance that would make me leave. If you think I'm chicken enough to run at the first sign of trouble, you're wrong. And if you think I'm going to let someone get away with this, you're wrong there, too. And there's another thing. I haven't accomplished what I came here to do."

"Finding out who killed Sadie isn't worth risking putting yourself in danger."

"I think they're just trying to scare me, not hurt me."

"Use your head, Memphis. Whoever is doing this is not a nice person. It's hard to imagine what they will do next."

"I feel perfectly safe here with Nelsey around, and Leroy at the bottom of the hill."

None of which was entirely true.

The lights still appeared in the woods from time to time, and she still heard the woman humming "What a Friend We Have in Jesus." The woods had seemed a friendly enough place when she had searched for a Christmas tree with Katie and Cutter, but she hadn't been in them since and avoided even looking in that direction. And despite Nelsey's opinion that the "presence" in the darkroom was a friendly one, it was still unsettling to hear a ghost humming a hymn and making you feel heartbreakingly sad.

He closed his eyes and shook his head as if in pain. "You are one stubborn woman. You'd make everyone happy if you left."

"Including you? That would make you real happy, wouldn't it?"

A long silence followed and they stared at each other grimly across the table.

"No. It would make me miserable," he said softly. "But how I feel isn't important. Memphis, I'm begging you to leave."

"No. Not until I get what I came for. Not until I right a wrong committed years ago, which no one has ever atoned for, and clear the slanderous rumors that have followed my grandmother's name all these years." His expression grew grimmer and her stomach turned, but she finished bravely. "I'm sorry if I seem obsessed with it, but I think maybe that I am. I'm being pushed by some unknown force to finish something started long ago."

Cutter stood up abruptly, and his chair fell backwards with a loud bang. He righted it, then walked around the table and bent to kiss the top of her head. Taking her by the shoulders, he lifted her to face him, then locked her head between his hands and studied her face.

Finally, his mouth came down hard on hers. His kiss was long, harsh, and searing, his mouth merciless in its lust, and her treacherous body responded with trembling need. But he finished with a soft kiss to each of her eyelids, then set her from him.

"I'll be gone a few days," he said, and walked out.

§20§

Patches of black, grime-encrusted snow spotted the shoulders of the highway to Twenty-Two Mountain, but the road itself was clean and safe. Would spring never come? There seemed a promise of it today. The air was biting cold, but sunny, and the sky reflected shades of acute winter blue. A beautiful, beautiful day, thought Memphis.

A day to enjoy, no matter what. She wouldn't worry or wonder about Cutter's long absence, or about who hated her so much that they would brutalize an innocent kitten.

The heartsickening memory of Miss Priss twisting listlessly in the cold cruel winter twilight came back, and she almost stopped the Jeep to turn around and return to the safety of the house. To the safety of Nelsey's and Katie's company.

No. She'd promised Vanta Lou she would visit Up Run on Valentine's Day. She wouldn't allow anyone to terrorize her into hiding behind closed doors.

The note Vanta Lou left for her at Christmas had intrigued her. Memphis had made this trip in January before the roads became impassable, but snow in the higher regions hadn't allowed her to get any further than Up Run. She'd left Vanta Lou a note saying she would return. This time Nelsey had packed a lunch, and tucked a thermos of hot tea into the basket. The women would share lunch, and she would catch up on Opal Marie and the other children, and discover the information Vanta Lou had for her.

Memphis slowed, and turned onto the steep road that led up the mountain. In her rearview mirror she looked for the blue pickup, which always seemed to be in her vicinity lately. No sign of the truck today. The idea that she was being followed must be a figment of her imagination created by fear.

Relax, Memphis. Remember, you're going to enjoy today.

Two hours later, she sat on a boulder next to Up Run Creek and waited. Vanta Lou had fashioned a little wooden mailbox for their note passing and secured it in the crook of the large evergreen that held the raft. The box was empty, and the raft was on the other side of the creek, so Memphis knew Vanta Lou had gotten her note.

Memphis wouldn't have retrieved the raft and crossed the creek anyway. The creek roared and rushed with large chunks of ice and debris.

She got up to move around. Drifts of snow that had accumulated through the winter remained undisturbed here in the dimness of the forest making passage of the Jeep impossible, so she'd had to leave it under a pawpaw tree miles back. The hike to the creek had kept her warm for a while. Now it was too cold to sit still for long. She stomped and huffed and puffed like a horse, then removed her gloves and blew on her hands. There was little sun here in the deep forest, and the day had become overcast. The sky was gray and forbidding.

Finally, Vanta Lou appeared on the other side of the creek and hailed her.

"Howdy, Memphis," she called. "I'm comin' over."

"Are you sure it's safe?"

"I've crossed when it was worser."

Memphis watched in amazement as the mountain woman deftly maneuvered the wooden craft through the icy flotsam and jetsam. When she reached the bank safely, Memphis helped her off, and they secured the raft.

"You shore are a sight fer sore eyes. Ain't seen you since before Christmas," said Vanta Lou, and hugged her.

"I brought some lunch for us, but first let me give you the boxes of powdered milk I brought, and also new pads of paper, and some pencils."

"Thank you kindly, Memphis. The childern really enjoy the paper, and I use it to teach them some readin' and writin'."

They talked while they ate the lunch.

"Preacher Elkins got snakebit a while back, and I went to help nurse him. He was feverish fer days, and then got the chills. We thought he weren't goin' to make it, thought he would be crossin' to the other side right soon. But he didn't. The Lord decided it wasn't time fer him to go yet."

"I'm glad. He seems like a real nice man."

"Yep. Thing is, you never know what snakebites is goin' to do to you. Preacher got to rememberin' things from his young days."

Memphis sat up straight, listening hard.

"Did he remember anything about digging graves?"

"Yes. Now, he don't remember today what he said then, but he was tellin' true then, I know it."

"What did he say?"

"He'd been in a delirium, but he woke up and said he wanted to talk to you because he'd done you wrong. Said he truly didn't remember when you asked him, but he does now. I told him you was far away and he'd have to tell me."

Vanta Lou chewed on her tuna fish sandwich and took a drink of tea. Memphis waited anxiously.

"He said he helped ol' buryin' man, Nathan, bury Sadie Maynard, but he'd made himself fergit it 'cause Nathan said they'd cut out his tongue if he ever said anything. Said he saw the body. They took it out from a real fancy coffin and put it in a cheap wooden one. The funeral parlor man in Yancey wanted his good coffin back. Preacher said he couldn't see her face because they was a black cloth tied around it, but Nathan told him her face had been cut all up like a raw piece of meat. But more than anything, he said she only had a thumb and her pointer finger on one hand."

"They cut three fingers off when she was murdered?"

"No. He said it looked like they'd been gone a long time. Like since she was a child."

"But I've never heard anyone say anything about my grandmother missing any fingers."

Vanta Lou frowned, and wiped her mouth clean with a paper napkin.

"Well, I've had a lot of time to think since Preacher told me that. I ain't said nothin' to Granpa because he ain't been feelin' too good." She looked around as if the woods had ears, which in this case Memphis knew they might. Then she whispered, "My great-aunt Opal Marie had the same fingers chopped off when she was ten years old. She was holdin' wood for her brother. Granpa told me that long ago. When did your granma git murdered?"

"In May, 1936."

Vanta Lou's eyes got big as saucers. "That's when my aunt disappeared. I think they was buryin' my auntie instead of your granma."

Memphis's heart tripped faster.

It made immediate sense to Memphis. Claytie had said that Opal Marie disappeared the same night Sadie was murdered.

"If that's true, then what happened to Sadie's body?

Did you ask him if he remembered where the grave was?"

"Yes. He said he went back thar once, 'cause he felt bad about not sayin' any of God's words over the grave. But they was nothin' thar. The earth was all messed up, and when he got to diggin' around, he knew someone had come and got the coffin and must have took it someplace else."

Of course, thought Memphis, probably the murderer himself. He wanted to make sure no one knew where this particular body was buried.

Words from the argument between her mother and grandfather echoed through the years, clamoring for her attention.

"I know where she's buried . . ." her grandfather had said angrily. "Leave well enough alone. Don't be lookin' for her last restin' place."

No, no, no. She was not going to start believing that her grandfather murdered her grandmother. But try as she might, the horrible possibility had been suggested and would forever gnaw at her until she found out the truth. *Damn.*

Vanta Lou looked about her worriedly. Fluffy snowflakes were falling around them. Memphis had been so intent on their conversation that she hadn't paid any attention to the changing weather.

"Granpa said we was goin' to have a big snow. He ain't never wrong. I better git back home. Why don't you come with me? Be a heap easier than sliding back down the mountain."

"I don't think it's that bad yet, do you?" *Besides, there's no way in hell I'm going to cross that swinging bridge again.*

Vanta Lou studied the sky, then held out her hand and caught a flake on her palm to look at its size before it melted quickly. She wet her finger and held it up to find which way the snow was blowing.

"No, it ain't too bad yet. You should be okay. You should make it back to your truck before it comes in bad. Jest remember that the storm is comin' from the west, and the best thing to do is keep your back to it. Yancey is to the east anyway, so you'd be heading in the right direction. And if you get lost, jest follow Up Run. The creek looks wicked now with all them ice chunks and sech, but them waters is good waters. Baptized all my babies in Up Run. It'll take you someplace safe, I promise."

She gathered up the boxes of milk, the tablets, and pencils and zipped them inside her faded brown quilted jacket. Memphis gave her a big hug.

Vanta Lou said good-bye with tears in her eyes. "You're the only woman friend I've ever had. God bless you."

Memphis waited until she'd crossed the creek, then they waved good-bye again and Memphis turned to start her trek back to the Jeep.

At first the path was easy to follow, but then the snowflakes grew smaller and the snow began to stick and obliterate the tracks she'd made on her way up. She hurried. She knew she was heading south, but had to make a turn to the east soon. Thank God, her frequent trips around the mountains had given her some sense of direction. She came to a fork in the path and stopped, undecided about which way to go. The snow was hitting her from her left side. Vanta Lou had said to go east, so she headed down the right fork.

The wind pushed her along from the back now, which was nice, but the snow flurried faster and thicker. She could hardly see a foot in front of her. It didn't take long for her to realize she was lost.

Don't panic, Memphis. Stop and think. Should she continue forward and try to find the Jeep? But she had no idea where it was.

Vanta Lou had said that if she got in trouble she should follow Up Run. Mountain people knew about these things. At least she had a vague notion of the creek's location, and she was closer to the creek than she was to the Jeep. She would trust Vanta Lou's advice. She turned around and headed back the way she had come. Remember, she said the snow blew from the west, so the creek is to your north.

Thanking God that she'd worn her snow boots, she fought her way back toward the creek. The drifts were still maneuverable, and sometimes she found a trace of her recent footsteps, so finding the creek wasn't as difficult as she'd thought. Soon she heard Up Run's rushing roar and followed the sound until she reached it. She stopped for a moment and looked longingly across the creek, wishing she had gone home with Vanta Lou, despite the rope bridge and Grandpa Chafin's animosity.

She moved east along the creek's bank, stepping like a Prussian soldier, lifting her feet high, then plunging them down into the foot-deep snow. She needed snowshoes.

Nelsey had said that the snowfall this year was way above normal. That wasn't hard to believe.

The wind was to her back again and she was grateful for that. Her nose felt like Katie's Frosty the Snowman nose, frozen and orange. Zipped inside her down jacket, the thermos of hot tea rested reassuringly against her waist. At least she wouldn't freeze to death . . . for a while anyway. Despite her protective boots, her feet felt like chunks of lead. She stopped within the teepeelike, ground-hugging branches of a large evergreen to fortify herself with tea, and to check her watch.

She'd been moving east for over an hour. Fear began to swim within her, stirring feverish waves of nausea.

Closing her eyes, she tried to picture in her mind where she might be. Fairly familiar with three adjacent mountains, Macauley's Mountain, Twenty-Two, and Aracoma, she imagined their configuration in her mind. She broke a twig from the tree and knelt to draw a map in the snow to help her get a better idea of where she was.

Dredging up every piece of information she could remember, she finally hit upon what she needed to give her some hope. When Senator Brady had told her about Uncle East's cabin, she'd said something about Up Run Creek running close behind the mountain refuge. But the cabin was on Aracoma, and she was on Twenty-Two. She closed her eyes again and tried to see the very concise map Senator Brady had drawn for her.

There was a tricky transverse path between Twenty-Two and Aracoma. Up Run ran beneath the ground for a while and then resurfaced as a trickle, coming to full waters again about fifty yards further on. Three ancient chestnut trees had fallen in on each other, forming a drunken X, as if X marked the spot where the creek reemerged and Aracoma Mountain began.

The three fallen chestnuts that marked the transverse path to Aracoma would be her goal.

The fear that zigzagged through her spurred her to action and she trudged on, hugging the bank of the creek where she could, trying not to think ahead.

Just put one foot in front of another, Memphis. Vanta Lou said these were good waters. Said they would take you someplace safe. Believe that, believe that.

Remembering the conversation with Vanta Lou drove her on. Anger fed her. Excitement led her. Her anger stemmed from discovering that her grandmother's death had been even more duplicitous than she'd imagined. Knowing she was close to the truth now excited her. She was eager to get back to Yancey and begin tying it all together.

The wind lessened and the heavy snowfall thinned to light flurries. Her steps quickened as the depth of the snow on the ground became shallow and almost kickable, almost walkable, but her knee hurt like hell. She checked her watch again. Another hour had gone by and it was getting dark. She listened for the rush of water but couldn't hear it. The creek had gone underground.

She hurried now, looking for the chestnut trees. There they were. Blessed, blessed trees, forming an odd X. And there was the trickle of Up Run telling her she was on Aracoma. If she followed the creek faithfully she should find the Bradys' cabin.

Cutter brooded before the fire.

Dusk cast long shadows in the log cabin. The amber firelight chastened the darkening shapes and flickered a welcoming warmth on the honeyed pine walls.

He ran a hand over the four-day stubble on his chin, then tossed back the remaining brandy in his snifter. He knew he was sulking, feeling sorry for himself, being nonproductive about solving his problem, but he didn't care.

He'd brought work with him to the cabin, a brief on the Cavendish case, and plans for his new greenhouse, but he'd worked little on either in the four days he'd been here.

The first day he'd gotten drunk. The second day he'd nursed a daddy of a hangover. The third day he'd immersed himself in the work he'd brought, but Memphis's face intruded on every paper, her laughter floated about the small cabin, the feathery moan that slipped from her throat when she climaxed tormented his ears. He'd finally shoved the work aside, and tried to read *Angela's Ashes*, but despite McCourt's sense of humor and gifted writing, the subject matter depressed him even more.

He'd given up. He sat before the fire now, brandy in hand, and faced his problem straight on, struggling for an answer. It was the reason he'd come here in the first place. All the joys and agonies of loving Memphis burned within him, as hot as the flames before him, and he allowed it to burn, let all the guilt eat away at him until he thought the flames would consume him. He let it all play through him, good and bad, taking each jolt as punishment or indictment.

He was a flawed man, as flawed as his grandfather.

Was there a way around this that would save them both, or would the tragedy be repeated again? The forces had been set in place so long ago. Forces that he gratefully acknowledged he'd had nothing to do with. He had, however, perpetuated them. But if he tried to right a wrong from sixty years ago, he would lose the love he'd searched for his entire life. Was Lady Fate going to insist on a replay, or would she nod her head in blessing and have an end to this Greek tragedy?

A sound outside the door caught his attention. Had to be a deer, or maybe a bear. No one knew he was here except Black, and he and the rest of the Brady clan were skiing in Austria. He took the shotgun from the wall and started for the door, but it opened before he reached it.

Shocked, he stood locked in place.

Memphis stood before him, looking like a frozen winter princess the snow had blown in. Ice crystals beaded her eyelashes and eyebrows, and her cheeks were pale-blue parchment against the contrast of the silvery fur that lined her hood.

"Cutter, oh God, I'm so glad you're here. I figured it was enough of a miracle that I found the cabin." Her voice was thin, and he knew she was exhausted. "Couldn't believe it when I smelled wood smoke, and then saw light from the windows and knew someone was inside."

"Memphis, holy Christ, how did you get here?"

"Well, I went to see Vanta Lou, and it started snowing again, and so—"

"Never mind, we'll talk later." He took two huge strides, shut the door behind her, and said, "Go sit in front of the fire and defrost. Do you want coffee or something to eat, or both?"

"Something hot to drink would be fine for the time being."

While Cutter heated coffee on the Coleman stove, he watched her untie her hood and remove her jacket. She moved shakily, her body adjusting in stages to the sudden warmth. He couldn't believe she was here, the object of his flights of fantasy and the object of his depths of despair for the last four days. She struggled with her boots and he wanted to help her so badly that he hurt, but he couldn't allow himself to touch her, couldn't even come close to her.

He had visualized her here with him, had wished her here, and the minute after wishing would know it was the worst thing that could happen.

Is this another one of your cruel jokes, God?

She looked around for a place to put her jacket and boots.

"There are hooks on the wall in the bedroom."

She nodded, disappeared for a moment, then returned. She was limping, and he knew her knee was hurting, but she hadn't complained. She wore an old green flannel shirt and blue jeans, and was barefoot. He noticed she'd hung her damp socks on the back of a rocking chair.

The coffee was ready. He had to leave his corner sanctuary and cross the floor and give it to her.

She stood close to the fire warming her hands, then turned around to warm her backside. He handed her the mug of coffee. She wrapped her hands around it gratefully, and closed her eyes as she took a sip. The ice crystals had melted, and her eyelashes were shining wet. He wanted to touch them with his tongue to see if they tasted as sweet as they looked.

"This tastes better than the finest champagne," she said, opening her eyes and smiling.

He stepped away from her.

"So this is where you've been. I was beginning to worry about you."

"Yes, well, Nelsey usually guesses where I am."

"I didn't think to ask Nelsey, and she never volunteers any information."

He smiled. "No, she doesn't."

Her hand shook when she drank again, and he saw her shiver.

"I think you'd better sit down. Here, sit in the rocking chair and I'll get you a blanket."

He covered her with a Navajo wool blanket that always hung over the back of a pine settle close to the fire. As he tucked it around her, his fingers itched to caress her cheek, to brush the hair away from her forehead, to follow and smooth the molded form of her breasts within the flannel shirt.

"Thank you, Cutter. You have gentle hands."

I'm not thinking gentle thoughts.

"I think I'm beginning to revive. You wouldn't, by any chance, have any soup around, would you?"

"Chicken broth."

"Just show me where it is and I'll heat it myself."

"No, stay where you are."

"Okay. For once, you won't get an argument from me."

"Brandy would probably be good for you, too. There's a decanter on the table beside you."

"Thank you."

She sipped the brandy while he heated the broth.

"Vanta Lou told me that while Preacher Elkins was

sick, he remembered burying Sadie Maynard. He saw the body, and—"

"Hey, stop talking, Maynard." *Was she preparing to tell him what he already knew?* "You need to rest awhile, get your strength back. We'll talk later."

"But it's so important . . ."

"Later."

He handed her the mug of broth, and sat in the chair opposite her in front of the fire.

"Okay." She smiled and looked around the cabin while she drank the broth. "What a lovely old cabin. It looks as if it's been well-loved and taken care of."

"Yes, and there's an interesting history behind it, which I'll tell you someday."

She yawned, and set her mug next to the empty brandy snifter.

"I wish there was a way to let Nelsey know I'm okay."

"There is. I'll use my two-way. Nelsey keeps a receiver with her most of the time, even at your house."

She nodded, and he went into the bedroom where he kept a small battery-operated radio, wishing that his cellular worked here on the mountain, and hoping that someone would pick up his signal. He'd told Memphis a small lie so she wouldn't worry. Nelsey's big two-way receiver was at her house. Only occasionally did she attach the small one he'd had made for her onto her belt and take it with her to Memphis's house. But someone would hear and call Nelsey to tell her to patch in.

Leroy picked up his signal, and Cutter told him to let Nelsey know that Memphis was safe with him. Hard to tell who was listening in. He didn't like all of Yancey knowing Memphis was on the mountain alone with him, but there was nothing to be done about it.

When he returned to the other room, Memphis was asleep in the rocking chair.

His first urge was to sit at her feet and inspect every inch of her, but he knew he had to keep his distance so he took the opposite chair and feasted his eyes. Her head rested on her shoulder, and her loose hair spilled down her arm. It was all gingery and sparked with gold as it caught the firelight, alive with vibrant energy as Memphis was. Her lashes, still dark with dampness, rested peacefully against porcelain cheeks slowly gaining rosy color as she rested and warmed. She'd tucked the blanket close beneath her chin, and he watched as her hand loosened and her arm slipped to rest in her lap.

She sighed and her lips parted, her bottom lip forming a small moue, and he gave up trying to control a growing erection. The ache to have her, to fit himself within Memphis again, to feel, caress, and kiss every silky warm inch of her, had become overwhelming.

He jumped from the chair, poured himself another cup of coffee, and paced the room.

Well, now you have two dilemmas. How to stay away from her, and how to tell her.

He thought about taking off his clothes, going outside, and throwing himself in the snow to cool off, then had to laugh. He'd done crazy things before, but he didn't need to catch pneumonia at this stage of the game. But he did step out onto the porch and lean against the railing post to gaze up at the midnight-blue sky dashed with millions of radiant stars. The snow had softened any night sounds, and the land was hushed. The mountaintop staged a variety of dramas in outrageous proportions: storm and lightning shows, wildlife cavorting in its natural habitat, the voluptuous colors of spring and summer. Tonight the production was one of wondrous peace and beauty, and Cutter drank it in gratefully.

He pitched the remaining dregs of the coffee into the snow and returned with a purposeful stride to Memphis sleeping by the fire. Wrapping the blanket carefully around her, he carried her into the bedroom and placed her gently on the bed. Unable to resist, he pressed his cheek against hers for a moment, and kissed her hair, then quickly left.

He stoked the fire, rolled up in one of the many blankets the Brady family kept in the cabin, and prayed for sleep.

Memphis woke up in the middle of the night and knew where she was. She lay quiet for a while and gazed happily through the window at the play of starlight on the drifted mountain snow. She was alone, but knew Cutter was close.

Why isn't he here with me? He belongs next to me.

She remembered how he'd looked when she arrived, and how for a moment he'd frightened her. He was unshaven, stormy-eyed, and troubled. He'd looked like a wild animal that had hidden away because it was injured. The cabin was charged with his power. He'd looked about as sexy as a man could look, and despite his storminess and her tiredness she'd wanted him immediately. Wanted all that power and wildness pumping into her, enveloping her, loving her, renewing and renourishing her body.

What had driven him here?

She got off the bed, and blanket trailing behind her, padded into the sitting room. Cutter was sleeping in front of a dwindling fire, the coals cooling and graying. She added wood, found the poker, and stoked it until it burned high and warm again.

He stirred and turned over as the flames leapt, and she took the opportunity to kneel beside him. She dropped her blanket, unwrapped Cutter's blanket and crawled in next to him.

He lifted his head for a moment, then lay back down and grew still.

"Memphis," he growled into her ear, "if you know what's good for you, you'll leave and get back into bed."

"No, this is where I want to be."

"Then *I'll* leave."

"No you won't," she said and kissed his stubbled chin.

He groaned.

He fumbled with the buttons on her shirt, then his hands grew sure and he swiftly unfastened the rest of her, almost ripping off the buttons. She shuddered as his fingers traced around her hardening nipples, and then followed the taut line of her belly to the top of her jeans, then back again to her breasts. He licked around her nipples like a cat lapping milk, then sucked one breast deep into his mouth, taking all of it until she ached with wanting him. He let it go slowly, tongue caressing her until the breast lay free again, and he turned to the other one.

His unyielding erection prodded hard against her hip.

He sucked until she was breathless, and then released her, and ran his finger lightly down her trembling belly to the top of her jeans.

"Unzip them," he whispered.

She did, and he shoved her jeans down to her ankles.

"Now unzip mine."

She did, and his erection leapt out of its restricted quarters.

His fingers sought out her most sensitive sweet spot, and he stirred the creamy juices that had wet her from the first moment she'd come into the cabin. His fingers teased and taunted until she moaned, and without preamble, disregarding their entangling clothes, her jeans around her ankles, his around his knees, he took her then. His cock fiery hot and rigid, he entered her, hard and demanding.

She held back for a moment, unwilling to give all of

herself yet, and he slowed his strokes, teasing now, taunting with his tip, playing with her entrance, until she moaned again and a sob escaped her.

"Give it to me, Memphis, let go. Let me have it," he murmured.

He sank deep within her again, then drew out and entered fast and hard.

Her ankles were imprisoned and she couldn't move, so his hips were tight between her thighs. The feel of his muscled hips in his jeans sliding against the silk of her thighs excited her to the point of frenzy and she let go.

He slowed again, and she whimpered, "No, please, I'm ready."

He plunged into her, rocking her fast against the floor.

They were both out of control now and neither cared.

"Yes, yes, yes," she cried.

His answering roar as they both came engulfed her, empowered her, and they reached the brink together, clasped in a feverish embrace.

His body slick with sweat, he fell to her side, brought her back to him quickly, and locked her to his chest. Her ear rested against his wildly beating heart.

"Sorry, sweetheart," he panted, "I've been fantasizing about you for days. I'll never do that again.'"

"Do what again? I wanted you just as bad. I loved it. I've missed you so much."

"Yeah, well, maybe next time we can get our clothes off before the urge hits us." He laughed, and his warm breath stirred her hair.

"Shucks, won't be near as much fun."

He laughed again. She loved the sound, and hoped their lovemaking had alleviated the pain she'd seen in his eyes when she'd first arrived.

He cuddled her close. "Warm enough?"

She nodded, and burrowed deeper into his embrace.

They lay quietly, while their breathing slowed and their hearts found a sensible rhythm. Finally, he got to his knees and undressed her. She loved the way his eyes roamed her body in admiration. He bent to kiss a mole on her tummy, and another on her thigh, and his rough stubbled beard scratched pleasingly against the silk of her skin. When he reached her knee, he massaged it lightly, putting pressure in just the right places until all of the pain was gone.

After he'd undressed her, and inspected, massaged, and kissed her body in out of the way places, he rewrapped her in the blanket.

"Lie still," he murmured. "I'll be right back."

He returned with a warm damp cloth, unwrapped her, and cleaned his come from her sweet parts.

"Ummm, feels wonderful," she said. Memphis sighed with release and happiness, but felt the fever mounting again. Thank you, God. She couldn't remember ever being this happy. "But I want to taste you."

She captured his penis in her palm. It stiffened immediately. She formed a fist and milked it, then raised herself on her elbow to taste the bittersweet liquid that oozed from the tip.

He groaned, and smiled. "Be careful, darlin', or you'll get no rest from me."

"Don't want any rest. Want you," she managed to get out.

A spasm shook his body. He removed her hand, and parting her legs, lowered his head to taste of the milky nectar that had gathered where he had just cleaned. He buried his face between her thighs, delving with his tongue into her honeyed opening. Memphis gasped as surges of pleasure soared through her, rippling every nerve ending in her body.

Relentlessly, Cutter's tongue searched for every hidden portion of her female center. He laved her vulva, and sucked the tiny nodule there until she screamed.

"Enough. Please come to me here."

He slid gently up her body, and for a while they only held each other, their bodies fitting perfectly. They rolled from side to side feeling their hips engage, their chests meet, and his hard cock rest in the bush of her mound.

He kissed her mouth with gentle, voluptuous movements, pulling her bottom lip between his lips, then releasing to lick it with tiny hard licks.

"We taste of each other."

"Yeah. Hush. I want to taste more of you."

As he kissed her mouth, he rotated her nipples. Memphis stayed his hand, and raised her head to take one of his nipples in her mouth and sucked until it hardened. She reached for his engorged cock and loved it with her fingers as she sucked at his nipples, until they both moaned with urgency.

Cutter slipped into her, and she gasped with her need for him, but he eased into her slowly, minute movement by minute movement, and she knew that he intended savoring her this time. Finally, he reached the center of her and they were joined in a pulsating stillness, anchored at the core of their beings.

He rocked her back and forth, and they made slow, easy love, tasting, touching, relishing, and celebrating the other.

Cutter quickened the pace. His strokes drew in and out fast and hard, and he pumped into her until she felt an age-old tide pull her into its primeval flood. He swept her out to sea along with him. Together, they reached the horizon, soared for an eternal moment on a wave of ecstasy, then floated back to shore.

He rested on top of her, then rolled on his side, taking her with him in the shelter of his arms.

The hiss and crackle of the dying fire, and their uneven breathing, were the only sounds in the stillness of the peaceful cabin.

"I'll never get enough of you, sweetheart," he whispered, when they could breathe again.

"Nor I, you." She smiled. "Look at me."

She studied the silver of his eyes, and found them still foggy with sex, but glistening with happiness. Satisfied, she said, "Good. Just checking."

Satiated, they slept.

§21§

Memphis drew the sleeves of her flannel shirt around her hands, and hugged her arms to her chest. There was a chill in the cabin. The heat of Cutter's newly stoked fire hadn't reached the table yet, but the chill of his attitude was even more unsettling.

What had happened to the satisfied glow she'd seen in his eyes before they slept? He'd said "good morning" and uttered a few other pleasantries and that was about it.

"Drink the coffee. It will warm you up," he ordered.

She curved her fingers around the thick white cup, welcoming the warmth it offered, and watched as he heated biscuits on a small flat gas griddle.

"I have so much to tell you that I hardly know where to begin," she said.

She told him then of finding the valentine signed with the initial M., and Vanta Lou's disclosure indicating there was a strong possibility the grave diggers had buried the body of Opal Marie Chafin, instead of Sadie Maynard as they had thought.

He sat across from her and ate his biscuits and listened. She expected more of a reaction. He nodded now and then as she talked, but his jaw was set and rigid.

"Well, what do you think?" she asked.

"She said Preacher Elkins told her the coffin had disappeared when he returned to visit it?"

"Yes."

Interest crossed his face, but soon disappeared, and the implacable set of his jaw returned. He said nothing.

"Cutter," she hesitated, afraid to ask yet knowing she had to. "Do you suppose our grandparents were romantically involved?"

He wiped his mouth with his napkin and stared at her for a long moment, then got up and left the table. He returned and placed a bundle of letters in front of her.

"Yes, they were."

Excitement leapt through her as she gingerly picked up the letters. They were frayed and yellowed, but seemed well taken care of.

"You knew? What are you saying?"

"Read the top letter first. It will explain a lot." He turned away, and walked to the window with his coffee.

Her hands shook as she untied the bundle and separated the first letter from the rest.

Dearest Mac,

I miss you beyond knowing. The mountains here are tall and masculine, unlike our voluptuous, green West Virginia mountains. The desert is brown and stark, and I miss the valley. My heart hurts when I think of Faith. Oh, God, why didn't I take her with me that horrible night? Too late for second guessing. My only consolation is that she is safe with Rose and you are keeping an eye on her.

The one thing that sustains me, and that keeps me going is knowing that soon we will be together, you and me, and Faith. I know it isn't safe now, but I pray every night that soon the way will be clear for you to come. I don't have to tell you to be careful. You know he'll kill all of us if he ever finds me. I've put the list in a safe-deposit box here.

God, the arrogance of the man is unbelievable. To think he would go to such lengths to cover up my leaving him. I wish we knew who was murdered that night so I could say a prayer for them, and I wish we knew the murderer. I'd feel safer about you if you knew. Don't ever turn your back. If James knew about us, then others did, too. I wish we could do something about poor Amos. Do you really think he'll go to prison for something he didn't do? Sometimes I think I've done the wrong thing, but if I return to help Amos, he'll kill you, me, and Faith.

I go crazy thinking about you, and I've cried so hard and so often that my face is a mess.

The last two years have been the happiest of my life. God loves us, Mac, and he meant for us to be together. Don't ever doubt that. A glorious love like ours will never be denied. I keep our volume of Edna St. Vincent Millay on my bedside table. I wait for your letters everyday. It was wise of you to arrange for your friend in Charleston to be our mailbox. How often do you go? Must be about twice a week because I receive your letters twice a week in big bunches.

Twenty-one days and the divorce will be final. I pray every night that you and Faith will be able to come to me then.

All of my love and soul to you,
Sadie

Wild happiness flooded through her. Good Lord, it was true. Sadie and Mac had loved each other deeply. Her heart knocked hard against her chest. Sadie hadn't been murdered, and Sadie and Macauley Tate loved each other. The letter said so much, and it whirled around and around in her mind.

But then the questions came. Hundreds of questions.

Was it possible her grandmother still lived some-where? Who had wanted to kill Sadie, and her own mother, Faith? Why hadn't Macauley Tate told the truth and saved Amos Washington from going to prison?

Trembling with apprehension, she raised her eyes and found Cutter still staring out the window at the miles of endless snowcapped peaks before them.

"Is Sadie alive somewhere?"

"No." He turned to look at her, his face pale and still, the lines about his mouth and eyes etched deep and sharp. "A particularly virulent flu bug swept through the Western states in 1936. The divorce came through, but Sadie died from the flu two months after she wrote that letter. Our grandparents were never reunited, and Faith eventually left Nelsey's mother and went to live with her father and a sitter until he married Alma."

"But what does all this mean?"

He took a deep breath. "The rest of the letters explain more, but they're mostly wonderful love letters, meant to be read with enjoyment . . . and gratitude that such a love existed. They should be savored on some rainy afternoon or night with a cup of hot tea, or some fine brandy. Perhaps it would be better if I tell you what happened that night. It took me a while to piece it all together, from things my grandfather said, from the research I did among the microfilms of the trial, and from the letters."

"Please do."

He poured himself another cup of coffee from the battered tin pot, and took a quick gulp, as if he needed to fortify himself.

"Some gossipmonger in the town eventually discov-ered Mac and Sadie's two-year affair, and told your grandfather. He evidently had his deputies spy on them, and realized Sadie was planning to leave him."

"If you're implying that my grandfather murdered

someone to cover up my grandmother's desertion, that's ridiculous."

"No, but that's about half true. A fog of evil hung over Yancey that night. Lives and situations came together at a crossroads that created a night of mayhem, and the results have affected some of us down through the years to this day."

He shoved a hand into his rear jeans pocket, and with a cup of steaming coffee in the other, he paced the floor in front of her as he talked.

"Sheriff Maynard beat up Sadie, threatened to kill her and Faith if she went on with the affair, or if she tried to leave him. I knew that he'd gotten a phone call then and had to leave the house in a hurry. It wasn't until I heard Claytie's story about Opal Marie and Root, and saw the pictures you'd taken, that I knew who had phoned that night. It completed the puzzle."

"How so?"

He flashed her a look, and she could have sworn his eyes held a note of fear.

"Unfortunately, your grandfather was not a nice man. Some of the more prominent men in Yancey had formed a 'key club.' The members had keys to a room in the bank building where they gathered twice a month with various women and girlfriends to have sex, group sex, and whatever else you can think of. A few daring wives participated, trading husbands and men back and forth like baseball cards. Harvey Root's father, H. A., headed the organization . . . and your grandfather not only knew of and participated in the orgies, but covered up and protected any knowledge of the group's existence."

Memphis's face flushed hot, and her head reeled. If what Cutter said was true, her grandfather, who had sworn to uphold the law in Yancey County, had been a wife beater and a crooked cop. Defiance reared within her.

"How do you know these things are true?"

He gave her a tired smile. "With what you've already discovered on your own, you'll figure it out for yourself as you read the letters. Do you want me to continue?"

She nodded.

"Mac and Sadie had heard rumors, as had everyone else, but they were so in love and involved in trying to see each other undetected that they weren't interested. Until the night the sheriff beat Sadie. As well as I can figure, this is what happened."

He sighed, and drew a hand down the dark shadow of his jaw.

"Right after the sheriff knocked Sadie around, he got a phone call from young Root, whose father let him come to the sex parties sometimes. Young Root had brought an underage mountain girl that night, Opal Marie Chafin. Opal Marie didn't like what was going on, and he'd gotten a little rough with her—in other words, he'd raped her. Not knowing the sheriff was involved, she told Root she was going to the sheriff's house for protection, and she ran away. That's when Root called your grandfather. Opal Marie couldn't be allowed to babble about what she'd seen that night, so the sheriff locked Sadie in their bedroom and left to find the girl before she arrived at the house. The locked door meant nothing to Sadie. He'd locked her in before, but she'd learned to crawl through the window, cross the roof, and shinny down the porch pole.

"She woke up Faith and took her to Nelsey's mom, Rose, intending to come back in a few days when her husband had calmed down. She met Mac to tell him what had happened. He convinced her to go back and get Faith and leave town right away, and he would meet them later. They decided that she would go to Reno for a quick divorce."

Cutter stopped pacing. He stood still, concentrating,

glaring at the floor as if it were responsible for everything.

"Her mistake was in returning to the house to pack
some clothes. When she arrived she saw lights flashing,
moving through the woods in back of her house.
Thinking hunters were trespassing, she ignored them
and went into the basement for a suitcase. She found
blood on the steps and floor. Beginning to panic, she
ran upstairs to pack, heard the midnight train whistle,
and knew she had to hurry even faster."

Memphis went weak with fear. She lowered her cup
and placed it carefully on the table, knowing her numb
fingers would soon lose their grip.

"Sadie saw lights, and heard the train whistle?"

"Yes."

"Did she hear screams, too?" she asked shakily, but
already knew the answer.

"Yes." He looked at her oddly. "Are you okay?"

"Yes." She dropped her head into her hands. "My
God, all this time I've been reliving that night through
my grandmother's memories. She's been trying to tell
me something."

Cutter circled the table and gripped her shoulder.
"Hold on, we're not finished yet."

He started to remove his hand, but she grasped it and
held it tight against her shoulder.

"As she finished packing, she heard a woman
screaming in the woods behind her. She knew then
there were no hunters in the woods, and that the blood
in the basement was not from an animal carcass. She
heard a—"

"A shot, and then another, and the screaming
stopped." Memphis's head whirled, and her stomach
heaved with waves of nausea as she finished the story
in an otherworldly trance. "I knew something hideous
was happening. I ran to James's desk to see if he had

any cash, and that's when I found the list of key club members. It tore as I ripped it from the drawer. I stuffed it in my pocket along with some money, and called Mac."

She was barely aware of Cutter's presence, but knew he gripped both her shoulders now as she and Sadie together relived the nightmare from sixty years ago. Reedy and faint, her voice haunted her as she recited the events that plunged all of them into some sort of fateful hell. Her heart pounded like the hooves of a horse racing to the finish line.

"I called Mac. He told me to leave right away. He said not to even get Faith, that he would keep an eye on her and make sure she was safe. He said to drive my car to church. Amos would meet me there in the old limo, and take me to Charleston to catch the train to Nevada. He would follow later, bringing Faith. Just before I drove down the hill, I looked in the rearview mirror, and saw two men coming from the woods. It was too dark to see who they were for sure, but I thought it was James and young Root. Root had a body slung over his shoulder. As I crossed the bridge, I saw car lights come down the hill. They were following me. I made it to the church, got into the limo, and Amos took off like a bat out of hell. I'll never forget the smell of old blood in the limo, or the stink of stale cigars, and gun oil."

Hazy, then bright, then hazy again, the figures and images came to her. The rancid odor of hunters and their dead trophies in the hearselike car turned her stomach. She made a choking sound, and a sour salty taste puckered her mouth as it filled with saliva.

She spit into her paper napkin, then crushed it in her palm.

"They followed us. Amos had to go so fast around the mountain curves, and through the back alleys of Charleston that I was sick when I got on the train. All I could think of was you and Faith. I was so scared, Mac. Oh, God, Mac, I was so scared and lonely."

An eery wail circulated through the cabin, and Memphis lost focus. She blacked out.

A terrible thirst woke her up. She lay on the old twig bed, and Cutter sat beside her with a worried look on his face. He put a cool cloth on her forehead and bent to kiss her cheek.

"Okay?"

"I'm not sure. Could I have a drink of water, please?"

"Right here," he said, and poured a glass from the bedside pitcher.

He helped her sit up. The water tasted like honey from heaven.

"Did I just speak for Sadie? Did I just tell you what happened that night?"

"Yes. You're shaking. Lie back down."

He lay beside her and held her close, soothing her, smoothing her hair back from her temples, and kissing her softly around the ear.

"I've had other slips through time recently. In church on Christmas Eve, in the attic in a dream, and when we danced in New York. Cutter, does this mean I'm my grandmother reincarnated or something?"

"I don't know, darlin'. I don't believe in reincarnation, but there's a case for it here. Either that, or some strong inherited genetic memories passed down from your grandmother."

She shivered and clung to him.

"But that doesn't explain what I feel in the darkroom, or the humming."

"I think that's Opal Marie. They've both been trying to tell you something. Six months ago I would have said you were crazy, but now I . . ." He cleared his throat. "Opal Marie arrived at the house while you . . . your grandmother was taking Faith to Rose's. Finding no one home, she probably hid in the basement where Root caught up with her. I would guess that he tried to scare her into coming with him, by nicking her with his knife. She ran again, this time into the woods. Afraid she would expose him and his father's nasty organization, he hunted her down and shot her.

"The sheriff must have arrived back home as Root and Opal Marie ran into the woods. He went after them. He witnessed the murder, and he and Root came out of the woods with the body as you . . . as Sadie was leaving."

"But why didn't he arrest Root, and why did they make it look like it was Sadie who was murdered?"

"Ahh, well, this I don't have to guess at. It's quite clear in the letters between Sadie and Mac. The sheriff found the note Sadie left saying she was leaving him. He also realized Sadie had taken the list of club members with her and had the 'goods on him,' so to speak. In the meantime, Root's father had arrived at the house and decided to blackmail the sheriff. Said if he told anyone what happened there that night, he would tell everyone the sheriff not only protected the club, but that it was his idea. So, not only was Sheriff Maynard facing humiliation because his wife had deserted him, but he faced the loss of his job, criminal charges, and a jail sentence."

"He saw his whole life crumbling around him," guessed Memphis. "He knew about the Chafins' weird religious beliefs, and that no one else would worry much about the disappearance of a mountain girl, so he hatched the scheme. They would make everyone believe the body was Sadie's. That way he escaped humiliation and exposure, and no one would know it was Opal Marie who was killed. Young Root had openly spent the whole evening with her, so it wouldn't have been hard to prove he murdered her."

"Just about what I figure."

"They slashed up her face even more, put one of Sadie's dresses on her, and dumped her on Twenty-Two Mountain."

"Right."

"But why didn't your grandfather Mac tell what he knew?"

"Because Sheriff Maynard and the Roots threatened to harm Faith, and any children she bore, if Mac ever told what he knew. Bear in mind that Grandfather didn't know who had been murdered. He never did know, nor did Amos. They only knew it wasn't Sadie. Amos told Grandfather that when he returned from Charleston that night, they threatened to slash his dog's throat if he didn't follow orders. They put Opal Marie's body in the old limo and told him to transport it to Twenty-Two Mountain and get rid of it. So, no matter how much he denied it, Amos was now implicated in the murder. They had a proper burial for the people of Yancey, then later, they ordered him to dig up the coffin and transport it to a secret burial place."

"So Amos was in trouble all the way around. He knew about Sadie, and he knew about the body, and he knew where it was buried."

"Right. I think Amos thought prison might be the safest place to be. The Roots were blackmailing your grandfather, and he was blackmailing them. Grandfather couldn't leave town because he was afraid they would follow him to Sadie, and also Sadie insisted that he stay in Yancey to make sure Faith wasn't harmed."

"But after Sadie died, why didn't your grandfather speak up?"

"Again, because of Faith, and because he'd promised Sadie he wouldn't." He hesitated. "I think he was wrong. An innocent man spent years in prison because Grandfather didn't tell what he knew. He didn't have any claim to Faith, and he couldn't even pretend to without raising suspicions. However, it seems to me that a resourceful man would have searched for a way to help Amos, without telling the whole story."

She heard the pain in his voice. Accepting the idea that his grandfather was less than perfect had been difficult for Cutter.

"I can only guess that at first he must have been so leveled by Sadie's death that he was incapable of action," he continued. "Later, it was easier and safer to maintain the status quo."

The shock was wearing off, and the calamitous fear she'd been fighting since Cutter had first given her the letters reared its ugly head. She moved away from the sheltering comfort of his body and sat up.

"You knew all along."

He rolled off the bed and walked away. "Let's wash our faces and make fresh coffee. I think there's soup we can heat."

She ran after him, and planted herself in front of him.

"All this time you knew and you didn't say anything. You didn't tell me."

"I knew they were lovers, and that Sadie hadn't been murdered, and that there might be some sort of threat to you, but I thought that everyone involved had probably died. It wasn't until recently that I suspected Root, especially after you told me about his threatening remarks regarding Katie. I didn't know for sure until I heard Claytie's story that night in Ruby's, and saw the pictures of Opal Marie and Root. Then it all came together. Since then, I've tried to stay as close to you as I could, and I hired a man to keep an eye on you when I couldn't be around."

"The man in the blue truck."

He nodded.

Colossal anger boiled fast from the bottoms of her feet to the crown of her head. Her whole body went rigid with fury and hurt.

"My God, how could you keep this from me? All these months. How could you not tell me?"

A muscle in his jaw rippled as he set his teeth and glared back at her.

"Grandfather showed me those letters right before he died, but said I wasn't to read them until I was older, and that I must never tell anyone about them. They would be a secret between the two of us. He said I would understand better when I was older. He put them in a safe-deposit box. Our family attorney gave me the key when I was twenty-one."

"You should have told me."

He turned away from her. "Yes, I should have. I know that now. But the enduring love in those letters was an inspiration to me. And they were a sustaining private link to my grandfather. He'd told me not to tell, and I believed the secrets would go to the grave with me. It wasn't important for anyone else to know about them."

"I had a right to know."

"Yes, you did, but I didn't realize that at first. To me you were just a nosey journalist poking around to stir up trouble. It wasn't until I began to . . . see you in a different light that I knew I should tell you, and then . . . I was afraid to. But after what happened in New York, I knew I had no right to keep it from you any longer."

"You're damn right, you didn't. You never did. You were wrong, as wrong as your grandfather."

"I know that now. I can only ask your forgiveness, Memphis."

Her heart shriveled, dried, and crumbled like dead and brittle rose petals. She stepped away from him.

"I'll never forgive you. God, I could kick myself for trusting you in the first place. My head told me no, my heart told me yes. Stupid, treacherous heart."

The minute the vicious words came out of her mouth, she was sorry she'd said them, and racked with misgiving agony. But she couldn't take them back. Her pride fought with her misery. All these months, Cutter had known the answers to what she searched for, and hadn't told her. How could she forgive that?

His eyes had half closed, and only slits of silver showed between the narrowed lids. His face was stony, unreadable.

"I've never asked anyone to forgive me before, and I never will again."

"It wouldn't matter if you did. Just one question, Cutter. Where *is* Sadie buried?"

"Reno, Nevada." He attempted a smile, but it turned into a bitter grimace. "Everyone thought Grandfather was a gambling man. Every other month he flew out there to visit her grave. The next month he would go to Moundsville and visit Amos."

"How noble of him," she said sarcastically. "I'm leaving this minute."

"Get your things together. We'll leave while the weather's good."

"You're not coming with me. I don't want to be around you anymore."

His body drew as taut as his bow and arrow, and his hands curled into fists as if he wanted to hit something. Probably her, she thought.

"You'll never make it off this mountain without me, Memphis. Sorry, but you'll have to endure my odious presence a few hours longer."

As painful as it was, she had to admit he was right.

"Fine, I'll pay you for your excellent guide services, Mr. Tate."

The cabin, unaccustomed to hostile feelings and

words within its warm honeyed walls, expelled them out into the cold. The intricate trek down the mountain took forever. Neither of them spoke a word, and by the time they reached the bottom, the wet and chill of the weather had not only seeped into the marrow of Memphis's bones, but also into the cavern of her aching soul. She knew their relationship was irrevocably broken.

Nelsey could tell from Memphis's pale face that something was wrong. She had scarcely spoken since her arrival home late yesterday afternoon. Cutter had dropped her off. In his hurry to leave, his tires had spit gravel, as they dug into the slush and snow. Memphis had stormed into the house, swept Katie into her arms for a prolonged hug, said hello to Nelsey, and that was it.

"Weatherman says no more snow." Nelsey stirred the oatmeal, and watched from the corner of her eye as Memphis helped Katie eat scrambled eggs.

"That's good. Maybe the roads will be clear enough for Leroy to take me to get the Jeep," Memphis said listlessly.

The fire that had raged in her yesterday was gone. Looked like she was depressed today.

"Probably."

"I hope so. I have to deliver a message for Vanta Lou before we leave."

"Leave?"

"Yes. As soon as I finish the article for *Vanity Fair*, Katie and I will be going back to New York. In fact, I would appreciate it very much if you would begin gathering things together for me. Find our duffel bags and see if Leroy has empty boxes we can have."

The arthritis pain in Nelsey's elbows flared and fired and surged right to her heart. She gripped the oatmeal ladle so she wouldn't drop it.

"Kind of sudden, ain't it? I mean, you haven't found where Sadie was buried, and, eh, well, you've never seen spring until you've seen it in these mountains, Memphis."

"I found out all I needed to know, and you and everyone in Yancey will know when my story comes out this summer. As for spring, it will have to wait for another year, Nelsey." She sounded sad now. "I don't have time or the inclination to wait for it."

"I see." *Change the subject. You'll have to tell me how to deal with this hurt later, Lord.* "Root called this morning. He wants you to meet him at the church. Wants you to serve on the fundraising committee for the new church steeple. You can use my car if you want."

She ladled oatmeal into Memphis's bowl.

Memphis gave a short bark of a laugh. "Okay. I was going to see him today anyway. What time did he say?"

"Eleven this morning."

"Great. I can't wait."

Later, as Memphis passed Leroy's, the blue truck pulled out and followed her as she crossed over the bridge. Angry, she screeched to a halt and jumped out of the car to confront the man.

He rolled down the window as she approached, and smiled sheepishly.

"I appreciate your watching over us, but there's no need anymore."

"Cutter called this morning and said he wanted you watched closer than ever. Sorry, miss, but them's Cutter's words, and I do what he hires me to do."

"But I don't want you. I'm perfectly capable of taking care of myself and my daughter."

"I'm sure you are, but Cutter seems to think you need help. Why don't you jest be a nice lady and let me earn my keep. Ain't nobody gonna bother you or sweet Katie while Buddy's around. And as long as you know about us now, I want you to rest easy about Katie. There's a man in the woods watching the house for me."

She sighed and looked at her watch. She didn't have time to argue with this man. Damn Cutter. "Okay, if you insist, but just for the day."

He nodded and gave her a big gap-toothed grin.

When she got to the church she found Harvey Root waiting for her in a small prayer room next to the sanctuary. He was alone. She wished she had a brief-case filled with torturous weapons. How pleasant it would be to stick needles beneath his fingernails, then tear them halfway off and watch them bleed, or to plunge his feet in boiling water and watch the red creep toward his knees as he screamed for mercy. She was sure she could think of even more ingenious ways to make the evil old man suffer.

"Sit down, Memphis." He indicated a wooden chair near his wheelchair.

His pig eyes were hooded, and his hands and arms were folded neatly over a plaid lap robe.

"I'll stand, thank you. I don't plan on being here long. Why did you want to meet in church? Do you seriously think God's going to give you a break, Harvey Root?"

"Cutter Tate visited me early this morning."

So Cutter had beaten her to the punch. That explained why he'd retained the bodyguards.

"Yes, and I'm going to expose you, Harvey Root."

"Cutter said that you would. Said he knew you well enough to know that you would confront me. But I wouldn't do anything to embarrass me publicly if I were you. You can't be positive of this little fairy tale you and Cutter have stitched together. I'm not admitting anything, and you can't prove anything. No grave, no bodies, no way to do DNA tests."

"That's true, I can't prove a thing. But I sure can hint, implicate, and generally make life miserable for you, which is exactly what I'm going to do. After I'm through with you, the people in this town won't return your phone calls, will turn their backs when you approach, maybe even spit at the ground you pass over."

Even in the gloom of the windowless room, she saw his face pale. His palsied hands twitched violently. He slid them beneath his blanket. Did he have a weapon in his lap? No. He was too smart for that. If he killed her here in the church, everyone would know and then the whole story would come out. Cutter would make sure of that.

"I warn you, Memphis, you'll be sorry if you soil my name. Cutter told me he has bodyguards close to you, but there are ways I can get to you."

"I'm not afraid of you anymore, Harvey. You're just a useless, evil, impotent old man who has never been loved by anyone. Unless it's Minnie Jo, who probably waits on you hand and foot to insure her inheritance."

She loved every grimacing twitch in his folded-up frog face. This was fun, maybe even more fun than the article he would read in *Vanity Fair* this summer. She decided to pour it on. She would use the ancient voodoo method of applying suffering by suggestion.

"In fact, Harvey, you're going to die soon," she hissed in a menacing tone, loving every syllable she uttered. "I'm sure of it. I can see death in the green of your skin, and hear it in the rattle of your breath. Everyone *knows* they're going to die, Harvey, but no one really *believes* it. Believe it, Harvey, you haven't got long. Just long enough to suffer as the people of Yancey point fingers at you."

He blanched and shuddered, but soon gained his equilibrium.

"Stay away from Yancey and you'll be fine."

"Oh, I plan to." He didn't know about her magazine article and she wasn't going to tell him. The whole world would know his sordid story. "We're leaving soon, but not because I'm afraid of you. I'm leaving because I don't want to live in a town that harbors people like you. Which reminds me, Harvey, you can stop your dirty tricks now. They're no longer necessary."

"I have no idea what you're talking about."

"Yes you do. The bloodied sheets, the Halloween visitor, and my . . . cat."

"What happened to your cat?"

"Didn't your hireling tell you he'd hung my kitten?"

A smirk twisted his thin lips. "Not my style, Memphis. In fact, none of those nasty little deeds were of my doing. If I were you, I'd look closer to Cutter. You know Birdy was a sneaky little brat as a child, and she thinks she owns Cutter."

"What do you mean? Are you saying that Birdy Harless is capable of such hatred?"

His smirk spread to his eyes, as he said with malicious delight, "I attended a birthday party Nelsey gave for Cutter once at the picnic grounds. Cutter took a shine to a pretty girl with blond hair. They were all swimming in the lake. I saw Birdy hold the pretty girl's head underwater when she thought no one was looking. She would have drowned her if someone hadn't called the girl's name, looking for her. The girl told her mother, but no one believed her."

"I don't believe you."

He gave a grunting chuckle, and coughed phlegm into his handkerchief. "You should. There was a girl Cutter dated fairly steady in high school. One night after a date with Cutter, the girl's house caught on fire. Fortunately, the family escaped without injury, but the house burned to the ground. Birdy reported the fire. Said she was walking her dog, but Birdy lived clear across town, and had no reason to be in the neighborhood. Draw your own conclusions."

"I have, and they are not the same as yours. Only an evil, dirty mind could come up with such thoughts."

"Think what you want. The wisdom of old age tells me you'll regret it."

§22§

"Jake the Snake," muttered Memphis.

Katie toddled to the television and patted the screen.

"Unca Jake," she said.

"Right," said Memphis under her breath. "Treacherous Jake Bishop. Your infamous father. Yuck!"

Memphis, Katie, and Nelsey sat in the living room watching the *Today Show*.

"*The Maynard Murder* has already hit some of the bestseller charts," said Katie Couric on the split screen. "Why do you think people buy these books you write about old unsolved murders?"

Jake, standing in front of Carpozzoli's Pizza, flashed Couric his devilish white smile, and said, "To our detriment, Katie, people are always interested in the sordid, and especially mysteries. This book has a little of everything: murder, sex, a picture of a small southern town and its ingrained racism, and mysterious overtones about prominent men and who was really guilty."

"We spoke with Memphis Maynard earlier. She declined a live interview, but said a rebuttal will appear in *Vanity Fair* this summer, and a book of her own later in the year. It sounds like she's not happy about your book, Jake."

"No, she isn't. But I can't blame her. It is her grandmother who was a 'tainted woman,' as they called them sixty years ago. So her article isn't likely to be very objective."

Nelsey said, "You should have talked on TV. Seein' that fool up there talkin' like that makes me mad."

"I know I should have, but I'm so depressed that I was afraid I would embarrass myself."

Certainly in no mood to debate Jake on television, she thought. *But Jake's going to look like a real monkey after the facts come out. That will provide me with endless pleasure.*

"I've heard enough." She pressed the remote and switched to the Weather Channel.

An attractive young woman who'd received inadequate elocution lessons pointed out areas of concern on the big map.

". . . and in areas of the Midwest and South, West Virginia, Kentucky, and parts of Alabama, melting snow and rain may set up dangerous flooding conditions, which we will most certainly keep an eye on and most certainly keep you informed."

Memphis turned off the television. In front of her, on the Early American coffee table Jake had once made fun of, rested her printout of Sadie's story. She flipped a finger hard at the offending sheets and the pile of papers toppled to the floor, flying over the braided rug. Katie laughed and chased them.

"This stinks. It says little of what I really want to say. I'm going to be here longer than I thought, Nelsey." She sighed, and dropped her head in her hands. "I'm going to have to rewrite this whole thing, and I don't want to go back to New York until it's perfect. So unpack whatever you've packed."

"I'm sorry the article isn't comin' well for you, but I'm mighty happy you and Katie will be here a while longer."

She heard relief in Nelsey's voice and raised her head

in time to catch her happy smile. Memphis had been so engulfed in her own misery that she hadn't thought of the effect their departure would have on Nelsey.

She squeezed the older woman's work-worn hand and said, "Katie will miss you terribly, and I'll be lost without you. Why don't you come to New York with us?"

"Lordy, no. Thank you, but me and New York would fit like a Catholic at a Baptist meetin'. I'm jest hopin' you'll visit me sometimes."

"Of course we will. You're the grandmother Katie never knew, and I can't tell you how much you mean to me."

Tears welled in Nelsey's eyes, and Memphis felt her own watering. "Oh, well, none of this now," Nelsey said gruffly. She got up and began to gather Katie's toys from the floor and put them away in the toy box in the corner. "We'll all be jest fine, I'm sure. You been mighty listless lately. Anything wrong?"

"Not really. Maybe a case of spring fever."

It was true. She was listless. She couldn't seem to recover her original anger and sense of injustice. When she sat at the computer to revise her article, the screen glared back at her as if affronted at her efforts. A monumental sense of futility hit her every time she thought of her inability to punish Root legally. There was no body to dig up and use for DNA testing, no way to prove that it was Opal Marie who was murdered and not Sadie. No way to prove that she had been buried in a secret location, and then later moved and buried again by her paranoid murderer. There was no one alive now, except Ruby and a few others who were either too young at the time or too old now and remembered nothing, who could testify in a court of law.

The angry words she'd hurled at Cutter echoed

endlessly in her ears. *"I'll never forgive you."* The implacable set of his face. His freezing words: *"I've never asked for forgiveness before, and I never will again."* Oh, dear God, how she missed him. She hadn't known until it was over how important he'd become to her. The cold clear facts were that the words they had flung at each other, though said in anger, had been meant at the time.

They had failed each other, and she had failed her grandmother. She had fallen short by not exposing the truth before Jake's misinformed book came out. She also understood now that part of her assignment in Yancey had been Sadie's wish that Cutter and Memphis be given the gift of a life of love together, which Sadie and Mac had been denied. Memphis's failure to achieve an amicable closure with Cutter had defeated her grandmother's hopes.

The tears she shed at night soaked her pillow, but did nothing to relieve the endless suffering. She felt disconnected from everything and everyone, except Katie. Life had become a dull anxious feeling of inner detachment. Every hour, every activity was a chore, superficial and routine.

Margo was the only person she'd talked to, but she'd been of no help. She was even more furious than Memphis. Her sister was not only angry with Cutter for not revealing what he knew earlier, but was enraged that he had hurt her little sister. When they talked, instead of commonsense advice, all they did was commiserate with each other.

"A nice cup of Red Zinger tea is always good fer what ails you," said Nelsey, looking at her worriedly. "Come on. Let's go to the kitchen and I'll fix you some."

"Might as well. I sure don't feel up to writing."

The tea lived up to its name, and the feel of Katie dozing in her lap was comforting.

Nelsey set a plate of fresh-made butterscotch chip

cookies in front of her. They were still warm, the chips melting and golden gooey. Nelsey folded her arms tight aross her chest until the bodice of her starched gray housedress caved in. She leaned back against the sink counter.

"Okay, maybe you better tell me what's going on."

Memphis sighed. "I've been wrestling with that decision. I haven't told you because I didn't want to involve you in any unhappiness."

"Well, balls of fire! You think I don't know unhappiness? One of the reasons we're put together here is to help others."

Memphis told her of how a strange juxtaposition of events came together to form a heinous night in 1936, and of how Cutter had known all along. Nelsey didn't move a hair while she listened. When Memphis had finished, she hung her head.

"So the hauntin' in the cellar, and the hummin' are Opal Marie, wantin' you to expose Harvey Root," she murmured to the floor. "And your bad dreams is your grandmother Sadie relivin' that night sixty years ago."

"I believe so."

When she finally looked at Memphis, her eyes blazed with indignation.

"I always knew Harvey was evil, but I never knew how bad it was. But Cutter didn't have no control or say over any of this. He promised his grandfather he'd never tell, jest as Macauley Tate had promised Sadie that *he'd* never tell. Don't be so blamin' mad at Cutter."

"He betrayed me."

"Not in my thinkin'. He did what he thought was right until he saw that it wasn't right no more."

Memphis didn't trust herself to speak, and shook her head in denial. Inside of her weak, wanting, treacherous body, she trembled violently. She was grateful Katie's heavy weight anchored her in place.

"You're really hurtin', ain't you, child?" asked Nelsey softly.

Determined not to cry, she set her teeth and pressed her lips tight together. She hated for anyone to see her cry.

"You in love with Cutter?"

Memphis started to shake her head in denial again, but unstoppable tears spilled from her burning eyes, and she avoided the painful question by looking past Nelsey and out the kitchen window. Through her crystal blur the beckoning spring day mocked her. She hugged Katie and rocked back and forth.

Nelsey knelt on the floor at the side of her chair, wrapped her arms around both of them, and laid her cheek on Memphis's shoulder. The three of them rocked together while silent tears coursed down Memphis's cheeks and Nelsey made soothing sounds. Katie slept on.

"I love you and Cutter like you were my own children. You're breakin' my own heart, Memphis. God has His ways. He'll bring you back together."

"No. Cutter should have told me."

"You're bein' childish. He was keepin' a promise, and you were a stranger to him. When he got to know you, I guess he had to decide about keepin' a secret about someone he loved or tellin' it to someone else that he loved. Try to put yourself in his shoes."

"He doesn't love me. You don't do that to someone you love. I don't want to talk about it." She freed an arm and wiped tears from her cheeks with the back of her wrist. "The sky is so blue. Sure doesn't look like rain or floods."

Nelsey gave her one last squeeze and stood up. "Yep. Spring blue. So blue you want to join the birds up there somewhere. But the rains will come in a few days, and what with all that snow we had this winter there'll be a few floods."

"Anything to worry about?"

"Nope. We have a pretty good one about every twenty years, but the dam up Grady way holds. Maynard Creek floods up to Leroy's doorway sometimes, and the river rises in town a few feet, but that's about it."

"I have to do some revisions. I'll put Katie in for her nap."

"Fine. Good luck with the writing."

Memphis stood, adjusting Katie's deadweight in her arms. "Thanks, Nelsey. I need all the encouragement I can get. It's so frustrating not being able to get to Root legally. But, by damned, I can sure crucify him with words. I can jab, hurt, embarrass, and generally mortify him. His reputation and standing in the community are his most precious possessions. When I'm finished, the people of Yancey will hate him."

All of a sudden her own words galvanized her, and she was eager to get to the computer. Her apathy was gone. The telling of the story to Nelsey, and the release of tears, had unlocked the latch she'd placed on her emotions. Indignation and anger were back, for the moment anyway.

Nelsey frowned. "Be careful, Memphis. 'Vengeance is mine, saith the Lord.'"

"Yeah, well, I'm going to help God a little bit."

"No matter what you do, God has His own ways of makin' justice."

"By the way, I don't want anyone to know about any of this. It would lessen the impact of my article. I've only told Margo, and I sent a letter to Vanta Lou by Leroy when he went to get the Jeep. So the Chafin family knows what really happened to Opal Marie."

Nelsey drew herself up haughtily. "I never tell nothin', Memphis. You know that."

"I know, I'm sorry. I just want to make sure you don't put yourself in any danger. Cutter has men guarding us. I wanted to send them away, but have decided I'll let them stay for you and Katie. So don't be concerned about Root hurting any of us."

"I wasn't worrying about that. I'm worried about you and Cutter."

Memphis froze up. "Don't be praying over that, Nelsey. You'd be wasting your time with God."

Nelsey frowned. "I'll be prayin' over anything I want to, Memphis Maynard."

Memphis sighed. "There is one thing, though, that I could sure use your help with. Root implied that Birdy has been behind the dirty tricks, even Miss Priss's hanging."

"No! Never."

"That's the way I felt at first, but the more I've thought about it, the more I think he might be telling the truth. What do you think?"

"Well, we've always known they wasn't bein' done by no ghost." Nelsey shook her head. "I'd hate to think Birdy was capable of such cruelty, but she does have a mighty attachment to Cutter. I've watched it get stronger through the years. Tries to hide it, but she's always been jealous of Cutter's girlfriends. I figured it might cause trouble someday. Cutter loves her like a sister. That ain't the way she loves him."

"If it's true, I'd like to choke the life out of her, but it's obvious she needs psychiatric counseling."

"You better tell Cutter what Root said about Birdy."

"No. I'll be happy if I never have to speak to Cutter Tate again."

"Well, it don't look like that attitude is makin' you happy."

"Cutter is already part of my past. I'll be fine."

Nelsey frowned, and Memphis could tell she didn't agree with Memphis's brave statement. But Memphis had no more time to look back and regret. The irreparable damage had been done.

*   *   *

Cutter polished another glass and placed it on the mirrored shelf behind the bar.

It was four o'clock in the afternoon. Ruby's was empty and quiet.

"I wish you'd let me buy you a dishwasher. These part-time dishwashers you hire are as reliable as a pair of deuces in a poker game."

Ruby flipped her damp dish towel over her shoulder, and lit a cigarette. "Believe I'll take you up on your offer this time. I'm gettin' too old for this shit."

"Great. I'll have Billy deliver one today."

"What are your plans for the weekend?"

"Not that it's any of your business, but I'm going to see Alison."

Ruby blew smoke and squinted at him through the haze. "Thought that was over with."

"It was, it is."

"You ain't seen Memphis since you came down off the mountain couple weeks ago."

"Right."

"How come?"

"It wasn't working out the way we hoped, Ruby. Leave it at that."

He hadn't told Ruby what he and Memphis had figured out, or about the secret letters he'd had all these years. If Ruby knew the story, she was capable of literally cutting Root's balls off. The only way he could help Memphis now was to keep quiet so her magazine article would have some impact, then be prepared for strong rebuttal when the media descended on Yancey for interviews as the dissension between Memphis and Jake grew.

"Alison ain't for you, Cutter."

"I know that, but I'm sure you'll tell me anyway, so I'll bite. Why?"

"She's all frosting. No cake."

"You're right."

"Then what the hell you foolin' around her for?"

"I need to laugh and have a good time for a few hours. Alison is a good friend, a good listener."

"Seems to me like you're kickin' in the wind."

Later, on the drive to his office, Cutter thought "kickin' in the wind" appropriate words: twisting in the wind like Memphis's kitten, and kicking futilely to loosen the noose that hung him.

He'd realized too late that love was an energy source like the air you breathe. If you withdrew or endangered that love, you took your breath away, and he was choking. The sense of inner potency and vitality that he'd always possessed had been energized by his love for Memphis, and now the power was gone. He knew he would survive, would regain himself, but for what and why?

The surrounding landscape did nothing to help his lousy mood. The last major melt of snow had left the ground sodden. Hillsides slid onto roads and inched onto lawns. Half of the roads were impassable. The Range Rover threw mud on everything it passed, as did every other vehicle. Shoes, boots, parcels, and sidewalks were mud-spattered. Too wet to plant. The only positive thing he had to look forward to was visiting his new greenhouse soon to set some seedlings into their birth pottings.

Memphis haunted him everywhere he turned.

He saw her profile in filigreed shadows on his bedroom wall at night, and in certain curves of sunlight on the patio in the morning—the delicate turn of chin, the high, fragile cheekbones. He heard her laughter in a Mozart concerto and her throaty moan in a Patsy Cline ballad. He looked for the summer green of her eyes in the river, but the river ran too fast and muddy now, and he always turned away disappointed.

His fears had come to fruition, and he deserved the hell he was going through. He'd been tried and found guilty. His sentence was to spend the rest of his life in hell.

He was surprised to find Birdy's new tomato red Lexus, which her indulgent father had given her for her birthday last month, parked in his private spot behind the office. Her hours were from nine to two. If he had a particular problem or case to work on, he often came late in the afternoon when he knew she would be gone. She meant well, but couldn't seem to refrain from constantly interrupting him for the smallest of reasons.

His office was dim. The light on his desk provided the only illumination. Where was Birdy?

He headed for the file drawer that contained the material he'd written on Root, and his grandfather's letters. Ordinarily he kept the letters in the trunk at the greenhouse, or in a locked safe at his house, but he'd brought them to the office to incorporate the information they provided into the Root file. The reason he'd come here so late this afternoon was to retrieve them and put them back into his safe.

The lock was broken, and the drawer gaped open. The files were out of order, and his letters were gone. He really didn't care about the files. He didn't care if the whole world knew about Root, which they would soon enough anyway. But the letters were Mac's and Sadie's, and he realized then that they belonged to him and Memphis also. The thought of anyone else reading them enraged him. It was as if someone watched as they made love, as if someone observed the progression of their shattering souls, and then poked about amongst the ruins with a disinterested finger.

Birdy hurried through the reception room door with the letters in her hand. She didn't see him in the shadows.

She went to where the Chafin photos hung. The shaft of light coming through the door from the other room was like a spotlight, illuminating every expression. He should announce his presence, but something in the way she held herself, and the incriminating letters in her hand made him hold his tongue. She looked at the Chafin photos with such loathing that Cutter was startled.

She picked up the heavy crystal ashtray he kept for cigar smokers and hefted it as if she was going to throw it at the photos on the wall, but then thought better of it and replaced the ashtray on the butler's table. Then she stared at the letters in her hand, and fanned them like a deck of cards, as if she hadn't decided what to do with them. She picked up the cigarette lighter and flicked it on and off a couple of times, then replaced it on the table also.

Was she going to burn the letters? What was wrong with her?

"Birdy."

Her hand went to her mouth, and the letters fell to the floor.

"Oh, my God, I didn't see you. You scared me half to death."

"What are you doing?"

"Oh, well, just some filing I've been meaning to do for ages. I thought this would be a good time because you're usually not here this late."

"That's my personal file and there was a lock on it."

"It was unlocked, so I figured I might as well start working in it."

He stepped out of the shadows and bent over to pick up the nail file that lay in full view next to the lock.

"Were you doing your nails while you sorted files, Birdy?"

"Well, my goodness, for heavens sakes, how did that get there?"

He stared at her, not saying a word.

"Cutter, if you're implying that I picked the lock, you're wrong."

"I don't think so." He saw the desperation mount in her eyes, and for a moment he felt sorry for her. After all, this was Birdy, his childhood playmate. "Did you find the letters interesting, Birdy?"

"Oh, well, I just glanced through them. Didn't really have a chance to read much. . . . Uh, I . . . very romantic, aren't they?"

She was red-faced now and played with the curl above her ear, the same gesture she'd used as a child when she was caught in a lie.

Any sympathy he'd felt for her disappeared.

"Pick up the letters and give them to me."

She did as he'd ordered, but her voice trembled when she tried to maintain her accustomed perkiness. "There you go, delivered all safe and sound with a seal of forever friendship."

"Now clean out your desk. You're fired."

Her flushed cheeks turned pale, and her hand went out to him. "No, this is one of your jokes, right, Cutter?"

"No. You violated a sacred trust between employer and employee, but even worse, you broke a trust of friendship. Friends don't intrude where it's obvious they aren't wanted."

Her knees began to buckle, and she caught the back of a chair.

"But we're more than friends," she whispered.

"You were like a sister to me, Birdy, but this is not acceptable. You better leave before I say more than I want to. And I warn you, if I hear anything that faintly suggests you've told anyone about the letters, you'll sincerely wish you hadn't."

She drew herself as tall as her tiny frame would allow. Loathing pinched her face. "It's Memphis, isn't it? She's the reason you don't like me anymore."

"Memphis has nothing to do with this." The fragile letters in his hand seemed to warm with the mention of her name. "You brought this on yourself."

"No, it's Memphis. I told you when she first came that she'd be trouble. Remember, Cutter? You wouldn't listen."

"Leave, Birdy, before you destroy the last of whatever friendship might remain."

She marched primly away, but stopped in the doorway to turn and have the last word. Her face ugly with malice, her tone raspy with hatred, she said, "Memphis Maynard will be sorry she ever came to Yancey."

Jake sank his teeth into Carpozzoli's Super Pizza. This was about the only thing he would miss about Yancey. Through the smudged plate-glass window, he watched reporters from CNN and ABC interviewing citizens of Yancey in the town square.

Across from him, his local cameraman, Pete, drank a cup of coffee.

"I'm surprised you're still here, Jake."

"Me, too. Living in this town is like scraping your dick across a screen door."

"Thought you'd move out real quick after the *Today Show* interview. People around here don't like the book, don't like reporters coming into town, and they never did like you."

"The good citizens of Yancey won't suffer long. It'll be a few days of sensation, just long enough to give my book a nice push, and then it will fade. I'm still here because I had a little unfinished business to take care of."

"Memphis and Katie?"

"No. Memphis won't speak to me."

"Must be Sally Junior then."

"Yep. She's like a booger on the end of your finger, sticky and hard to get rid of."

"At least you have the decency to say good-bye. You're not as big a jerk as I thought. Good luck. Here she comes. See ya around, pal."

Sally Junior slid into the seat Pete had occupied.

"Hi, sugar-hunk. This is all so exciting. I've never known anyone famous before. God, I taped the *Today Show*. You were s-o-o-o great. Do you think anyone will be taking my picture? I mean, after all, I will be with you sometimes, won't I? I don't want to be in the hotel room all the time when we're on this book-signing tour."

For one redeemable moment, Jake felt guilty about letting Sally Junior think she was going on tour with him, but the guilt faded fast as he worked to ease his way out of the sticky situation he'd created.

"Look, Sally J., about this tour, it would be easier for me if I was by myself. I move fast and I won't be good company."

"That's okay. I'll be as good as a little mouse. You won't even know I'm there, except at night when we're in bed."

"Yeah, well," he cleared his throat. He *was* going to miss sex with this skirt. "My publisher says it's going to look bad if you're with me. Bad form, he says."

"But I have my bags packed and everything."

Her lips got all trembly, and her eyes glistened with unshed tears.

Ahh, jeez, she's not going to cry, is she? He'd never seen Memphis cry, but it just about killed him when Katie cried.

He finished the last bite of pizza, thinking hard. Sally Junior pulled a Kleenex from her windbreaker, and blew her nose.

"Look, tell you what. You can meet me along the way. Like when I get to San Francisco, I'll call you and you can fly out to meet me."

"But I don't have the money to be flying around on my own."

"I'll send you the ticket. Ever been to San Francisco?"

"No." A note of excitement lifted her voice.

Bingo.

"You'll love it."

"Oh, I can't wait, Jake. When will you be in San Francisco?"

"Uh, I don't remember. I don't have my itinerary with me."

"You'll call me every night, right?"

"I'll try." He glanced at his watch. "Gotta go, baby. Gotta catch a plane."

He gathered his duffel bag and briefcase and stood up to leave. Sally Junior clung to him like wet toilet paper.

"Oh, God, I'm going to miss you, sugar-hunk."

He gave her a big lippy kiss and said, "Me, too, honey, me too. See you in San Fran."

He hurried out onto the square with a sigh of relief. *Mission accomplished. Congratulations. You did it again, Jakey ol' boy.*

§23§

"Rain, rain, go away, come again another day," recited
Memphis.

Katie laughed as they clapped hands and repeated
the rhyme together.

"Again," she implored. "Itsy bitsy spider?"

"Katie, me girl, you don't give up, do you? No more
rhymes. It's bedtime."

"Where's Miss Priss? I lonely in my bed."

Memphis's heart flickered then resumed a steady
beat. Miss Priss had slept with Katie, and Katie asked
the question every night.

"Miss Priss had to visit another little girl, but Nelsey
and I are looking for another kitten for you. Okay?"

Katie shook her head sadly. Memphis diverted her by
beginning their counting game.

They climbed the stairs together, Katie counting as
she negotiated each step, reaching the number five and
then starting all over again. Except for the unbroken
beat of the incessant rain, the house was quiet and
Katie's undersized voice echoed in the stairwell.

Memphis placed the rag doll, Opal Marie, in her
arms, and tucked the covers around her. She stared at
the doll for a moment, the doll she'd named so blithely,
innocently, when Katie was an infant, not knowing at
the time that the name had been sent to her for a

reason, and how important the name would become in her life.

Katie asked for Nelsey.

Memphis kissed her cheek and sat next to her so they could cuddle. "I miss her, too, love. Nelsey's at a church convention in Richmond. We'll just have to do without her for a few days. I'll read *The Ducklings*, okay?"

Katie smiled and nodded, her lids already beginning to close. After two pages, Memphis closed the picture book, gave the sleeping child another kiss on the cheek, turned off the light, and left the room.

Downstairs, she prepared a tray with hot tea and a stack of Nelsey's cinnamon cookies, and settled into the large armchair in the living room. She turned on the television, but soon decided it was one of those "wasteland" nights. There was nothing worth watching, and an annoying flash flood warning message kept traveling across the bottom of the screen.

"Shouldn't affect us. Especially me, here on the hill." She pressed the off button.

Her time here in Yancey was almost over. The darkroom had been dismantled, and all of her equipment and files were on their way to her Manhattan address. She and Katie would leave for their apartment in the big city next week. The *Vanity Fair* piece was finally in the hands of her editor. Margo had called from Miami earlier in the evening, so she'd already had the pleasure of a long chat with her sister. Accustomed to Nelsey's presence, or frantic phone calls from her agent in New York, work to do in the darkroom or at the computer, Memphis was at a loss for something to occupy her.

For the first time since she'd arrived months ago, she felt isolated and left out of things. She wished for Miss Priss's curled warmth about her feet. Even Leroy was gone, visiting a brother in Charleston.

For a brief irrational moment, she wished she hadn't sent away the men whom Cutter had hired to watch her. Knowing Cutter was away, she'd ordered them away from the property yesterday . They had protested, but she had fibbed, saying, "Cutter called from New York and said you were to take the weekend off." The thought of two days' vacation must have been enticing because they chose to believe her and drove away.

She'd taken great pleasure in countermanding his instructions. The sight of their night-lights, one in the woods and one at the bottom of the hill, used to be irritating, but in retrospect would have been welcome on this lonely rainy night.

Wonder what Cutter is doing in New York? Is he in his hotel room right now? Does he remember our night there?

Stop this, right now.

But she couldn't help herself. These were the thoughts she'd been warding off all evening. He was in New York cementing the last of his agreement with United Mining. She always knew where Cutter was. She couldn't help it. It was like osmosis. She decided her condition was akin to an unwanted radar alert. In spite of efforts not to, she eavesdropped on Nelsey's phone conversations, listened to men gossiping at Leroy's, and struck up conversations with people at the hardware store who she'd never talked to before in hopes of acquiring dribs and drabs of information about Cutter.

Every morning she woke up with a dull anxious feeling that stayed throughout the day. Her feet felt lead-weighted, and a stark inner detachment made life seem superficial and mundane. She heard music, but her feet didn't itch to dance. The spreading oak at the corner of the house had sprouted green nodules, and brave yellow dandelions nodded for attention on the lawn, but they might as well have been plastic. She looked at the changing colors of the mountains, but didn't really see them.

This new emptiness was frightening. She hated it. The rest of her life yawned abysmally before her. No. Surely this wouldn't last forever.

"Come on, Memphis. Chin up," as Faith used to say. "Read a good book." Reading a book had been her mother's solution to everything.

She turned on the CD player, hoping Pachelbel's Canon in D Major would catch her up in its drama, and scooched back in the soft confines of the chair. She picked up Ben Bradlee's *A Good Life*, which she'd been meaning to read for ages, and opened the book with determination.

Bradlee's book absorbed her for a time, but she caught herself listening automatically for sounds that she knew couldn't be there. The bad dreams had stopped. No more ghostly night trains whistling at midnight. No more screams in the woods.

Her grandmother must know that Memphis knew the truth now, and had entrusted the tragic story to her care. Sometimes she still heard Opal Marie humming on the breeze, which saddened more than frightened her. She'd told Vanta Lou how Opal Marie really died, and short of finding the girl's grave, Memphis didn't know how else to help her.

She forced her attention back to the book. Soon, like Katie, her eyelids drooped, and she fought sleep. But suddenly her eyes popped open, and she shot straight up in the chair. Had that been the crunch of gravel as a car pulled around the house into the woods? There had been no flash of headlights on the living-room wall as there usually was if someone came at night.

She settled back with the book again. Pachelbel's Canon ended and the rhythm of the rain lulled her into a light doze.

The metallic rattle of the rusty twister doorbell sounded loud in the silence.

Her book fell to the floor. Next to her, the teacup tipped over as she caught the edge of the tray with her arm when she jumped to her feet. She rubbed her face with her hands, trying to wake up.

Her heart beat fast with alarm, and she shivered violently. The temperature must have dropped ten degrees while she dozed.

Who would be way out here on a night like this? Birdy? No. Birdy had gone to the Harless's cottage at Myrtle Beach. Nelsey had made sure of that before she left Memphis alone. Rumor had it that Cutter had fired Birdy, and she'd left town the next day.

The bell rang again. *Don't stand here wondering. Answer it.*

The pebbled-glass window of the door revealed nothing outside. Another prank? She opened the door.

Nothing. No one there. She shut the door and re-locked it, and stood in the hall wondering if stress from the last month had driven her insane.

"Memphis."

She whirled around. A young girl stood behind her, between Memphis and the now-open door. She was barefooted, and wore a summer-white dress, and she was dry. Memphis rubbed her eyes. The girl should have been wet, but she was dry. It was hard to see her face because sheets of rain fell behind her and reflected rainbows from the porch light. The multicolor crystal rays circled around her.

But I just shut the door. Memphis broke into a cold sweat.

"Memphis," said the girl again, softly. "You must leave the house."

"Ahh, who are you?" But Memphis suddenly remembered. This startling apparition standing in her living room looked like the hitchhiking girl she'd picked up on Twenty-Two Mountain the night she and Katie had first arrived in Yancey. "How did you get in here?"

"Leave afore the bridge washes. You'll be stranded fer days."

"Surely the creek won't come to this level."

"Evil is hyar tonight."

"What do you mean?"

"Hurry, hurry. Git the baby and hurry."

Suddenly Memphis knew who this wavering creature of the light was.

"Opal Marie?"

"Leave, leave, leave." The figure began to dissolve, and the humming came, then singing. "What a friend we have in Jesus, all our sins and griefs to bear . . ."

The small voice grew strong, then diminished as the figure faded from the hall, floated through the open door, and into the torrential downpour.

Memphis reached into the space where Opal Marie had stood, then stepped onto the porch and groped for what had been there and now was not. There remained only a strong sense of heartbreaking sadness, which always heralded Opal Marie's comings and goings. Bewildered, she stepped back into the foyer, closed the door, and leaned against it, shaking so hard that her elbow rattled the frosted glass of the door. She shook with fear, not of the apparition, but of the evil that Opal Marie had warned her of, for she knew it was here. She felt it close enough to touch, and she trusted the young girl instinctively.

"Hurry, hurry, hurry." The words echoed faintly through the silent house.

She tore upstairs two steps at a time.

Don't think, just do as she says.

She threw a change of clothes into the weekend bag she kept filled with toiletries. As a traveling photojournalist she'd learned to keep a small case ready to go. In Katie's room she hastily packed clothes, diapers, and the rag doll, Opal Marie.

"Hurry, hurry, hurry."

In the kitchen, she slipped on her yellow rain slicker and snatched a flashlight from the pantry. The Jeep wasn't far from the back door, but far enough for her to get soaked as she ran for it. She pulled it close to the kitchen door and ran back inside and upstairs where Katie still slept peacefully. Memphis grabbed the two bags she had packed, and went down to deposit them in the back of the Jeep.

Katie's car seat was fastened in the rear seat where all the experts said it was safest. But for reasons unknown to her, she wanted Katie close to her on this trip.

The rain tore at her as she undid the straps and clamps and yanked the carrier from the backseat. It was impossible to hold the flashlight and install the child carrier properly in the front passenger seat. Working with only the weak overhead light to guide her, her wet fingers slipped and fumbled with the important locking devices until she was satisfied they were secure.

Soaked through now, when she reentered the house she replaced her slicker with Nelsey's dry one, then bounded up the stairs to Katie. Katie murmured sleepily when she bundled her up. As she tore through the kitchen she grabbed an old orange windbreaker that hung on a hook next to the door and threw it over the child.

"Shhh, it's okay, love. We're going for a ride."

The rain woke Katie up, and she whimpered while her mother fastened her in the carrier.

"Don't worry, Katie. I know you're a bit wet, but you'll be dry in no time. We're going on an adventure.

You'll have fun." She stuffed Opal Marie into Katie's arms, and shut the passenger door, out of breath and trembling.

For the first time she glanced around her. Was she being foolish? Had she panicked? Everything seemed to be in order. The dark woods were wet with rain, and the house sat innocently still, yet she shivered with the sensation that someone watched her. Evil surrounded her, icy in its intent.

"Hurry, hurry, hurry. Leave, leave, leave," whispered Opal Marie.

She ran to the other side and jumped in, afraid to study the woods or the house any longer. She pulled the Jeep around the house, and headed toward the hill. Halfway down, she had the impression of movement behind her, but had no time to look and attributed it to her imagination. Negotiating the descent, which had washed out in places, took all her attention.

They reached the bridge and she stopped, stunned with disbelief. Opal Marie had been right. A foot of water curled at Leroy's back door. The creek, once a peaceful flow of placid water, had become a broad roaring river. It rushed noisily above the sound of the rain, and had risen until it slurped angrily onto the bridge.

As close as she could tell, maybe two inches of water ran over the surface of the bridge. Was it safe to cross? There were no guard rails, never had been. How sturdy were the old supports that held it? Maybe she'd better go back and take her chances at the house.

No, she felt the creeping chill of evil that insinuated itself around the entire hill. If she drove carefully, they should reach the other bank safely. She leaned tight over the steering wheel, peering beyond her headlights to spot the other side of the creek. *Dear God, I can't see a thing but water.*

Should she cross, or shouldn't she? If she were alone,

she would just dash across, to hell with the consequences. She glanced at her precious cargo. Katie had blessedly fallen back to sleep.

A jar against the rear bumper startled her. Her eyes jerked to the rearview mirror. A large car, headlights off, sat dead against her bumper.

What on earth?

The car jolted the Jeep again, and they inched toward the bridge.

No, dammit.

She put the Jeep in reverse and tried to shove the car back. It wouldn't budge. She set the emergency brake, and prepared to leave the Jeep to confront the driver of the car, but thought better of it when she glanced at Katie. She couldn't leave her alone, and she couldn't get into a confrontation with the child in her arms.

The headlights of the big car flashed on and off a few times, as if mocking her. In the reflection of the headlights against her dashboard, she saw that the car was tomato red.

There was only one car that color in Yancey County. Birdy Harless's new Lexus.

The Lexus bumped hard this time, throwing her forward, and sending the Jeep onto the bridge.

Okay, damn you. You won't take charge here. We'll make it across before you can do any harm.

She released the emergency brake, shifted into second gear to moderate the powerful push of the Lexus, and swallowed hard. Heart pounding, she pressed the gas pedal. The Jeep moved toward the center of the bridge, and she held her breath. Behind her, the Lexus hung tight to her taillights. Suddenly, Birdy switched her headlights on high, and the full blast of light filled the interior of the Jeep so Memphis could see barely a foot in front of her.

The old bridge creaked and groaned with the weight of the two heavy vehicles and the rush of runaway water against its rotting supports. The wrenching sounds terrified Memphis. Her breath came in short gasps. There was no escape. She was trapped on the bridge with Birdy. The only way out was forward. She steadied her jittering foot and pressed on the gas pedal with determination.

Birdy accelerated, pushing harder, and the Jeep moved faster over the water-covered surface.

As the two cars, locked now at the bumpers, moved recklessly across the bridge, Birdy sounded her horn over and over again in some sort of gleeful, triumphant message. The crazy trumpeting of the horn in the midst of this crazy trip across the slippery span made the whole scene surreal to Memphis. Katie, whose eyelids had been drooping, was now wide awake and screaming with fright.

She gripped the steering wheel, praying they would reach solid ground before the structure gave way.

A distant roar caught her attention. She chanced a glance upstream. She could see nothing through the night blackness and the downpour. Katie still cried, and Memphis had no time to comfort her. The brightness of Birdy's headlights highlighted the gold in her blond curls, and caught the glistening of her tears.

The roar grew louder, as if something drew closer.

Oh, God, that's water coming this way. The dam has broken.

She pressed hard on the gas now, asking for more power, but the Lexus locked to her bumper was too heavy a load. The noise was deafening, and the bridge lurched and tilted with the extra surge of power that pushed at its aged supports.

Memphis's stomach flipped sickly.

"No, no," she cried.

The wall of water from upstream hit, and the bridge tore loose from its restraints, carrying the Jeep and the

Lexus with it. Katie wailed with fright, and held her arms out to Memphis.

The two cars rode the span down the careening creek. Memphis's stomach settled and her heart stopped its erratic, panicked beat. She went into command-alert. Cool as a cucumber now, for she knew their survival depended on her, she quickly took stock of the situation.

Would Katie be safer in her arms or in her car seat? She decided to leave her in the seat. As she realized she had little or no control of their fate, her hands reluctantly loosened their death grip on the steering wheel. She tightened the straps around Katie, and said as calmly as she could, "It's okay, Katie, love. I can't take you right now, but Mom's right here. We're riding down the creek. You hold tight and we'll be done in no time."

Memphis realized Katie probably couldn't hear her, but the child watched her mouth, and read the expression on her face. She smiled reassuringly, and anchored herself by holding to the steering wheel with one hand, and holding Katie's arm with the other.

Logs, branches, and other debris tore past them. Memphis wanted to close her eyes, afraid to see what new danger approached them in the roiling waters. But she couldn't close her eyes, for she suspected their time floating on this fragile span of old tarred logs was limited. Again she worried whether she had done the right thing with Katie. The thought of Katie strapped into her seat with water swirling around her blond curls panicked Memphis again. If water entered the car, Katie would be better off in her arms.

"Dear God," she sobbed out loud. "Somehow we'll get through this."

The wild honking of a horn made Katie scream again, and she squeezed Memphis's hand in terror.

Memphis had forgotten about Birdy. She twisted her head to see the Lexus still attached to the Jeep.

All coherent thought left as the bridge smashed broadside against an immovable object and tore in two, and the rear of the Jeep sank. The front section still clung to a portion of the floating span. Water leaked into the rear, slowly at first, then quickly rose to the backseat, and lapped noisily at the two front seats. Memphis had an impression of the Lexus sweeping swiftly by, going ahead of them as they swept faster and faster downstream.

For a second, the Jeep headlights caught a glimpse of Birdy clawing at her window, her eyes wide with terror, her mouth open in a scream that Memphis couldn't hear. The Lexus disappeared in the downstream blackness.

The sight drove Memphis into action. Water now lapped at her feet. She undid her seat belt, which had served her well until now, and grabbed Katie's carrier. The water rose rapidly now. It circled her knees and swirled over the passenger seat, wetting Katie's shoes. She worked feverishly to undo the straps that held Katie in the seat. Katie's crying had quieted to hiccups and tired sobs.

"That's a good girl. This funny ol' trip down the creek will be over in no time. You'll see."

The straps wouldn't loosen. She commanded her fingers to find the right combination to undo the damn things.

"Steady on, Memphis. Steady on," said a strange voice. Faith? Are you there?

Not her mother. Not Opal Marie, either.

Water swirled at her waist and Katie's knees.

"Oh, God, help me."

They wouldn't loosen. The straps wouldn't loosen.

The Jeep twirled around and around in a whirlpool.

The front door of someone's house smashed hard against the windshield, followed by a refrigerator. The refrigerator was the crowning blow. It broke the glass and the raging river poured in on Memphis and Katie.

She held fast to Katie's car seat, knowing they would go down together. She would die with Katie. Her last coherent thought before the water pulled them under was to give the child seat a yank.

It gave and floated free. They sank with the weight of the Jeep to the fast-running bottom.

Memphis felt with her feet for the opening at the smashed windshield. She couldn't find it. Everything was black, and upside down, and backwards. Was the Jeep upright or had it turned over?

"Try again," said the voice. She knew it was Sadie.

She kicked again. There was an open space of some kind. With a death grip on Katie's seat she kicked her way free of the Jeep and fought her way toward the surface. The swift run of water pulling at the deadweight of Katie's seat yanked painfully at her arm.

Fast-moving rubbish struck her breast. A mess of wire teased her legs, caught an ankle for a moment, and then moved on. Her air was gone, but she fought upwards, her knee killing her. Foggy gray cobwebs of thought moved in and around her, and then they were gone, too.

"Kick!" said Sadie.

One last mighty kick. Blackness took over.

When Memphis regained consciousness, she was still gripping Katie's seat and bobbing with the rest of the debris down the tumultuous river.

Sputtering, protesting coughs and angry cries from Katie were the sweetest sounds she'd ever heard in her life.

Thank you, God.

She was a good swimmer. The water was cold, but not icy. If they could avoid major injury from the lethal spoilage hurled at them from upstream they might make it. She pulled the child seat to her, hoping Katie could see her face.

"I'm here, Katie, I'm here," she yelled.

A large jar conked her on the head, then caught Katie, too. Katie wailed anew. An onslaught of rubbish hit them—a carpenter's saw, a wooden case of empty bottles, a white Clorox carton, and numerous unidentifiable articles. There was no protection from the dangers that flew at them.

Memphis wished futilely for light to see their way. If it were daylight, at least she could try and aim for a tree or some solid object that had held fast during the flood.

Something swiped across her cheek, and she knew she'd been cut. The blood dripped warmly across her chin and then was washed away by the dirty river. She pulled Katie as close as possible, trying to shield the defenseless child, but knew it was useless.

"Kick, kick, kick."

Stay afloat.

A swirling eddy took them around and around. Memphis was sick to her stomach, and the rapid whirl must have taken Katie's breath, because she was silent. The whirlpool tossed them in the air. They landed with a thump on top of a large object, which seemed anchored a few feet below the surface. Memphis scrambled for a toehold, but found nothing. She reached into the air and quickly latched onto a sturdy tree branch. She curved her free elbow around it and struggled again to find something to hook her feet onto. The object they had landed on was wedged between a large tree and an abutment of some kind.

Finally, her frantically searching feet found a smooth opening that felt like metal. She angled her feet through and around it, and could stand for few seconds of time before the water pushed her out of place again. She sought for better purchase above her. The tree offered a surplus of branches and leaves. She inched her way toward the trunk as far as she could without losing her toehold beneath the water. She found an angled branch that she could lock onto and hold Katie, too.

The swift powerful tide of the dam water seemed to be ebbing somewhat, but the tug of it pulled and pushed at her body as if she were a strand of seaweed washed back and forth in a restless tide. But she had to hang on until daylight. They had a chance in the daylight. She could figure a way to dry land, or someone would see them.

She gagged, then threw up river water and bile.

A two-by-four swiped her calves, and she almost lost her footing.

"No. This is were we landed, this is where we'll stay. We'll make it through the night, Katie. I promise we will."

Katie hadn't made a sound. Memphis brought her as close as she could, and bent her ear to the carrier. She couldn't hear anything above the rush of water, but she pressed her forehead against the child's chest and felt it move. She was breathing.

She wished she could tie Katie to her, fasten her tight to her body so she wouldn't lose her should she fall asleep during the night.

But it was impossible. She couldn't loosen her hold on either the carrier or the tree. She inserted three fingers through the strap slots on the rear of the seat and held on for dear life. She found the seat floated, so that helped. Katie wouldn't sink, but she might float away from her.

Pain from her knee kept her awake part of the night, sending jolting avenues of agony through all her limbs.

Through the terror-filled night she alternated periods of extreme painful alertness with terrifying moments of hazy nightmares or fog-filled dreams. Shadows gathered around them, and voices keened softly. Who were these women who touched and encouraged and kept her awake? Faith blew her a kiss, and Sadie . . . was it Sadie? Sadie looked sad, but she smiled, her eyes filled with love. Memphis would awake with a start, listen for Katie, and then she would sing. The singing kept her from falling into deep sleep. Someone sang with her.

Cutter's silver eyes shimmered through the haze. *Hang on. Hang on for me.*

Would morning never come? She hurt all over.

The sun on her face woke her.

Her fingers and arms had lost all feeling, but Katie was still hooked to her. Memphis pushed the seat around with her nose until she could see Katie. Her golden curls were brown with coal silt, and black mud filled every plump-baby crease of her arms and hands, but her chest moved up and down and she slept the sleep of the exhausted.

Memphis looked around, anxious to see what their situation was.

The immovable structure in front of them was the railroad trestle that spanned the Tow River south of Yancey. The iron trestle had held. The tree, which she had imagined rooted and whole, was actually a mammoth broken branch caught fast in the arched trestlework. There was no tree holding them. Had a larger object hit it, the sturdy limb could have been swept away at any time during the night.

Thank God I didn't know.

The water had ebbed enough for her to discover what she'd hooked her feet around in the blackness of the night, the solid mysterious object that had anchored them.

The muddy water eddied lazily over and around it now. Small circles came and went on the top of Birdy's Lexus. Memphis had her feet hooked through the narrow opening of a window.

Birdy was nowhere to be seen.

§24§

"Lord have mercy, how did he git up there? Ain't no way the waters was that high," said a woman.

Memphis, like everyone else in the ragtag crowd that gathered in the few dry spots the town square offered, stared skyward at the bell tower of the Episcopal Church of the Good Shepherd.

Harvey Root hung nude, and obviously very dead, from the arched scaffolding.

Memphis sat in the rear of Leroy's truck, which had stalled in water above its tires. Two coal miners had rescued her early this morning, and left her in the care of a family whose mountainside cottage had been high enough to escape damage. Leroy had found her as he maneuvered his way on back roads and byways around the floodwaters toward Yancey.

The small crowd who gawked at the spectacle of Harvey Root were those who had been anxious to get into Yancey before the National Guard arrived and took over. Mountaineers would never allow others to do for them what they felt was theirs to do. They floated in canoes and rubber dinghies in the deeper water, or stood in knee-high boots, or sat in stalled vehicles like Leroy's. Leroy stood next to the truck with Katie high in his arms.

"Well, somebody's gotta go up and cut him down," said a man.

"Hell, no. Let the old bastard hang there 'til he rots."

Memphis, repelled by the macabre sight, yet fascinated like everyone else, felt a surge of elation and triumph. It was wrong to feel so good about someone else's misfortune, even Harvey Root's, but in this case she couldn't be happier. Harvey Root hung in the town square, shorn of the dignity, honor, and respectability he had so prized all his life. She surprised herself by wishing Cutter were here to share this moment with her.

"What's he got hangin' around his neck?"

"Looks like a big ol' snake, and it ain't the kind of snake we'll be findin' in the waters either."

"Naw. Someone hung him, sure enough, but why would they put a dead snake on him?"

"That's what it is, swear to Gawd. And there's a paper tied to the snake."

From the moment she had seen Root hanging limply in the still air, lewdly outlined against the bright blue sky, Memphis suspected who had murdered him. Now, squinting to get a better look, she knew for sure. She started to climb down from the truck, but Leroy stopped her.

"Stay put. There be snakes all over, Memphis."

"But I want to climb up there."

"No way. Too dangerous. We'll cut him down later. There's other stuff to be doin' first. Wish Cutter was here. He'd know where to start."

"Leroy, promise you'll let me know when they bring him down. I think that's a note attached to the snake, and I have to read it."

"I promise. Now, let's git you and the baby somewhar dry. Someone said Ruby's place didn't git too much damage. I'll borrow someone's boat and take you out thar."

"Hey, hey, look at his dick," giggled a young man.

"What dick? He ain't got no dick."

"That's what I mean. It looks like one of Ma's dried-up biscuits, all flat and sunk in the middle."

"Okay, okay, everybody. We've got work to do," said Leroy. "There's people what needs our help. Joe Bob, you be findin' a place where we can set up a soup kitchen, and Gus, thar's probably goin' to be some people hurtin'. We need someplace to take care of them. Check out the Baptist church. It sits high enough that it might be okay. I know the rest of you want to be checkin' your homes, so go ahead. National Guard will be here purty soon, and we don't want much bossin' from them, so let's get busy. I'm takin' Memphis out to Ruby's in Claytie's boat. Anyone else want to go?"

Another mother with a child accepted his offer. As they transferred mothers and children to the boat, Claytie looked at Memphis with knowing eyes.

"You thinkin' what I'm thinkin', Miz Maynard?" He pointed to Root's corpse.

"Yes, Claytie, I am."

A broad smile split his seamed face.

"I know there's a bunch of misery around us, and more in the days a-comin', but I'm tellin' you that I couldn't be happier right now."

"Me too, Claytie. We'll talk later."

Cutter took a swift inventory of his landing strip on top of Cat Teeth. No one here, and he really hadn't expected anyone. Everyone was in the valley helping with the cleanup. He'd spent two frustrating days trying to get back to Yancey. A stubborn fog layering the northeast had detained him in New York.

Phone service had been restored early this morning, and he had tried to reach Memphis and Nelsey with no luck at either house. He suspected both houses were still inaccessible. Frantic with worry, he finally connected with Ruby.

"Things is bad here," she'd said. "The Tow has receded some, but people who lived next to the river have been wiped out. There's mud and garbage everywhere. Stinks to high heaven. And there's more son-of-a-bitch snakes than you can imagine."

"No one answered at Memphis's place, or Nelsey's. Are they okay?"

"Yep. They're both stayin' with me, but they ain't here now. Nelsey arrived yesterday and is running the soup kitchen from the Baptist church, and Memphis is giving tetanus shots somewhere."

"What do you mean 'somewhere'?" he'd asked in alarm. "And who's taking care of Katie?"

"I'm baby-sittin' Katie," she'd said with a note of pride in her voice. "And I'm not sure where Memphis is because she's been all over the place. She got the whole damn rescue operation organized. I never saw anything like it. You'd think she lived here permanent."

"My father?"

"That weird nurse of his, Victor, got him over to a hotel in Charleston before things got serious." She paused. "Hope you make it back soon. We need you real bad."

"I'm cleared to take off in thirty minutes."

The Range Rover performed admirably, taking each swoop with ease as he drove at dangerous speeds down Cat Teeth. The foul smell of rotting debris and coal-filled silt and muck met him as he neared the bottom.

When he reached the valley, the damage inflicted by the rampaging river soon became evident. Traffic was one-way on the narrow road leading into Yancey. Pockets of deep filthy water still stood, and debris-filled mud layered everything. Houses had shifted off their foundations, and trucks and cars were filled with muck up to their steering wheels.

Cutter knew the sunlit azure sky was a relief to rain-weary flood-stricken Yancey residents, but it seemed an affront to the gray-brown devastation that lay beneath it.

He showed his proof of residency to the National Guardsmen on the outskirts of town, and they waved him on through. The town square was dry, clean, and the center of activity. A Red Cross mobile unit sat next to the courthouse. National Guardsmen gave directions, protected shops still uninhabitable, and kept news media from climbing to the Episcopal Church belfry.

AP wire services had spread the bizarre story of a respectable banker found hung in a church belfry high above floodwaters in the small coal-mining town of Yancey, West Virginia. The accounts included the contents of the odd note found attached to the copperhead, which was wrapped around the old man's neck.

"Here hengs the evil soul of the merderer of Opal Marie Chafin. Hervey Root will burn in hell ferever."

The coroner said Harvey Root had been boxed up in an enclosure of some sort and bitten several times by the snake. He'd sufffered horribly before he was taken out, still alive, and hanged. No information or clues as to the perpetrators of the hanging had been forthcoming, a wire report said, and the town was so intent on cleaning up after the flood that they didn't seem to care a whole lot about their former prominent citizen, Harvey Root.

Cutter paused to stare up at the now infamous bell tower, and smiled. Opal Marie Chafin's family had served retribution in full measure, and in a very befitting manner. Few people would recognize Grandpa Chafin's handiwork in Harvey Root's diabolical death, and if they did they would keep it to themselves.

Gotcha, you son of a bitch.

He donned a pair of waders provided by the Red

Cross, and went in search of the face he wanted to see most in the world. Heart in his throat, he looked in vain for Memphis, but always seemed to be two steps behind her. Eventually he found Nelsey at the Baptist church. She finished piling a plate high with peanut butter sandwiches, gave a child an apple, then turned to give him a heartfelt hug.

"Lordy, we been missin' you, son."

"Where is she, Nelsey?"

She hooked an errant hank of white hair behind her ear.

"Hard to tell. Probably somewhere she shouldn't be. She told me to take charge here yesterday, and then she took off. I know one thing. She's plumb wore out. Got about three hours of sleep last night, and was off again at six o'clock this morning. We couldn't even get her to eat nothin'."

"What do you mean, she's somewhere she shouldn't be?"

Nelsey smiled. "Reminds me a little of you. Doesn't listen to nobody and does as she darn well pleases. She had several skirmishes with the National Guard until she charmed them to pieces. Now they let her in and out of everywhere."

"But where is she?"

Nelsey's smile faded. "I'm tellin' you true, Cutter. I don't know. The thing that worries me most is the snakes and the infected places she goes into."

"What the hell for?"

"Well, one time she heard a child whimperin' in a place no one else had took the time to check out, so she went in and found the Akers girl hidin' in an upstairs closet, safe but scared to death. The parents had gone away for a few days and left her alone. Memphis carries a machete with her and killed two cotton-mouths in the Akers's house." Nelsey sighed. "But if I were to guess, I'd say she was near the river helpin' clean out the muck in the houses that's still standin' down there."

Cutter gave her a quick kiss on the forehead and turned to leave, but she held his arm, an odd look on her face.

"Cutter, Birdy didn't go to the beach like I thought. She's missin'."

Pain knifed through him, and guilt rode high in his chest.

"Damn. I'll look for her. I fired her right before I left. She was probably feeling pretty low."

"I think you better talk to Memphis about Birdy. She has some things to tell you."

"I don't know if Memphis will ever speak to me again. I just want to see her and make sure she's okay."

"Then get a-goin'."

The people he spoke to as he searched for Memphis lit up when he mentioned her name. A look of respect came into their tired eyes, and they always took a moment to say something nice about her.

Leroy was down by the now docile Tow River in serious discussion with several men. They stood near the defunct bridge that had led across the river to Cutter's home and several other large estates, including Birdy Harless's and Cle Hutton's and Sally Junior's.

"Whew. You're a sight fer sore eyes, Cutter. These here men are engineers the governor sent down to help us rebuild, and I don't like the way they're talkin'. Says it's goin' to take months to rebuild this bridge, and the one over Maynard Creek down by mine and Memphis's place. Don't sound right to me. I'm an uneducated old man, but I wish we could get things done quicker than that."

In his search through town, the immediate need for heavy earth-moving equipment, building materials, and trained carpenters had become quite evident to Cutter. He'd already called his TEC, Inc. men into action. They were on their way into Yancey right now.

At first the engineers with their blueprints and slide rules were reluctant to listen to Cutter. But when they understood who he was, they realized he knew what he was talking about. After some sketchy planning and respectful nods, Cutter clapped them on their backs, shook their hands, and generally made them feel as if they were going to be a large part of the rehabilitation of Yancey. Cutter was happy for the help, but knew that Yancey would do most of its own rebuilding in its own way.

The two men walked away to inspect the bridge site again, leaving Cutter and Leroy alone.

"The bridge by your place is damaged, too? How's your store?" asked Cutter.

"My place slud off its foundation. Have to build a new one. The creek riz up to Nelsey's doorstep, but didn't come near Memphis's. The bridge ain't no more. Plumb gone. It washed away down creek and into the river with Memphis and Katie on it."

"What are you talking about?"

Leroy took off the miner's hard hat, which he wore for protection, and scratched the back of his balding head. "Well, she ain't told no one what happened 'cept me, Nelsey, and Ruby. I don't reckon it's no secret though, and I reckon she wouldn't mind if I told you."

"Jesus," Cutter said, and he gripped Leroy by the arm. Alarm beat like a tattoo in his throat and his head ached. "What happened? Were they hurt?"

Leroy told him then of Memphis and Katie's harrowing ride down the flooded creek and into the rampaging river. He told him of how Memphis had held on through the night, and of the rescue by the two miners in the early dawn.

Rigid with fury, but confused, Cutter asked, "Who was the son of a bitch in the Lexus? There are only a few in the county, and one of them is Birdy's."

"I better let Memphis tell you the rest. She was here helpin' shovel muck out of Mitchell's Hardware. The stuff was way too heavy fer her, so I run her off by tellin' her they needed her to give tetanus shots up at the clinic, which weren't no lie. The children like Memphis doin' it better than anyone."

He finally found her on the second floor of the courthouse, which had been converted into a makeshift clinic. The walnut-railed jury box held tables with supplies. The counsels' tables had been discarded, and the space was filled with hospital cots. People sat in the viewing seats waiting for attention, or eating.

Memphis took a squalling child from the arms of its mother, and laughing and cajoling, she had the child smiling in no time. She administered the injection smoothly. Cutter leaned against the doorjamb. Now that he'd found her safe and sound, he wanted to take a few moments of pleasure in watching her before he had to leave. Dressed in an oversized blue-plaid shirt of Ruby's, and trousers too big for her, Memphis padded around the once dignified courtroom in thick socks so large that the toes flopped emptily. He suspected that one of the pairs of muddy waders left outside the door belonged to her.

Everywhere she went, she brought smiles and laughter.

"Hey, Miz Maynard, you eat anything today?"

"I'm fine, Bodie, I'm fine," Memphis replied as she tried to spoon soup into an elderly woman's mouth.

The woman refused the soup.

"Now look here, Emma Lee," said Memphis, "you don't want your Buster getting well and going home before you, do you? You going to let that old man watch your new television without you there?"

Emma Lee took a quick look at the old man next to her in a wheelchair, frowned, and shook her head. She took a sip of soup, and Cutter watched as Memphis coaxed the whole bowl into her.

She acted as if she'd known these people all her life. She knew their names, and they knew hers. Whether she liked it or not, Memphis Maynard had become a part of Yancey County, and it had become part of her. He wondered if she would ever admit that to herself.

"You ought to be goin' back to your house for some rest, Memphis," someone said.

"Can't go home," she said, and tossed her head to clear her forehead of a strand of bronze hair. "Can't, Imogene. I'd have to get a boat to bring me back and forth to town, or swim across the creek and hire one of those army trucks with mammoth tires."

"Well, go to Ruby's then."

"I will pretty soon."

Memphis patted Emma Lee on the cheek, then straightened up, rubbing the back of her neck as if it ached, and rested her forehead against the wall. Cutter itched to give her a massage and then make love to her until she slept satiated in his arms. She bent to pick up a child, but paused and stood still. Somehow he knew she sensed his presence, as he always sensed hers. He should leave, but found he couldn't.

She turned and saw him. Her face was pale with weariness and marred with bruised half-moons beneath her eyes. A nasty abrasion crossed one cheek.

Their gazes linked. Time shimmered and held its breath. It happened then, that moment of recognition when all the seasons of time crest and hearts leap with revelation. In the space of a heartbeat, fellow travelers discovered each other. Cutter wondered then how he ever thought he could give her up. Her summer-green eyes glistened with unshed tears. She extended a hand toward him, but she began to fold like limp linen. She slid quietly to the floor before he could reach her.

Imogene came running to help, but Cutter picked Memphis up and held her like a child. He hugged her to his chest and welcomed the rapid beat of her heart against his. He laid his cheek against hers and felt the sweetness of her breath feather his ear.

"Lord God, is she okay, Cutter?"

"I think she's fine. She's just exhausted. Needs food and rest. I'm taking her home."

"You mean to Ruby's."

"No. I'm taking her home. See if you can locate Claytie, or someone with a boat."

"I'll try, but some phones are working and some aren't."

"If you reach him, tell him to meet me at Big Bridge." He headed toward the door, but called over his shoulder, "And find someone to tell Nelsey to get Katie and bring her to the bridge."

He carried her, sometimes through mud that came midknee, across the square, past Carpozzoli's Pizza, down Church Street past the Baptist church where people waited in line for food, past Mitchell's boarded-up hardware store, around the devastated warehouses close to the river, and finally to the river. As he made his way determinedly through the ruined little town, tired men doffed their miner's caps in respect, and weary women waved and asked if Memphis was okay.

"Fine, just fine," Cutter would answer. "We're going to take care of her."

"Glad you're home, Cutter."

Cutter nodded. *Me, too. Me, too.*

Claytie and Leroy waited for him at the site of ruined Big Bridge.

"Leroy, barges will be coming downriver soon with my men, heavy equipment, and supplies. Send them on downriver and into Maynard Creek."

"But Cutter, don't we want them here first? We gotta git Big Bridge rebuilt."

"Nobody needs that bridge except a few families like mine and the Huttons, and people going to the Country Club. We'll leave it until last. I'm taking Memphis home, and then we're going to build her a bridge that will last for generations."

"But people use Big Bridge to git to the four-lane back and forth to Charleston."

"We're surviving fine without the four-lane. My men will bring whatever supplies are needed here in town from Charleston. We're building Memphis a bridge first."

Memphis woke up to the sound of hammers, pile drivers, and men yelling orders. Yellow sunbeams striped the ceiling, and the leaf-laden branches of the big oak cast lacy shapes on her bedspread.

She sat up, amazed to find herself in her own bed. She vaguely remembered someone spooning soup into her at some point. Cutter? No, couldn't have been. Someone had put her favorite green silk pajamas on her, too. How had she gotten here? She swung her legs over the side of the bed and stood up, but her head swam from the sudden motion, and she quickly sank back down.

"Well, had enough beauty sleep?" asked Nelsey. She bustled into the room with a huge smile on her face.

"What's going on? How did I . . . how did *we* get here? Is Katie okay? What's all that god-awful noise?"

"I'll answer your questions soon as you lie back down."

"I will not. I want to know what I'm doing here. I should be in town helping out."

"You've been here sleeping the sleep of the dead for almost three days, missy, and everyone's gettin' along jest fine without you."

"Where's Katie?"

"Downstairs with Ruby."

"Thought you and Ruby didn't like each other," Memphis said grumpily.

"Well, we didn't. But now we share a grandchild. Ruby adores Katie." Nelsey plumped up the pillows. "Now put your head back down here. I'll get your lunch."

"I'm not going back to sleep. I've had enough rest. I just need food. And I want to know what's going on outside."

"I, I, I, I. Is that all you can do, talk about yourself? You do what I tell you, or Cutter will come up here and get real bossy."

"Cutter?"

"He's down the hill."

Memphis swung her feet over the side of the bed again and stood up. The room whirled for a second then righted itself, and she took a step.

"Get back in bed."

"No, I want to see what's happening outside."

Nelsey sighed and said, "If you insist, but I'll help you."

She took Memphis by the elbow, but Memphis shook her off. "Nelsey, I'm not sick."

"Humph, no, but you was mighty tired, and you're stubborn as a mule."

Nelsey was two protective steps behind her as she walked to the window. At first, all she saw was the welcome sight of the green carpet of her lawn. The knowledge that her home had survived intact was exhilarating.

"Thank you, God."

"Yes, we have much to be thankin' Him for," said Nelsey softly.

"Nelsey, I'm so glad to be home. The minute I woke

up this morning, I felt like I'd come 'home.'" She felt the pressure of tears behind her eyes. "Looks like maybe I have too much invested in Yancey to leave now."

"Looks like."

"But your house was spared, and mine, too. If Opal Marie knew the bridge would be wiped out, why didn't she know Katie and I would be all right here in the house?"

"Because you wouldn't have been. The cellar door was open, and Cutter found a can of kerosene, oily rags, and matches down there." Nelsey cleared her throat nervously, and her voice turned sad. "Birdy was gettin' ready to torch the house. Don't know how she thought it was going to catch, with the rain and all, but she would have hurt you and Katie in some way that night."

"Oh, my God." Memphis saw tears glistening in Nelsey's eyes.

"She must have been hiding in the basement. You caught her by surprise when you packed up and left so quickly. She jumped in her car, which we figure was hid behind the shed, and followed you."

Memphis shivered.

They stared at each other in horror, realizing what could have happened. Yet there was an element of poignant sadness remembering chipper little Birdy, and a childhood love that had gone awry somewhere along the way.

Nelsey answered her unasked question. "They found her body caught in a culvert downriver near Charleston."

"But where is she? I mean, her family . . . ?"

"Cutter's pretty torn up about Birdy and how she turned out, and the fact that he didn't see the signs of a disintegrating soul. After he brought you here, he went to Charleston, got her body, and brought her home. Her family is home now takin' care of buryin' her and sech."

Memphis put her head on Nelsey's shoulder, and they shared a hug of sadness and love.

The roar of heavy machinery drew Memphis's attention down the hill. The site where Leroy's Store had sat was a beehive of activity. Construction workers operated big yellow backhoes and bulldozers back and forth near the creek, and carpenters worked industriously on a bridge.

"A bridge? Nelsey, they're building a new bridge already?"

"Yep, and they're almost done."

"But that's impossible. It would take a month at least, I mean . . . how . . . and they should be working in Yancey."

"You take that up with Cutter. They've been working on that durn bridge since he carried you up here three days ago."

"Cutter carried me home?"

"Yep. He and Claytie brought you in the dinghy, then Claytie come to get me and Katie. You were here in bed sleepin' like a baby by the time we got here, and Cutter was already shoveling mud down at the creek."

"Well, who . . . I mean, it was Cutter who fed me?" She remembered now, the feel of strong but gentle hands feeding, then bathing her, then dressing her in the pajamas. "He cleaned me up, too?"

Nelsey raised an eyebrow and blushed. "Guess he did, lessen it was your ghost angel, Opal Marie."

"No, it wasn't Opal Marie. I think we've seen and heard the last of Opal Marie."

"You get back in bed. I'll bring your lunch up."

"Dammit, I can't spend the rest of my life in bed."

"That's fer durn sure, and stop cussin'. But indulge me and Cutter this once. He ain't left here, ain't hardly slept. He has two crews of men working through the night. He only comes to the house to eat sometimes."

"Nelsey, nothing he can do will ever make up for what he did. I'll never forgive him."

But her heart said otherwise. She remembered vividly now the look they'd shared before she fainted, how something in her heart had whispered that "love forgives."

"Frankly, missy, I don't think Cutter cares what you think. Now climb back in that bed."

An hour later she'd eaten her lunch and found to her chagrin that Nelsey was right. The thought of an afternoon nap was delicious and she drifted off.

When she woke up, twilight shadows cut friendly figures on the walls, and Cutter sat beside her bed. He held one of her hands in both of his, his head bowed wearily and propped against their interlaced fists, his mouth pressed against her fingers. His eyes were closed. She studied his rugged face, the rumpled fall of his dark hair against his tanned forehead, the determined square of his jaw, the strength of his mouth. It must have been a week since he'd shaved. The stubble on his face had grown to almost beard length.

She loved him irrevocably, now and forever. Any doubts or misgivings were gone, replaced by abounding, absolute knowledge. Would that be enough? Could it take them past the rough place in which they found themselves?

She sighed, and he opened his eyes. As he looked at her—his silver eyes filled with pain, worry, and love—everything that had been slightly off center for her suddenly slid into place. Her love for him cut across eternity to the beginnings of time, as if they'd been together before and would be hereafter.

"Thank God, you're safe," he said.

"*You're* thanking *God?*"

"Yeah," he murmured. She could barely hear him.

"He and I kind of met and got to know each other the last few days."

"I'm glad."

She couldn't tear her gaze away from him, and he drank in the sight of her like a drowning man sighting shore.

Finally, he said softly, "We'll have to forgive each other, you know."

"I know."

He kissed her knuckles, then her wrist.

"What else do you know?"

"That I love you, and love forgives."

He smiled and the glow in his eyes filled her with joy.

"And I love you, and love trusts."

He lay down beside her then, took her in his arms because she was his to comfort and give comfort, and fell into an exhausted sleep.

Memphis woke up the next morning with Cutter's arm flung heavily over her waist. One look at him convinced her that he had several more hours of sleep to go. Energized and rested, she was ready for the brightness of a beautiful spring day. The smell of bacon and fresh-baked cinnamon rolls coming from downstairs made her mouth water.

She kissed Cutter's rough chin, maneuvered from beneath his arm, and slipped out of bed. She dressed in jeans and big white shirt, then hurried downstairs.

A note from Nelsey dangled from the spout of the coffee pot.

"Me and Ruby took Katie for a walk in the woods."

Yes, it was that kind of day. She savored her breakfast, all the while glancing eagerly out the window at the freshness of the sky, and the mauve-and-sapphire limned mountains in the distance. Finally she cleaned up her dishes, put on her hiking boots, and slipped out the back door. Her ultimate destination was the new bridge, but she would walk through the woods first to find Katie, then loop back along the creek to the bridge.

She entered the cool woods without fear. Wildflowers of all kinds and colors made a colorful carpet beneath the tall evergreens and hardwoods. Coreopsis seemed to bob their yellow heads in greeting as she passed, and the shorter lavender dwarf iris nodded shyly, welcoming her to the forest she'd so long avoided. There was no sign of Katie, or her adopted grandmothers, so Memphis headed for the creek.

Careful not to sink into the dangerous muck left by the high water, she edged along the tree line. The water was still high, but had receded eight or ten feet, at least. Stumps, branches, and debris from upstream cluttered the banks of the stream, but Memphis knew she and Cutter would clean it up in no time.

She stopped abruptly. Ahead of her, a rotting rectangular wooden box lay on its side, halfway exposed in the deep mud. It looked suspiciously like a homemade coffin. She approached with caution. The ragged remnants of a filmy white dress were sucked in and out of the moist creek bank. A partial skeleton spilled helter-skelter from the open lid.

Memphis drew a sharp breath.

She didn't have to move any closer to know it was the earthly remains of Opal Marie Chafin. One whole arm lay exposed telling all the story Memphis needed. The small, delicate bones of the hand extended into the bright spring sunshine. The last three fingers were missing, leaving only the thumb and pointer finger.

The sheriff had moved the pitiful coffin close to him so he could keep an eye on it. All this time, the grave site Memphis had searched for had been right under her nose. It had taken the flood to flush it from its hiding place next to the woods.

Opal Marie had haunted Memphis because she

wanted her story told, and because she wanted to go home.

"I'm going to take you home, Opal Marie. I'll make sure you get home to Chigger Hollow."

She heard Katie's voice down creek. They must be at the new bridge site. She skirted the coffin carefully and hurried toward the bridge Cutter had built for her.

$Epilogue$

Summer 1997

In a mountain glen near the swinging bridge, Vanta Lou Chafin gave the rough-hewn wooden cross one last blow with the hammer and stepped back to join the rest of her family.

"We deliver Opal Marie to you, Jesus," said Grandpa Chafin. "We thank you fer savin' her from the spirits and bringin' her back to us who love her. We know she's happy now, hyar with us. Praise be to God."

"Praise be to God," they all repeated after him.

Vanta Lou raised her voice in song. The comforting refrain of "What a Friend We Have in Jesus" lifted high through the glen and floated over the trees, reaching the blue of the hot summer sky. The soft white light that accompanied the hymn wasn't seen by anyone, but they all felt the sweet smile of the presence that accompanied it.

Memphis Maynard Tate ran her hand lovingly over the letters engraved on the stone. "Sadie Maynard, friend and lover, rests in peace." She glanced around the green leafy bower that she and Cutter had chosen for the final resting place for their grandparents. It was lush with wild crimson roses, and lay protected and private in a vine-covered spot in the woods.

Memphis patted the stone next to Sadie's, identical

in size and wordage. "Macauley Tate, friend and lover, rests in peace."

In the distance, hammers and saws, the sounds of remodeling going on at the house, could be heard, but the peace here in the bower seemed untouchable, inviolate.

"Looks like I'm going to have to build you a bench here."

Cutter approached with Katie in his arms.

"It's a nice place to visit."

He put his arm around her waist, and they headed back to the house.

"Happy?"

"Happy."

**POCKET BOOKS
PROUDLY PRESENTS**

We'll Meet Again

LINDA ANDERSON

**Coming soon in paperback from
Pocket Books**

**The following is a preview of
We'll Meet Again. . . .**

He WALKED out of the prison gates without a backward glance.

The odors, the weak-green institutional stain of the walls, and the miserable moaning during the long nights would be forever imbedded in the seams of his patched-up soul. He stopped his slow deliberate pace to survey the moss-draped oak trees surrounding Raiford Prison, then closed his eyes and took a deep breath. The north Florida air, though hot and thick, was free, and the blistering June sun on his face energized him.

From the prison bus he heard jeers and name-calling. They wanted him to hurry and board the bus into Starke. He flipped them a finger. Let 'em wait. He deserved this moment. He'd waited for deliverance ever since he'd stepped into his cell, and now that his attorney had engineered a pardon, he intended to savor every second of freedom.

The jeers and chants grew louder but he ignored

them. His eyes closed, he thought of the woman who'd falsely accused him of attempted rape, assault, and kidnapping ten years ago. Her form and face were sharp and clear in his mind. He even caught the light fragrance of her signature perfume, as though she stood right in front of him. She didn't, of course, but he knew where she was and soon he would confront her. He'd dreamed of the confrontation every night for nine interminable years.

Sophisticated DNA testing, not available when he'd been accused, said he'd never raped anyone. She was a liar. Someday the whole world would know what he knew: the bitch was a liar. The governor had signed his pardon yesterday.

"Come on, you dumb sum-bitch! Looka him. His first day out de' walls and he stands there like a fuckin' retard!"

He opened his eyes and grinned at the yelling, waving men, then ambled toward the dusty yellow bus. He was in no hurry. She was in North Carolina, a day's drive to the north. He'd get there in due time, but first he had things to take care of, errands to run, and people to see. He knew she would still be there when he was ready. After all, he'd kept an eye on her for nine years.

He would always know where she was and what she was doing.

He boarded the hot bus. It reeked of body odor and cigarette smoke. For a finite second, he missed the chill air-conditioning of the prison, but then laughed, sucking in a huge breath of freedom as he headed to the rear where he could be alone to dream his dreams. He tugged at the window until it gave with a reluctant squeal. A big blue-black June bug buzzed in and circled his head. He swatted it away and slouched down in the seat.

As the bus pulled away from the penitentiary, he

stared out the window and saw her face again. He went over the plans he'd made and his excitement mounted.

The fly returned and whined at his ear. He caught it in his fist and held it for a moment, feeling its angry vibrations against his sweaty palm. He knew just how it felt, captured and helpless. He squeezed the bug slowly until the vibrations stopped, then dropped the lifeless thing on the littered bus floor. He took an immaculate white handkerchief from the pocket of his new khakis and scrubbed the sticky yellow residue from his hand, then folded it meticulously and returned it to his pocket.

He closed his eyes and again conjured up her face and her fragrance. Soon. Not now, but soon, he would see her.

Children drown silently.

The toddler reached for the ball and toppled softly into the pool. Her arms and legs flailed valiantly as she fought a desperate solitary battle to survive. She opened her mouth to cry out, but gulped water instead. Instinctively, she locked her jaws to stop the overwhelming rush of water from invading fragile lungs. Her blue eyes widened in heart-catching fear, and she had a moment of bewilderment at the betrayal of the mother who should have been there to keep her safe. She began to lose consciousness, and the irises of her eyes rolled back until only the whites showed. As the water closed over her ears, the pretty song of the bird nearby became a muffled trill, and soon dissolved completely. It was the last sound she heard. All was quiet. Air seeped from her delicate nostrils, and she sank until she drifted lifelessly, like a formless amoeba, along the bottom of the pool.

The red ball she'd reached for bobbled merrily on the crystal blue surface.

"Noooooo."

Lannie woke with the familiar cold sweat beading her hairline.

"Damn."

She sat up, drew up her knees, and wrapped her arms around them. Eyes still closed, forehead pressed hard against her knees, she rocked back and forth.

"Dammit, dammit, dammit."

Lannie hadn't been there when her daughter, Gracie, drowned, but she knew this was how it had happened. She'd suffered this vivid nightmare almost every night since Gracie's death three years ago.

But she deserved the nightmare. She deserved to suffer every damnation that came her way. She should have been there for Gracie.

A gruff bark and then a soft whine made her smile. She stretched out a hand and found the wiry head of O'Bryan, the Irish wolfhound who had slept at her bedside for the last two years. The reassuring feel of his rough, warm coat soothed her.

"It's okay, Bry," she whispered into her knees. "Only twice this week. I'm getting better, huh?"

He whined again.

She lifted her head and laughed. "Okay, okay. I know it's time to get up."

Early June sunlight streamed through the square screened windows. The one-room log cabin faced the east. When she'd first arrived she'd resented the cheery intrusion of the sun first thing every morning and had kept the shutters closed, preferring the dreary dimness of the primitive interior. Now, though the nights were still cold high on this North Carolina mountain, she kept the shutters open and welcomed the light.

Five minutes later she was following her morning routine: letting O'Bryan out, slipping on her soft moccasins, poking up the embers that remained in the fireplace from last night, making coffee in the old tin pot and placing it on the Coleman camp stove to boil, pulling on her threadbare jeans and blue-and-orange Florida Gators sweatshirt.

O'Bryan barked, and she opened the screened door to sit on the stoop with him. Coffee mug in hand, she surveyed the colorful scene before her. The only sounds this morning were the distant wheezy cheee-up of a pine siskin, and close by, the energetic whir of a hummingbird.

She held her breath and froze as the ruby-throated hummingbird hovered over the vivid red Indian Pinks, which grew wild next to the stoop. She could have reached out her hand and touched its tireless body. For a blessed, sacred moment she and the hummingbird existed alone together, and then the tiny bird took impatient flight.

This had been her solitary domain for two years, but she hadn't really begun to appreciate it until the last few months.

Waves of blue-green spruce and hemlock stretched before her for endless majestic miles. Budding mauve and deep-rose hardwoods blended their colors artfully with the evergreens. A dawn mist drifted, weaving lazy blue ribbons haphazardly through the summits. The effect was ethereal and soothing.

June might be heading into early summer elsewhere, but here near the top of Fodderstack Mountain early spring flowers and trees still blossomed. Yellow dog-tooth violets radiated over the ground all around her and disappeared into the sharply sloping tree line.

Bry's tail began to thump rhythmically.

"Yes, I don't know how you know, but yes, we're going into town today."

She tossed the dregs of her coffee onto the ground and stood up.

"Okay, you big brute, give me a few minutes to perform my pitiful beauty routine, and then we'll leave."

Inside the cabin, she washed her face, brushed her teeth, and drew a brush through her thick red hair. A quick glance in the small rectangular face-sized mirror that hung on the wall told her that she should, at least, tame her hair in some manner. Where was the green ribbon she'd had a month ago? She rummaged in a drawer, found a worn shoestring, contemplated its use, but then discarded the notion. She'd promised her friend Nell that she would work on her appearance. The crumpled ribbon, saved from a birthday present from her brother, finally showed itself in the rear corner of the drawer. Quickly, she bunched the mass of hair into a ponytail and secured it with a rubber band and the ribbon. She had no idea what she looked like from the neck down and didn't care. Grabbing her shopping list, she left the cabin.

Bry waited for her beside the olive-drab army jeep parked at the rear of the cabin. He sprang easily into the passenger seat, and they tore down the mountain, gears screaming, brakes straining and protesting noisily. They splashed through the shallow creek that ran near the cabin, followed a barely discernible two-track path, and finally emerged onto a rocky dirt road that led to the main highway two miles away.

Her brother, Tom, made fun of the 1950s army-issue jeep.

"If you insist on staying up there by yourself, at least buy a reliable new Jeep," he'd said. "One with a top, and sides, and one that doesn't grunt and pant at every stop sign."

"Sorry I embarrass you, brother dear," she replied. "But I don't go to the country club. I drive into town a few times a year for supplies, and that's about it."

Tom had visited her once in the beginning and never returned, which suited Lannie just fine. The arduous trip up the mountain to the cabin had inflicted several deep gashes on his expensive Grand Cherokee, and he'd always hated the isolated cabin anyway. Letters from her father indicated that Tom and his wife, Cynthia, had visited friends at High Falls Country Club several times in the past year, but, per her explicit instructions, he had not tried to communicate with her.

Only three people knew where she was: her father, Tom, and her friend Nell. And only Tom and her father knew how to get to the cabin.

As she approached the highway, the road smoothed to a rocky crumble instead of a boulder-strewn, spine-shattering ride, and she shoved into fourth gear.

The Panoz AIV Roadster's swift and powerful passage up the curling mountain highway pleased and matched the personality of its owner. Drum Rutledge pressed the accelerator, and a small smile lit his grim face at the immediate response of the small car. He didn't want to be here in the first place, so he took extra pleasure in the performance provided by the special-built roadster. He also had to admit that the cool bite of mountain air was a refreshing relief from the hot weather in Charlotte.

Other than the brisk invigorating air, he found no enjoyment in his first trip to High Falls in five years.

Two reasons brought him here today: one, a business favor for a friend in New York, and the other in response to an urgent phone call from the caretaker of his summerhouse here. A violent storm, not unusual this high in the mountains this time of year, had caused extensive damage, and the man wouldn't take responsibility for repairs until Drum inspected the lodge.

He chanced a quick glance at the passing terrain and realized he was probably passing some of his own land. Usually a small, discreet dark-green sign anchored close to the ground, which said "Rutledge Timber" in pewter letters, marked the boundaries of his properties. But he'd let this area go untended and uninspected for a long time. So it wasn't surprising that he couldn't identify anything.

Rutledge Timber's enterprises were far-flung. He owned millions of acres of prime timber, lumber companies, and paper mills all over the world, but Drum knew that Rutledge employees swore he knew every tree on every parcel, every lot line, the particular whine of every buzz saw that felled a tree, and every hand that planted a new tree to replace the old. But he'd ignored this land in North Carolina. He surmised that longtime employees knew why he didn't spend more time at the beautiful summer lodge that he'd once loved. Newer employees didn't even know it existed.

It was unlike him not to protect what was his, and not to keep a close watch on his investments, but Drum had a deep aversion for the place.

He shifted into fifth gear and swooped around a looping curve, loving the swift obedience of the small car. The mostly aluminum custom-made car had a low center of gravity, so it hugged the road and handled well at high speeds. It was Saturday, and traffic was light at this time of the morning. The tourists hadn't found their way up the mountain yet. Except for a few pickups filled with locals on their way to construction sites, and a few retirees wending their careful way to town to buy a newspaper at the convenience store, the looping, dangerous highway was his to conquer. He'd passed them all easily, smiling when the construction workers shook their fists at him.

He took the next curve on two wheels, but the joy he received in the skilled maneuver turned to fear and caught in his throat as a vehicle shot onto the highway from his right.

He stood on the brake and the clutch, downshifted, and swerved to his left. He caught the shoulder of the road but corrected enough to stay half on the road and screeched to a halt, gravel flying. A jeep careened wildly across the road in front of him, bounced off a tree, then back onto the hard surface and to the center of the highway, rocking from side to side until it came to a complete standstill.

Suddenly, he remembered a lumbering old Cadillac he'd passed about a mile back. It would be coming around the curve any minute. They were all in danger.

Choking back his anger, he yelled at the driver of the jeep. "Move that piece of junk out of the middle of the road before we all get killed."

A huge brindled dog, thrown from the jeep when it hit the tree, stood protectively next to the vehicle, barking at the driver. The woman raised her head, shook it as if to clear it, and looked around her.

Drum pulled onto the shoulder and shut off his motor. He leaped over the side of the Panoz and ran toward her. The Irish wolfhound turned its head, growled menacingly, and bared its teeth. Drum saw the fur on the dog's ridge rise, and he backed away a step.

"It's okay, sport. I have to get your mistress out of the middle of the road." He spoke calmly and softly, hoping the dog would back down. He loved dogs, and was good with them, but he knew this huge brute was deadly serious.

Drum heard the purr of the Cadillac coming toward them.

The wolfhound heard it also. The dog nudged roughly at the stunned woman's side, then gently took her wrist in his big mouth and pulled her from the jeep.

"Good dog," said Drum.

As the dog tugged the woman to the shoulder of the highway, Drum jumped into the decrepit contraption, stomped on the clutch, yanked protesting gears into place, and moved it onto the shoulder in front of his car as the Cadillac rounded the curve. When it passed, an elderly couple gawked in curiosity.

Emergency over, Drum's anger surged again.

The redhead stood at stiff attention with her hands on her hips, glaring at him. The dog sat docile at her side.

"What the hell did you think you were doing?" she yelled at him. "You've got to be crazy, driving that fast on these mountain roads."

Every foul epithet he'd learned as a young lumberjack surged forth and threatened to erupt, but he fought to keep his cool.

"Look, lady, I'm the one who had the right-of-way, and I'll be damned if I'll apologize. You, and that dangerous thing you're driving, came out of nowhere. It's a blind curve, if you haven't noticed."

"Yeah, and you're the one who's blind," she spit back at him. "I've been using this road for two years, and this is the first time I've had any close calls."

"Has that contraption you're driving been registered lately? Do they even license jeeps like that anymore?"

She flushed guiltily, and he figured she was driving it illegally. She stuck her hands in the rear pockets of her ragged jeans and threw back her shoulders.

"You lowlanders with your fancy cars come racing through here like you own the place. Go back down to Atlanta, or Charlotte, or Charleston, or wherever the hell you came from, and stay there."

Strands of her red gold hair had fallen into her face. She stuck out her lower lip and blew at them, but they fell back across her eyes, and she swatted at them impatiently, finally managing to tuck them behind an ear. Her toe tapped rapidly against the gravel. Her ragged Reeboks had holes in the toes and were wet, as were her jeans halfway to her knees.

"So, a redhead with the proverbial temper." He folded his arms and raked her over with his eyes. "What a shame. You look like you'd be nice to take home tonight."

He could have kicked himself. He hadn't said anything like that in years, but something about her infuriated him. He was angry enough at the close call they'd just had, and she was only fanning the flames.

She paled, and raised her hand as if to slap him, but drew back. "Why you . . . you . . ."

"Bastard?" he supplied.

"Among other things," she gasped. Her dusky gray eyes silvered as tears threatened, then dried quickly as she seemed to will tears away.

Drum sucked in a quick breath. There was a mystical quality about her lovely eyes that drew him. The velvet-gray ovals were fringed by thick black lashes, but it was what the eyes portrayed that interested him. Behind the angry, defiant curtain of silver, he caught haunting shadows. He knew that look. He'd seen it before.

He took a new appraisal of the woman standing before him, and his curiosity grew. She looked like a derelict, a homeless creature of sorts, but beneath the frayed jeans and grubby blue-and-orange sweatshirt, he noticed how regally she held herself. She was of average height, but stood tall, lifting her chin imperiously. The bulky sweatshirt camoflaged her chest, but torn tight jeans revealed long slim legs.

He hated the brief tears he'd seen and knew he'd been acting like an ass.

"I'm sorry. My apologies. I shouldn't have said that. We're just lucky we didn't kill each other, but you should look before you shoot out of side roads like that. Where were you coming from anyway?"

She glanced across the highway at the dirt road she'd emerged from, and his eyes followed hers.

"None of your business."

Drum spotted a Rutledge Timber sign lying half-buried and askew in the weeds along the entrance to the dirt road.

His waning anger returned. This strange woman had been on his land. Of course, he knew people hiked and crossed the acreage from time to time as they did in the mountains, not realizing it was private land, but that had never bothered him before.

"Maybe it is my business," he said, but decided not to pursue it. They weren't getting any friendlier, and he was wasting time, something he abhorred. He looked at his watch. "I have an appointment in town. Do you think you can get that excuse for a conveyance off the shoulder and onto the road, or should I do it for you?"

She gave him one last dirty look, ordered the dog into the jeep, and climbed in herself. He noticed that she walked with the grace of a dancer, with an airy bounce, on the balls of her feet, toes turned slightly out. Spitting gravel against his polished shoes, she roared off toward High Falls, the jeep's smelly exhaust coughing noxious fumes. What remained of the tattered canvas hanging from the rusted metal frame over her head flew in the wind like last year's football pennants.

Drum climbed back into the Panoz. Putting one hand on the body, and the other on the center console, he slid his long body in under the wheel. He had planned on stopping by the lodge first to change into casual clothes, but he wouldn't have time now. He needed to buy food and other essentials for the weekend before his ten o'clock appointment. Underneath this reasoning, he knew that he was simply putting off his arrival at the lodge.

Spencer Case, the director of the High Falls Summer Playhouse, had asked if they could meet at the theater at ten this morning. An ungodly hour for anyone in the theater, thought Drum. But from all he'd heard, Spencer Case wasn't your usual run-of-the-mill Broadway director, and this was summer theater. Robert Keeting, his producer friend in New York, had said the show "was in crisis," whatever that meant.

He switched on the ignition and pulled back onto the highway with a heavy heart. The weekend had started badly, and he didn't expect it to get any better. The tragedy that had changed his life, the tragedy that had taken Ann-Marie and Chip from him and kept him away all these years, now beckoned like an evil cancer that must be cured before he could live.

Look for
We'll Meet Again
Wherever Books
Are Sold
Coming Soon
in Paperback from
Pocket Books

Look for
We'll Meet Again
Whitney, My Love
Are Still
Coming Soon
in Paperback from
Pocket Books